YOU

HAD

IT

COMING

ALSO AVAILABLE FROM B.M. CARROLL
AND VIPER

Who We Were

YOU
HAD
IT
COMING

B.M. CARROLL

First published in Great Britain in 2021 by
VIPER, part of Serpent's Tail,
an imprint of Profile Books Ltd
29 Cloth Fair
London
EC1A 7JQ
www.serpentstail.com

1 3 5 7 9 10 8 6 4 2

Typeset in Palatino by MacGuru Ltd
Printed and bound in Great Britain by
CPI Group (UK) Ltd, Croydon, CR0 4YY

A CIP catalogue record for this book is
available from the British Library.

ISBN 978 1 78816 419 1
Export ISBN 978 1 78816 420 7
eISBN 978 1 78283 648 3

For my family, near and far.

Ladies and gentlemen of the jury, Megan Lowe has failed, at various junctures during the police investigation and the course of this trial, to tell the full story. She has left things out ... Important details that reflect badly on her decision-making, her actions, her reputation and, ultimately, her credibility.

1

MEGAN

The radio crackles just after 7.30 p.m., a half-hour before their shift is due to finish. The streets are quiet, deceptively benign. Megan is enjoying the pleasure of driving for once. Not having to race against time, or worry about taking a wrong turn, or curse other drivers for holding them up.

Lucas is smirking beside her. 'You have to give it to the old fellas. They know how to turn on the charm.'

The old man they've just dropped off to Royal North Shore Hospital said she was 'just his type' and if he were forty years younger and not married to his beautiful wife, he'd take her out to dinner.

Lucas played along while he took the man's temperature and blood pressure. 'So what's your "type", Barry?'

'Dark eyes, with a bit of mystery to them. And a nice smile. Keep smiling, love.'

Lucas is right: the old men tend to turn on the charm. Bravado to disguise their vulnerability and fear.

'I couldn't help noticing that his wife had *blue* eyes.' Lucas is still laughing.

They're stopped at an intersection on Pacific Highway. Megan is thinking about the cup of tea she'll have back at base before signing off for the night. Her thoughts fast-forward to tomorrow, her mum's birthday, which should be a joyous occasion but won't reach the bar. Megan is taking the day off work and they're going out for a fancy lunch. Because if you don't manage to make an effort for birthdays you might as well give up.

Car 482, intrudes the scratchy voice on the radio. *Category 1B in Killara. A shooting. Details coming through.*

Megan glances at Lucas, seeing her own anxiety and adrenalin mirrored on his face.

'ICP on the way?' she checks. An intensive care paramedic is usually dispatched as well as an ambulance if the situation is high acuity.

ICP is on another job.

Oh God.

'Male, fifties, several gunshot wounds to chest and abdomen …' Lucas reads from the mobile data terminal while Megan turns on lights and sirens and executes a U-turn at the intersection. They're five minutes away, according to the MDT.

'Nonresponsive and bleeding heavily,' Lucas

4

continues, intermittently glancing up to help navigate. 'Assume substantial internal damage ...'

'Only the one patient? Is the scene secure?' Megan's heart pounds just from the thought of what they're about to walk into.

'Shooter is believed to have driven away. Police attached and in transit. Neighbour giving assistance ... Watch out for the P-plater, Megs.'

The P-plater changes lane at the last minute, and the road ahead is clear. Megan accelerates: two minutes away. Sydney doesn't have much gun crime. This will make the 9 o'clock news.

Lucas exhales audibly. He has four years' experience to her six. Car accidents, house fires, domestic violence, heart attacks: they've dealt with everything ... except this.

Megan scrambles to assimilate what she knows in theory, if not in practice. Thorough visual inspection (it can be easy to overlook wounds if there are multiple entry and exit points). Possible tissue damage to lungs, liver, spleen. Possible rupture of heart, bladder or bowel. Shattered bones can become secondary missiles.

No more time for theory. They're here. This is real. A squad car has pulled in ahead of them.

'Just need to make sure it's safe,' one of the officers says, through the open window. 'Sit tight till I give you the nod.'

A short unbearable wait until they're given permission to enter the scene. The victim is laid out at the entrance of a driveway, a wheelie bin close by. The sight of the bin – something so innocuous and routine – brings a lump to Megan's throat. In this job she has become desensitised to many things, but seeing catastrophe juxtaposed with the ordinary gets her every time. A resuscitation on a kitchen floor, inhaling the smell of roast dinner. A dead-on-arrival motor-vehicle accident, pop music playing obliviously on the radio. Tuesday night, bin night.

Two people, a man and woman, are assisting the victim, trying to stem the flow of blood using jumpers and jackets. Several others are huddled in a group nearby.

'What's his name?' Megan asks, kneeling down on the cold rough concrete of the driveway. The injured man is wearing a dark suit and what was once a white shirt. Someone had the presence of mind to turn him on his side to manage his airway. A quick glance establishes that his colour is bad – pale and grey – and his breathing is shallow. She knows even before she checks his pulse that it will be barely there.

'We don't know,' the woman replies in a quivery voice.

'I'm Megan and this is Lucas. What are your names?' They're trained to do this: exchanging names establishes an immediate connection and fast-tracks the flow of information.

'I'm Sarah. I live in the apartment block across the street. I was putting out my bins too.'

'Darren,' the male adds. 'I was parking my car. Heard two loud bangs, then a motorbike roaring away.'

Megan cuts open the man's clothes to assess his wounds. One entry point in the right-hand side of the chest and one in the abdomen. Two exit points in his back. Blood clotted on the skin and clothing. Distension of the abdomen.

'When did he become unresponsive?'

'After a couple of minutes,' Sarah says. 'He was moaning and muttering, then he just faded away.'

Lucas packs the abdominal wound with haemostatic dressing, in an attempt to arrest the bleeding. Megan checks the head, feeling for skull deformities with her fingers. Appearance and alignment of trachea and jugular veins seem okay. She inserts an oropharyngeal airway. Next priority is oxygen.

A second squad car arrives. Two male local-area detectives.

Megan supplies them with a brief update. 'External and internal haemorrhaging. Need to get his blood pressure up before he goes into irreversible shock.'

The fact that he's already unconscious is a sign that he's lost huge amounts of blood.

Megan and Lucas work quickly, issuing abrupt instructions to each other.

'Here's a vein.'

The IV has Hartmann's Solution, a temporary fix until his blood type is cross-matched at the hospital.

'Keep applying pressure.'

Extensive bandaging, trying to stem further loss of blood, probably futile considering the extent of internal bleeding.

'Blanket. Keep him warm.'

This man's life is in the balance. Time is of the essence, yet they can't cut corners. If he dies – and that seems likely – their actions will be analysed to the very last detail.

His blood pressure is improving as a result of the crystalloid fluids. A small window of time: another deterioration is likely en route to the hospital. Load and go. Lucas hurries to get the stretcher.

'One, two, three.' The patient is on, and they're mobile, the stretcher bumping over the stencilled concrete of the driveway.

'I hate when we don't know their name,' Lucas says.

Megan knows what he means: it's hard to reach the patient if you don't have a name to use as an anchor. But she's only half listening. In her head she is planning the quickest route to the hospital. She'll call ahead as soon as she gets behind the wheel. Warn them of myriad internal injuries and the need to have the right resources standing by for immediate surgery.

The rear doors of the ambulance are open, bright light spilling out. The stretcher is ready on the hydraulic lift and it's only then – in those few seconds as the stretcher is rising and the patient is fully illuminated – Megan realises that she knows his face. She knows it from a different world, a different life. This face has haunted her, belittled her, broken her. Those thin lips, the hateful words they spat out: lies, terrible lies. Behind those eyelids are eyes that are pale blue, cold and contemptuous.

She checked this man's body from head to toe, trying to envisage the bullets' trajectory through his tissue, bones and internal organs, all without properly looking at his face. His hair has whitened; his skin is the colour of death; the poor lighting on the driveway: these are the reasons she failed to recognise him. And she never imagined she'd see him again.

Her conscience wrestles with her deep hatred. The reinvented Megan wrestles with the old, devastated one. This man doesn't deserve comfort. He doesn't deserve Lucas's murmured reassurances, trying to reel him back to consciousness.

'His name is William Newson,' she blurts out, against all her instincts.

Then she shuts the doors on Lucas's questioning face.

Members of the jury, this trial has revealed some harsh truths about Jessica Foster. In courtrooms we talk a lot about character, so we can understand and judge behaviour in a wider and fairer context. This young lady is not as innocent or indeed as vulnerable as she maintains. This young lady was engaging in provocative and risk-taking behaviour.

2
JESS

Tuesday nights are reserved for the serious fighters. They warm up with stretches, skipping and some work on the punching bags, before being paired off in the ring.

The first pair tonight – Billy and Lachlan – are in their mid-twenties and have similar ability. The purpose of sparring is to practise punching, positioning, posture and footwork, without hurting one another.

'Go easy,' Jess reminds Billy, as she helps him on with his gloves. 'Save the aggression for the real fights.'

She loves being a coach. Teaching better technique, eradicating weaknesses, giving praise when it's been earned. She loves it, and the members love it too. Some of them are like family to Jess.

Billy adjusts his headgear, patches of sweat under

each armpit from the warm-up. Tones and I's 'Dance Monkey' is playing on the sound system. Vince, her boss, is in Lachlan's corner. The buzzer emits five rapid-fire beeps to indicate the start of the round.

'Billy, you're too straight on the front leg. *Bounce.* Knee over foot.

'Sit. Sit. He's putting pressure on you. You're giving him too much time.

'Jab only. Find your range. You're coming up too late. Jab to the body. Set it up. Good shot, mate.'

Vince calls out similar advice from the opposite corner. Twelve years ago, Jess arrived at this gym, spitting with rage and the desire to hurt someone as profoundly as she'd been hurt. Her rage earned her three Australian titles and two split-decision losses on the world circuit.

The most rewarding part was fighting battles she at least had some chance of winning.

The sparring finishes at 8.30 p.m. The boys unwrap their hands before starting core work on the exercise mat. There's a strong smell of sweat, probably the only thing Jess doesn't like about her job.

'That's it for tonight. Good work.'

'Billy is coming along well,' Vince comments, as the boys pack up their things. His wiry physique and skewed nose provide clues to his former career as a professional boxer. His hair was charcoal when Jess first met him, now it's fully grey.

'Yep. He just needs to bend those knees when he's punching. He's still not sitting low enough. I'll tape his knee next time.'

'He's nearly ready, though.'

'Yep.'

Vince will organise Billy's first amateur fight in the next month or so. He is already putting out feelers to find the right opponent. Too good, and Billy could get scared off. Not good enough, and Billy won't learn much from the experience.

The boys leave, one by one, through the garage roller door. The gym is located in an industrial estate in Artarmon, neighboured by warehouses and factories. Each departure is pre-empted by a series of fist bumps: the club's version of a handshake.

Billy catches her eye on his way out. 'See you, Jess. Thanks.'

He makes no secret of the fact that he likes her. He's an associate lawyer with one of the big firms in the city. Every day he puts on a sharp suit and plays games with the truth.

'See ya.' She gives him an abrupt nod.

There is no obligation to like him back. She is his coach, not his friend.

Her hatred of lawyers is so ingrained, no amount of charm or good looks can get past it.

Home is a five-minute walk through the industrial estate, followed by a fifteen-minute train ride. The industrial estate is poorly lit, deserted, but that doesn't bother her. She is more than capable of defending herself. In many ways she'd welcome the challenge.

The 8.48 arrives as she's scaling the concrete stairs to the bridge. She sprints, takes two steps at a time on the descent, and flies through the open doors just in time. The carriage is virtually empty: rush hour has come and gone, it's just the stragglers left. She pulls out her phone from the inside pocket of her backpack; she hasn't looked at it for hours. The fact that she can take a long time to answer messages is a long-running complaint of friends and family.

Two new messages. The most recent one is from Alex.

Hey, babe. Just gone for a few beers with Ramsey. Don't wait up! A

She sighs and smiles at the same time. This is what Alex does: works hard and plays even harder. While one part of her wishes he would grow up, another wants him to stay the way he is: always living life to the fullest, a daily reminder that she should have the same aim. She has an early shift in the morning, doesn't want him waking her up when he stumbles in the door. But there's no way to say that without nagging so it's easier to say nothing at all.

The second message is from a former friend. Just seeing Megan's name brings a rush of guilt. It's been a few years since they last had contact.

> Something weird just happened. Got called to a shooting
> in Killara and you won't believe who the victim was.
> William Newson!!! He's badly wounded. Don't know if he's
> going to make it. Thought you'd like to know.

She's so startled she almost drops the phone, fumbling to re-establish her grip on it, then brings it closer to read the message again. William Newson has been shot. Maybe there is justice in the world, after all.

A whoosh of cold air brings her back to the present. This is her stop. She exits the station, crosses the road, takes the second left. Her pace is slower than usual; her legs seem to have lost their power. William Newson! Someone has actually done it. Taken action. All Jess was capable of was fantasy. Who? Why? How many lives has he ruined this time?

Home is a one-bedroom 1970s apartment, its proximity to the station equating to a hefty price tag. She used her prize money to pay the deposit, with a small amount left over for furniture. Most of her neighbours are well into retirement. The lift judders upwards, an old-people smell lingering within its confines. Jess doesn't mind it; better than the smell of sweat in the gym.

She decides to eat before composing a reply to Megan. Nutrition is a constant battle. So many calories burned in training, fitted in during quiet periods at the gym, along with whatever she expends instructing classes. Calories out always seem to outweigh calories in, despite her best efforts.

Dinner is a toasted sandwich in front of the TV. The food sits in her gut. She can't stomach the last few bites and pushes the plate aside. Megan will be waiting for a response. It takes a few attempts to come up with one.

Someone else must hate him as much as we do.

She puts the phone down and goes for a shower. The water cascades over her face and along the sharp angles of her body. She shampoos her hair, massaging the lather into her scalp as images flash through her mind. Megan, her eyes swollen and accusing. William Newson, every reproachful word and gesture. The police, the parents, the jurors. The lies, the shame, the injustice.

The bathroom is freezing when she exits the shower cubicle. She rubs her skin roughly, before wrapping the towel around herself. The mirror is condensed and she uses her fingers to clear a circle. There she is. Platinum-blonde hair darkened from the water. Her nose, kinked from three separate breaks. A scar under her left eye and another above her right, where she's had stitches. Her face is just the half of it: fractures of the wrist and thumb, dislocation of both shoulders, ankle and finger sprains, and three concussions, the last one signifying the end of her career. But it was worth the pain.

When people find out that she was a professional boxer, they automatically assume a rough background. Her father is a heart surgeon, her mother a concert pianist turned piano tutor. Rough is about the last word in the dictionary that applies to them.

Boxing saved her, albeit not from a poor background. It provided a release. It gave her focus, goals and a training routine to cling to. More than anything, it rebuilt her self-respect, which William Newson had done his utmost to destroy.

'You had it coming,' she says, as though it were his reflection in the mirror and not her own. 'You had it fucking coming.'

3
BRIDGET

Jesus. A shooting in *Killara*. A suburb associated with corporate executives, sky-high real estate prices and insidious wealth. Bridget pulls into the street, flashing blue and red lights heralding the precise location about two hundred metres ahead. Three squad cars flung at odd angles, offending her innate sense of order. She parks next to the kerb, cuts the engine and takes a steadying breath before getting out: you never know what you're about to face. The wind lasers through her, a command to zip up her jacket.

'Bridget.' Detective Sergeant David Nesbitt is an old friend from her academy days in Goulburn. It seems incongruous that his party trick on drunken nights out was the Moonwalk. Bridget's party trick was sculling a schooner in under ten seconds. Now Dave works out of police command in Chatswood and she's with the Homicide Squad. His dancing would be limited to the jostle between family life and work demands. Her drinking constitutes a half-hearted glass of wine before falling asleep on the couch.

'Hey, Dave.' They shake hands, even though a hug would feel more natural. 'Give me the run-down.'

He's slightly breathless as he complies. 'Male, late fifties, identified as William Newson. Apparently, he's a barrister with a number of high-profile cases.'

A barrister? It's usually the drug dealers or gang leaders who're shot down outside their homes. Forensics have taped off the area. They've commenced swabbing, dusting and searching for holes and defects from projectiles that may have missed the target. She's not sure they'll find much, other than bullet casings, blood spatters and perhaps footprints and tyre marks. A police photographer is present too, crouched down as she photographs the bloodstains on the driveway.

'Two gunshot wounds?' Bridget says, repeating what was relayed over the phone: it's amazing how many inaccuracies infiltrate that first swathe of information. People find it hard to be factual when confronted with traumatic situations.

Dave nods. 'Alive on arrival to Royal North Shore but in a critical condition. Mr Newson lives alone. There's an ex-wife and three grown-up children. The family are being informed.'

'Witnesses?'

'Two neighbours who came to his aid. We've taken statements and sent them home. They heard shots, saw the motorbike speed away, and could offer nothing more than the fact that the driver was wearing dark clothes and a black helmet. We're door-knocking every house. Someone might have seen something in the lead-up.'

She glances at her watch: 8.45 p.m. Twenty minutes ago, Bridget was in her fleecy pyjamas watching 'bathroom week' on *The Block*. Regardless of the inconvenience, and the jarring change from cosy living room to this hastily constructed quadrangle of police tape, her heart rate has increased and her mind has started flying off in different directions. There is nothing quite as invigorating as a new case. Technically not homicide, but it will be by morning: the victim is not expected to make it through the night.

'Make sure that counselling is offered to the witnesses. Hard to get over something like this. So close to home, too.'

She steps back from Dave to look up and down the length of the street. Jesus, that wind feels like it's from the Antarctic. Occasionally, Sydney produces a genuinely freezing winter's night, as though to say, *Don't ever get complacent*. A group of neighbours are watching from outside the tape perimeter. There's not much to see; she has a strong urge to tell them to get in from the cold. It's the mother in her. Hard to quell, even when she's acting in a professional capacity.

The street is located within a maze of similarly quiet streets. No traffic lights or shops in the immediate area, which essentially means no CCTV. The main road is nearly three kilometres away. How many motorbikes zoomed past during the period in question? How many intersections will need to be reviewed? How long did the perpetrator lie in wait? Did he – or she – come to anyone's notice? It sounds like the witnesses didn't have much detail to offer; the door-knock might be more successful.

Dave takes her arm and guides her to a spot where there is a clearer view of the front garden. 'Looks like he hid behind that gum tree, waiting for his moment. Bang, bang, then back on the bike and away.'

In Dave's mind, it's already a 'he'. A dangerous assumption.

The gum tree is one of those huge ones that give you vertigo just from looking up at it. Its trunk is substantial, and that area of the front garden is dark and murky: perfect for stealing up on someone.

Bridget turns her attention to the victim's house. A steep driveway leading to what appears to be an architect-built home. Three levels. Two balconies.

'Big place for just one person,' she says, a little enviously. 'Have we had a look inside?'

'A quick squiz to make sure it was secure. Nothing untoward. No sign of a struggle or forced entry. The garage door was open. He must have come out that way to access the bins.'

'We'll send forensics up when they're done here. Seize his laptop and any other devices. I'll go to his workplace first thing in the morning.'

She assumes that his chambers are located in the city centre, close to the courts: she deals with her fair share of lawyers. He'll have an assistant, probably a pretty young thing, but now she's guilty of making assumptions. Regardless, Bridget knows exactly what she wants from the assistant. Details of the cases that William Newson has been working on, the clients he's been meeting with, and if he's done anything to upset anyone.

'Random or personal?' she asks Dave.

He blinks. 'Doesn't look very random to me.'

'Me neither. Let's hit the ground running. Let's talk to colleagues, friends, family, neighbours, lovers, doctors, anyone who can vouch for Newson's state of mind and if he was worried about anything or anyone in particular. But first things first – the bins. Contact the council and suspend collection tomorrow morning. Sort out some extra manpower. We need to search each and every bin on this street, and the next street, and probably the entire area.'

Dave's mouth drops open at the magnitude – and messiness – of the job, but the necessity is indisputable: the weapon or clothes of the perpetrator could be discarded in any one of those bins.

Another car has arrived, a familiar silver-haired head alighting: Katrina, Bridget's boss.

'The detective inspector is here … One more thing: we need an address for the ex. We'll call on her tonight. Don't want to give her too much time to think about things.'

William Newson, by the nature of his job, might be moving in the same perilous circles as criminals and other shady characters. A crime like this – involving a motorcycle, an assumedly illegal gun and at least some degree of target surveillance – suggests outlawed bikie gangs, drug wars or some other organised crime. Nevertheless, Bridget always, *always* starts with the wife – or ex-wife, in this case.

Cold hard fact: we're more at risk from our beloved than anyone else.

4
MEGAN

Megan wakes up with the sensation of not knowing where she is, which happens quite a lot. It's been nine years since she returned to Sydney. It doesn't make sense that her body – after all this time – thinks it's in Europe or Asia or South America.

You're here, at home, where you always are!

Next is the pervading feeling that something really bad has happened, another throwback to waking up in those foreign cities, listening to the babble of strange voices and sounds, her stomach clenching at the thought of what had driven her there.

Oh God, William Newson!

It's happened twice before: arriving unsuspectingly at the scene, heart plummeting at the realisation that she knows the patient. One was a former friend of her mother's, a glamorous and devout woman who collapsed at Sunday church. The other was someone from school, a boy she used to like. Both occasions were extremely disconcerting. Trying not to be distracted by her personal feelings. Trying not to be thrown by the abrupt change in context and roles. Her mum's friend shuddering, frightened and looking ten years older than her age. The boy from school: a grown man, filthy drunk and concussed. Now a third occasion: William Newson.

A knock on her bedroom door. Her mum sticks her head around.

'Oh good, you're awake. It's gone eleven. Might want to shake a leg, love.'

Eleven? That late? Oh God, her mum's birthday lunch!

'Coming,' she promises, and swings her legs out of bed. 'Happy birthday, Mum!'

'Thanks, love.'

None of last night went to plan. An hour late clocking off work. Exchanging late-night texts with Jess. Would have been simpler to phone, but they haven't spoken in years. Then awake into the early hours of the morning, reliving the shame, the unfairness and, like a scab wanting to be picked at, the apportionment of blame.

Toiletries, bathrobe, fresh underwear: her body is stiff and uncooperative as she moves around the room. This happens. Paramedical work is strenuous. Lifting

25

and manoeuvring bodies on and off stretchers, and up and down stairs. Crouching, kneeling, bending over. You need to be strong, physically and mentally.

The bathroom is a draughty walk down the hallway. Her hair – dark brown, shoulder length – needs a wash but she is not sure there's enough time. Would William Newson have recognised her last night if he'd been conscious? Twelve years is a long time. It's the difference between a hopeful seventeen-year-old and a hardened twenty-nine-year-old. It's three years of running away (in the guise of travelling), three years of intensive studying and training, and six years on the road as a qualified paramedic. In those twelve years she has seen the best and worst of life. What happened to her and Jess wasn't the worst. But it was close.

In the end, Megan washes her hair because if she doesn't her mum will be quick to read things into her lack of effort. Back in her bedroom, she uses two fingers to separate the horizontal window blinds. It's one of those stunning blue-skied winter days: warm in the sun, cold in the shade, with an air quality that's pure and rejuvenating, unique to this time of year.

She surveys the contents of her wardrobe and eventually chooses a maxi dress she bought in Portugal. The dress is old but doesn't look it. Large hoop earrings, a light cardigan, open-toe espadrilles. She is ready with a few minutes to spare.

She should ring the hospital, find out if William Newson lasted the night. She *should not* ring the hospital. She did her job, gave him the care he needed and got him to A&E in record time. Way more than he deserves.

Step back, don't get sucked in, pretend he's someone else. But following that logic, she always checks on critical patients, phoning the next day to see how they're doing. Sometimes there's been a miracle and they've pulled through. If the news is not good, it's closure: she says a prayer for them, and moves on.

Her phone is in her hand. She is still see-sawing – call, don't call – when a message comes in from Lucas.

He died during the night. How did you know him again?

Lunch is at a modern-Australian place in Turramurra. Megan is distracted, her mum is forced, but after a couple of glasses of wine they both relax and somewhat enjoy themselves.

'Isn't this lovely?' Roslyn exclaims, blotting the napkin carefully to her lips. Her lipstick and finger-nails are in matching pinks, complementing the tiny dash of pink in her floral dress. She's from that generation who're obsessed with matching their outfit with their shoes and accessories. Roslyn is a receptionist with a busy car rental company, her uniform of white blouse, navy trousers and flat shoes thwarting her love of accessorising.

'Yeah. We should come here again.'

Megan had asked if she wanted to invite any of her

friends today but she'd insisted she wanted only the two of them. The truth is, Roslyn doesn't have many close friends. Some fell by the wayside during the trial, appalled by the unpleasantness and unwanted publicity. Her husband's death was another layer of contagion; people were sympathetic but they didn't know how to act so it was easier to keep their distance. It's the same for Megan. Her mother is her closest confidante as a result.

'You seem a bit tired, love,' Roslyn says now, her gaze becoming more scrutinising.

'Is that your way of saying I've got bags under my eyes?'

'You know it isn't. But it must have been a difficult shift for you to sleep in so late.'

Roslyn was in bed by the time Megan got home last night. She's an early-to-bed, early-to-rise type, which fits well with 7 a.m. starts at the car rental company. Megan was relieved not to have to face her last night, and she has no intention of bringing up William Newson now: that would be one way of completely ruining her birthday. But it feels so odd and discombobulating to keep something this big from her mum. *He's dead … Someone actually shot him … I was one of the last people with him.* She has to concentrate to keep the constant inner dialogue from spilling into spoken words.

'I'm so full. I really shouldn't have dessert.' Not the most subtle change of subject but Roslyn falls for it and convinces Megan to order the pavlova.

Megan is slightly tipsy on leaving the restaurant. An Uber and fifteen minutes later they're home.

She stifles a yawn. 'I'm just going to have a lie-down.'

'Don't fall asleep or you'll have trouble tonight,' Roslyn warns.

Twenty-nine years old and still being told what to do by her mother. It's wrong, but fixing it is complicated. Her whole life is complicated.

Megan's bedroom is her haven, albeit cramped and drastically over-furnished. Double bed with bohemian-style pillows and cushions. A writing desk where she laboured over school homework, before her bachelor of paramedic practice. A long low-level bookshelf, which complicates access to the window. A built-in wardrobe and two crammed-in bedside lockers. Unfortunately, there's no other viable layout for the furniture. Her father used to talk about knocking through the wall to Seb's old bedroom, affording her more space, as well as installing a modern kitchen and much-needed second bathroom. The plans were a mere fantasy: there was never the money. His death arrested any further thought of renovations. His death arrested every-thing. Three years later, Megan and Roslyn still haven't regained rhythm to their lives. Everything feels flat and kind of pointless.

Megan kicks off her shoes and moves some cushions on the bed: the wine has wiped her out. Two glasses are her limit. Lucas calls her a lightweight.

She types a text to Jess.

He's dead. I know I should feel sympathy but I can't.

How odd if someone else, a stranger, were to read the message. What would they make of such a callous statement? Does Jess tell people about what happened to them? Is she open about her history? Megan isn't. She tried with some of her earlier boyfriends; it quickly killed dead any romance.

Seventeen: *so young*. Megan picks up a lot of teenagers in the ambulance, most of them comatose drunk or high on drugs. In between checking their vitals and giving them fluids, the same refrain repeats over and over in her head: *You're too young, you're just a kid; go home to your parents where you'll be safe.*

She searches the news headlines while she waits for a reply from Jess. All the channels are headlining the story.

A well-known barrister was shot outside his home at approximately seven thirty last night. Mr William Newson was taking out his bins when residents heard two gunshots ... The motivation for the shooting is not yet known and police are appealing for witnesses.

It's only a matter of time before Roslyn hears about it, but hopefully not today.

Megan closes her eyes. Her limbs feel both heavy and weightless. Fragments of last night begin to replay in her head. The concrete unyielding against her knees as she bent over his body. Blood glistening on the grey-white skin of his torso. Light escaping from the rear doors of the ambulance, revealing the face from her nightmares. Doing over a hundred on the Pacific Highway, siren screeching. At one point she clipped the kerb and almost sent the vehicle over on its side. Never has she driven so recklessly, putting everything on the line to get William Newson to hospital. Trying to save his life. Which is completely inexplicable because he destroyed hers.

5
JESS

Alex is still in bed when Jess gets home from work, just after lunch. He came in from the pub at 3 a.m. – she heard the front door creak, checked the time on her phone and sighed. In fairness, he tried to be quiet, whispering swear words when he dropped something in the kitchen. He navigated his way to the bathroom, using the torch on his phone to avoid turning on the lights, but still managed to trip over something, which resulted in more swearing. Stealth is difficult when you're six foot three, not naturally light-footed and three sheets to the wind.

It's always good to open the front door and come home. Jess loves this place, the high ceilings, big windows and generous proportions giving her space to breathe. Her things, her décor, her rules. Alex knows this and doesn't interfere. As far as she's aware, Megan still lives at home. Jess doesn't know how she can stand it. She'd live on the streets before going back under the same roof as her parents.

Food is always her first thought when she gets home, and her stomach makes a weird noise to remind her it needs filling. A quick scan of the fridge and pantry before assembling a punnet of cherry tomatoes, a jar of pesto and a packet of dried pasta. The pasta will replace her lost calories as well as settle Alex's stomach when he decides to surface.

The pasta is bubbling when her phone pings from somewhere. She looks around for it before remembering it's still in her backpack. A plummeting sensation when she sees Megan's name again.

He's dead …

The question has been at the front of her mind since she woke up, and here, finally, is the answer.

He's dead. I know I should feel sympathy but I can't.

Alex chooses this precise moment to appear and she drops the phone guiltily.

'Hey, babe.'

He's wearing an old pair of work shorts, possibly yesterday's, and his chest is bare and tanned, defiant of the fact that it's still winter. Alex is a horticulturist and spends his days outdoors in the sun, often without his shirt. He should be at work right now, mowing someone's lawn or yanking weeds from neglected garden beds. His clients rarely make use of his consulting skills or expansive horticultural knowledge. He says it doesn't really bother him: 'Money is money, babe. Don't care if I'm the most expensive lawn boy in the city.'

He sits down on one of the kitchen chairs with an elongated groan. 'Bloody hell. Big night. Hope I didn't wake you.'

'Think of a giraffe trying to move quietly and you'll get the picture.'

'Sorry, babe. Got stuck with Ramsey. He's having a hard time at work.'

Alex is the friend who gets called when someone needs to drown their sorrows. Jess is not sure about the quality of his advice, but he can be counted on to listen and stay until they're ready to go home; his loyalty can't be faulted.

'Nothing on today?' she asks, tipping the pasta out of the pot and into the waiting colander.

'Nothing urgent. You know how it is, they always seem a bit surprised when I come at the agreed time anyway.'

Alex, like other tradesmen, has to battle against a blanket reputation for unreliability. He's usually good for turning up on time or at least phoning if he's been delayed. Today excepted.

Jess plonks a bowl of pasta down in front of him. 'Here, this should help some.'

34

'Thanks, babe. You're so good to me. I'm a lucky bastard.'

In fairness, she's lucky, too. She can be herself around him, she can be honest: one glance or touch can replace a thousand words. They're different, though. Jess is ambitious, intense, introverted, and obsessed about fitness. Alex is none of the above; he just wants a good time. But they fit well together. Jess doesn't know how, they just do.

She sits down opposite him and prongs her pasta with her fork. She needs to tell him about William Newson.

He's dead … He's actually dead …

William Newson has always had the effect of making her boyfriend – the most laidback person she knows – extremely angry. She decides to wait a couple of hours, until his hangover subsides.

It's a pretty bad hangover. Alex declares himself unable to do even a few hours' work and makes a sheepish phone call to his client. Jess prescribes fresh air and some gentle exercise. The closest national park is a fifteen-minute drive; they often go there on weekends.

Alex's ute looks incongruous next to the luxury vehicles parked along the street. Its paintwork is riddled with rusty scratches and dings, mostly from encounters with letterboxes as a result of driving too fast up and down driveways.

'I'm driving,' Jess states in a tone he knows not to

argue with. It's late afternoon now, but she's still not confident that his blood-alcohol is below the legal limit. Last thing he needs is to lose his licence.

She hoists herself behind the wheel, before adjusting the seat and mirrors: his legs are a lot longer than hers. Take-off is jerky: it always takes a while to get used to the manual gearbox. The sun is starting to drop behind the trees by the time they reach Bobbin Head Road.

'Park closes at five thirty,' the ranger says gruffly when they stop at the entrance to pay the fee.

'Just going for a short one, mate,' she assures him.

She swings the ute into one of the marked spaces; there's nobody else around. They jump out. The air is clean and pure, the only noise the sound of wind in the trees and a few chirps from native birds: this is why they come here. A number of walks, of varying lengths, begin from the car park. They decide on one that's an estimated hour's round trip, according to the mounted noticeboard and map.

It's a narrow path, winding through gum trees and bush. Jess leads and Alex brings up the rear. It works better like that, otherwise his long stride would leave her behind. The first section is fairly level and she sets an easy pace, a nod to his fragile state. They don't speak, other than a warning she issues when they come to a slippery bit. Her thoughts are far away from the bush.

He's dead … He's actually dead …

The urge to see Megan has been building all day. They were such unlikely friends. Megan went to public co-ed in Hornsby while Jess went to a private ladies' college in Pymble. They met at karate, weekly classes in Turramurra, forced there by their fathers, who knew Sensei through different channels. Jess's dad wanted her to learn self-discipline, Megan's dad wanted to build her confidence. They were often paired together, being the same age and gender, and Megan used to giggle whenever she stuffed up the moves in the katas (there were so many bloody katas to learn). They were prone to chatting, which got them into perpetual trouble with Sensei. After class, they used to walk together to the train station, before going to their different platforms, Jess's southbound, Megan's northbound. If there weren't any trains blocking the view, they would wave across at each other. Megan was sweet, uncomplicated, and quite naïve in comparison to Jess's other friends. Her house was a ramshackle weatherboard on a sad block of land, while Jess's family home had a tennis court, an enormous pool and extensive gardens. Jess liked their differences. She liked Megan and started to invite her to things. A sleepover for her sixteenth birthday. A weekend away for her seventeenth. For her eighteenth they were both in a courtroom, on the receiving end of William Newson's insinuations and outrageous lies.

The path reaches an incline, with uneven steps hewn from rock and sleepers. Up and up and up. Jess's breath is ragged, her thighs burning. She knows she's alive; Alex probably wants to die.

After ten minutes of climbing they come to the top. A stunning vista of bush, water and sky.

'Let's stop here a minute,' she says, sinking down on to one of the sandstone boulders.

Alex immediately looks suspicious. They don't usually stop: they're both dogged like that.

'What's wrong?'

'William Newson is dead.' Something releases in Jess when she hears those words out loud.

'What?'

'William Newson. The barrister. He was shot dead last night. It's been on the news.'

'Fucking hell.' Alex runs a hand through his hair, which is especially unkempt today. Jess's mother comes to mind: she is constantly suggesting he get a haircut, or at least run a comb through it.

'Fucking hell.' His hands are hanging by his sides now, clenching and unclenching with emotion. 'Pity they didn't put a few bullets in those other two bastards while they were at it.'

6
BRIDGET

Jesus, teenagers! Bridget's children are pressing her buttons. They don't go to bed at night therefore don't want to get up in the mornings. She's had to call Cara three times this morning. *Three!* They're deaf to her voice, her refrains that they wash up after themselves, keep their rooms clean, do their homework, not spend too long on Netflix. Seventeen and fifteen years old, incompetent in many respects, but brimming with opinions and contrariness. Who knew that life would be ten times more difficult now than when they were toddlers?

'Homicide is way easier than this,' is Bridget's parting shot as she leaves the house. The only person who hears is her husband, Shane, not the person to whom the remark is directed but he is used to getting caught in the line of fire.

Homicide is obviously not easier. Bridget has been given the Newson case, which she was hoping for the minute she got called out on Tuesday night but didn't dare take for granted. This is a big, high-profile case: many of her colleagues had their hand up too. Bridget's team consists of Patrick, an experienced detective senior constable, and Sasha, a hardworking junior. Dave and the other local detectives at Chatswood are helping on the ground.

Bridget opens the car window to let in some air. The traffic is making her agitated. Megan Lowe's shift started at 8 a.m., and Bridget's plan was to get to the ambulance base ten minutes before. Time enough for a quick chat to establish if Megan and her colleague have anything to add to the narrative of the shooting. But the traffic is not complying. Her phone rings. It's a welcome distraction from the fact that only two cars have progressed through the intersection and now the lights are red again.

'Hey, Bridge. It's Dave.'

'I was just thinking about you. How are you getting on with the bins?'

He groans. 'Still at it. Not popular with the neighbours or the council or the poor sods rifling through the rubbish.'

'Popularity is overrated,' Bridget says.

'Any more news on the wife?' he asks after a small pause. It's clear that he's itching to be involved in the case at a deeper level.

'You mean *ex*-wife,' she corrects tetchily.

The ex-wife of a barrister comes with certain preconceptions: someone with innate poise and confidence; someone immaculately groomed and dressed; someone 'well-to-do', to borrow a term her mother would use. Suzanne Newson was none of the above. A plump woman in her mid-fifties, eyes gritty from crying, a tremor in the hand that shook Bridget's and Katrina's (the detective inspector paired up with her for the late-night visit). Suzanne's hair was grey, short and practical. Her house, a modest bungalow, smelled of dogs. Most surprising was her honesty.

'I don't know what to do.' Her eyes darted between Bridget and Katrina. 'Should I go to the hospital, or stay here and wait for news? Our split was acrimonious, you see, so it doesn't feel authentic to rush to his deathbed. Joshua, my middle son, is there, talking to the doctors. He said it isn't looking good. The oldest works as an accountant in London and the youngest is studying politics in Canberra. They're booking flights home. Oh, I'm so devastated for the boys.'

They asked Suzanne if she had been out that evening: she said she hadn't. They asked if William had any known enemies: she said that his cases were often 'controversial', but she couldn't really comment on the recent ones. They asked if William had any money problems: she shook her head emphatically.

The traffic lights change to green and Bridget puts her foot to the pedal, not caring if she gets caught in the middle of the intersection: the fine is worth her sanity any day of the week, plus there's a good chance she'll get off.

'We're checking Suzanne's phone records and financial situation but first instincts are that she isn't involved. Three sons, though, so lots of potential there. I'm particularly interested in the middle one, Joshua, who is a junior barrister in the same chambers as his father.'

Bridget and Patrick visited the chambers yesterday. Joshua wasn't at work, obviously, and they were told that William Newson's assistant was away on her honeymoon. They came away empty-handed.

'Patrick is doing some background checks on Joshua Newson. Seeing if he has any questionable friends, or if there was known friction with his father. And Emily, the executive assistant, phoned me from Fiji. She's going to email details of the cases he was working on.'

'That's dedicated.'

'I know! I like her already. I'm on my way to talk to the paramedics. Don't expect to hear anything new but always good to speak to those first on the scene.'

Bridget reaches the ambulance base at 8.25 a.m. Three ambulances are parked in the bays. A slow morning for emergencies? Normally she'd be with a colleague, but this is a tick-the-box exercise and a small detour on her way to work (if the traffic had complied). Before getting out of the car, Bridget uses the rear-view mirror to fix her hair and apply a slash of red lipstick.

'Detective Sergeant Bridget Kennedy,' she says to a good-looking man who is holding a clipboard and pen and checking the tyres of one of the ambulances. 'I'm looking to speak to Megan Lowe and Lucas Halliday.'

'I'm Lucas.' He smiles and she's immediately conscious of her thrown-together appearance. Is her lipstick even on straight? She sighs at the unfairness.

'Hey, Megs,' he yells. 'Out here.'

A woman – thirtyish, dark-brown hair tied in an up-knot – emerges from the ambulance. She's also holding a clipboard. The pair appear to be doing some sort of inventory, checking the vehicle and equipment.

'Good morning.' Megan Lowe has watchful brown eyes and a quiet capability. 'I just need a few minutes to finish off in here. Do you mind waiting in the kitchen?'

'Not at all.'

Lucas points her in the general direction with another smile. He has the dark good looks that Bridget has always been susceptible to. Shane, like her, is a redhead, as are their children; providing them with yet another reason to resent their parents.

The kitchen has a rectangular table and six chairs. A large glass window looks into an adjacent room, which contains several paramedics watching television.

'Feel free to put on the kettle,' one of them calls out.

Bridget is dying for a coffee – she only managed a few sips of the one Shane made for her this morning. She fills the kettle and lines up three mugs.

'Tea or coffee?' she asks Megan and Lucas when they appear about five minutes later.

Looking surprised and pleased, they both request tea with milk, one sugar. Bridget can't help wondering what other things this pair have in common. Their hair, eyes and skin come from the same palette of browns. Even their physiques seem to match: strong, muscular. Something about them fits together.

'I just wanted to have a chat about Tuesday night,' Bridget says, setting the mugs on the laminate table before sitting down. 'Thought it was a good idea to cross-check my facts and see how you're both doing.'

Megan cups her hands around her mug. Her fingernails are short and unpolished. Bridget notices a small tattoo – some sort of symbol – on her inside wrist. 'We did everything we could – we've nearly ten years' clinical experience between the two of us – but it was obvious at the outset that his injuries were extensive. Normally we'd have the back-up of an intensive care paramedic, but even if an ICP had been available, I don't think it would have made any difference.'

Bridget writes down the fact that an ICP was unavailable in her notebook.

'The patient was unresponsive when we arrived,' Lucas adds, folding his arms across his navy short-sleeved shirt. 'There were two neighbours assisting. Sarah and Darren, from memory.'

Bridget flicks back through the pages of her notebook, cross-checking the names. 'Yes, we've spoken to those witnesses. Neither was acquainted with Mr Newson. Can you tell me what you observed about his injuries?'

Bridget expects to receive the results of the forensic autopsy later today, confirming the number of bullets, the order in which they were fired, and their trajectory within Newson's body. A personal account from the paramedics will complement the scientific details in the report.

'Two close-range gunshot wounds,' Megan says in her softly spoken voice. 'Entry wounds in the chest and abdomen, exit wounds in the back. One bullet was located in the skin of Mr Newson's back, the other was located between the skin and clothing.'

A call comes through on the ambulance station's radio system.

Car 410, says a disembodied voice. *1A cardiac arrest in Gordon.*

Bridget sees activity through the glass window: two male paramedics leaving the room, a fleeting picture of authority and controlled calm. What scenario awaits them? No matter how much you condition yourself to expect the worst, some situations defy the imagination. Policing and paramedical practice are similar in that regard: you have no idea what you're about to walk in to.

'How long have you two been working together?' she enquires out of casual interest.

Lucas answers. 'Almost three years, on and off. We

change partners every couple of months but we work in the same region, so we get stuck with each other fairly often.' He pulls a face and Megan rolls her eyes at him.

A siren sounds as the departing ambulance begins its wrangle with the rush-hour traffic. Bridget gets back on track. 'So, Mr Newson didn't regain consciousness at any point?'

'He became restless on the way to the hospital,' Lucas supplies. 'Not exactly conscious but not that far from it. It can happen when the patient's blood pressure goes back up. I sedated him. The last thing I needed was for him to pull out the IV.'

Bridget writes down the word *sedated* before snapping her notebook shut. 'Well, thanks for the chat and corroborating my information. I'll be in touch if we need to know anything else.'

'Wait!' Megan Lowe commands just as Bridget is on the verge of standing up. 'There *is* one more thing.'

Her tone is quiet and firm. Both Lucas and Bridget look at her questioningly.

'You should probably know that Mr Newson and I were acquainted.'

Bridget's hackles rise. She reopens her notebook. 'In what capacity, exactly?'

A pause. Megan shifts in her seat. The subject is obviously difficult for her. 'William Newson was the defence barrister in a case where I was the complainant.'

'What was the case regarding?'

Megan's gaze flits from Bridget to Lucas before

drifting downwards, to her hands, clasped together. Her discomfort is painfully evident.

'It was a rape trial.' The kitchen is deathly quiet. Lucas seems as shocked as Bridget is. How well does he know his colleague? There's an obvious rapport between the two, but at the same time Bridget can understand how this subject matter was never discussed. The stigma. The embarrassment. Bridget dealt with a few rape cases before she transferred to homicide. Categorically the most frustrating cases of her career; six offences, not a single conviction.

'Twelve years ago now,' Megan continues in a voice that sounds very far away. 'It took me a while to recognise him. He looked a lot older. And he was the last person I expected to see. I still can't believe the coincidence …'

Bridget is on high alert. Cold hard fact: coincidences are often not coincidences at all.

She has a thousand questions to ask but suddenly there's the crackle of the radio.

Car 482. Category 2A, construction-site fall … Lucas and Megan are on their feet and already halfway out of the kitchen.

'What was the verdict of the trial?' Bridget calls after them.

A beat before Megan turns around. 'Not guilty … Aren't they all?'

Ladies and gentlemen of the jury, we have it on account that Megan Lowe has a quiet nature. We have heard evidence from her pastoral care teacher, Mrs O'Neill, who read us an excerpt from last year's school report: 'Megan is a hardworking and introverted student who sometimes finds it difficult to voice her feelings and thoughts. Next year I hope to see Megan grow in confidence and I will be encouraging her to speak up both in class and with her friends.' Megan has a history of being passive, of not voicing how she truly feels, and of internalising her thoughts and true opinions. We all know that introverts are good, intelligent people. But no amount of thinking can substitute for talking. There are times in life when we need to articulate what we want, and – more crucially – what we don't want. Megan didn't need to give chapter and verse on the night in question. Monosyllables would have done the job. She could have said 'No'. She could have said 'Stop'. She could have said 'Don't'. She said none of the above, and my clients should not have to pay for the fact that Megan Lowe, at age seventeen, had trouble speaking up.

7
MEGAN

'Right at the lights. All clear.'

It's Lucas's turn to drive today, which is a relief because Megan feels off-kilter. She is in charge of navigation and the MDT, which require less decision-making.

'Another right coming up. Watch that white car.'

Lucas hasn't brought up what happened in the kitchen. He's waiting for a lull and there hasn't been one. A construction-site accident. A schoolyard concussion. A pedestrian versus a reversing car. Now they're on the way to a multi-vehicle accident. One of the drivers, an elderly woman, is reportedly unable to leave her car. She hit her head on impact. God knows what other harm has been done: her bones will be more brittle than a young person's.

'Here we are.'

Three crumpled cars in a neat row of destruction. The first one appears to have stopped suddenly, the vehicle behind rear-ending it before getting rear-ended itself. Relatively high speed, going by the concertinaed bonnets and splintered windscreens. The elderly woman is in the middle car, damaged from both ends. The other cars appear to be empty. A brown-haired girl is sitting on the kerb. A man, with a cut on his forehead, stands back to allow access to the old woman. She's leaning forward, into the airbag. Conscious. Wincing in pain. The car door is open, which is a bonus. In accidents like these, the doors often become crumpled and stuck, requiring the assistance of Fire and Rescue: extra levels of stress and complexity.

'Hello there. What's your name?' Lucas asks her.

'Shirley Wallis.'

'I'm Lucas and this is Megan. What day is it today?'

'Thursday.'

'Do you remember everything?'

'I do … Unfortunately.'

Her sense of humour seems to be intact. That's a good thing.

'Was anyone else in the car at the time of the crash?'

'Just silly old me.'

Megan goes around to the other side of the car and opens the passenger door.

'Just pulling up the handbrake and putting the car into park, Shirley,' she explains, sliding in next to her. 'Are you on blood thinners?'

'I am.'

'Can you run your tongue around your mouth for me?' The old woman complies. Megan presses fingers gently against her forehead. 'Pain?'

'Oh, yes. Gave it a right wallop. Saw stars. It was like one of those cartoons.'

'How about your chest? Is it hurting?'

'Yes. Didn't know the airbag would be so bloody hard. Took the wind right out of me.'

Lucas is taking her blood pressure while Megan continues her assessment.

'Any neck pain?'

'No.'

'Pelvis area and legs?'

'Just as rickety as usual.'

Megan uses scissors to cut open her top. 'You have some nasty seatbelt abrasions there, Shirley. Now Lucas is going to hook you up to the ECG so we can check your heart.'

'I haven't got a heart!'

Megan laughs. 'How old are you, Shirley?'

'I'm ninety-one, but in my head I'm still nineteen.'

Lucas and Megan share a smile. It's moments like this that make it all worthwhile. Shirley – battered, bruised and after the fright of her life – still able to joke around.

Lucas turns his smile on Shirley. 'Considering you don't have a heart, it's beating just fine.'

Megan leaves Shirley temporarily in his care. Time to quickly check on the other drivers. Make sure that their

51

injuries aren't serious. You can't be too careful. Sometimes it's the people who appear to be okay who are
hurting the most.

'Coming for a drink?' Lucas asks after they sign off for
the night.

Oh God. He wants to talk. Megan doesn't want to
talk. She is depleted, particles of her left behind with
each of today's patients. What she needs is an early
night: sleep puts her back together.

'Nah, too tired.' She hitches her bag on to her
shoulder.

They're always tired at the end of a shift. Impossible
not to be. But one look at his face is enough to tell her
that he's not going to let her get away with that excuse.

'You can't avoid me for ever, you know.'

True. And there is a part of her that wants to get this
over with. Blurt out the full story in all its ugly, mortifying detail. It has been so long since she has spoken
about it to anyone.

He senses that she's torn. 'Come on. Just one. Daniella's expecting me home by nine, anyway.'

Daniella is his long-term girlfriend. She's a dentist,
very precise in everything she does. Lucas deviating
from an agreed plan would annoy her intensely.

'Okay, okay. The usual?'

'The usual' is a wine bar in Pymble.

'Yeah, I'll see you there.'

It's a ten-minute drive. On the way, Megan passes

the stretch of road where today's car accident occurred. Some left-over debris is scattered near the traffic island: shards of broken glass and part of a wheel arch. Dear old Shirley, all that vulnerability and bravado. Hopefully, she has family and friends who can visit her in hospital. It's quite shocking, the number of elderly people who are truly on their own. Some of them never married or had children. Others have kids who are interstate or overseas or can't be bothered. At Shirley's age she's likely to have outlived her siblings and most of her friends. Perhaps even her children. It's one of Megan's biggest fears. Getting to that age and being on her own.

Lucas – probably due to some lucky guesswork regarding routes and off-peak traffic lights – gets to the bar first and even has a glass of red wine waiting for her. The place is only half-full: plenty of free bar stools. Megan dumps her bag and jacket on one, sits on another. They clink glasses, wordlessly toasting to another day survived.

He doesn't make small talk. He's waiting. There's nothing but kindness in his brown eyes. His body is angled towards hers. *Tell me. It's okay. Tell me.*

A gulp of red wine. A ragged breath.

'We were seventeen, in our last year of school. Two stupid girls who thought they knew everything. It was a house party, there was a lot of alcohol ...'

Her gaze slides away from his, towards the entrance, where a group of women are in the process of coming in. It's easier not to look at him.

'To tell the truth, I can't remember much. I got very drunk very quickly. I remember wanting to go home but Jess wanted to stay. I remember staggering into one of the bedrooms, craving sleep. Then I have vague memories of someone kissing me, lying on top of me. I must have passed out after that.'

What a silly young girl! Drinking so much, inviting trouble, laying herself open to all sorts of risks. Less painful to pretend that the 'silly young girl' is someone else, a stranger.

'It was light when I woke up, about six a.m. My head felt like it was going to crack open. I was shivering, I had no clothes on, neither did Jess … She was asleep next to me on the bed. We weren't the kind of girls to sleep naked next to each other. Like most teenagers, we were horribly self-conscious about our bodies …'

Confusion. Acute embarrassment. Where were their clothes? What had happened? Megan couldn't get her thoughts to gel. Her head was weighted to the pillow. Her throat was raw and swollen; it hurt to swallow. In the pit of her stomach was a weird sensation, something she would later identify as foreboding. For years afterwards, she would wake up with that sensation: something terribly bad – but as yet unidentified – had happened.

'My clothes were strewn on the floor. When I stood up, I saw bloodstains on the sheets. And I realised that it wasn't just my head and throat that were sore …'

Shame. Horror. Dressing clumsily before shaking

Jess awake. Seeing her face as the truth hit home. Nothing would ever be the same again. Least of all their friendship.

Lucas has put his arms around her. His embrace is warm, solid, dangerously addictive. It would be nice to stay here. It would be nice to pretend that they're more than friends and colleagues. To forget about Daniella. Megan remembers an instant spark of liking and attraction on their first job together, before being devastated to learn that he had a girlfriend. The irony was that he'd met Daniella only a month earlier. A month!

He pulls back, chocolate eyes brimming with sympathy. 'So, William Newson got them off?'

Megan blinks, unable to hold his stare. 'He twisted the facts so that Jess and I looked like criminals instead of victims. We were liars. We were risk-takers. We had been excessively and illegally drinking. He was so good at his job even I believed it was all our fault by the end of the trial.'

Ladies and gentlemen of the jury, Jessica Foster's school reports had comments of a different kind to her friend's. Mrs Goulding, her school principal, read some of the following excerpts to the court. Semester 1, 2006: 'Jessica is extremely disruptive in class and fails to show respect for her teachers or for the learning environment of other students.' Semester 2, 2006: 'Jessica's behaviour has deteriorated this year. She has failed to meet uniform standards, attendance standards and behaviour standards. We hope to see a significant improvement in her final year.' Unfortunately, there wasn't an improvement: there were numerous detentions and a suspension for drinking alcohol on school premises. Mrs Goulding confirmed that Jessica was pushing boundaries for a girl her age. We all have friends like that, don't we? The reckless ones. The ones who talk us into stuff we know we shouldn't do. The ones who look for excitement, for trouble, and can't comply with the rules, no matter how many times they're punished. We all know people like that, and I'm not saying a girl like Jessica is unusual. What I'm saying is, don't go breaking rules and then look for someone else to blame when it all goes wrong. Step up and take ownership for your actions. Admit that you knowingly engaged in risk-taking behaviour. Don't point the finger at two young men who did nothing wrong. Don't ruin their lives because you broke one rule too many.

8
JESS

Saturday mornings are busy, with back-to-back classes mostly populated by corporate types whose long work hours make it difficult to come during the week. Each Saturday they arrive with a week's worth of frustration and angst. An hour later, they're red-faced, sweating profusely and realigned for the week ahead. Jess finds the transformation gratifying.

'One, two, rip ... One, two, hook ... Pick it up ... Fast hands. Great work ... Swap it over. Let's go.'

Each class operates on a rotation system. Five people per station: punching bags, skipping ropes, agility ladders and squatting against the brick wall. Rounds of two minutes, with short breaks to get from one station to the next. The usual soundtrack: the thwack of gloves making contact, the whistle of the skipping ropes, grunts and moans, Rihanna playing at full blast.

'Whoever's on the right moves first. Don't cross your feet over. Try to catch up with each other. Quick feet.'

Jess smothers a grin as she observes the disarray on the agility ladder. Performance tends to be directly related to age. The younger ones are nimbler and scurry along the rungs without having to stare at their feet the whole time. For the older ones it requires more concentration. Five push-ups are the punishment for tripping up.

'Pump it up. Keep it tight. Last thirty. Faster. Nice work. Swap it over.'

Saturdays attract more women, in vests and leggings and hitting the punching bags with such ferocity you've got to give them credit. The men tend to be grey-haired, mostly in their forties and fifties. Many are overweight and unfit. Some are decidedly weak. A few weeks of training, and the improvement is substantial. Improvement in the serious fighters is more subtle, and they're not as grateful for it.

'Has everyone been twice around the circuit? Okay, let's get on the floor and do some core work.'

A flurry as they unwrap the strapping from their hands and spread out on the mat. The more experienced ones grab a balance ball.

'Everyone on your elbows and toes. Push down your lower back. Now hold the plank. Twenty more seconds. Hold … Ten … Hold …'

Sun is spilling through the large corner window on to the blue exercise mat. Twenty people are on the floor, holding their plank position with varying degrees of success. Their faces are set with concentration and resolve. Vince is sitting at the desk, tapping at the keyboard with two fingers, catching up on admin. He glances up and points to the kettle. Jess nods: she could kill for a coffee. Vince is always looking out for her, in small ways and big. He'll have her coffee ready at the end of class and she can sip it while chatting to everyone. Eventually, this lot will leave and the next lot will arrive. Full of angst and surliness. Another transformation to begin.

Jess's shift finishes at lunchtime. There's a text waiting on her phone from Alex.

Job bigger than I thought. Won't be home till after five.

She and Alex left home at the same time this morning: 5.30 a.m. He dropped her to the station on his way, his stubble scratching her face as they kissed goodbye. Saturday mornings are busy for him, too: working mums and dads keen to get stuck into their gardens, seeking help with mowing, weeding and pruning. He thought he might be finished by early afternoon, but a job turning out to be bigger than expected is a common occurrence. They're meeting friends for dinner tonight; still plenty of time to get ready if he's home by five. A shower, an optional shave, any old thing to wear. Alex's lack of vanity is one of the things Jess loves about him.

She pops her phone into her backpack before slinging it over her shoulder. 'I'm off, Vince. See ya Monday.'

The gym is closed on Sundays. Vince is old-fashioned like that. In his view, Sunday is a day for rest, families and religion. If it were left to Jess, she'd open up in the morning at least. For the people who don't want to rest or visit their families or go to church. For people like her.

Vince glances up from the computer screen. His gaze is bleary and affectionate. 'Take it easy, Jess.'

The roller door is at half-mast; Jess ducks underneath. When she straightens, Megan is there, right in front of her. She stifles a scream: not the best greeting after all this time.

'Shit! You scared me.'

'Sorry. I was just about to knock.' Megan glances dubiously at the roller door.

An awkward silence, where they size each other up. Megan has put on some weight: her face is round and glowing with health. She's in her paramedic uniform. The navy suits her. She looks clean, crisp and competent.

'Sorry,' Megan says again. 'I should have texted. I came on impulse.' She looks around at the other warehouses, most of which are closed for the weekend. 'Look, is there somewhere we can go and talk?'

'There's a coffee place on the main road. This way.'

They fall into step. It's like walking next to a stranger, a wary silence and distance between their bodies. Jess hasn't spoken to Megan since her father's funeral, but the friendship was gone long before that.

'Here we are.' The café is nothing special. Clean and utilitarian. Metal tables and chairs, which are uncomfortable if you sit on them too long. Basic menu and order at the counter.

'What do you want?' Jess asks, more brusquely than intended.

'Just a tea, thanks.'

There's no one else in the café. The order is placed and Jess is sitting back down in less than a minute.

'A detective came to see me,' Megan says carefully.

Jess hurtles back in time. Detectives hammering her with questions, different ways of asking the same thing, trying to catch her out for inconsistencies. Detectives sending her for a medical examination, which was excruciatingly intrusive and embarrassing, until she learned that a courtroom can be more intrusive than any medical procedure. All at her own instigation. Megan wanted to keep it between themselves, to get on with their lives and not make the same mistake again. But Jess wanted her day in court. She wanted justice. And because she was the stronger personality, that's what happened. A full-scale brawl. Detectives, lawyers, journalists, the public, a judge and jury. She got her fight, her day in court (three weeks, actually). And they lost. A unanimous verdict. A knock-out, to use a boxing analogy.

'Her name is Bridget Kennedy,' Megan says, bringing Jess back to the here and now. 'She asked pretty standard questions. We often have to talk to police, especially if we're first responders … But—'

'But what?' Jess is not usually this abrupt. Megan's putting her on edge. She's going somewhere with this, taking her oh-so-careful time about it.

'I had to tell her that William Newson was known to me.' Megan is gently spoken in contrast to Jess's terseness. 'Then I had to leave before I could fully explain the circumstances. And I knew, just by looking at her face, that she was going to rush off and request the court transcripts.'

The waitress chooses that moment to arrive with their drinks: tea for Megan and a latte for Jess. The mugs are ridiculously oversized: the caffeine will have Jess buzzing for the rest of the afternoon. She takes a cautious sip, scrambles to gather her thoughts. The court transcripts! She can actually remember the court reporter's face, sitting next to the judge's assistant at their own special table, lips pursed as her fingers flew across the keyboard. Jess would spend hours looking at her, but she never so much as glanced in her direction. She had an air of disapproval; it was probably just that she had to concentrate on what was being said.

'So, I should expect a visit from the detective too?'

Megan's response is loaded. 'Maybe … Are you ready for that?'

Jess bristles. 'What the fuck do you mean?'

Her gaze is scrutinising. 'I'm just remembering some of the things you said …'

Jess's mug clatters against the metal surface of the table when she puts it down too forcibly. 'Just because I said I wanted to kill him doesn't mean I'd actually fucking *do* it.'

9
BRIDGET

William Newson's chambers are located in Elizabeth Street, opposite the Downing Centre Court. It's the usual fare: sombre atmosphere, plush carpets, statement pieces of art in the foyer. Bridget is accompanied by Patrick, one of the homicide detectives on her team. Patrick is the nice guy of the department: nothing's too much trouble.

'Detective Sergeant Bridget Kennedy and Detective Senior Constable Patrick Yandle to see Joshua Newson.'

'Take a seat,' the receptionist says in an efficient tone. 'I'll let him know you're waiting.'

Bridget rang ahead to make sure that Joshua was due in the office today. His father has been dead less than a week, the body not yet released to the family. Unfortunately, the legal world cannot press a pause button to allow for grief. Joshua's clients still need to meet with him, or see him across at the court. A lot is at stake: their futures, their families, their financial stability. In Bridget's view their worthiness is up for debate: according to the website, Joshua Newson specialises in drug offences.

Bridget and Patrick sit down in the waiting area. Patrick scrolls through his phone while Bridget gazes at the enormous artwork on the far wall. It's an abstract piece, vivid splashes of colour in the background, white chevron-type slashes in the foreground. Are the chevrons meant to be stick figures? Is the artist trying to depict people dancing? She uses her phone to take a photo. Cara, her eldest, is hoping to get a place in a visual arts degree next year. This is something they can talk about when Bridget gets home. She is constantly on the lookout for ways to prise herself into the closed worlds of her teenagers.

Bridget and Patrick are shown to Joshua's office ten minutes later. He stands up to greet them. Early thirties, glasses with dark frames, distinctly overweight. He sticks out his hand; it feels clammy in Bridget's grasp.

'Sorry you had to wait. This is my first morning back.'

They all sit down. Patrick takes out his notebook. Another impressive piece of art is hung on the wall directly behind Joshua. A portrait of some description. Bridget can make out eyes, a distorted mouth and the swish of hair.

'Thanks for seeing us,' she says, realigning her gaze

to William Newson's middle son. 'It must be difficult, returning to work so soon. Did you and your father work closely together?'

He blinks. Bites on his lip. Takes a few moments to get his emotions in check.

'No. Different areas of speciality. Dad's office is on the other side of the floor. Some days we didn't even set eyes on each other. But we caught up for lunch at least once a week.'

'Did your father mention anything of concern to you? Something or someone he was worried about? Or anything difficult or controversial?'

'Nothing he mentioned. Dad dealt with a lot of sexual assault cases, which are controversial by nature. His assistant – Emily – would know the details.'

Bridget spoke on the phone to Emily Wickham last week. She was in Fiji, on honeymoon, but that didn't stop her from being startlingly efficient. Within a few hours, Bridget received an email, summarising William Newson's open cases as well as recently closed ones, including all the relevant names and phone numbers.

'Yes, we've been in touch with Emily. Poor girl, having something like this happen while she is on her honeymoon.'

Bridget honeymooned in Fiji, too. Elaborate breakfast banquets before languishing by the pool. Cocktails at sunset followed by three-course dinners. She came home with four extra kilos and a life-long love of passionfruit mojitos.

'Are you aware of the Malouf–O'Shea trial in 2007?' she asks, watching Joshua carefully.

'Yes … although I was still in university then and more focused on my social life than my father's cases.'

'But you know about it?'

He nods and sighs simultaneously. 'It caused a stir – the female students were furious about the outcome. There were protests on the campus. Action groups were formed. It didn't do a lot for my popularity.'

Bridget can picture it. Placard-holding students pleading for justice. William Newson's son an unwitting target for their anger.

'The case catapulted my father's career,' Joshua continues in a brighter tone. 'Suddenly he was the go-to person for sexual assault offences in New South Wales.'

Bridget takes a moment to digest Megan Lowe's significance to William Newson. She played a pivotal role in his career; it could be argued that his success came at the cost of her trauma. She was someone who inspired protests in universities around the state. Of course, her identity was protected, as is mandatory with sexual assault complainants; she and Jessica Foster were known to the media as 'Girl A and Girl B'.

Bridget has conducted some cursory checks into Megan, as well as the control-centre operator who answered the triple-zero call. Both individuals are extremely well regarded and trusted by their colleagues. Bridget doesn't like the coincidence of Megan being one of the paramedics at the scene, but this past week has been about gathering evidence while it's fresh. A twelve-year-old rape trial is hard to prioritise over so many other – more recent – lines of inquiry. Yet it still niggles.

Bridget stares at the artwork while she's thinking. The portrait is beautiful and ugly at once. Equally repelling and fascinating.

Joshua notices her interest and turns his seat sideways so that he can see it too. 'I'm still getting used to this one. I like it. At least, I *think* I do. We rotate the pieces between offices, so as wide an audience as possible can appreciate them.'

Joshua's clients are drug addicts and traffickers. Bridget imagines them as pale and emaciated, with skittish eyes and thoughts. Hardly capable of appreciating a complex piece like this. Maybe she is underestimating them.

'My daughter wants to be an artist,' she confides. 'She's building her portfolio, in between studying for her HSC. The pieces look good to me but apparently the standard is extremely high. She gets super defensive when I give praise. "You've no idea, Mum." I suppose I don't.'

Bridget catches Patrick smiling to himself. His kids are really young and cute. Oh, to have those days back again.

'Dad thought that law wasn't right for me,' Joshua says softly. 'In his mind I wasn't assertive enough. I guess I proved him wrong ...' Another blink and the sheen of tears in his pale-blue eyes. A few moments to compose himself. 'I hope I made him proud.'

Bridget waits a while, then asks, 'Were *you* proud of *him*?'

'What do you mean?'

'I've had a look at some of the court transcripts online. The prosecution had compelling evidence in many of the cases but your father somehow managed to convince entire juries otherwise.'

'Dad believed that everyone is entitled to the best defence they can get. That includes rapists.' Joshua pauses. Bites his lip again. 'This is hard to say, but even the murderer who shot Dad deserves a defence. Legal representation is a civil right, as is the assumption of innocence.'

Bridget glances at Patrick's notebook. The page is blank, bar a few words. Joshua Newson is not giving them much to grab hold of.

'How many cases did your father lose in recent years?'

'None. His success rate was phenomenal. That's why he was so in demand.'

'How many charges were withdrawn before reaching trial?'

'The vast majority,' he concedes, and Bridget notices beads of sweat above his full lips. 'But that's the nature of sexual assault. It's one person's word against another's. Most of the time only two people know what really happened, and their perceptions of reality are often very different.'

Bridget is aware of this, from the half-dozen cases she handled in her early career. She remembers one particular girl, shaking uncontrollably as she made her statement, genuinely distraught but at the same time failing to provide the confirmatory evidence required for the matter to be referred to the Director of Public Prosecutions.

'Only one in ten reported cases results in a conviction,' she says, quoting a statistic that Joshua Newson is probably already aware of. 'But with your father on the case, the odds were even better than that. Or worse, depending on whose side you're taking.'

Joshua smiles ruefully. 'You sound a bit like my mother. It really got to her in the end. I remember her saying, "Some of those boys must be guilty, William, because all those girls can't be lying."'

Bridget's heart quickens. Patrick suddenly starts writing. Joshua has finally given them something to grab hold of.

10
MEGAN

Tuesday is unusually quiet: a visit to an aged care facility to deal with a suspected stroke, another to the home of an octogenarian who fell and broke her hip. Megan's had far too much time in her head, analysing that weird meeting with Jess on Saturday. Jess was still that odd mix of scrawny and tough. Her hair was dyed a paler shade of blonde, her face white and sharp; she looked like she could do with a solid meal.

They didn't know how to act around each other. As a result, Jess was even more brittle and Megan more reserved. The metal table rattled every time they put down their mugs, adding to the tension. Megan had wanted to see Jess's face, to check that she wasn't lying. Because she remembered what she'd said. Because she hadn't said it just the once. Because she'd said it like she really, really meant it.

I want to kill that cold-hearted bastard. He's worse than any rapist.

Had she killed him? Had something snapped in her after all these years?

Jess acted like it was a crazy notion. 'Just because I said I wanted to kill him doesn't mean I'd actually fucking do it … For God's sake, I was at the gym that night. There are dozens of people who can vouch for me.'

An accusing silence before Megan changed tack. 'How's Alex?'

'Good. Moved in with me last year.'

This was a surprise. Megan hadn't picked Alex as the cohabiting type, but what would she know?

'Still in the landscaping business?'

Jess rolled her eyes. 'A glorified gardener, in my mother's eyes.'

Jess's parents maintain that they're ordinary people. Her father is one of the leading heart surgeons in the city and her mother used to be a concert pianist. They own a six-bedroom home in one of the most affluent suburbs in Sydney, a boat that's moored at Bobbin Head, and a holiday house in the South of France. Not ordinary by any definition of the word.

'How *are* your parents?' Megan asked from ingrained politeness more than a desire to know.

Jess shrugged and grimaced at the same time. Her shrugs always had a vocabulary of their own. 'Dad's preoccupied with work, Mum's preoccupied with her

73

students. Both of them seem perpetually disappointed with me and suspicious of Alex … They think he's after my money – *their* money – which is laughable …'

Is it so laughable? Is Alex impervious to money? Megan's head was turned by their wealth. The Fosters were rich in a real-life way. Dog hairs on the custom-made sofas and expensive rugs. Towels discarded in the cabana next to the 25-metre pool. Designer clothes and shoes overflowing from closets to bedroom floors. A set of mud-spattered Range Rovers in the drive-way. Mrs Foster admonishing her untidy children in a mildly exasperated manner, all the while knowing that the cleaner would come on Friday and make the place spick and span. Mr Foster unperturbed about the household chaos, possibly quite refreshing after a day spent in the sterile confines of a hospital theatre.

There is something intoxicating about wealth that's scruffy and real-life as opposed to the showy, cringy kind. So, yeah, Megan can admit that her head was turned. She was impressed, a little envious. But the downside of that kind of careless wealth was revealed to her during the trial. The danger that comes from not having to clean up after yourself, not having to worry about bills that need paying, from having the luxury to pursue something that is ultimately going to lose you a lot of money, just to make a point. It cultivates selfishness, a poor grasp of reality.

Jess didn't ask after Megan's family; there's a point where politeness becomes farcical.

'I still can't believe I was the first responder,' Megan said, steering the conversation away from the minefield of families. 'It feels too coincidental.'

All she got was another shrug, one that said: *Don't ask me.* Surely, Jess could understand why she was here, trying to have this conversation? For God's sake, she had vocalised her desire to kill Newson! More than once. Admittedly after hours of intense cross-examination, riled by the barrister's audacity.

Did you make eye contact with the defendants?

Did you smile at them?

We have testimony from several witnesses that you were being sexually overt with these two men.

The idea that Jess might be somehow involved didn't occur to Megan immediately. The notion crept in later, lodging itself in her brain, arguing its case. Jess hates losing a fight. Her crooked nose is proof of her determination, her ability to prevail over pain. How many other bones did she break when she was fighting professionally? How many times did she pick herself up off the floor and resume the match? Or take a bashing against the ropes until the bell went? If there's anyone in the world who could hold on to a grudge for twelve long years, it's Jess. Her incredible doggedness. Her actual words: *I want to kill that cold-hearted bastard* …

Megan could have asked more questions as they sat there, the only two people in that soulless little café. In the end, she wasn't ballsy enough to persevere.

They said an awkward goodbye and went in separate directions outside the café.

Megan and Lucas are playing cards with another crew, Kaz and Sakar. The day has dragged on. Only two more call-outs: a great-grandmother with a suspected heart attack, and a withered old man suffering from a dizzy spell. On days like today it's the elderly who keep them in a job.

'Hey, Megan. You've been to Italy, haven't you?' Kaz asks as she shuffles the cards.

'Yeah. Ten years ago, though.'

They're playing Twenty-one, each chip worth ten cents. The small bet generates excitement, which passes the time while nobody is at risk of losing more than a couple of dollars.

Kaz deals the cards deftly. 'Can you give me some recommendations, darl? Tripadvisor's driving me crazy. Too many reviews, too many opinions, too much bloody whinging. If you read it all, you'd never go anywhere.'

Megan is the resident travel advisor at the base. Everyone knows she spent three years hopping from country to country, and even though it was a long time ago, they still ask her for recommendations.

'Sure. I'll look through my stuff when I get home.'

Her 'stuff' is in dusty boxes under her bed. Bus tickets, tour brochures and other keepsakes. Photo albums, with place names and dates meticulously written in the margins. Pictures of churches, town squares and sunsets. The wizened faces of old men and women sitting outside their homes, and the soft laughing faces of children. Megan's in very few photographs. She hated herself at the time.

Megan surveys the cards in her hand. Bust. Again.

'What cities did you go to? I've only got six days.'

Six days isn't enough, but it's obvious Kaz already knows that. Not everyone has what Megan had: an open-ended ticket and nothing worth returning for.

'Well, if you're short of time you should concentrate on the major ones, Venice, Florence, Rome …'

Lucas wins the round, scooping up the chips with a whoop. Kaz deals another hand and Megan's thoughts drift back in time. Italy was crazy roads, dry red wines, and men with sexy accents. She caught the train from Geneva to Milan, where she spent a week touring with a Swedish boy she met along the way. After gorging on cathedrals, museums and the Swedish boy, she crossed over to Venice, with its canals, history and romance. Next was Florence, then Rome, where she got a cleaning job in the hostel where she was staying. The hostel was next to the train station, a rough area, not safe to walk at night-time. She spent many of the nights entwined with Raimondo, the owner, twenty years older than her. After a month, she caught a bus to Naples, but no matter how far she travelled, or how many handsome European men she kissed, she couldn't get away from it. It was there every time she closed her eyes. It was a weight in her stomach when she woke in the mornings. It was present in her parents' voices when she phoned home.

While Megan was fleeing from country to country, Jess began her career as a fighter, notching up titles along the way. Fight or flight, they say. Eventually, Megan stopped her flight and came home. The question is if Jess ever stopped fighting. She hates being the loser. God knows, she can hold a grudge. According to her, she was at the gym on the night of the shooting, and has witnesses who can confirm it. What about Alex? Where was he? Does he have witnesses, too?

Alex's parents have a cattle farm in the Hunter Valley. Jess used to talk about the farm; Megan can remember seeing some photos. The farm is large, several hundred acres, and, like many farms in New South Wales, besieged with kangaroos, rabbits and foxes. This translates to two things: dirt bikes to access far-off acres and livestock; and guns to control the pest animals.

I want to kill that cold-hearted bastard. He's worse than any rapist.

Jess didn't *have* to leave the gym. She could have asked Alex to take on this fight for her.

11
JESS

Jess wakes up with a cracking headache, one of the worst ever. It feels like someone is tightening a vice over the front of her skull. The prospect of moving one centimetre to the left or right seems catastrophic. She lies perfectly still, fantasising about an ice-cold glass of water and a tiny white pill, but unable to mobilise herself to rise from bed to fetch them. She can hear the shower running. Alex will be out in a few minutes. She'll wait for him.

Her eyes close, shutting off the brightness slicing through a crack in the curtains. Nausea rises up her throat. The migraines come at random times. She can have a month without any, then suffer three in a row. The medication is effective if it's taken at the onset. Waking up with one is the worst-case scenario, its stranglehold already established.

'Hey, don't you need to get going?' Alex says when he emerges from the bathroom and notices that she's still in bed.

'Migraine,' she mutters, keeping her eyes half closed. 'Can you get me some water and my tablets? And when you've done that, can you call Vince for me?'

'Sure, babe.' He brushes his calloused hand against her forehead before heading to the kitchen. The sound of the fridge door opening and water being poured. Then the sound of cabinet doors opening and closing, thuds that resonate disproportionately in her head. He's looking for her box of medication.

'Second shelf above the toaster,' she calls out.

He's back. She forces her head off the pillow, pinching the tiny tablet before placing it on her tongue and glugging back most of the water. The liquid sloshes in her stomach. Another wave of nausea.

'Vince,' she reminds him as she flops back on the pillows. 'Tell him I'll be fine in a few hours.'

Vince understands better than anyone. Concussions cause hypersensitive areas of the brain, which cause migraines. Vince had his fair share of concussions, too.

Alex calls Vince while he's making breakfast. Disjointed words float back to the bedroom; Jess's brain hurts too much to segue them together. He sticks his head around the door when he's done.

'Vince says take the full day off. He doesn't want to see you till tomorrow.'

'All I need is a couple of hours.' She sighs, hating the

thought of inconveniencing her boss, who is always so accommodating.

Alex leaves shortly afterwards, the front door crashing behind him. Jess winces on her own behalf, and on behalf of their elderly neighbours. Alex doesn't do it on purpose. A certain clumsiness comes with being so tall.

She falls back asleep. It's ten when she wakes for the second time. The headache has receded, leaving her body tender, her mouth thick-tongued. Sunlight pours through the crack in the curtains, and she can cope with the brightness, which is a positive sign.

She uses the toilet, splashes water on her face, and brushes the gunge from her mouth. In the kitchen, she fills a glass with cold water and takes it outside to the balcony, where she sits down gingerly on one of the deckchairs. The sun is filtered, winterish. Deep breaths in and out, each intake opening up those defective vessels in her brain. Alex has built a vertical garden on one of the walls, Boston fern interspersed with white and purple violets. The opposite wall has shelves laden with pots of rosemary, thyme and other winter-proof herbs. This is the only part of the apartment that has Alex's stamp on it. This and the bathroom sink, the white enamel perpetually stubbled with his facial hair.

She sends him a text.

Feeling much better. Sitting outside and enjoying our urban garden.

He must have his hands dirty because his reply takes about fifteen minutes.

> Great you're feeling better. Just heading out to your parents' now. Want to tag along?

Jess's mother asked him to quote on some landscaping around the pool. She has never used his services before, other projects coming and going without any mention of whether Alex might be suitable for the job. Jess and Alex are not sure if this change of heart means that she has finally accepted that he's here to stay, or if it's coming from a belated sense of politeness. Maybe it's a means for her to keep an eye on him and come up with a fresh list of reasons why he's all wrong for her daughter.

It should be an easy answer. Jess has nothing pressing to do. The fresh air will be good for her. God knows, she is overdue a visit home. But it's not easy. It never is with her parents.

> Okay. If you think you need a bodyguard.

Jess slides back the passenger seat of the ute, so she can stretch out. There's something tucked underneath: a black puffer jacket.

'Where did this come from?' she asks, holding it up.

Alex gives it a quick glance, takes a moment to think. 'Ramsey must've left it when we were out last week.'

Jess brushes loose soil from the polyester fabric. Small brown stains persist. 'Well, it's going to need a wash.'

'Ramsey won't care. Probably something he wears at work.'

Ramsey works in construction; Alex is right, he won't be put off by a bit of dirt.

Jess rolls it up and puts it on the middle console, where Alex is more likely to remember to return it.

Alex pulls out from the kerb, pressing heavily on the accelerator. He usually drives with little regard for the rules of the road, but today is another level. Orange lights are a challenge, as is the slight loss of control on rounding corners. Of course, he's driving too fast on entering her parents' driveway. Gravel sprays in all directions. Jess can picture her mother's pained expression.

'Fucking hell, babe.' She gives him an angry stare. 'Stop giving her something to complain about.'

The front door opens before they're even close to it. Yep, she definitely heard their arrival. Margaret Foster's frown says more than any words.

'Jessica, I wasn't expecting you. Don't you have work?'

'Day off,' Jess replies in a tone that doesn't encourage further questions. She doesn't want her mother to know about the migraines. She'll only get started on all the reasons why she should never have stepped into a boxing ring in the first place.

'Come through,' Margaret says, waving them into the hall.

Alex glances at his work boots. 'I can go around the side if you want?'

'Oh, it's fine. The floors need a wash anyway.'

Margaret has never been pedantic about cleanliness, which probably saved her sanity when the house was full: four children, two dogs, school friends constantly coming and going. Jess's dad used to call the house Central Station. Now it's so quiet it's like a morgue. Even the dogs are gone. Her mum and dad like to travel, so when Poppy and Samson died of old age, they decided not to replace them.

Jess and Alex follow Margaret down the hall. Framed photographs line the walls on either side. Natasha and Edward receiving their Doctors of Medicine (Natasha is an oncologist now and Edward is in cardiology, like his father). A black-and-white photo of Angus in action with his clarinet at the Sydney Symphony Orchestra. They're a family of music and medicine. Even her father, when he's not performing bypass surgery, enjoys a tinkle on the piano.

Jess is last in the line-up of family photographs. Sweat glistening on her face, her lower lip swollen but still grinning from ear to ear. The referee is holding up her arm to signify the victory: her first Australian title. Not a musical bone in her body. Not a jot of interest in biology, chemistry or anything to do with medicine.

Where did you come from? Margaret used to ask in a

perplexed tone when Jess was younger. She still has the same question hovering on her lips, but knows better than to vocalise it these days.

The kitchen is Jess's favourite part of the house. White country-style cabinetry, pale-grey subway tiles and a solid wood countertop: rustic charm with a price tag. The kitchen always had the reassuring smell of food, a curry simmering on the stovetop, or muffins baking in the oven. If her mother wasn't with students in the piano room, she could be found in the kitchen, her bony fingers gripping a wooden spoon, preparing to feed the hordes.

Margaret yanks open the sliding doors that lead to the backyard.

'Over here,' she says, striding towards the pool. 'This whole area needs work, Alex. The retaining wall is crumbling away, and this garden bed needs rebuilding. I want to put in some screening, mature trees that won't take a lifetime to grow.'

'Planning on some skinny-dipping, Margaret?' Alex asks cheekily.

Jess smothers a laugh. He shouldn't tease her; their relationship isn't good enough to withstand it. Right from the start, she made it clear she didn't like him.

Very rough and ready, isn't he?

I suppose your connection is a physical one, rather than intellectual.

Little seeds of criticism, planted suitably apart, like fledgling trees!

What's in this relationship for you, Jessica? I see what's in it for him – free rent, et cetera – but what do you get out of it?

They were at a family barbecue when she came out with that one. Jess flounced off without vocalising her response. *This is what's in it for me, Mother: great sex, no criticism or hassle, someone who lets me be me.*

Alex runs his hands through the soil of the garden bed, presumably checking its quality. He uses his phone to take photographs of the wall, which looks like it needs to be repointed. Then he produces a measuring tape from his pocket.

'I'll leave you to it,' Margaret says abruptly. 'Come on, Jessica. Let's get the kettle on.'

Jess perches on one of the kitchen stools while her mother empties the kettle into the sink and refills it with fresh water.

'Been a while since we've seen you, Jessica. I thought you might have at least phoned when William Newson got gunned down outside his house.'

Fucking hell. Straight into it. Jess doesn't feel strong enough today.

'Look, Mum, I really, *really* don't want to discuss William Newson ... How's Dad?'

Margaret blinks. She's a bit like Jess: it's hard for her to walk away from something when her mind is set on it.

'Has he got theatre today?' Jess prompts her along.

Margaret's nod has more than a hint of reluctance. 'A triple bypass. Very complex from the sounds of it. How's work going for you?'

'Fine. Good. The gym keeps getting busier and busier.'

'You're looking a bit pale. Are you feeling okay?'

Margaret knows. She might not understand Jess, but she has always had the uncanny ability to see right through her. *What have you done, Jessica? Tell the whole truth. We can't help you if you only give us half the story.*

Jess adjusts her position on the stool. 'Woke up with a bit of a headache. But it's gone now.'

Margaret gives her a scrutinising stare. 'I wish you wouldn't—'

'Don't, Mum. Please don't. I'm fine. And I'm happy.'

Margaret turns sharply. She's rummaging in the freezer. A plastic container lands on the counter in front of Jess. Margaret extracts some frozen muffins.

'Banana and vanilla. Have to freeze them these days, otherwise they go to waste.'

The microwave door pings open. Jess's stomach constricts with hunger and memories. Sometimes she gives the wrong impression. It was a happy childhood. Yes, she was different from her siblings, but that didn't mean there wasn't warmth or love. Margaret made sure the pantry and fridge were well stocked, and there was always a cooked dinner that catered for a few hangers-on. Friends would come for a swim and stay for dinner, then reappear at the breakfast table the next morning. Banter and squabbles at mealtimes. Excitement from the dogs when they got home from wherever they were. The sound of Margaret's students playing their scales on the piano. 'C sharp,' she would correct them, in the same exasperated tone she used for her own children.

Jessica, life would be so much easier for all of us if you just toed the line!

Jess was the rebellious child. Pushing the boundaries, at school and at home. Ditching classes. Lying about her whereabouts. Raiding her dad's drinks cabinet (a predictable story that ends with vomiting on her bedroom carpet). Pretty normal teenage antics. Until that house party, until the rape, until the trial. That's when Jess recognised the dangers of having too much money, and the illusion that money can actually protect you. As a result, she keeps a distance from this life, and from her parents; too easy to get sucked back in.

She made herself a promise after the trial: her mother and father would never have to pay another cent for her. Make her own way, pay her own way.

Next time Jess fucks up, it's on her alone.

12
BRIDGET

Bridget is parked outside Suzanne Newson's house, waiting for Dave to join her. She's seeking a third opinion on William Newson's ex-wife. Is Suzanne as congenial and harmless as first impressions suggested? She admitted that the divorce had been acrimonious, and Bridget and Katrina didn't press for details. Her ex-husband's life had been hanging by a thread; she was upset and in no fit state to be interrogated. Now, her ex-husband is dead, and after meeting with their son, Joshua, Bridget has a better handle on what questions to ask this woman. For a start, the specifics behind that gnarly word 'acrimonious'. Was there a disagreement regarding assets or spousal maintenance? Or maybe bitterness generated by deceit or infidelity? Or perhaps it was years and years of ingrained resentment, leading to an inability to see eye to eye on anything at all, let alone the terms of a divorce. Or maybe, as Joshua alluded to, there were ideological differences.

All those girls can't be lying.

Dave pulls up in a squad car. He gets out, straightening his tie. He and Bridget converge on the footpath. Because it's just the two of them, they exchange a hug. He smells of coffee and sandalwood aftershave.

'Bridget! We must stop meeting like this.'

It's obvious that he's pleased to be working with her on the investigation. Homicide don't have to involve detectives from local area command but Bridget tries to whenever she can. If the shoe were on the other foot, she'd hate being frozen out. Besides, Dave has invaluable local knowledge: CCTV locations, hide-outs and rat runs, ex-cons and current criminals living nearby. He has also orchestrated the search of more than a thousand rubbish bins in the surrounding area. No evidence was found, but that doesn't detract from the gigantic effort or Dave's stoic approach to the task.

A bottle-green fence protects Suzanne's colourful, well-tended garden from the road. It's the tail end of winter, rainfall has been woefully scarce; someone has clearly put a lot of time and effort into this garden.

The front door is the same bottle-green as the fence. Bridget raps on it loudly. A growl resonates from somewhere inside, followed by loud barking.

'That sounds like a big dog,' Dave comments warily.

'It's the little ones you need to watch out for.' Bridget

met the dog – a Golden Retriever – last week. She can't remember its name, only that it was one hundred per cent friendly.

The dog bounds outside as soon as the door is opened.

'Come back here, Mabel ... Mabel! Mabel!'

The dog pays no attention to its mistress, heading straight for Dave, jumping up on its hind legs.

'Mabel! Mabel! Get down!' Suzanne is wearing similar clothes to last week: tailored pants, a long-sleeved cotton shirt, sensible shoes. Her short grey hair is neatly combed, her face plump and exasperated.

She smiles apologetically at Dave. 'Sorry about that. She's nearly ten and still acts like a puppy.'

'Don't worry about it. People aren't always so pleased to see me.' He sticks out his hand. 'Detective Sergeant David Nesbitt.'

The dog doubles back to Bridget. She gives its head a ruffle.

They follow Suzanne into the back of the house. The mid-morning sun illuminates the sparse furnishings: a floral sofa, a small table with two chairs, a TV perched on an old-fashioned wooden unit. The house and contents are in stark contrast to the multi-level architect dwelling of her ex-husband.

'Have you lived here long?' Bridget enquires, a question she didn't ask last week.

'I bought it two years ago, after the divorce. Still haven't got around to properly furnishing it.'

Haven't got around to, or not able to afford to? It doesn't look like Suzanne came out of the divorce particularly well.

'I was admiring your garden on the way in,' Bridget says, sitting next to Dave on the sofa. 'Mine's parched. Not sure how much longer the plants will last with this drought.'

Suzanne smiles. 'The water restrictions make it difficult. Most people don't have the time to hand water … Can I get either of you anything to drink?'

'No thanks, we're fine,' Bridget assures her without checking with Dave. 'We don't want to bother you for too long, Suzanne. It's been a difficult week for you and the family. We just want to follow up on a few things. Sorry in advance about the personal nature of these questions …'

Mabel lies down at Suzanne's feet. Her hand strokes the dog's coat. 'Go on,' she says softly.

'You mentioned last week that the split was acrimonious. Would you mind expanding on that? Was there a disagreement about money?'

Suzanne presses her lips together. 'You could say so, but not in the way you might think … William wasn't an ungenerous man, but I didn't want his money. I took only a fraction of what I was entitled to, just enough to buy this house and have a bit left over for a rainy day.'

Dave is scribe, his notebook balanced on one knee. He's a lefthander, his writing large but well-formed and legible, from what Bridget can see.

'Can you explain why you didn't want his money?' Bridget asks in a light tone that doesn't reflect how interested she is in the upcoming answer.

'I didn't like where it came from,' Suzanne says plainly, her eyes darting from Bridget to Dave.

All those girls can't be lying.

'You mean you didn't like that he earned some of it from defending sexual assault cases?'

Suzanne rubs her temples with the tips of her fingers. Bridget wonders if she has a headache coming on. 'I read some of the files he brought home at night. Saw the photos, the statements, the medical reports … It bothered me and bothered me until eventually I found the whole situation – and him – repulsive.'

Bridget and Dave exchange a glance.

'Can you tell us if you went out anywhere last Tuesday night?' Dave asks, knowing full well that Suzanne was asked this question previously. 'Did you pop out to the shops, or go anywhere in the car?'

She shakes her head, then gestures to the room around them. 'I was here all evening. I was watching *The Block* when I got the phone call from Joshua. He was on his way to the hospital.'

Bridget had been watching *The Block* too, before her phone rang. Everyone knows what time the show airs; this detail doesn't offer any reassurance that Suzanne was really here.

'When was the last time someone saw you on Tuesday?' Dave continues.

Suzanne takes a moment to consider this. 'I was in the garden that afternoon, between four and five. I think I said hello to one of my neighbours as she walked past. But I'm not sure if I have the right day.'

'Which neighbour? What number house?'

Suzanne provides the information but reiterates that she isn't sure. Now that Dave is asking the questions, Bridget can concentrate on reading Suzanne's facial clues and body language. Her colouring is high. She seems slightly flustered. But she is being cooperative and appears to be genuine.

'Did you use your phone to make any calls?'

'Only after I heard the news. I called Quentin and Riley and other relatives to let them know.'

Quentin is the son who works in the UK, Riley studies politics in Canberra. Back at headquarters, Patrick is examining Suzanne's phone records, as well as signals from her handset to the local base station, which should help in providing her approximate location. He's also doing some digging on her financial situation, although if Suzanne is to be believed she doesn't want any of her ex-husband's money.

Bridget gives Dave a nod, indicating that she is ready to take over again.

'How are your sons holding up, Suzanne?'

Her face crumples. 'It's hard on them. They've never lost anyone close – both sets of grandparents are alive. Me being estranged from their father is difficult, too. The boys are organising the funeral. I'm helping as much as I can from the sidelines, giving advice about what kind of coffin they should buy, who should speak at the service, what to do afterwards … But the responsibility rests with them.'

'Are Quentin and Riley staying here with you?'

'No, they're with Joshua. He's in Blues Point Road. Much better location. Lots of good restaurants on the doorstep.'

Bridget doesn't comment. Surely, the availability of good restaurants should be irrelevant in circumstances such as these?

'How do your sons feel about their father's cases? Are they as repulsed as you?'

Suzanne contemplates this for a moment. 'Quentin and Riley are very removed from it. They live in different cities, have different professions … I don't think they've ever stopped to think it through. Joshua isn't repulsed, but he *has* got caught in the crossfire more than once.'

'How?' Bridget prompts.

'Protesters outside the courthouse. Someone who spray-painted the reception area of the chambers. The Malouf–O'Shea case was the worst – Joshua was still at university then. A girl egged him while he was walking through the campus. Bloody underwear was taped to his locker. Turned out it was just fake blood, but Joshua was very upset. The stress made him overeat. He's still carrying around the extra weight today.'

Bridget's eyes flick to Dave, writing as diligently as

ever. There's a lot to get down. Hopefully, he's capturing it all. Of course, they could bring Suzanne in for a formal interview, hitting the record button and negating the need for taking notes, but in Bridget's opinion one can never replicate the benefits of an informal chat in the home. People tend to let their guard down. It's harder to sustain a lie in the place where they're at their most honest.

She looks around the room, granting Dave some time to catch up. Her eyes snag on a series of matching photo frames on the shelf above the TV. Suzanne and her sons, three dark-haired bulky men. Suzanne with another woman of a similar age, champagne glasses raised, a celebratory moment frozen in time. Suzanne shaking someone's hand at some kind of official gathering.

Bridget stands up to take a closer look. 'Is that the NSW Premier?'

'Yes. It was great meeting her. She's extremely witty in person. Not at all what I expected.'

'What was the occasion?'

'Oh, I just received an award, that's all.'

'For what?'

'Some work I do at the Rape Crisis Centre.'

All those girls can't be lying.

Bridget sinks back down on the floral sofa. Dave indicates that he has caught up, which is good because this tangent seems like a rather important one.

'What kind of work do you do at the centre?'

'Mainly fundraising. I also facilitate one of the support groups.'

'When did you become involved in the organisation?'

'Two years ago. Around the time of the divorce.'

'And what did William think about this?'

Suzanne folds her arms in a blatantly defensive action. 'Look, he wasn't pleased, but it was my business, not his. I didn't specifically want to make life difficult for him, and I tried to be discreet, using my maiden name so there was less chance of it having a negative impact on his practice.'

While William Newson was defending sexual assault offenders, his ex-wife was actively supporting the victims. How did these two remain married for so long? How did they end up on opposing sides?

'Can you tell me more about your divorce? Was there something specific that forced your hand, Suzanne?'

'Just the build-up of becoming more and more disillusioned with the work he was engaging in. And, yes, there *was* a tipping point. You see, he had this repeat client ... Unbelievable, isn't it?' Suzanne pauses, to register her incredulity with her audience. 'Suddenly it seemed inevitable that they would *all* reoffend at some point, because they had never been appropriately punished in the first place ... thanks to my husband. The same offenders reappearing again and again, like a conveyor belt, labelling the victims as liars, never being held to account for their behaviour, my husband facilitating their violence. I couldn't bear to be in the same house as him, so I packed my bags and went to stay with my sister. A few weeks later I offered my services to the Rape Crisis Centre and began divorce proceedings. Everything was handled through lawyers. William and I didn't speak to each other again.'

A whole new definition of 'acrimonious'. Bridget is both appalled and impressed. Impartiality is one of the hardest things she's had to learn in the police force. Hiding what she thinks and feels behind a mask of neutrality, striving to maintain an open mind, reminding herself that there are two sides to every story.

'So the burial is Friday?' she asks in what she hopes is a matter-of-fact tone.

'Yes, eleven a.m. at St Mary's. The body was released yesterday afternoon. I've decided not to go.'

Bridget is going. Dave doesn't know it yet, but he is too. The funeral is an opportunity to gain a deeper understanding of the family dynamic. The pink-faced woman sitting before them, who was so repulsed by her ex-husband she supposedly didn't even want her fair share of their assets. Joshua, the middle son, who was bullied as a direct result of his father's courtroom victories and the only family member to see him on a regular basis. His fly-in brothers, who have chosen not to stay with their mother, which Bridget finds peculiar. Boys, even the grown-up ones, yearn to be spoiled by their mothers. Do they resent Suzanne for shattering the family unit? Would they have preferred that she suffer in silence, live the rest of her life with a man whose moral compass was pointing in the opposite direction to her own?

'Thanks, Suzanne. We'll be in touch if there is anything else.'

13
MEGAN

'Ready to spend the day saving people from the jaws of death?' Lucas says in greeting. It's 5.30 a.m.; they're on the early shift.

'Buy me a coffee and we'll see!'

Megan is not a morning person. Winter mornings are particularly excruciating. Hauling herself out of bed in the dark, her bedroom an icebox. Like many houses in Sydney, they don't have proper heating. Nine months of the year, it's fine, but conditions are frigid from June to August. The fact that the house is a weatherboard and all the windows and doors are old and ill-fitting compounds the problem.

The crew they're taking over from are still in the process of cleaning the ambulance. Megan sticks her head inside the rear doors, the smell of disinfectant lodging in the back of her throat.

'Hey, guys. How did your shift go?'

A few car accidents and asthma attacks, a cardiac arrest and a suicide attempt: sounds like they had an eventful shift. The crew get to share their war stories, and at the same time help Megan establish what to pay attention to while completing the checklists. Medical kit, trauma kit and oxygen kit have all been restocked.

Lucas does the vehicle checks – tyres, fuel, oil levels, sirens, cabin. Once handover is complete, he drives them to the closest McDonald's. They sit in the deserted car park, sipping from their disposable coffee cups, watching dawn breaking across the sky, yellow and orange leaching into greyness.

'Heard anything more from that detective?' Lucas asks quietly.

Oh God. She should have guessed this was coming. Steeled herself.

'Not a thing.' Megan stares straight ahead, not trusting herself to meet his eyes.

To tell the truth, she thought she'd hear more from Bridget Kennedy. Maybe she and Jess are a long way down the list of people who had issues with William Newson. Maybe she has been worrying and casting aspersions on Alex for nothing.

'You okay, Megs?' She feels Lucas's eyes raking over her face, hears the concern in his voice. She's not okay. The reverberating shock of recognising William Newson's face, that prickly dissatisfying meeting with Jess, speaking about the rape after so many years of silence: her façade is well and truly cracked. One look at Lucas and he'd know that she's not okay. Then he would take her in his arms, like that night in the pub. It's tempting.

'Course I am. Tough as old boots!' She takes a large glug from her cup. The caffeine courses through her bloodstream. 'How's Daniella?'

Nothing as grounding as bringing up his girlfriend's name.

'Yeah, fine. She's thinking of going back to university to study orthodontics.'

'How long will that take?'

'Another three years.'

Daniella works in a busy dental practice in Chatswood. Orthodontics would suit her; she's very up-close and detail-oriented.

'Maybe she'll give me a discount. My dentist wants me to get braces. Too old, too expensive, I said.'

Lucas turns her chin towards him. 'Let's see. Smile.'

Their faces are so close Megan can see the gold flecks in his brown eyes. She sticks out her tongue before baring her teeth at him.

'Definite overbite,' he declares. 'I'll ask her about the discount.'

'Well, she can practise on your wonky teeth before touching mine.'

They're still laughing when the MDT lights up. The mood changes instantly.

'Six-month-old baby with febrile convulsions,' Megan reads out loud.

Sirens and lights. Their coffee break is over.

The mother is hysterical, the sick baby propped in her arms while a little girl pulls at her leg. Both children are red-faced and howling. Everyone is dressed in pyjamas.

'He wasn't well last night. I thought it was just a cold. Oh God, is he going to be okay?'

Lucas is in the process of removing the baby's one-piece pyjamas.

'He's very hot,' Megan says, speaking slowly because fear makes it hard to listen. 'Have you given him any medication in the last few hours?'

'Baby Panadol, a few minutes before he started fitting.'

'How long did the seizure last for?'

'Six or seven minutes? I don't know exactly. Oh God, I should have brought him to the doctor last night. I'm so sorry.'

Her face is blotched from crying. Her hair hasn't been combed. She looks like she needs a hug, a strong cup of tea, and being sent back to bed for the shock. Poor woman. It's a scary thing, seeing a child having convulsions, even when you aren't related to them. The toddler is still howling and adding to her stress levels.

'No need to be sorry. You did the right thing, calling us. Have you got anyone who can come and help?'

'My husband's away on business. We're new to the area. I don't even know where the hospital is.'

The pitch of her voice rises with each statement. The toddler's volume rises in conjunction, feeding off her distress. The baby, down to its nappy, is kicking and screaming. Megan can barely hear herself speak.

'No problem. We can take you all with us. Grab your bag and whatever you need.' She gives the toddler a smile. 'You want to come for a ride in the ambulance?'

'No!' she wails, not the response Megan was hoping for. 'I don't want am-blence. *I don't want am-blence.*'

'We have lollies in am-blence,' Lucas says helpfully.

'Lollies! Lollies!' The transformation is instantaneous.

Megan and Lucas share a smirk. If only adults were so easy to manipulate.

The young mother reappears in record time, wearing jeans in place of her pyjama bottoms and sneakers instead of slippers. She wrestles the toddler into a pair of sparkly pink shoes.

'Do you need a bottle for the baby?' Megan prompts. 'Nappies?'

'Oh God, yes.'

'Keys. Phone. And don't forget jackets, it's cold out there this morning.'

Both kids have perked up by the time everyone's loaded into the ambulance.

The toddler is ecstatic with the lollipop Lucas presents to her. 'We're going to the hob-ital,' she announces cheerfully.

'Yep,' Lucas says. 'We're going to the hob-ital in the am-blence.'

The baby's cheeks are less red and his eyes have regained some of their twinkle. Curious fingers reach out to touch Lucas's nose.

'Hey, little fella. Think you can just poke me in the face now that you're feeling better?'

'Do you have kids?' the mother asks Lucas, smoothing tousled hair back from her tear-streaked face.

'Nope. Just practising.'

He's going to make a great father one day. This is why Megan finds it so hard to like Daniella: she is plain jealous of her. Daniella doesn't appreciate how good he is with the kids, or how kind with the old people, or how caring to just about everyone. Megan feels the envy contorting her face; she bangs shut the ambulance doors before anyone notices.

'That's a wrap,' Lucas declares, twelve hours later. They've completed the handover to the next crew and are walking back to their cars. It's dark and chilly, like early this morning when they started their shift. He looks as tired as she feels.

'Enough people saved from the jaws of death for one day.' Megan smiles. 'Four days off, though. What're you going to do with yourself?'

'Sleep. Call and see the folks. Take Daniella out for a nice meal.'

Daniella. That ugly stab of jealousy again. Can he

see it on her face? Oh God, she hopes not.

'Well, enjoy the break,' she says, disguising the jealousy with cheeriness. 'See you next week.'

Next week they're rostered for 10 a.m. to 10 p.m. Preferable to getting out of bed in the dark, but no chance of doing anything outside work. This job is hard on families as well as social lives. The long shifts, which can be day or night or straddling both. Home for either breakfast or dinner, but never both meals. When everything goes to plan, and there are no extra shifts to cover sicknesses or other absences, Megan is rewarded with four days off in a row. Her mum goes from not seeing her at all to falling over her at every turn. Does Daniella feel wrong-footed too?

In the car, Megan turns the heating and the radio up high. Lucas is ahead of her as she exits on to the road but they turn in different directions at the first intersection. After a few minutes her phone rings, shutting off the music. It's Roslyn.

'Hi, love. Just checking where you're at?'

'Just left five minutes ago.'

'I'll put the dinner on, so. We're having fish.'

'Anything you want me to pick up on the way?'

'No, we seem to be fine for everything.'

Mother and daughter have regimented roles. Roslyn does the cooking and gardening, Megan takes care of shopping and cleaning. Tomorrow Megan will call into their local real estate agent, to see if they can get out of this rut. The longer it goes on the more strangulated she feels.

Roslyn hangs up and the music comes back on. Megan likes the song, it's new and catchy.

The phone rings again.

'Yes, Mum? Forget something we needed?'

'Megan, it's … it's … Dylan O'Shea.'

The shock is intense. Her chest tightens. It's hard to draw air. A red light looms out of nowhere. She slams on the brakes at the very last moment.

'Megan, I'd like … I'd like … Can we … can we meet …? I just want to talk.'

Speak. Answer him. Tell him what you think. Speak, *for God's sake.*

'No.' An explosion from her mouth. Her hands grip the steering wheel, knuckles white and protruding.

'No,' she repeats, because she wants him to hear loud and clear, because she wants him to know that she has learned to speak up for herself.

'I do *not* want to meet you. I do *not* want to talk to you. Not now or ever. I've told you this before. Do *not* call this number again.'

Megan ends the call. Then the shaking starts.

14
JESS

Thomas Malouf and Dylan O'Shea: their names are like invisible scar tissue. Year-twelve students at Barwood College, a school for rich and privileged boys (Jess's school was for rich and privileged girls, so she can't exactly criticise). She met Thomas through friends of friends. Floppy hair, dimples when he smiled. The kind of boy who wore shirts instead of T-shirts. The kind of boy who sauntered rather than walked.

The party was in Thomas's house, in September. Those last few weeks of school, when assignments and trial exams were behind them and study leave for the real exams hadn't yet begun. They were stir-crazy from a year of hard work combined with very little play. Freedom had never felt so close or so far away.

'Sixty?' Jess gasped when he told her how many

people were going to the party. Her group of school friends were hanging out with his group at the local shopping centre. 'Your parents okay with that?'

Jess's parents had an open house when it came to friends calling round or sleeping over, but any requests for parties had been met with a flat refusal.

'Don't be stupid,' Thomas smirked. 'My parents are in Melbourne for the weekend. As far as they're concerned, I'm studying and looking after Leo.'

Thomas's younger brother was fifteen, but Jess didn't know that at the time. She was imagining a much younger boy; little did she know what a pivotal role Leo would play in the whole debacle.

'What if your brother tells your parents?'

Thomas's laugh was the nasty kind. 'He wouldn't dare. He learned a long time ago what happens to squealers.'

A warning sign she should have heeded. Questions she should have asked: what happens to squealers? Do they get hurt? How far do you go to get revenge, Thomas? Is your brother afraid of you?

At this point, Jess and Thomas hadn't kissed, but there was an expectation that something would happen at the party.

'Can my friend Megan come? She's from another school.'

How Jess wishes she could go back in time and retract that question.

'Only if she's good-looking.'

He laughed when he said this, but Jess should have seen it for what it was: another warning sign. Girls were commodities to Thomas Malouf.

'Hey, O'Shea,' Thomas called to one of his friends. 'Might have a girl for you. From another school, so she won't know you're such a dumbo.'

Jess knew Dylan vaguely. Pale-skinned, an extremely nervous speaker. She was pretty sure Megan wouldn't find him attractive. Megan didn't have much experience with boys. Neither did Jess, beyond a few casual hook-ups, but she was ready to step things up a notch with Thomas.

'Saturday night, then,' she said, adopting some of his swagger. 'See ya there.'

It's excruciating to look back on it. Jess wants to shake that girl, scream some sense into her.

Open your eyes. Can't you see he only wants one thing? Choose some other boy. Choose someone who's not as cruel or vindictive. Choose someone who's not going to ruin your life.

There's no going back, though.

Jess smiled at Thomas and her fate was decided. Megan's, too.

Youth classes run from 4 p.m. to 5 p.m., Monday to Thursday. It's an eclectic group of kids. Eight boys and two girls, aged between twelve and sixteen. A few of the kids are agile, strong and show real potential. One kid, Andy, is overweight and being bullied about it; he's here to gain some respect at school. Another kid, Tyler, is as uncoordinated as he is unenthusiastic; he's here because his parents want him here. As per usual, some of them have forgotten their mouthguards. As per usual, Jess and Vince take a tough stance: no mouthguard means no sparring. Discipline, discipline, discipline.

'Okay, we're going to punch off now. Up top, fast … Underneath, slower … I want to hear those bags being hit.'

Fifteen minutes later everyone is thoroughly warmed up. They split the class, one group heading towards the ring with Vince and the others – the ones without mouthguards – staying with Jess to do activities on the mat.

'Tyler, take off your school shoes, mate.' Tyler is a repeat offender when it comes to forgetting his mouth-guard. It's obvious that he forgets on purpose.

The first activity involves bouncing tennis balls, and is particularly challenging for the uncoordinated kids. Balls rebound out of reach. Hands and legs quickly go out of sync. It's hard not to laugh. Vince's voice carries over from the ring, where the first pair have started to spar.

'Throw hard, Andy. Like you mean it. Stop waving it at him. Up on your toes. That's good. Long arm … Hands back to your head afterwards. Good boy.'

Sounds like Andy is landing a few good ones. Jess has a soft spot for that kid. He's very overweight, lacking in natural athleticism as well as confidence. He puts in the hard work, though. Listens carefully to everything they say. Never forgets his mouthguard.

The beeper goes off and another pair of kids jump into the ring.

'Sit in a line, feet balanced off the ground,' Jess says to her own group. 'This is a concentration and reflexes game. When I throw the ball at you, you've got to catch it and throw it back.'

This time it's a soccer ball. She gives each of them an easy throw to start off with, moving in order up the line. Then she throws harder and more randomly, tricking them with dummy throws before firing it at another person.

'Pay attention, Tyler. If you don't pay attention in the ring, you're going to get hit!'

Every class finishes with core work, with the two groups reunited on the mat. Andy finds the core work really difficult. Sweating and panting, he's giving it his best. In the meantime, Tyler is doing everything he can to cheat the system, not coming the full way down for push-ups, or maintaining position for the entire duration of the planks. Tyler reminds Jess of Thomas Malouf's younger brother, Leo. Similar in both looks and manner. Sometimes it's hard to get past the similarity. It can be easy to get caught up feeling sorry for boys like that, even easier to mistake their true motivations and loyalties.

Tyler's mother has arrived to pick him up. She's hovering by the roller door, in her trendy jacket and gym wear. Vince ambles over to speak to her, probably to let her know that Tyler's forgetfulness meant he was limited to activities on the mat again. Tyler hurriedly unwraps his hands, a stream of red bandaging spiralling downwards. He shoves the wrapping into his school bag without stopping to rezip it; it's obvious he can't wait to get out of here.

'Hey, mate, hold on a minute.' Jess touches his arm to get his attention.

'Yeah?' He eyes his mother, who is still talking to Vince, an earnest expression on her face.

'If you don't like sparring, just come out and say it, okay? It's not compulsory. And if you don't like coming here, even to do the activities, you should tell your mother. The worst thing you can do is go along with things.'

That's what Leo Malouf did. Went along with things. Went along with his brother's lies.

15
BRIDGET

The weather is far too beautiful for a funeral; it's the kind of day when things are begun, rather than ended. Bridget feels a trickle of sweat running down her back: her jacket is too heavy. Who knew that the cold morning would transform into this glorious day? Her face will be pink, never a good look with red hair. Mourners are making their way from the car park to the church, men in black suits and women in dark dresses and heels. She's waiting for Dave, which is becoming something of a pattern. Organ music drifts from the church. Was William Newson a religious man? Did he speak about his wishes with his sons, or with Suzanne while they were married? Some people can't bear to talk about death and their relatives have to resort to guesswork. Bridget knows what she wants: a cremation and a non-religious service. Her husband, Shane, is planning to donate his body to science.

'Ugh! Does that mean we'd only get some parts back for the funeral?' Cara asked, when the topic came up during a family meal. Cara looked disgusted. Ethan looked bored. Bridget felt mildly turned off her food.

'When the science faculty are finished dissecting me, they'll return what's left for burial or cremation. It could be months or years later. None of you will really care by then.'

A squad car swings into the car park, driving slightly too fast. Dave's face is flushed. Another hug to greet each other: his squishy stomach and the scent of coffee mingled with aftershave.

'Come on,' Bridget says. 'We're late.'

The church, old and sandstone, is dark and restful inside. It's less than half full. Bridget and Dave slide into one of the pews towards the back.

The Reverend is bespectacled and surprisingly young. 'We are gathered here to say farewell to William Newson and commit him into the hands of God.'

Some of Bridget's colleagues don't attend funerals, fearful that their presence would be intrusive to the family, or might jeopardise the investigation in some unforeseen way. Bridget attends primarily out of respect. Over the coming weeks and months, from investigation to – hopefully – court proceedings, she will come to know this family quite intimately. This is the start of a journey they will take together. She also attends because it gives her a unique opportunity to observe all the players. The immediate family are seated in the front row: an elderly man and woman sitting alongside the boys, presumably their paternal grandparents. Extended family – aunts, uncles and cousins – are pressed close together in the seats directly behind. Friends are identifiable by the fact that they're sitting further back, the gaps between bodies noticeably wider. A few lawyer types here and there: arms folded and heads bowed, probably lamenting the fact that this isn't billable hours.

The Reverend says a prayer, followed by a short reading from the Bible. Then Quentin, the oldest boy, is called on to deliver the eulogy. He stands rigidly at the pulpit. Silence: it's obvious he's trying to control his breathing. Bridget's protective instincts are stirred. Ethan, her fifteen-year-old, was an emotional young boy. Any sign of tears equated to relentless teasing by his classmates, which only made him more upset.

Walk away, Bridget used to advise him. *Walk away until your emotions are back under control.*

I can't walk out of class, Mum.

Say rats. Say it over and over, under your breath. You won't be able to cry while you're saying it. It's something to do with how you have to use your mouth to form the words.

Now, Bridget can't remember the last time Ethan cried, or sought her advice.

Quentin composes himself. He begins to speak, haltingly. 'Dad was a man of conviction and loyalty ... When he loved something, he loved it wholeheartedly … He loved cricket, and instilled that love in us, his sons. He could always be found scoring our Saturday games. In fact, he was so good at scoring, all the other parents made up excuses when it was their turn.' Laughter from the congregation. 'Dad paid an exorbitant amount for his membership at the Sydney Cricket Ground, and rotated which one of us went with him. I have vivid memories of those days. Sunburn and sweltering heat. Ice cream and hot chips. Dad's undivided attention … during the tea breaks, at least.' Another round of laughter. Quentin is warming up. 'Dad loved his job. He was disappointed that Joshua was the only one of us who followed him into law. He didn't have much time for accountants. "How's the number bashing going?" he would ask me. "Come across an honest politician yet?" he would tease Riley. To him, nothing was purer or more worthy than law.

'And Dad loved family. He loved Mum …' Bridget feels Dave stiffen by her side. Did William really love Suzanne or is Quentin saying it out of politeness? If he did, his feelings certainly weren't reciprocated. His ex-wife made a statement by deciding not to come here today. She used the word 'repulsive'.

'He loved his parents, Virginia and Ron. And he loved us, his sons – me, Joshua and Riley. "You're all that matter," he would say. "You three are all that matter." Dad, I hope you know how much you mattered to us …'

Joshua and his brothers are standing outside the church, shaking hands with people as they leave.

'Detective Kennedy,' he says, looking both surprised and displeased to see Bridget.

'Hello, Joshua.' His hand is clammy, like last time. 'This is my colleague, Detective Sergeant Nesbitt.'

'I'm sorry for your loss,' Dave murmurs. He has a natural way with people. Slightly gruff voice that suggests depth of feeling. Cuddly physique that implies approachability. 'These are very difficult circumstances.'

'This isn't a good time if you need to talk to us.'

'We're just here to pay our respects,' Bridget assures him, offering her hand to Quentin, who's next in line.

Quentin smiles tremulously. His handshake is warmer than Joshua's.

Riley, the youngest boy, doesn't make eye contact as she shakes his hand. His eyes are trained downwards, on his black leather shoes. Considerably younger than his brothers: the age gap must be at least ten years. Was he a much desired third child or an 'accident'? What was the state of the marriage by the time he was born?

Bridget shrugs off her jacket as soon as she and Dave are a respectable distance from the church. 'How about a sandwich and a debrief?'

He jerks his head towards the shopping precinct. 'Let's leave the car and walk. Funerals make me think too much.'

Bridget knows what he means. It's hard not to apply

118

'what ifs' to your own family. What if Bridget or Shane died unexpectedly? What if Cara and Ethan had to sit in that desolate first pew, their grief and vulnerability on tragic display? What if one of them had to deliver the eulogy? God, it doesn't bear thinking about. Bridget will subject them to an extra-tight hug when she gets home tonight, even though they'll hate it.

Bridget updates Dave as they walk. 'The forensic autopsy report didn't turn up anything new. First bullet entered the abdomen and travelled in a parallel direction to his back. He was beginning to fall as the second bullet was fired. It entered the chest cavity and, again, travelled to his back. Thirty-two-calibre Federal bullet casings.'

Despite strict gun control and border security, there are thousands of untraced weapons on the black market in Sydney, many stolen from licensed gun dealers or owners.

'Forensics have checked his laptop. No suspicious files or internet activity. Nothing to report in terms of his phone calls or texts. House and car have been extensively searched. No large sums of cash or anything else suspicious. There's no evidence that William Newson was engaged in any kind of illegal activity.'

'Do you have a firm timeline?' Dave asks, slightly out of breath.

'He spent most of the day in court, returning to the office at four, then working till six thirty. Commute home took about fifty minutes. CCTV along the route indicates he was alone in the car. He parked in the garage on arriving home, went to take out the bins before going inside. We think we've identified the motorbike on a camera at the 7-Eleven in Lindfield. Yamaha, very common. No registration plates, of course, and the rider wasn't wearing anything we can use for identification purposes. Can't even tell if it's a he or a she. I'm getting the images enhanced.'

'Send them to me and I'll post them on our Facebook page,' Dave says. 'We get a great response rate from the public, even when the images are blurry … Here we are. This should do the job.'

He opens the door and steps aside so Bridget can enter the café ahead of him. Pale green walls, white wrought-iron tables, and the combined smell of toasted sandwiches and coffee beans. Their order is taken by a girl who's a similar age to Cara. Wide smile, friendly demeanour. Maybe not so like Cara after all.

'So that's where we're at. No alarm bells ringing from Newson's bank transactions, internet activity or physical movements. We're also formulating a timeline for Joshua and Suzanne and checking their bank and phone records. Sasha, one of our junior detectives, is looking at Newson's will and life insurance policies.'

'Sounds like you have things well in hand.'

'That's one way of putting it … Another would be to say we have bugger all to go on.'

Their order is delivered by the smiley waitress, two flat-white coffees and overfilled sandwiches held together with toothpicks.

'How about your end of things?' Bridget asks. 'Anything to report?'

She tasked Dave with going back around the neighbourhood, attempting to jog memories in relation to unusual occurrences in the days leading up to the shooting.

'I've talked to the next-door neighbour, Mrs Simon, who wasn't at home that night. She and her daughter were at the theatre, came back about eleven. Mrs Simon is close friends with Suzanne Newson. She described her relationship with William as "civil", which leads me to believe there wasn't a lot of love lost between them.'

'She probably took sides during the divorce,' Bridget surmises. 'Did Mrs Simon notice any unusual visitors or activity next door?'

'Apparently, the only regular visitor was Joshua. He dropped in the Sunday before and had a brief chat with Mrs Simon, who was out in her garden when he arrived. She said he seemed a bit distracted. He looked over his shoulder once or twice while they were speaking, as if he were expecting someone else to turn up.'

Bridget is immediately suspicious of such extraordinary detail. 'Is there a Mr Simon in the house?'

'He died four years ago.'

'How about neighbours on the other side?'

'A young couple who moved in a few months ago.' Dave dabs the corners of his mouth with his napkin. 'They never got around to meeting Newson.'

'Any insights on whether there was a girlfriend or partner on the scene?'

'Mrs Simon doesn't believe so. If there was, it doesn't look like she came to the house very often. Then again, if Mrs Simon is Suzanne's friend, Newson might have been extra discreet.'

The waitress is back, brimming with enthusiasm. 'How's your sandwich? Can I get you anything else?'

She must be barely out of school. Perhaps this is a part-time job to supplement her first year of university. She looks like an arts student, History or English or something like that. Bridget's thoughts automatically jump to Cara. Her daughter went to a party last weekend. Her outfit – an indecently short denim skirt with a lace crop top – made Bridget blush and Shane immediately avert his eyes to a far-distant spot over her shoulder.

'Are you going to allow her to go out like that?' he demanded of Bridget when Cara left the room to get her jacket.

'She should be able to wear whatever she wants to wear,' Bridget retorted, even though she was inwardly aghast. Her daughter's breasts were spilling out. The skirt barely covered her knickers.

'I know that … But I'm her father and I can't find anywhere safe to put my eyes. What hope do other blokes have?'

Bridget turned on him furiously. 'Why is it always about the blokes? It's *nothing* to do with them. It's Cara's business what she wears. It's her body, her choice, her way of expressing herself.'

Now the argument is niggling at her. Because the way Cara was dressed screamed vulnerability as much as sultriness. The young waitress is wearing a short skirt too; not quite as skimpy as Cara's, but short nevertheless. Her midriff is exposed, showing a piercing in her navel. She exudes sweetness rather than sexuality. Yet, if anything untoward were to happen, her choice of clothing would be dissected and questioned. She could even be accused of smiling too much, or being flirtatious rather than plain friendly. Sexy or sweet, the girls should be able to wear whatever they want. Sexy or sweet, the girls should be *safe* from unwanted attention. More than anything, they should be safe from *blame*.

'Time for another coffee?' she asks Dave.

He looks at his watch. He's hesitant. Other work awaiting his attention back at the station? Bridget knows the feeling; she has been neglecting her other cases. Unsolved homicides invariably reach a point where they stall. Once stalled, they're in danger of being usurped by new cases coming in. It's a constant battle to keep the older cases ticking over while giving the new ones the oomph required in these critical early days.

'I want to tell you about the Malouf–O'Shea trial. It had a big impact on Newson's career, twelve years ago.'

Dave nods and Bridget smiles at the young girl. 'Two more coffees, please.'

The waitress – oblivious to the fact that one of her customers has cast her as a potential rape victim – bounces away.

16
MEGAN

Megan has blocked the number Dylan used last night, but she is still on edge, eyeing her phone warily in case it produces another nasty shock. It's not the first time he has tried to make contact. Maybe half a dozen phone calls over the years? Not enough for her to change her number. Not enough to accuse him of stalking her. Not enough to expect it when it happens, so there's always a profound shock, a sense of violation and powerlessness. He uses a different number each time, so blocking him won't prevent it from happening again, but she has to do *something*. She knows what he wants: to clear his name, to rewrite history. Too damn late for that.

Her phone stays silent. At noon, Megan slips it into the back pocket of her jeans, and walks to the real estate agents. The walk puts her in a better frame of mind: the healing powers of fresh air and a cloudless blue sky.

The agent is called Paula Mason. Middle-aged, sharply dressed, heavy on make-up and jewellery. A framed certificate on the wall declares her as the highest-selling local agent last year.

'Megan, so nice to see you again,' she says, standing up from behind her desk, her rings squeezing Megan's fingers as they shake hands.

'Hello, Paula.' Megan pops in every few months, to chat about the market and the saleability of their house.

'Got the day off work?' Paula is the kind of woman who remembers not only your name, but where you live (is it a good street or bad street? How many beds, baths, etc.?) and what you do for work (full time or part time? Professional or trade? Cashed-up or a potential credit risk?). This level of retention is exactly why she's ranked as the highest-selling agent in the area.

'Four days off, actually. Almost makes up for the six a.m. shifts this week.'

'Hats off to you. Couldn't do what you do. Nearly fainted when my grandson cut his knee the other day … I assume you're after a market assessment?'

'Yeah.' Megan smiles and sighs simultaneously. 'Just wondering if there's any improvement since we last spoke.'

'Clearance rates were up last weekend. It's the tail end of winter and buyers are coming out of hibernation. Not a lot of supply yet, so that would work in your favour. I think September and October will be quite strong.'

'How strong?'

'Better than six months ago. Maybe even better than twelve months ago.'

They should have sold after her dad died, when the market was at its peak, but they weren't emotionally ready to say goodbye to the house and were unaware that prices were about to plummet. Even so, they wouldn't have come out with much money. Her dad had been out of work, her mum caring for him full time. They'd been paying mortgage interest but not any capital. Megan should have insisted on taking financial stewardship earlier. After all, it was her fault that they'd ended up owing so much.

'Look, it's a weatherboard and crying out for renovation, if not knocking down.' Paula is especially blunt. This is why Megan likes her, trusts her. 'You're not going to get a premium price, but who knows what will happen if two buyers are genuinely interested in the property!'

'I'll talk to Mum.'

Roslyn will be conflicted, too. They love the house. They hate the house. It's seen them through the best of times and the worst of times. It's where everything fell apart for Megan, and then for her dad, but it's also the place where she and Roslyn recalibrated and got back on track. The bottom line is that it's bigger than they need and costing more than they can afford.

It's time to move on. Megan is just hoping her mum won't fight it.

'How much did Paula say?'

'She didn't … But I'm hoping we'll clear the million. Otherwise, it isn't worth doing.'

Roslyn has showered and is wearing a pink towelling robe and slippers. Her laptop is resting on her knees, her fingers clicking on the plastic keys; she's searching for recent sales of three-bedroom houses in Hornsby.

'It says here the average price is one-point-two.'

'Most of those houses are brick, Mum. And renovated.'

The bathroom and kitchen are in original condition, the roof needs replacing and there's asbestos in the wall cavities. As Paula pointed out, there's a strong argument for knocking down and rebuilding, which means they should be seeking land value only.

'We have a big block. That's something, isn't it?'

'Yeah, Mum, that's something.'

Maybe someone will fall in love with the garden. Megan and Seb used to have a swing-set, a cubbyhouse and plenty of room left over for ball games and hide-and-seek. It's nice to think of other children filling the garden with their noise, toys and games.

This is the right thing to do.

'Where would we go if we sell?'

Her mum looks so vulnerable with her shiny face and baby-pink towelling robe. Megan hates hurting her. At work they're taught to inflict pain quickly. Don't dither sticking in the needle or applying antiseptic. The more protracted it is, the worse for the patient.

'I might move closer to the city.' Megan's voice is raspy with guilt. 'And you might stay around here or try somewhere new?'

Realisation dawns on Roslyn's face. She's shocked and upset, then understanding and resigned; she has one of those faces that shows every thought and feeling. During the trial, Megan had to avoid looking in her mother's direction. Roslyn's face would crumple when something hurtful was said about her daughter. It flared up with anger and indignation when the defence went on the attack. And filled with despair when it became evident that the verdict returned would be 'not guilty'. Looking at her mum was too much like looking inside herself. Megan used to look at Jess's mum instead: Margaret. Stony faced, chin resting on her hand, her long bony fingers concealing one side of her face. Megan used to imagine those fingers slapping her. She deserved a slap for being so stupid and reckless.

'I'll sleep on it,' Roslyn says now, putting down her laptop on the couch. She stands up with an exaggerated yawn. 'Goodnight, love.'

'Night, Mum.'

She's definitely hurt. It's not even 8.30 p.m.; she's not going to bed, she's going to lick her wounds, perhaps cry a tear or two. The bathroom door opens and closes. The sound of running water; she's brushing her teeth. Megan sends Seb a text.

> Mum and I talking about selling again. I think we're
> actually going to do it.

Seb lives in Melbourne with his wife Cassie and baby daughter, Tia. He's been encouraging them to sell for years. The fact that the sale price needs to be enough to cover the loan and selling costs is lost on him. He's a musician, hopeless with numbers and money.

> Do it! You're far too old to be living at home.

Megan smiles. There's nobody like her brother for issuing an insult in the same breath as his undying support. Seb has been gone from Sydney fifteen years and can only see positives from selling the house. Megan's more realistic. Selling is a big deal: a lot of preparation, hard work and uncertainty lies ahead. Assuming they're successful, she'll miss her mum terribly: Roslyn's her best friend. Megan will have to cook for herself every day, and do *all* the chores (not just the half she prefers). She's not even sure what she'll be able to afford to rent. Freedom has a price. She is willing to pay it, though.

Roslyn has left her laptop open on the couch. Megan picks it up, and clicks on some of the recent sales in the area, looking for houses like theirs. The few she finds seem to be in much better condition, freshly painted and well presented. Megan will start work tomorrow, cleaning out cupboards and choosing paint colours. Something stirs in her. Excitement with an underlay of treachery.

Stop feeling guilty. This is the right thing to do!

Roslyn's laptop is slow and clunky: she has too many tabs open on the internet. Megan closes some down. Recipe websites. Medical websites. Nine news.

Neighbours shocked and frightened after well-respected barrister gunned down outside his home.

Police still looking for leads in the shooting of defence barrister, William Newson.

CCTV images released to media in appeal to find person of interest.

Roslyn knows. Oh God, she knows.

Megan should have brought it up the day after her birthday. Or that weekend, when they had breakfast together. 'Mum, you'll never guess what happened …' But she couldn't get the words to form and now it looks like Roslyn didn't need her to break the news. A quick check of her history confirms that she has been following every single development.

Family, friends and colleagues gather for the funeral of William Newson. Oldest son, Quentin, says that his dad loved his family, his job and cricket.

Detective Sergeant Bridget Kennedy appeals to the public for help. 'Someone somewhere has seen something. You might think it's too small to matter, but

I can assure you nothing is too small. Anyone with information is urged to contact Chatswood Police Station or Crime Stoppers.'

It's suddenly difficult to breathe. Roslyn doesn't just know about it: she's all over it.

There's a reason Megan couldn't bring herself to mention William Newson; it's the same reason she failed to mention Dylan's phone call. It's because these men have the ability to transform Roslyn – an ordinary, softly spoken suburban mum – into an explosive, unpredictable stranger.

17
JESS

Jess makes her first coffee of the day and takes it out to the balcony. Leaning over the railing, she observes the Sunday-morning bustle of the neighbourhood. Lawnmowers droning, hand-held hoses hissing water on to parched lawns, neighbours chatting over fences, probably discussing the weather forecast. The week ahead is meant to be sunny, cool and dry. Dire predictions are being made about future water supplies in New South Wales. Some large country towns are facing the prospect of running out of water within the next couple of months. If it doesn't rain, soon and significantly, Sydney will be upgraded from Level 2 water restrictions to Level 3. This will be bad news for Alex's business, because who wants to put in a new garden or plants in conditions such as these?

Fortunately, Alex is not the type to worry about it.

'Can't control the weather, babe,' he shrugs.

He's sleeping off last night's hangover while Jess attempts to banish hers with coffee and fresh air. They were at a thirtieth birthday party and stumbled home in the early hours of the morning, Jess trying to steer Alex into bed.

'Shush. You're going to wake up the neighbours again.'

'You care more about the neighbours than me,' he grinned and slurred.

'That's because they're fragile and sweet and you're just a big drunken oaf.'

Alcohol makes Alex sleep like the dead while Jess invariably wakes up early, feeling seedy and annoyingly alert. The coffee is starting to take effect, though, and the fresh air, which she breathes in deeply. This afternoon there's another birthday party, her niece's, and a full family gathering at her brother's house. Jess and Alex need to be one hundred per cent hangover free. Her mother will be watching as closely as ever.

She turns around from the railing. A half-full watering can is next to the vertical garden in a deliberately prominent spot. Alex built the garden; it's Jess's job to keep it alive. She lifts the can just as she hears the sound of a door sliding open. Then the shuffle of feet. There's someone on the balcony next door.

'Is that you, Helen?'

A disembodied voice answers her question. 'Yes,

dear. Another lovely morning. Not a cloud in the sky. Such a shame.'

The desire for rain is reaching manic level. At this rate there will be celebrations when it eventually happens, street parties in the deluge.

'Sorry if we were noisy last night.'

'Don't be sorry, dear. Enjoy your youth.'

Helen's such a sweetheart. Always smiling. Nothing seems to perturb her. Then again, Jess has done nothing to *really* test her patience. Maybe she's tougher on her grown-up children. Jess's thoughts are dragged back to her mother. She's too hungover to pass Margaret's scrutiny today; she's really not looking forward to this birthday party.

'Our parsley and rosemary are thriving, if you need any?'

'That would be lovely, dear.'

'I'll drop some over.'

Jess finds it easier to face the woman next door than her own mother. She doesn't know what that says about herself, or her mum.

Alex drives with one hand resting on Jess's thigh, and the other draped casually over the steering wheel.

'Did you give Ramsey back his jacket?' Jess asks, noting its absence from where she left it on the middle console.

Alex shoots her a confused look. 'What jacket?'

'The one he left behind last week.'

'Oh that … yeah.'

Her boyfriend's tone is decidedly unconvincing. Something tells Jess that the jacket didn't make its way back to its owner. Probably rolled up in a ball somewhere else. Typical.

They're last to arrive at her brother's house. The kids adore Alex. He's totally unlike the other adults; he doesn't try too hard or get in their faces. They respond to his slight air of unavailability by climbing all over him.

'Why is your hair so long?' Tilly, the birthday girl, promptly begins to plait it.

'My daddy doesn't have any earrings in his ears.' Charlie, her cousin, touches the gold stud with stubby fingers.

'Are you a real-life giant?' Noah asks guilelessly.

Jess has two nephews and two nieces, ranging between two months and five years old. The baby, Lucy, is the only one oblivious to Alex; she is ensconced in her grandmother's arms. Margaret soothes Lucy in that brisk way of hers, all the while keeping an eye on things. What stage is the barbecue at? Are all the condiments ready on the table? Are her grown-up children on their best behaviour? Jess's dad has a glass of red wine in his hand and a satisfied smile on his face. Richard loves his brood of children and grandchildren.

'Big night out?' Natasha, mother of baby Lucy, sits down next to Jess.

'God, is it that obvious?'

'Only because I'm a trained doctor.'

Natasha is an oncologist, currently on maternity leave.

'Hopefully not obvious to Mum, then.'

'Mum's eye is keener than any doctor's! You're probably busted, but at least she can't lecture you while she has Lucy to keep her busy.'

Natasha is the oldest sibling. When Jess was at primary school, her sister was at high school. When Jess was at high school, Natasha was off at university. Now she's a new mother and – judging from her washed-out face and bleary eyes – finding it a challenge.

'You look a bit hungover yourself, mate.' Jess smiles, to take the sting out of her words.

'I wish,' her sister laughs harshly. 'I've woken up so many mornings thinking I must've been out the night before, but all I've been doing is feeding Lucy, and changing Lucy, and settling Lucy. Sleep deprivation is worse than any hangover.'

'Can Oliver help?'

Natasha's husband is a stockbroker who works crazy hours and always looks like he's rushing somewhere. He's talking to Jess's dad and her brothers, near the barbecue. Alex is notably missing from the circle of testosterone. He's inside, splayed on the couch, three young children on top of him.

Another harsh laugh from Natasha. 'Not a lot Oliver can do. Unless he can grow some boobs.'

Lucy has started to grizzle. Margaret props her

against her shoulder. 'Natasha, I think you're needed over here.'

'Coming.' Natasha stands up. She has an odd expression on her face. 'Keep doing your own thing, Jess. Don't let them pressure you into anything.'

What does she mean by that? Does she regret having Lucy? Did Oliver or Margaret apply pressure, or make loaded comments about her biological clock that prompted her – for once in her life – to make a decision that she had not properly considered? Or maybe she thinks she isn't succeeding in this new role, floundering when she is used to flourishing. This family is hard on underachievers; Jess knows this first-hand. Natasha was the standard setter. Frighteningly clever, possessing both the focus and the work ethic to see her through years and years of study and training. Maybe if she'd been a little less accomplished, their parents wouldn't have expected so much from the rest of them.

Twenty minutes later, the men declare the meat to be cooked and everyone gathers around the outside table. The food settles Jess's stomach, and her headache loosens its grip, which is illogical given the noise levels – Lucy is crying heartily against a backdrop of children and adults laughing and talking over each other.

Richard booms from the other end of the table, 'So, Alex, Margaret tells me you're going to do some work for us around the pool?'

'Well, um, that's not confirmed,' Alex says, not

knowing which direction to look, his face flushing under his tan. 'Margaret hasn't accepted my quote.'

'Oh.' Margaret's fork is suspended mid-air. She's feigning surprise. 'Did I need to accept? I just assumed ... Sorry, Alex, when can you start?'

Her mum does it on purpose. Puts Alex on the back foot and puts him in his place at the same time. Thankfully, he's oblivious to her games; he's just glad to get the job.

'I have a gap later this week. Should knock it over in four or five days.'

After dinner there is a Disney princess cake, and they all sing Tilly happy birthday. Jess and Alex help with the tidy-up before making their excuses.

Jess gives Natasha – who looks as wan as one of her chemo patients – an extra-tight hug. Oliver did not offer to take his baby daughter once all afternoon. Why didn't her dad or brothers nudge him in the right direction? Margaret would have noted what was happening yet failed to comment. How come Oliver makes the grade and Alex doesn't? Where does doing your fair share come in the criteria? Good thing Alex doesn't really care about making the grade.

At home, Alex slouches in front of the television with a beer and Jess lies on the bed with her phone, which she hasn't looked at for hours. There's a text from Vince, asking if she can work an extra hour tomorrow, and a couple of missed calls from an unknown number. A voice message has been left. She presses the phone against her ear, and the halting voice on the other end brings a rush of bad, bad memories.

'Jess, this is … Dylan O'Shea. I just want to … t-talk. Can you m-meet me somewhere? Please say yes. Call or text this … num-num-number.'

18
BRIDGET

Another Monday morning in the Kennedy household. Two comatose teenagers who won't get out of bed. One flustered husband who can't find his Opal card (probably due to the comatose children, who borrow the bus cards of other people when they can't locate their own). One frazzled wife-mother-detective who doesn't have time to assist her flustered husband in the frantic search of likely places.

'Jesus, Shane, I wouldn't know where to start looking. Try Cara's backpack. Or her jeans pocket. Gotta go, love. Make sure they're out of bed before you leave. Bye-ee.'

Bridget is on her way to meet Emily Wickham. The newly married young woman is back from her honeymoon and Bridget is hoping she'll be able to help narrow down their lines of inquiry. Traffic from Willoughby into the city is predictably awful. Bridget uses the time to make a few calls relating to other cases and court matters. One call is to a bereaved mother, the woman's distress and anger filling the car. Bridget opens the window, petrol fumes and sound pollution diluting the mother's grief and her own sense of failure that the case has hit an apparent dead-end.

The door-to-door journey takes more than an hour. Patrick is already waiting in the ground-floor café, sitting at a table that's suitably out of the way.

'Morning.' Bridget flops down across from him. 'How long have you been here?'

'About ten minutes. All good.'

Bridget shoots Emily a text to let her know they've arrived. Patrick slides a printed document in front of her: the list of cases that William Newson recently worked on. Bridget quickly refreshes her knowledge.

'Here she comes,' Patrick murmurs.

Blonde and slender, Emily's wearing a dark-blue shift dress, showcasing her figure and tan. Her nude-coloured shoes are extremely high with pointy toes; Bridget's back aches just from looking at them.

'Thanks for seeing us,' Bridget says, shaking Emily's hand, which has long fake nails painted a light-peach colour. 'This is my colleague, Detective Senior Constable Patrick Yandle. We know it's your first morning back, Emily. We'll try not to take up too much time.'

'It's fine.' She sits down, flicks her very straight hair over her shoulder. 'I came in early out of habit. I always tried to be in the office before William, in case he needed me. But he's not here, and I'm not sure what to do with myself. I'm not even sure what's going to happen with my job. So, take as long as you need.'

It must be disconcerting for the young woman. Away on honeymoon, which is suspended reality in itself, and then returning to this very strange set of circumstances. Will she be redeployed to one of the other barristers in the chambers, or made redundant? Who will make the decision about her future?

'Would you like to order something?' Patrick asks kindly. 'Tea or coffee? Cake?'

Emily shakes her head. 'I'm fine, thanks.'

Bridget commences. 'Just for the sake of background information, can I ask your age, please?'

'Twenty-five.'

'And you've been working for Mr Newson how long?'

'Three years next month.'

'We've started investigating the list of cases you compiled. Thank you for doing that while you were on holiday – it's been really helpful. Can you tell me if there was anything particularly controversial or heated among the cases? Any victims who might have felt aggrieved by Mr Newson's actions? Anything that stands out?'

Another flick of her hair, which seems to be an

unconscious action. 'Emotions run high in almost every case. Accusers and defendants are scared and humiliated, having their dirty laundry aired, their bad choices being discussed by lawyers, judges and juries. But the people who are the most emotional – the angriest, I suppose – are the fathers. Sometimes it's the fathers of the defendants, the boys who've been accused. *Their child's life is ruined, there's no coming back from this, the other party is telling lies* ... More often it's the fathers of the victims, the girls. They can turn violent. Threaten all sorts of things ... It's really ugly.'

'Did it ever put you off working for Mr Newson?'

She shrugs, as though the answer is obvious. 'Of course. It's impossible not to be affected.'

'But you didn't leave. Why is that?'

'Because William believed in his work and in everyone's right to have legal representation. He used to say, "It's dirty and upsetting work, that's why it's even more important to do it well." That really resonated with me, and after a while I got to see that sometimes the accuser was acting out of embarrassment or revenge, and William was actually stopping a miscarriage of justice. He was a good boss. I'm paid well, and he gave me extended leave last year when my mum was sick.'

Bridget and Patrick share a wordless glance. A good boss. A man committed to the justice system. A man who was generous, empathetic and altruistic. Does Emily have a case of rose-tinted glasses?

'Okay, let's read through this list together and see which cases incited the most backlash … Nichols?'

'Never made it to court. Phone records proved that the woman was lying about her whereabouts.'

'Davis?'

'University student and his former girlfriend. Charges were withdrawn.'

'R v Smith?'

Her face scrunches with distaste. 'That one was nasty. DNA analysis confirmed sexual activity but no evidence of bruising, scratches or any other signs of forced sex. The accused was committed for trial but William made a successful application to the DPP to discontinue due to the unreliability of the evidence. The girl's father went ballistic. He accosted William outside court the following week. William had to get an AVO.'

'The father's name?'

'Fergus Herrmann.'

'How long since the incident outside the courthouse?'

'Two or three months.'

Fairly recent, then. Is the father still furious? How long does it take for such blinding anger to abate? Does it ever?

Bridget continues to ask questions while Patrick takes notes. Emily flags another case – and complainant – as difficult.

'Laura Dundas met our client on a night out, and went back to his place. You could say that the two of them were on very different wavelengths. The case went to court but not enough evidence for a guilty verdict. Laura was beside herself. She protested outside the Downing Centre Court wearing a bikini! Then somehow got past the security doors here and graffitied reception.'

Jesus. Poor Laura. And not very pleasant for William Newson either. Did he take the threats seriously? Was he cautious about walking alone at night? Watchful on his way in and out of court? Did he take any additional security precautions?

Bridget sets the list to one side. She'll have a closer look at Fergus Herrmann and Laura Dundas back at headquarters.

'How about repeat offenders? Did Mr Newson have any clients who were accused more than once?'

Emily blinks. 'Not while I've been working for him.'

Bridget is recalling that disturbing conversation with Suzanne Newson, where she compared the offenders to a 'conveyor belt'. Was Suzanne exaggerating?

Bridget steers the conversation towards the family. 'Do you have much to do with Joshua, Mr Newson's son?'

'Not much. Just slotted him into William's diary once a week for coffee or lunch.'

'Do you like Joshua?'

A slight pause. 'He's okay, I suppose … But he's not the same calibre as his dad.'

'Is that your opinion or general opinion?'

'General.' She shifts in her seat. It's obvious that this

topic is making her uncomfortable. 'I've heard that he's not very thorough, doesn't always do his homework and his clients have suffered the consequences. And he has a temper. He blows up, shouts at his secretary, slams doors. William never lost his temper.'

Interesting. The question is whether it's relevant. Joshua's temper tantrums could be superficial or a sign of him being troubled at a much deeper level. His lack of thoroughness could also be interpreted in different ways.

'Did Mr Newson's ex-wife ever call him at the office?'

'Suzanne? No, not since their divorce.'

'Did he ever speak about her?'

'He asked me to organise flowers for her birthday, and for Mother's Day. That's about all.'

Sending flowers can mean lots of things. Affection. Contrition. Control.

'Any other women in his life? A girlfriend or partner?'

'No, strangely. He was such a nice man. Clever. Thoughtful. Kept himself in good shape. If I were twenty years older …'

Emily smiles, and suddenly all Bridget can see is insincerity. She's not sure whether she should believe this young woman. About William Newson being so perfect, about Joshua's temper and shoddy standards, about anything.

Her phone buzzes in her pocket. She knows without looking that it'll be Cara, calling about the missing Opal card and protesting her innocence.

'Thank you for seeing us, Emily. Here's my card. Call me if anything else comes to mind. Make a record of Mr Newson's files and who asks for them over the coming weeks. Make sure they're all accounted for. We may need to organise a warrant at some stage.'

'Sure. Of course. Anything you need, anything at all.'

They shake hands again, her long fake nails curling around Bridget's hand. Cara would probably like the peach-coloured polish. Cara would definitely like her hair, that bright blonde, straight but somehow voluminous too.

Bridget watches Emily stride through the foyer in her high-heeled shoes, heading towards the lifts that will take her up, up, up to a job that strictly no longer exists: executive assistant to a dead man. Did she really come in early out of habit, or was there another more sinister reason? Is this list that she has given them complete?

Bridget raises an eyebrow at Patrick. 'What do you think?'

He clicks the top of his pen a few times. 'Not sure. She seems too good to be true.'

*Your Honour, members of the jury, I want to take a moment
to talk about lies. Why do we lie? Two main reasons. We lie to
get what we want. And we lie to protect ourselves, or others.
Some children learn how to lie from a young age and are
naturally adept at it. Some never learn; they just can't pull it
off, not even as adults. Megan Lowe and Jessica Foster are in
the former category – we have heard compelling evidence that
these girls are accomplished liars. Megan told her parents
she was staying the night at Jessica's. Jessica told her parents
she was staying at Megan's. Both sets of parents testified
that they would not have given their daughter permission to
attend an all-night party with boys who were barely known
to them. These initial lies were to get what they wanted: to
be able to go to the party. Of course, that was just the start
of it. They told lies about how much they'd had to drink that
night. They told lies about how they ended up in the master
bedroom. They told lies about what was said, or indeed not
said, while they had sex with my clients. Why all these lies?
Well, it was to protect themselves, of course. Megan stated
that she felt embarrassed and regretful the next morning.*

But it was to protect their parents, too. Megan and Jessica didn't want to disappoint their parents. They didn't want to shock or disgust them. They wanted to give them a narrative that was more palatable than the ugly truth. Ladies and gentlemen of the jury, my clients engaged in what some of you regard as morally questionable behaviour; however, their path to this courtroom has at least been an honest one. Lies cannot prevail over honesty ... no matter how difficult it is for these young ladies and their families to face the truth.

19
MEGAN

Nobody likes being called a liar. It's humiliating, insulting, disempowering. In a courtroom there's no opportunity to immediately defend yourself, to respond with something to negate the accusation before it settles in people's heads and forms an irreversible part of the narrative. It's true they lied about where they were that night, but it was within the range of normal teenage behaviour. William Newson called them 'accomplished liars', as though they had been honing their deception skills for years. That was extremely unfair, and untrue.

Every muscle in Megan's body aches. There's paint in her hair and in the cracks of the skin on her hands. Her fingers are raw from scraping sandpaper on wooden trims and scrubbing walls with sugar soap.

She is hoping to get two coats on the skirting boards and doors today. Probably too ambitious.

Music is playing from her phone, which is hooked up to portable speakers. There's a lot of time to think. About William Newson and his assault on her credibility and character. About this house and all the good and bad memories within its faded walls. About the disquieting Google history on her mum's laptop.

Police uncover threats on William Newson's life.

Detectives looking for Yamaha WR450F motorbike in relation to shooting.

Family and public left without answers.

The problem is that Roslyn isn't just mildly curious. Her reactions to William Newson were never mild. On one mortifying occasion she had to be escorted from the courtroom after standing up and screeching at him.

'Stop! Stop saying those terrible things about my daughter.' Her finger stabbed the air in front of her. 'How can you call *her* a liar when *you* haven't said a word of truth since the day we came in here?'

The judge cautioned her but she was oblivious.

'How can you live with yourself?' Her face was contorted, almost unrecognisable. 'How can you assassinate the character of these innocent young girls?'

The judge called for one of the court officers, who unceremoniously steered her from the room. She was allowed to return the next day only because the judge felt sorry for her; he could see that this was a woman to be pitied, not punished.

On the day the jury handed down their verdict, Roslyn lost control again. Spitting with disappointment and rage on the steps outside the courthouse, newspaper and TV cameras capturing her reaction and broadcasting it around the country. Megan's parents were firm believers in the establishment. They respected school teachers, police officers, law and order. They kept to the rules, drove below the speed limit, never parked illegally or took an illegitimate sick day. The trial crushed their belief in the establishment. Rapists could get away with the most heinous crime. Defence barristers could tell shameless lies. What was the point of keeping to the rules?

Painting the skirting boards is back-breaking, fastidious work, albeit strangely therapeutic. Slow precise strokes of the brush, the clean smell of paint, the satisfying improvement after the first coat. The Fray's 'How to Save a Life' is playing on her phone. The song was popular around the time of the trial. Megan remembers hearing it on the car radio on the way into court in the mornings, her dad driving in his careful way, her mum fixing her hair in the sunshade mirror, both of them still hopeful about the outcome.

William Newson chipped away at their hope, day by day, week by week, until it was extinguished. He chipped away at their belief system, until it crumbled around them, leaving them looking foolish and naïve. Worst of all, he chipped away at their fortitude.

It's no surprise that Roslyn has been compulsively following the news. She is selling her house because of William Newson; he is still impacting her life, all these years later. It makes Megan uneasy, that's all. Something snapped in Roslyn that day in the courtroom. Her pain was excruciating to watch. Her outrage was both magnificent and deeply disturbing.

For the first time in her life, Megan was frightened of her.

Dinner is salmon and salad. Roslyn is complimentary about the simple meal as well as Megan's progress with the painting.

'The place is starting to look really good, love. Amazing what a lick of paint can do.'

'Walls next– that should make a *big* difference. I spoke to Seb. He's going to fly up Saturday and help with the outside.'

Roslyn is thrilled; they haven't seen Seb since last Christmas, when he, Cassie and three-month-old Tia visited. Tia is almost one now and starting to bear weight on her pudgy legs, using furniture to pull herself up and into all sorts of mischief. Not a lot of painting would get done with her around so on this occasion she will be staying at home with her mother.

After dinner, Roslyn starts decluttering the kitchen cupboards. Now that she has committed to the sale, she seems to be a mixed bag of emotions. Nostalgic. Excited. Terrified. Just like Megan. But the important thing is that they're finally doing this.

While Roslyn works in the kitchen, Megan attacks her wardrobe. Her approach to fashion has always been random, acquiring single pieces rather than complete outfits, mixing and matching clothes and accessories from all eras of her life. Now it needs to be culled to fit the limited storage space of a one-bedroom apartment, her future accommodation.

Roslyn comes to say goodnight about two hours later.

'Are you planning on sleeping in there?' she asks, eyeing the bed, which is buried under mounds of clothes.

'Yeah. Being ruthless is harder than I thought.'

Her mum puts her hand over her mouth to contain a yawn. 'The kitchen is a mess too, but I've run out of steam. Hopefully, it won't get in your way.'

'It'll be fine. Night, Mum.'

The clothes are more than just a jumble of fabric, colours and styles. They hold memories of foreign cities and nights out with friends. A leather jacket purchased in Barcelona, even though the weather was unbearably hot. The green maxi dress she wore to Seb's wedding. It's a wrench, but both items haven't been worn for years.

It's another hour before Megan emerges with two black garbage bags destined for the charity shop. As Roslyn forewarned, the kitchen is in disarray. Megan navigates her way through half-full boxes and lifts the kettle to establish its water level: just enough for a cup of herbal tea.

Roslyn's phone is charging on the kitchen counter. Megan looks at it, and quickly looks back to the kettle, which is starting to make noise. She glances at the phone again, before swinging around to extract a cup from the wall-mounted cupboard behind. One last, prolonged look before sighing and giving in; her mum's passcode is Seb's birthday.

Megan checks the pages that have been left open on Safari: headline after headline about the shooting. Between the laptop and the phone, there are dozens and dozens of news articles, all recent except for one that's a few months old.

Young woman uses shock tactics to draw attention to low number of convictions for rape cases. 'I want people to know my name,' said Laura Dundas. 'I want people to see my face and my body. I have nothing to be ashamed of. I am telling the truth.'

The accompanying photograph shows a young woman standing outside the Downing Centre District Court, wearing a bikini. She's holding a placard, I'M NOT A LIAR in red block capitals. Her gaze is unflinching, even though she must be shivering with the cold; it's the middle of winter. Her bravery and vulnerability bring a hard lump to Megan's throat. She feels her pain, the powerlessness that drove her to these lengths.

William Newson up to his old tricks, calling girls liars. Roslyn would have gone ballistic on reading this.

Megan taps on the next page that's been left open: a map, with a red location pin. Killara! She uses her fingers to widen the zoom. William Newson's street address.

The kettle whistles as it comes to the boil.

Why has Roslyn been looking at this map? How does she know Newson's exact address? She must have found it somewhere on the internet. But *why*? Some sort of macabre desire to see where it actually happened?

Then a nauseating, treacherous thought: what if this map, with its ominous red pin, has been open since before the shooting?

20
JESS

The youth class is winding up and the serious fighters are trickling in. Billy arrives in his suit, looking every inch the lawyer from the city. He disappears into the changing room and emerges a few minutes later in black shorts and grey T-shirt. He smiles at Jess while he wraps his hands with protective strapping. He has a nice smile and knows it. She bets he uses it a thousand times a day as he tells his clients things they don't want to hear.

'Hey, Jess.'

'Hello, Billy.' It's a struggle to be friendly. She can't get over the fact that he's a lawyer, one of *them*. 'How's your day been?'

He pulls a face. 'Pretty crap, actually.'

'Well, you're in the right place to release some frustration. Go extra hard on the bags.'

Vince runs the warm-up session – a twenty-minute routine of punching, skipping and squatting – while Jess catches up on admin at the desk. Music pumps through the sound system. Fists pummel the punching bags. Vince, hands stuffed in the pockets of his track-suit pants, yells out orders. He's tough on this group. If they want to fight at an amateur or semi-professional level, they've got to put in the work.

The warm-up finishes. Jess is needed at the ring for the sparring. The first duo is Billy and Matt. Jess positions herself in Billy's corner. He's the first person she has coached to this level, from complete novice to the precipice of being an amateur fighter. Despite her personal misgivings, she's proud of his progress and work ethic. She helps him on with his gloves.

Vince presses the buzzer and it starts the thirty-second countdown. Dua Lipa is playing on the sound system: 'Don't Start Now'. Billy and Matt are bouncing around, readying themselves. The buzzer sounds.

'Find your range, Billy … Jab to the body, set it up …

'Don't put yourself on the ropes, get out of there … Good work.

'Great defence, mate. Yep, that's the way … Move to your right … Lean on the back foot.'

Billy's posture looks good today; he seems to be making a concentrated effort to sit lower. His defence has been faultless so far.

'Keep him away from you. Don't let him dominate.

This is bread and butter, mate. Get in there. Nice jab. One more. Go for it.'

The round finishes. Matt and Billy touch gloves before retreating to their respective corners.

'You're boxing really well, mate.' Billy deserves the praise. She needs to treat him like any other member of the club.

'Thanks, Jess.'

'Vince has a fight lined up in a couple of weeks. He'll talk to you about it later. We'll need to get blood tests organised and stuff.'

Billy's first official fight. He beams with pleasure.

Dylan O'Shea had a nice smile, too. It transformed his pale unhealthy face into something altogether more attractive. Jess remembers saying so to Megan at the party.

'He's much nicer when he smiles.'

'Doesn't make a difference,' Megan said flatly. 'I'm not into him.'

Jess's attraction to Thomas Malouf had also waned. His arm felt heavy around her shoulders. She had noticed his eyes assessing other girls at the party, checking if there were any better options.

Dylan had got them drinks. Another big smile as he shoved glasses into their hands. 'House s-s-s-special.'

The readiness of Dylan's smile could have been an unconscious compensation for the fact that his words were so hesitant.

Now Dylan O'Shea has got hold of her phone number

– probably from the gym's website or Facebook page – and he wants to talk. Well, Jess wants to talk too. She wants to know if he remembers practically forcing those drinks into their hands. She wants to know if he remembers Megan pushing him away when he tried to kiss her. She wants to know if his guilty conscience has caught up with him, or if he is still pleading a terrible misunderstanding.

'Lachlan and Jordy, you're up next,' she calls out, forcing her thoughts away from Dylan O'Shea and into the here and now.

The industrial park seems darker and more ominous tonight. Jess hurries, her breathing loud and sharp, her fists clenched in preparation. The night has echoes from two weeks ago, when she got that shocking text from Megan. Do the police have a suspect by now? What was the motivation? Some kind of moral issue? Money? Revenge? A family feud? There have been ongoing appeals for information, members of the public urged to come forward. Are the police floundering or hiding how much they really know? Jess hasn't heard anything from the detective who went to see Megan. She didn't really expect to. There must be plenty of other, more recent, lines of inquiry. Still, Jess wouldn't have minded asking the detective a question or two of her own.

The platform is freezing, a piercing wind preceding the arrival of the train. By contrast, the carriage is over-heated and airless. It's almost empty: a middle-aged man on the opposite side, who looks decidedly worse for wear; a younger man, a few rows back, with sleeves of tattoos on his bare arms. Doesn't he feel the cold? Jess pulls the sleeves of her sweater down and uses the reflection in the window to keep an eye on both of them. The younger guy gets off at Roseville. The middle-aged man seems to be fighting the urge to fall asleep. His head drops, then jerks back up again. The train pulls into Killara. A couple of kilometres from here is where it happened. Two weeks to the day.

Jess's attention is caught by a figure walking along the platform. Floppy hair, overcoat, scarf, smartly dressed. Fucking hell, is that Thomas Malouf? Did he just get off this train? Jess thinks she recognises the saunter. She squints through the window, but all she can see now is the back of him. Is her mind playing tricks? Conjuring up Thomas because William Newson and Dylan O'Shea have been so much in her head?

The train pulls away and Jess exhales, unfurling her hands. It's not Thomas. She's imagining things. Dylan made some noise here and there over the years, but not a squeak from Thomas. Jess likes to think that he is living overseas, so she is not constantly looking over her shoulder. Are Thomas and Dylan aware that their former lawyer has been shot? What does Dylan want to talk about? Maybe the shooting propelled him back in time, forcing a confrontation with his guilt.

Jess is guilty, too. There were actions she should have taken, actions that would have prevented what happened. She should have shrugged off Thomas's proprietary arm, let him know that she'd changed her mind. She should have said 'no thanks' to the drinks, and the ones that followed. She should have listened to Megan when she said she wanted to go home. And this is hard to admit, but she also should have respected Megan's wishes about not involving the police, or even their parents. Involving the police, going to court, *losing* … by the time they were done, the damage was tenfold.

Jess has decided to meet Dylan O'Shea. Maybe he has realised – finally – that Megan won't budge and Jess is his only option if there's something he needs to get off his chest. Well, Jess has some stuff to get off her chest, too.

Number one: she is not a liar.

Number two: how could he sit in that witness box, shaking and looking petrified, and at the same time being so fucking selective with his memory?

Number three: plying them with drink after drink, that was part of the plan, wasn't it?

Jess will meet him, although she hasn't told him yet. The when and where are her decision. This is on her terms. It's the least she – and Megan – are owed.

21
BRIDGET

Two weeks and not much to show for it. The detective inspector is visibly disappointed.

'I thought you'd have more than this, Bridget.'

Katrina is in her early sixties, her silver hair cut in a razor-sharp bob. She's an extremely elegant and intelligent woman, who maintains impeccable standards in all areas of her life. Bridget hates disappointing her.

'I thought I'd have more, too. All that door-knocking, those filthy bins, hours of CCTV … Plenty of lines of inquiry with the family and work-related threats – just nothing we can grab hold of and run with.'

It's a high-profile case and as a result there's pressure to make an arrest. The police commissioner has weighed in, as well as a few politicians. The law community has spoken publicly about their concerns. Loudest of all is the media, running the story daily, demanding updates and asking tough questions. A large whiteboard is mounted on the wall of the detective inspector's office. Katrina cleans it off and picks up a blue marker.

'Remind me where everyone was on the night in question,' she says.

Bridget complies. 'As you know, Suzanne Newson says she was at home, but we can't corroborate that. Her phone signal indicates that it was in the area but that's no proof of anything. She mentioned a neighbour who may have seen her in the garden in the late afternoon, but both she and the neighbour can't pinpoint the day with enough certainty. Joshua claims he was in transit from work. We have CCTV showing him en route to his car at 6.50 p.m., and footage of his car going over the bridge at 7.05 p.m. We've asked him to provide further details on which route he took from there. His phone signal implies that he went directly home but, again, phones and their owners can be in separate places. Joshua seems to blow hot and cold. Happy to talk when I called to his office but less than pleased to see me at the funeral. The other two sons are living in London and Canberra so we've eliminated them for now.'

On the whiteboard, Katrina has written the following in bright-blue marker: *Suzanne: Home? Joshua: Car?*

'Any strange payments or receipts in anyone's bank account?'

'Not that we can determine.'

'Changes to life insurance or the beneficiaries of his will?'

'No changes. All three sons will inherit equal amounts.'

Katrina draws a shaky line, splitting the whiteboard in two. 'Let's consider the work angle. The threats that were made.'

'Fergus Herrmann. Father of an eighteen-year-old girl. Very upset about an application Newson made to the DPP to drop charges. Grabbed him by the throat outside the courthouse. An AVO was taken out and it appears that Mr Herrmann kept to its terms and initiated no further contact. I guess he has form, though. I'll arrange a meeting with Mr Herrmann, see where that takes us.'

'Anyone else?'

'Laura Dundas. Twenty-two-year-old arts student. Classic case of he said/she said. Not enough evidence for a guilty verdict. Laura protested outside the courthouse for a few days. You might remember it on the news. She was in a bikini, holding a placard saying, "I'm not a liar". Early one morning, she managed to gain entry to Newson's office and spray-painted the reception wall. She was charged with damaging property and trespassing.'

'Did she ever directly threaten him?'

'Several witnesses heard her screaming all sorts of threats. The court imposed a community service order and there was another AVO.'

Katrina looks appalled. 'Good God! You've got to

ask, why did he keep taking those cases? How could it be worth it?'

Bridget shudders. It wasn't worth it. Very possibly cost him his life.

'Then there's his executive assistant, Emily Wickham. Away on honeymoon when the shooting happened. Something about her is not sitting right. Preliminary investigations about her salary and career trajectory set off alarm bells. She's paid thirty per cent more than the going rate for someone of her experience. She's half Newson's age, very beautiful and newly married. I don't think they were having an affair but something was going on.'

Katrina adds Emily's name to the second half of the board.

Bridget exhales loudly. 'Not forgetting the bizarre coincidence of Megan Lowe being the first responder, which I can't get my head around.'

Katrina is across the Malouf–O'Shea case. Bridget discussed it with her boss early on, when prioritising resources. She hasn't pursued this line of inquiry beyond some cursory checks. Megan – obviously – was at work at the time of the shooting and so was Jessica Foster. Besides, what are the chances of a twelve-year-old case still being relevant? Nevertheless, the two women – Girls A and B – still hover on the periphery of Bridget's thoughts.

Katrina adds Megan Lowe and Jessica Foster to the list, leaving a gap before their names.

The detective inspector flops down on her seat. Both women stare at the whiteboard. William Newson was a wealthy man. A multi-million-dollar house, hefty super-annuation balance, high-performing share portfolio, and various investment properties dotted strategically around the city. Wealth complicates things. There's more to gain, especially for family members. Contract killing becomes an option, and with that alibis become decidedly less relevant.

'Are we sure it's not a case of mistaken identity?' Katrina murmurs.

It's a fair question. The wrong house was targeted in a drive-by shooting in the western suburbs last month. Bullets peppered the lounge window of a ter-rified single mother, who, quite miraculously, wasn't hurt even though the sofa she was sitting on absorbed six of the bullets. Her children's bedrooms were at the back of the house, thank God, all four kids sound asleep. Extensive investigation found no links between the woman and organised crime. Her ex-partner was quickly cleared of suspicion. Everyone was bewildered until a note was left in the mailbox the following week.

Sorry. Wrong house. Hope your kids are okay.

This doesn't feel remotely the same. Bridget isn't bewildered with nowhere left to turn. Suzanne Newson, Joshua Newson, Fergus Herrmann, Laura Dundas, Emily Wickham: these names are legitimately on the board. Megan Lowe and Jessica Foster might look like an afterthought, with that gap before their names, but they have motive, too: it could even be argued that the passing of time has intensified their sense of injustice.

The problem is Bridget has too many directions to turn in.

She looks her boss straight in the eye. 'I'm one hundred per cent sure that the person who shot William Newson didn't make a mistake.'

'What are we searching for, exactly?' Dave enquires when he meets her outside William Newson's house in Killara.

'Inspiration,' Bridget replies sarcastically.

She's holding the crime-scene photographs. She studies them before positioning herself on the drive-way, on the spot where Newson fell. Her eyes scan from left to right. Front lawn on the left, driveway straight ahead, wooden fence on the right, garage directly behind.

'So, he hid over there?'

She is using 'he' for convenience; a female is very possible. Tyre marks on the night suggested that the killer (and motorbike) were hidden behind the large gum tree. Wouldn't have worked in the daylight, but more than ample screening for a dark night. According to the timeline, and allowing for travel time from the 7-Eleven at Lindfield – where the suspected vehicle was captured on CCTV – the killer waited for up to fifteen minutes.

What did William Newson notice when he walked down the driveway, the wheelie bin rumbling behind him?

Did he see a silhouette emerging from the shadows?

Did the killer say something before pulling the trigger?

Afterwards, he, or she, mounted the bike and drove it over the lawn, down the driveway and along the street at high speed. No CCTV images for afterwards, implying that the driver didn't go very far, or managed to replace the registration plates somewhere close by. No trace of the weapon or clothing being discarded anywhere in the local area.

Bridget strides across the lawn, towards the gum tree. The grass is dry, the ground unyielding. The tree is enormous, with the potential to wreak untold damage if it were to come down in a storm. A slight movement catches the corner of her eye. She stops in her tracks, looking up, her eyes training on one of the upstairs windows of the house next door. There's someone there, watching. A partially obscured face. Blonde hair. Bridget catches the woman's eye and she moves out of sight.

'What did you say the neighbour's name was again?'

'Diana Simon. Why?'

'She's having a stickybeak at us.'

Bridget recalls the very specific information Mrs Simon supplied about Joshua, who conversed with her on the Sunday before his father's murder; when he was apparently distracted and looked over his shoulder several times. Cold hard fact: being specific doesn't mean one is telling the truth. Is there an ulterior motive lurking behind those twitching curtains?

Bridget takes hold of herself. Mrs Simon was not home on the night of the shooting and her daughter has corroborated this fact. The woman is being nosy, and that – unfortunately – is not a crime.

Bridget stands behind the tree trunk and imagines herself in the killer's shoes. Shrinking to make oneself invisible. Waiting. Waiting. Probably feeling nervous. Hands shaking? What did he or she think about? How did they pass the minutes? Fifteen of them. Not a long time. Unless you're waiting to kill someone.

Bridget squints her eyes. What's that on the tree? Words! Something etched into the bark.

She steps closer. The letters are jagged and superficial, quite easy to miss. It takes a moment to segue them together. Her breath catches.

'Dave! Dave! Come over here!'

He arrives, breathing heavily. She points.

YOU HAD IT COMING.

22
MEGAN

'So, how was your long weekend?' Lucas is relaxed, chatty. 'Didn't even get the chance to ask yesterday.'

They're on the way to help an obese patient who can't get himself out of bed. It's not a lights-and-sirens emergency so they can afford to catch up. Megan missed him during her time off. She always does. The pathetic thing is, he doesn't miss her. Why should he? He has Daniella.

She smothers the flare of jealousy with a laugh. 'Had a paintbrush glued to my hand for most of it!'

'You should have called me. I'm pretty handy at cutting in edges.'

She glances at him; his eyes are full of a genuine desire to help. Her gaze falls to the lower half of his face; at some stage over the weekend he decided to ditch shaving. The bristle makes him even more attractive: that masculine, rough-and-ready look – the last thing she needs. She turns her attention back to the road, flicking the indicator for an upcoming left turn.

'My brother is coming on the weekend to help out.'

'How much older is your brother?'

'Four years.'

Megan is fond of Seb, and he's fond of her in return, despite having spent little time together as adults. She is looking forward to seeing him on Saturday. Giving him a hug, hearing all about his little family, and engineering some alone time so she can discuss her concerns about their mum.

Megan's foot is pressed on the brake pedal; she is driving down a narrow steep hill, with cars parked bumper-to-bumper on both sides of the road. As a child, she used to have a recurring dream about a hill like this one. Her mum, dad and Seb striding effortlessly up the incline, Megan sliding backwards, unable to get a grip with her hands or feet. Calling after them with increased desperation.

They've reached the address on the mobile data terminal. Steps lead down into a thickly forested hollow; one can only assume there's a house down there somewhere. Bad news if their bariatric patient needs a visit to hospital. She and Lucas won't be able to manage without back-up.

'Shit!' Lucas sighs. 'Well, this should be interesting.'

The sandstone steps are uneven and slippery.

Thankfully, the handrail is solid and Megan holds on firmly, the medical kit in her other hand. She counts the steps as they go: fifty-seven.

There's a slim middle-aged woman waiting at the bottom. 'Oh, thank God you're here. Be careful on that last step, it's the deadliest one. I'm Cathy, Ray's wife. This way. This way.'

The house has a surprising amount of light, and a stunning 180-degree view of the surrounding bush. It's hard to believe they're less than fifteen kilometres from the centre of Sydney. The master bedroom contains a large window (with another breathtaking view) and a large body lying flat on the king-size bed. Lucas starts chatting while Megan sets up equipment.

'Hi there. I'm Lucas and this is Megan. What's been happening here?'

Ray is about Cathy's age, somewhere in his fifties, and weighs around 200 kilos, if Megan's estimation skills are any good.

'Can't move my legs. Can't get up.'

'Are they numb?'

'Yeah. My hip, too.'

'Looks like you have some blood-flow issues. Has this happened before?'

'Not this bad.'

Ray is wearing pyjama shorts and the skin on his right leg is red and inflamed.

'Is that cellulitis causing you pain?'

'Bloody oath. Especially the abscess.'

The abscess, on the inside of his thigh, is leaking pus. There are several blisters in other areas, and some red streaks, an indication that the infection is spreading.

'Have you been given any medication for this, Ray?' Megan asks, leaning over him so he can see her face.

'Been taking antibiotics about a week now.'

Megan and Lucas exchange a look. If oral antibiotics aren't working, then an IV is required in hospital.

'You have a bit of a temperature, Ray, so we're going to give you something for that, which will also help with the pain. We want to get you to hospital so they can treat the cellulitis infection and the circulation problems. Plan A is to try to get you on your feet and very, very slowly up those steps. If that doesn't work, Plan B is a stair chair.'

Plan C is Fire and Rescue, but Megan leaves that possibility unsaid. She unclicks her radio and calls for back-up.

'Car 482. Can we get a bariatric ambulance, please?'

'Sorry.' Ray covers his face with two oversized paws. 'This is so bloody embarrassing.'

Lucas pats him on the shoulder. 'Don't be embarrassed. This is our job.'

'I'm just a fat bastard taking up too much space in the world.'

His wife chides him immediately. 'Stop being so down on yourself, Ray.'

'We've moved people much larger than you,' Lucas says.

This is an outright lie but it immediately makes Ray feel better. He comes out from behind his hands, even manages a self-deprecating joke. 'You mean I'm not the biggest fat bastard you've had to deal with?'

'No. Sorry. You're boringly average.'

They all laugh and the atmosphere in the room becomes positive.

'Right. The drugs should be taking effect now, Ray. We're going to try to get you into a sitting position. Slide your legs over this way. Take my hand and Megan's. On the count of three. Everyone ready?'

It takes more than half an hour to manoeuvre Ray from the bed to the hallway, then outside to the front path, and up all fifty-seven steps. He leans heavily on the handrail on one side, and on Lucas on the other. Lucas uses a combination of patience, cajoling and laughter, with Ray panting, swearing and guffawing in response.

The bariatric ambulance and crew are waiting at the top. Ray pauses to catch his breath and look around him. He's emotional. 'Been more than a year since I've come this far. Bloody oath.'

Megan and Lucas help get him settled before wishing him luck.

Cathy clutches Lucas's hand. 'Thank you for being so extraordinarily kind.'

The bariatric ambulance strains its way up the hill. Megan waits a few moments, giving it a head start. Lucas clears the job from the MDT before slumping back in his seat. Kindness can be exhausting.

The road is so steep it feels as though they're suspended in mid-air. Once again, Megan is reminded of that childhood dream. Losing traction, sliding backwards. Her hands flailing, her calls going unnoticed. Not one member of her family hears or turns around. She doesn't know what the dream signified at the time. She wasn't abandoned in any way. They were a happy family, a close-knit one. Maybe it was a premonition of what was to come.

Finally, the vehicle is on flat ground and Megan can relax somewhat. She glances at Lucas. His head is tilted back, his eyes closed in a momentary reprieve. The roster changes next week. They'll be assigned to new partners and go their separate ways for at least a few months, until the roster fairy reunites them again. The thought of being without him makes her feel untethered.

'Hey, Megan, there's been a delivery for you,' Kaz says when they get back to base.

The delivery is hard to miss. A long rectangular box tied with an elaborate white ribbon is taking up most of the table in the kitchen. Inside are a dozen roses, blood red, plastic water phials at the end of each elegant stem.

'Nice,' Kaz says. 'Secret admirer?'

Megan snorts. 'Probably an old geezer saying thanks for restarting his heart.'

Lucas and Kaz are watching as Megan opens the accompanying envelope.

Dear Megan,

Thank you for treating my father on the night he was shot. My family and I have some questions, the answers to which might help us come to terms with this awful tragedy. I would be grateful if you could call me on the number below.

Joshua Newson

Megan's legs go from under her. She sits down heavily at the table, pushing the roses as far away from her as possible. Joshua Newson knows her name and where she works. Something tells her he also knows that she is much more than one of the paramedics who treated his father. She is probably overreacting, but those perfect red flowers don't feel like a thank-you; they feel like a threat.

23
JESS

The train station is closed. An incident on the track. A relief bus is parked on the street outside, but has pulled away by the time Jess realises that she needs to be on it. She approaches the security guard, who is standing on the steps to the entrance, turning people away.

'When's the next bus?'

'About twenty minutes,' he says in an unconvincing tone.

She is deeply tired. It's dark and cold. Twenty minutes, if it's really that, is too long.

'Do you know when they'll reopen the station?'

'Not anytime soon. It's a fatality. Big clean-up, if you know what I mean.'

She's sorry she asked. Someone's remains are being scraped from the train and tracks. What a messy way to die. But when you're in that frame of mind you're not thinking about the impact on the train driver or the emergency workers or anyone else.

'Thanks,' she says, moving away. No taxis in sight, and a quick check of her Uber app shows nothing close by. She dials Alex's number.

'Babe, I'm stranded at Artarmon station. Any chance you can come and get me?'

He sighs. He's deeply tired too. Their jobs are physically demanding. She's had seven hours instructing classes, followed by a tough one-on-one training session with Vince. Alex spent the day digging and bricklaying at her parents' house. At this time of night, neither of them has much energy left in the tank.

'What's happened?'

'A fatality. The train line is closed and I've just missed a bus.'

'Okay.' Another reluctant sigh. 'I'm on my way.'

Jess sits on a bench and huddles into her hoodie. Vince added extra rounds to her routine tonight and demanded higher intensity. Both of them temporarily forgot that she's not a professional, or even an amateur; there's no need to push so hard. It felt good, though, pummelling the bag to his chant of 'harder, faster'. Now she's paying the price. Her shoulders are somewhere between aching and numb. She's dehydrated and slightly nauseous. A headache is threatening. At this stage it isn't an unpleasant feeling: a mild sensation behind her eyes, heaviness in her limbs.

She opens her backpack, extracting some migraine pills and her water bottle. She has learned, the hard way, not to ignore the warning signs.

'Act early,' the doctor has said. 'You're not being a hero if you wait.'

A white ute is coming down the street. She jumps to her feet before realising that it isn't Alex. Back down on the bench, the cold metal penetrating her Lycra gym pants. Her phone rings in her pocket. Alex? No, an unfamiliar number. Suddenly she knows, somewhere in the pit of her stomach, exactly who it is.

Breathe. Breathe. 'Hello.'

'Jess?'

'Yep.'

'This is … It's Dylan O'Shea.'

'What do you want?' she snaps.

'I just want to … talk. Can we meet some-some-somewhere?'

'Why do we have to meet? Can't you just say what you want to say?'

'It's com-complicated.'

Bullshit. It's pretty simple from where she's sitting. He wants one of two things: to make amends or to plead his innocence again. Well, Jess wants something too: answers.

'What about Megan? Have you been pestering her, too?'

A long pause. 'M-Megan won't … speak to me. I've tried and … tried … and she just won't …'

Typical Megan, turning the other cheek. Typical Jess, unable to resist confrontation.

'Do you know William Newson's dead?'

'Yes. That's what I-I-I …'

She doesn't owe him anything, not even the politeness of waiting for him to finish what he's trying to say. 'Okay, I'll meet you, but just so you know, the truth isn't complicated – it's simple, actually, so how about you keep that in mind when we have this talk.'

'Is t-tomorrow good?'

Tomorrow is far too soon. Next week, maybe. She needs time to prepare. 'I'll text you when and where. Don't call me again. Is that clear?'

No more halting voice messages. No more calls out of the blue. This is on her terms.

'Thank you … S-Sorry about your train …'

She has hung up before she realises what he said about her train. What the fuck? She swings her head from side to side, her heart banging with fear and adrenalin. A small crowd has gathered by the bus-stop, waiting for the next relief bus. Some cars are parked by the kerbside; they look unoccupied, but it's hard to tell for certain. The rest of the street is fairly deserted, apart from a few customers in the fast-food restaurants across the road. How the fuck does Dylan O'Shea know that her train didn't come? Is he watching her? Or is it an educated guess, intended to send her off balance? The fact that the train line is closed is likely to be all over the media. Typical Dylan. Always looking for a way to get his foot in the door. A disarming smile. A drink to offer. Condolences about the delay in public transport.

Another white ute materialises from one of the side streets, an older more battered model, driving too fast. Definitely Alex. Moments later she is inside, garden debris under her feet, and the safe smell of earth and hard work filling her with relief.

'All right, babe?' he asks, the engine growling as he accelerates away.

His hair is damp and he's wearing a checked shirt she's never seen before; Alex rarely buys new clothes. She can't tell him about Dylan O'Shea. He'll be so mad at her. *Why didn't you hang up on the dickhead? No fucking way are you meeting him!* They'll have a massive fight. She's too weary to fight, or to explain about Dylan. Even too weary to compliment him on his new shirt.

'Yep, fine.' The migraine tablets are starting to work; they make her dazed before they make her feel better. She closes her eyes, visualising her bed and the soft warmth of her pillow pressing against the side of her face. 'Thanks for rescuing me.'

24
BRIDGET

I want people to see my face and my body. I have nothing to hide or be ashamed of.

A quote from Laura Dundas, the bikini-clad protester. Bridget scours the accompanying photograph for clues. Laura's chin with its proud tilt, her eyes, unblinking and defiant. The placard – I'M NOT A LIAR! – shielding most of her body. Lawyers and other people passing in the background wearing overcoats; definitely not bikini weather. The journalist proclaimed her as admirable and courageous yet all Bridget can see is vulnerability and bravado. Laura's defiance is underscored with strain. This is taking an enormous toll. She is not a natural show-woman: she has been *driven* to these lengths.

Bridget emails the article to Patrick, along with a list

of questions: Did Laura finish her arts degree? Where is she living now? Has she staged any other protests? Links between Laura's family and criminal networks? Check social media for whereabouts and posts during the past few weeks.

Experience tells Bridget that a twenty-two-year-old female is unlikely to have either the resources or the know-how to procure a gun, or the mettle to point-blank shoot her adversary. Bridget is not being ageist or sexist, just realistic. Besides, Laura made her point, very publicly and effectively. She doesn't seem like the type to operate in the dark of night.

Fergus Herrmann is another matter. Mid-fifties, more likely to have knowledge about guns, target sur-veillance and how something like this could be pulled off. A man who has already been physically violent to William Newson. A father. According to Emily Wickham, it's the fathers who take it the hardest.

Fergus Herrmann lives in Mount Colah, a suburb that Bridget is not familiar with. Sasha, one of the dedi-cated young detective constables, is her partner today. They're parked outside a single-storey red-brick house. Weeds grow between the concrete slabs on the drive-way and the lawn is equally neglected. The garage door is askew, lending the impression that it can't be opened. No evidence of a car or, more pertinently, a motorbike.

On approaching the house, the detectives hear the muted sounds of a television. There's no doorbell;

Bridget knocks loudly. The sheer curtains on the glass panel are pulled to one side to reveal dark eyes and a bushy beard. The door is opened.

'Detective Sergeant Bridget Kennedy,' she says, offering her hand. 'This is my colleague Detective Constable Sasha McEvoy.'

'Come in. This way.'

They follow Fergus Herrmann into the front room. Matching sofas, nice cushions and pictures on the walls; the inside of the house appears to receive more attention than the outside. He turns off the television and gestures for them to sit. Taller than average height, black T-shirt and jeans, faded tattoos on his muscled arms, one of which looks like angel wings. An intimidating man. Bridget has no difficulty visualising him attacking William Newson outside the courthouse.

'Thanks for seeing us, Mr Herrmann. As I mentioned on the phone, we're investigating the death of William Newson. Can you tell us where you were between seven and eight p.m. on Tuesday August twentieth?'

Blunt fingers scratch his grey-black beard as he casts his mind back. 'Tuesday nights I'm at work. I do night deliveries for a supermarket. Start at six p.m., finish at midnight.'

Bridget is surprised by his answer. He has an air of unemployment, of long empty hours spent in front of a television and getting up to no good once darkness has fallen. The bikie beard has strong connotations; it's hard to shake the bias. She asks if there is someone who

can corroborate his whereabouts, and he readily supplies a phone number for his boss. Then she asks where
his daughter was that night.

'Jemma was at home. With my wife.'

'You sound very certain about that.'

'Jemma doesn't have much of a social life.'

This is Bridget's cue to bring up the rape charges. 'Is
that because of her bad experience?'

His jaw clenches. There's deep-rooted anger in his
dark eyes. 'She goes nowhere. Comes home from work
every day and sits exactly where you're sitting, a book
on her lap. It's fuckin' sad. For her. For me and her
mum. These should be the best years of her life. School
done and dusted, money coming in from work, no big
responsibilities yet … She should be having the time of
her life.'

According to Bridget's research, Jemma was assaulted
in the public toilets next to a beach. She met the man
in a bar, and had been talking to him for some time,
supposedly flirting. They left the premises together. To
go for a walk, Jemma thought; the man obviously had
other ideas. The DPP dropped the charges because it
was ascertained that Jemma did not clearly indicate
dissent to the man. CCTV footage showed her entering
the public toilets in a willing manner, holding his hand.

'She was innocent for an eighteen-year-old.' The
harshness of the father's tone barely disguises his
anguish. 'Sex wouldn't have been on her radar going
into those toilets. He was six years older than her – that's

a lifetime at that age. He knew what he was doing. He paid her attention at the pub because he could tell that she was easy to manipulate. Fuckin' dirty bastard.'

Bridget can't help transposing Cara into the same situation. Inexperienced. Trusting. A little bit flattered. Cara has no trouble being assertive at home, but how would she cope in the situation Jemma found herself in?

'I have a daughter around that age,' she murmurs sympathetically. 'They're so young and vulnerable. It scares the hell out of me to think that this time next year she can legally drink and meet men like that in bars.'

They share a look of solidarity.

Sasha asks the next few questions. 'Do you have a car registered to this address?'

'Yes. A Mazda 6. My wife has it at the moment.'

'Any other vehicles? Your truck? Any motorbikes or scooters?'

'The truck belongs to the supermarket. No motorbikes or anything else.'

Bridget holds his eyes for a moment. He *looks* like the owner of a motorbike. Has she got him all wrong?

'Do you mind if we take a squiz around the backyard and the garage? You don't have to say yes. It just saves us from coming back at a later point.'

He hesitates. She doesn't know if it's the inconvenience or some other reason.

'Sure. If you turn a blind eye to the mess.' His smile reveals a missing molar.

He leads them through the hallway and into a modern kitchen. Sliding doors open to a back patio and a rectangle of grass that's as overgrown as the front lawn. She pokes her head into the small shed that contains a lawnmower, gardening tools and several bags of potting mix.

'Just need a quick look at the garage and we'll be off.'

They double back through the house and access the garage via a door in the hallway.

He turns on a light but it's not much help. 'Sorry. The roller door is broken.'

Bridget peers through the gloom: a folded-up table-tennis table, a couple of push bikes, some fishing rods and an extensive collection of half-empty paint tins.

No Yamaha in sight.

Bridget instructs Sasha on the drive back to headquarters. 'Request a full history of registered vehicles from roads and maritime services, going back at least five years. Check Fergus Herrmann for connections to outlawed bikie gangs. Call his boss, see if the truck has a tracking device.'

Links to a bikie gang would give Fergus Herrmann access to any number of motorcycles ... and any number of illegal guns.

YOU HAD IT COMING.

Forensics were embarrassed to have missed the etching on the tree. Light of hand, most likely done using the blade of a key, definitely recent, was their analysis on re-examination of the scene.

Did Fergus Herrmann believe that William Newson got what he deserved? The assault outside the court-house happened three months ago. How did the distraught father use those intervening months? To calm himself down, or work himself up into a greater fury?

25
MEGAN

Lucas has offered to speak with Joshua Newson.

'I was the one with his dad on the way to the hospital,' he reasons. 'If anyone should speak to the family it's me.'

'Thank you.' Megan gives him a grateful smile.

Bereaved relatives make contact from time to time. The ambulance staff are not obliged to respond, but kindness prompts them to offer whatever solace they can. Maybe a quick chat will help the Newson family come to terms with their loss?

Saturdays are non-stop, sporting accidents compounding the usual volume of emergency calls. Their current patient, a middle-aged man who overestimated his agility on the soccer field, has broken his leg in multiple places. After dropping him at Royal North Shore, they finally get a lull. Lucas makes the call while Megan sits intently by his side.

'Joshua? This is Lucas Halliday from NSW Ambulance … Sorry, Megan is unavailable today …' Lucas holds her gaze while he speaks. 'How can I help?'

A pause while he listens. 'Your father didn't regain consciousness, Joshua … No, he didn't speak at any stage … Megan? Megan was driving, I was in the rear with your dad … Not a word, but at least he was spared the pain … Megan will be off for the next few days. Sorry, I need to get back to work. Please extend my sympathy to all your family.'

Lucas hangs up. 'Boy, he's really fixated on talking to you.'

She sighs raggedly. Joshua Newson knows exactly who she is, then. 'Does he think I didn't try my hardest or something?'

'No, not that. More that his dad might've had some dying words that he needs to know about. Don't worry about it, Megs. I'll handle any further contact.'

Joshua Newson is not going to let it go. Megan wishes now that she had just spoken with him. Hiding behind Lucas has made her feel like a helpless seventeen-year-old all over again.

Saturdays are full of extremes. From wholesome 'sporting' accidents to the substance-abuse variety. From unlucky or misguided to the self-inflicted and reckless. From blue skies and grass fields to nightclubs and neon lights.

Teenagers kick off the transition. *I can't wake up my friend … My boyfriend has taken something … I'm at a party and this guy is unconscious …* As the night goes on, the patients become more mature, in their twenties, thirties or even forties. Old enough to know better, but yet they somehow don't. The woman on the floor is called Rachel. She is twenty-five years old. Her friend – Sophie – relays these facts because Rachel is unable to speak for herself.

'How long has she been like this?' Lucas asks in a calm tone that belies his level of concern.

'I don't know,' Sophie replies hysterically. 'She was missing for a while. I went looking for her and found her in here, completely out of it …'

'In here' is the living room of a family home in St Ives. There's a piano, an expensive rug and family photographs on the walls. Rachel has been sick on the rug and on her Lycra dress, which has ridden up her legs. Megan pulls it down, protecting her modesty.

'What has she taken?'

'I don't know. I honestly don't know.'

'Find her purse and check to see if there's anything in it.'

Sophie scrambles away to do as she is asked. There's a small group standing in the room, watching with concerned expressions. It's confronting, seeing a friend in this condition; it might make them think twice about mixing drugs and alcohol in the future, probably what's happened here. Music is playing somewhere else in the house; someone doesn't want the party to end. There are always the nonchalant types, who assume that everything will turn out fine, that this is just a misadventure they'll laugh about tomorrow. The girl's vital signs are worrying: irregular breathing and heart rate, low body temperature and elevated blood pressure. Absolutely nothing to laugh about here.

'I can't find anything in her bag.' Sophie has upended the contents on to the rug: lipsticks, keys, receipts, a few pens.

'Check the coin area and pockets.' That's often where the pills are located, if any are left over.

'Nothing. Sorry.'

'Has she taken drugs before?'

A telling pause. 'Speed.'

'And what has she been drinking tonight?'

'Vodka.'

Speed stimulates the central nervous system while alcohol depresses it. Rather than balancing each other out, the combination conceals the effects of alcohol, with people becoming dangerously intoxicated without realising it. The end result can be alcohol poisoning or coma.

Lucas goes to fetch the stretcher. One of the bystanders, an attractive young woman wearing far too much make-up, smiles flirtatiously as he passes. Megan is both disbelieving and resigned.

'Can you come in the ambulance?' she asks Sophie.

'Yes.' Sophie rubs smudged mascara from under her eyes. 'Of course.'

'Get your things. We're leaving soon. And don't forget Rachel's bag. Do you have a number for her family?'

Somewhere in this city, there's a mother and a father who believe their daughter to be safe and well and perhaps too old to find herself in such a predicament. Their Saturday night is about to be blown apart.

Rachel is a dead weight. It takes four people – Megan and Lucas, with the help of two bystanders – to lift her on to the stretcher. Megan readjusts her dress again, pulling it further down her legs, which are tanned and strong. The music is still playing. Megan expects it will be turned up as soon as they leave.

They spend some time in the rear of the ambulance, stabilising Rachel before setting off. Sophie is on the phone, giving a sobbing account of what has happened to someone on the other end, presumably one of Rachel's parents.

'All good to go?' Lucas asks, looking closely at Megan.

She gives him a nod. He slides shut the side door and goes around to the driver's seat. He knows, without having to ask, that she prefers to stay with patients like Rachel. She feels protective of them. Sees herself and Jess in their young faces. Going that step too far. Paying the ultimate price. Waking up to a new, ugly reality.

'We're just on our way now,' Sophie says into the phone.

Sophie will never forget this night. This fearful

journey to the hospital. What will happen when they get there. The role she played and if she could have done anything differently. It's all flashing across her face. Fear. Guilt. Uncertainty.

Megan reaches across and smooths Rachel's hair away from her face. It's matted with particles of vomit. She uses a surgical wipe to gently remove what she can.

Megan and Lucas need to restock and clean the vehicle before handing over to the next crew. They work efficiently, ticking off their checklists and completing reports. This is their last shift together for the foreseeable future. Every moment of today has been precious. His willingness to field Joshua Newson's questions. His touching concern about Rachel. His banter with the middle-aged man on the soccer field. The chocolate muffin he bought her from the hospital cafeteria.

They leave the building together, pausing in the shadowy car park, their cars on opposite ends of the bitumen.

'Want to go for a quick drink?' he asks suddenly.

'Can't, sorry. Seb arrived this morning. Need to catch him before he crashes for the night.' The day has been so jam-packed, she's barely had time to think about her brother.

Lucas moves closer to give her a hug. 'See you around,' he says, his breath in her hair.

She pushes him away. 'Yuck! You smell of vomit.'

He's laughing as she walks towards her car.

She cries for most of the journey home, overtired and overwhelmed. The toll of seeing the girl, Rachel, in such a bad way. The guilt that all she can offer Seb tonight is a bone-tired husk of his sister. And scathing of herself for falling in love with someone unattainable, yet again.

26
BRIDGET

Laura Dundas was in the middle of her honours' year at the University of Sydney when she made her shivering near-naked protest outside the courthouse. According to Patrick, she abandoned her studies before the end of the first semester, returning to the family home in the Blue Mountains. Patrick has spoken to her mother, who initially said that Laura was burnt-out and needed a rest. On closer questioning she admitted that her daughter had a serious 'breakdown' and was undergoing psychiatric treatment. One night out, life-long implications.

'This is something I need to talk to the kids about,' Bridget says to Shane when she gets home late Saturday evening. They decide that the dinner table is the best place to broach the subject. Shane promises to steer the conversation in the desired direction.

'Hard day at the office?' he asks Bridget, shortly after

they've sat down with his homemade green chicken curry, a family favourite.

'Was it ever …' Her reply is deliberately lacking. She is hoping for one of the kids to notice, for their curiosity to be piqued.

Cara obliges. 'What are you working on, Mum?'

'That defence barrister who was shot outside his house. I've been looking into some of the cases he was working on … They're upsetting, that's all.'

Again, she stops herself from going further. It needs to come across as organic, rather than engineered.

'What kind of cases?' Cara again. Ethan isn't biting. But he's listening and watching, hooded eyes glancing at his mother.

'Sexual assault. The barrister was pretty good at getting people off. He was a hero to his clients but a lot of other people hated him.'

'Do you think one of the victims killed him?' Shane asks, his tone casual.

'Maybe. Or perhaps someone from one of the families. I saw a dad yesterday. He's devastated, and really, really angry.'

'Would you kill someone if I got raped?' Cara demands of her father.

Shane chokes on his food. Bridget winces. Ethan's eyes fly open.

'I'd want to,' Shane says when he recovers himself. 'But I don't fancy going to prison, so try not to get yourself into that situation.'

Cara, failing to hear the irony in her father's voice, immediately goes on the defensive. 'It's not as if I could help it! Rapes happen, like, all the time.'

'Yeah, you can help it.' Ethan joins the conversation with a tone that's somewhere between bored and pragmatic. 'Don't go off with strange men. Don't get so pissed someone can take advantage of you. Don't say yes if you mean no.'

'All good suggestions.' Shane nods diplomatically. 'Also, don't say *nothing*. Speak up. Some girls get raped because they don't want to cause a scene.'

'I wouldn't be one of those girls,' Cara protests, rolling her eyes. 'I'd knee him where it hurts if he didn't listen.'

Would she? Bridget is doubtful, but maybe now, after talking about it, the possibility is unlocked.

'Good,' says Shane emphatically. Then he turns his eyes to Ethan. 'And you, young man, should never take advantage of someone who is drunk or under the influence of drugs or just not very communicative. The girl must explicitly say "yes".'

'She'd have to be out of her mind to say "yes" to him,' Cara snorts.

Bridget and Shane smile. Jokes are allowed. Anything is allowed, once the children walk away from this table with a clear understanding of how to act if they should find themselves in a predicament.

Bridget guides the conversation back to her work. 'One girl had a breakdown and is getting psychiatric treatment. Another is a social hermit, her confidence shattered. The effects can last a long, long time. For both parties.'

Bridget is just as worried for Ethan as she is for Cara. What if her son were to misread the signals? He's withdrawn at the best of times; how will he find the words to navigate a sexual encounter with a girl? She suspects he would be mute, hoping that the girl was 'into it' but not brave enough to double check. Jemma Herrmann was on a different wavelength to her attacker – she thought they were going somewhere to kiss, he assumed they were going to have sex. She froze when things got rough and was too shocked to even say 'stop'. Bridget doubts Ethan's ability to read body language; he has enough difficulty with garden-variety spoken language.

'Most cases don't go to court,' Shane adds. 'It's because nobody *really* knows what has happened, other than the two people involved. That's why you need to do your best to protect yourself. Be clear about what choices you're making. Keep your wits about you.'

'He means don't get pissed,' Ethan quips.

Bridget resists the temptation to deliver a further caution about the perils of underage drinking. This is more than enough for one sitting.

'Does anyone want more rice? There's heaps left over.'

Ethan wants more rice. Like most teenage boys, her son is perpetually famished. Cara's appetite, while still healthy, seems to have stabilised during the last few months. Her body has the curves of a grown woman. With make-up and the right clothes, she could pass for early twenties. This line of thought is not helping Bridget's worry levels.

The kids clear the table and disappear upstairs. Shane migrates to the couch and turns on the evening news. Bridget starts cleaning up the kitchen.

'That went well,' she says, from her position at the sink.

'Yeah, very professional for a pair of amateurs.'

They share a grin – sometimes parenting feels like a challenging game of chess, every move requiring scrupulous forward planning.

Bridget finds the washing-up calming. A lot of people say the same about gardening. She sighs; she must really work out a watering roster before the lawn turns to dust. In all other areas, she and Shane manage to muddle along. The garden seems to have fallen through the cracks.

The news announcer's voice infiltrates her thoughts. 'The body of the man killed on the T1 train line on Thursday has been formally identified.'

Bridget looks up from scrubbing one of the pots. A female reporter is standing outside a train station, commuters swirling in the background.

'Thomas Malouf joined commuters waiting at the far end of platform one at about eight p.m. Witnesses say Thomas lurched forward as the train arrived, giving the driver no chance to stop.'

Bridget freezes. Thomas Malouf: she knows that name.

'Turn it up.' She abandons the washing-up and hurries across to the lounge area. Her hands are dripping wet.

'Police are reviewing CCTV footage and talking to witnesses. It's believed Mr Malouf may have conversed with someone on the northbound platform before changing to the southbound one. Anyone with information is urged to come forward.'

'One of yours?' Shane asks, his voice sounding far away.

Thomas Malouf. *Thomas Malouf and Dylan O'Shea.* Bridget has placed him.

'He is now!'

She rushes to find her phone. Two main players in the Malouf–O'Shea case are dead. Now that Bridget has finally found what direction to point herself in, she's frantic that Dylan O'Shea is next to be targeted.

27
JESS

Billy is warming up on the tear-drop bag, doing under-cuts, hooks and rips. He's wearing a black sweatsuit, along with headgear and a groin guard, which he needs to get used to before his fight. It's Sunday morning. The gym is deserted except for the two of them. Vince took some persuading to open up this morning.

'Billy can't come a few nights this week,' Jess whee-dled. 'He has to go interstate with work. If he doesn't get enough training, we'll have to cancel the fight. No point if we're not fully prepared.'

Vince gave in after a visible internal wrestle: his long-held belief that Sundays are a day of rest versus all the preparation that has gone into this debut. 'Two hours max. But we're not making a habit of it.'

'It's a one-off. Promise.'

Billy moves from the tear-drop bag to the uppercut machine. His face glistens with sweat, even though the gym is chilly enough to see your breath. Jess begins her own warm-up, skipping and some practice on the bag. After about twenty minutes they're ready to spar. Slipping through the ropes into the ring is always a good feeling.

She presses the timer on the wall, which starts the countdown.

'What're you waiting for, Billy? Don't be put off by the fact that I'm a girl. If you hesitate, I'm just going to hit you … Too late, mate. You've got to get in those right hands all the time.'

Sparring and coaching at the same time is challenging. Jess has to keep her wits about her, defend and attack, as well as pinpoint areas where Billy can improve.

'Last thirty seconds … You know where to go … I want left hooks … You're coming up too late … Time!'

They glug some water, catch their breath. Then she starts the timer again.

'That's good, Billy. But you didn't finish! Don't reach for me. In and out. That's it. Find your aggression. Pretend I'm someone you hate. That's better.'

Sometimes the person you're fighting isn't your enemy, but it helps to pretend that they are. Jess used to visualise William Newson and Thomas Malouf. Picturing their faces never failed to produce a fresh surge of hatred and aggression.

They're reaching the end of the third round when there's a loud banging on the roller door, which is at half-mast to let in some natural light.

'Come under,' she yells, without taking her eyes off Billy. 'Go right, Billy. Don't let me off the hook like that … faster hands … good pressure … One, two … That's it! … Time!'

Jess and Billy touch gloves before pulling off their headgear. A woman with shoulder-length red hair is observing them. She's accompanied by another, younger, woman, but it's clear which of the two is in charge.

'Jessica Foster?'

'Yes. What can I do for you?'

'Detective Sergeant Bridget Kennedy.' She's wearing a dark trouser suit. Up close there are fine lines at the corners of her eyes and around her mouth. 'This is my colleague, Detective Constable Sasha McEvoy. I was wondering if we could have a word.'

Sweat is dripping from Jess's forehead into her eyes. 'Just a minute, please.'

Billy follows her over to the locker area. 'Why does a detective need to speak to you?' he asks in a low, serious tone.

'I guess I'm about to find out.'

'You don't need to talk to her. You have a right to remain silent.'

'I know my rights.' Jess buries her face in a towel before using it to wipe around her neck and chest. 'Do ten minutes on the reverse climber. Get your heart rate up even more. Then start your core work.'

'I'm a lawyer. I don't think you should—'

'I *know* you're a lawyer. That's why I enjoyed beating the crap out of you just now.'

Bridget Kennedy is watching their exchange from her position next to the ring. Her fresh-faced colleague is looking around the gym, cataloguing the layout and equipment.

'Reverse climber,' Jess reminds Billy before sauntering towards them. She can do this. She's strong enough to deal with whatever they want to dredge up.

'We're not usually open Sunday mornings,' she says; they're probably wondering where everyone is. 'How can I help?'

Blue-green eyes bore through her. 'William Newson and Thomas Malouf. I believe both these men are known to you?'

'Yep. From long ago.'

'Have you seen either man recently?'

'No.'

'Can you tell me when you last had contact with them?'

That's easy to answer. 'The trial, twelve years ago.'

'How about Dylan O'Shea? When did you last have contact with him?'

'A few days ago, actually,' Jess admits with a frown. 'He called out of the blue.'

'What day, precisely?'

'Thursday, I think. Yeah, the trains weren't running. I was waiting for a lift when he called.'

The detective narrows her eyes, as though Jess has revealed something vital. 'And you're not in regular contact?'

'Fuck, no! He wanted to meet up for some reason.'

'Did you meet up?'

'Not yet ... Probably some stage this week.'

Billy is poised between sets on the reverse climber, blatantly eavesdropping. Jess glares at him until he resumes, his calf muscles flexing.

'So, you commute by train?'

Jess turns her gaze back to the detective. 'Yep, the station's a five-minute walk from here.'

'You say you got a lift on Thursday night. Who gave you a lift, Jessica?'

'Alex, my boyfriend.'

'What time was that?'

'Sometime after eight ...'

'And where was Alex before he picked you up?'

This is starting to feel like a cross-examination. Maybe she should have listened to Billy. 'At home ... Look, where is this going?'

'Thomas Malouf died on Thursday night.'

The shock is intense. 'What?'

'It was his body on the train tracks, Jessica.'

Blue-green eyes are raking her face for some indication that she already knew this. Suddenly, Jess sees herself, sitting on the cold metal bench outside the station, waiting for Alex. How could she have been so oblivious? Surely, she should have known, at some instinctual level, that he had been dangerously close to where she was sitting? Surely, she should have been able to tell, via some sort of physical reaction, that he was dead?

Detective Kennedy is asking a question. 'Don't you think it's odd that he died here, in Artarmon, at the very same station you pass through every day?'

It *is* odd. Extremely odd. Jess recalls the fleeting image of the man who could have been Thomas at Killara station earlier in the week. Maybe it *was* him. Maybe they've been sharing trains and part of their commute all along. Jess needs to sit down. She grips on to the ropes around the ring for support.

'I was here, at work,' she says in reply to the accusation embedded in the detective's question. 'Dozens of people can vouch for that. Same applies to the night William Newson died.'

Detective Kennedy isn't finished. 'And so odd that Megan Lowe was the paramedic who attended to William Newson.'

Jess takes a shallow breath. 'Sometimes life is like that. Weird things happen.'

The detective's expression is thoughtful. 'Does Alex have a motorbike, Jessica?'

'Not here. Back at the farm.'

'And where's this farm?'

'The Hunter Valley ... Look, I don't know what you're implying—'

'I assume they have guns at the farm, too?'

The question sends Jess reeling.

Billy stops pretending that he hasn't been listening and gets down from the reverse climber. He puts a supportive arm around Jess's waist. How could he tell that she needs help standing up?

'That's enough,' he commands, every inch the lawyer despite the sweatsuit and groin guard. 'I'll be recommending Jess gets legal advice before answering any further questions.'

28
BRIDGET

Bridget and Sasha debrief in the car. The young detective constable seems unperturbed about working the weekend. Bridget likes her dedication.

'Right, so we need some background checks on the boyfriend, Alex, and a list of the vehicles and firearms licensed to the family farm. Can you run with that, Sasha?'

'Sure thing.'

It's a twenty-minute drive to Megan Lowe's address, their next port of call. Another cloudless blue sky and a lazy Sunday-morning air. Sadly, Bridget has too much happening to enjoy the drive.

'Let's check in with Dylan, make sure he's safe.'

Bridget spoke to Dylan last night and relayed her concerns for his safety without sharing too many specifics about the investigation – a very delicate balancing act. Dylan would be on her visiting list today if he weren't away on the south coast for the weekend. Bridget considered driving down there until common sense – and her overwhelming workload – prevailed. A twenty-four-hour delay is tolerable, once she knows he's not in harm's way.

'Dylan? This is Bridget Kennedy again. Just checking in.'

'Everything's f-fine.'

'What time are you getting home tonight?'

'Ah … Ah … ten … May-may-maybe later.'

Too late to arrive on the doorstep of the family home; Dylan still lives with his parents.

'Look, can you send me a quick text when you get back? Just being cautious until we get to the bottom of what's happening here … And I'd like us to talk at some stage tomorrow. Can you come in to see me?'

They agree a time and Bridget ends the call. She's interested to see him face to face, this stammering man who was accused of sexual assault at the tender age of eighteen. What kind of impact did the case have on his life? *I haven't been able to sleep*, he said in his statement at the time. *I feel so guilty and embarrassed. I really liked Megan, and I thought she liked me. I was drunk, too. My judgement that night was pretty crap. I'm so sorry that I hurt Megan.*

Now that Bridget has spoken to him a couple of times on the phone, she knows that the statement would have been delivered in a very faltering fashion, with none of the fluency of the written version.

William Newson and Thomas Malouf are dead. Is Dylan nervous that he's next?

Megan Lowe's house is on a tree-lined sleepy street, two kilometres outside Hornsby's town centre. It's a weatherboard, a small house on a large block like most of its neighbours. A ladder leans against the gutter; there's a man standing three-quarters of the way up. A woman is painting the trims of the doorway, and another is engaged in vigorous sandpapering. Music is playing loud enough to be heard from a distance: Coldplay's 'Fix You', one of Bridget's favourites. Their arrival has been registered by the woman who's doing the sandpapering, presumably Megan's mother. She turns the music down abruptly.

'Can I help you?'

Her tone is hostile, which is off-putting because her appearance is so cheerful: pink lipstick, dyed brown hair held back from her face with a floral bandana.

'Detective Sergeant Bridget Kennedy and Detective Constable Sasha McEvoy, from the Homicide Squad. Just wanting a few words with Megan.'

Megan sets down her paintbrush. The hand she offers has spatters of light-grey paint on it. 'This is my mum, Roslyn, and my brother, Seb. Do you want to talk out here or go inside?'

Megan exudes an air of quiet capability that Bridget

remembers from last time. Her brother descends from the ladder, a tin of paint dangling from his hand. He has tattoos on both arms and a stare that's as hostile as his mum's. Megan's family are clearly not fans of the police. Is it because they felt let down by the justice system during the trial, or is it something more systemic than that?

'Inside would be good.'

Bridget and Sasha follow Megan inside. Cardboard boxes line the hallway. The walls are bare and freshly painted.

'Are you moving house?' Bridget asks, taking in the evidence.

'Yeah. Selling up after thirty years.'

Moving home after such a long time is a big decision. Are Megan and her family drawing a line of some description? Selling the family home, and at the same time settling old scores?

'Can I get you something to drink?' Megan asks, grimacing at the half-packed kitchen.

'We're fine, thanks. You're busy, so we'll try to keep this short. Are you aware that Thomas Malouf died on Thursday night?'

Megan's face is an open book: confusion wrestling with genuine shock.

'Oh my God! William Newson and Thomas Malouf are both dead?' Her voice is faint, incredulous.

Bridget nods and continues to scrutinise her face. 'I spoke to Jessica this morning. Actually, I thought

213

she might have called to let you know we'd been around.'

Megan rests one hand against the edge of the counter. Short nails. Sturdy fingers. Hands that have saved lives. 'Jess and I aren't in regular contact. We spoke when William Newson died but that was the first time in years.'

Bridget decides not to pussyfoot around. 'Did Jessica ever say anything to you about wanting either of those two men dead?'

Colour floods Megan's face. 'Emotions were running high at the time ... I said some pretty bad things too ...'

That's as good as a yes. The thing is, Jessica has a watertight alibi for both nights.

'How about Jessica's family? Did they make any threats?'

'Not that I'm aware of. Her family are the opposite of hot-headed. She's different from them.'

'What about Jessica's boyfriend?'

'You mean Alex?'

'Yes, Alex. Does he strike you as the type to take justice into his own hands?'

She blinks. 'I barely know him. As I said, Jess and I haven't been close.'

There's something in her tone. Why did these two stop being friends? Was it something to do with Alex?

Bridget hears the murmur of voices from outside. 'What about your family, Megan? Did they make any threats?'

Another surge of colour. 'As I said, emotions were running high, everyone was upset …'

'Do you know where your brother was on Tuesday twentieth of August?'

'Seb was in Melbourne – he lives there. He's visiting this weekend, to help. We haven't seen him since last Christmas.'

'How about your mother?'

'Mum was here. She's always here on weeknights. She's like clockwork.'

'Did you actually see her on that night?'

Megan takes a moment to cast her mind back. 'She was in bed when I came home. I remember feeling relieved. I wasn't in the mood to talk.'

Bridget can easily imagine herself in Roslyn Lowe's shoes. A man hurting her beloved daughter, and escaping justice. Her rage would have no boundaries.

Megan frowns, her gaze hopping between Bridget and Sasha. 'There's something that might be important … Joshua Newson tracked me down. He sent flowers and a card saying he wanted to talk. Lucas, my colleague, spoke to him. Joshua seemed very concerned about what his father might have said during his last moments …'

Bridget is momentarily thrown; Joshua Newson hasn't been much on her mind the last few days. 'But Mr Newson didn't regain consciousness, did he?'

'That's what Lucas told him. I think Joshua knows exactly who I am. He didn't really want to talk to Lucas – he wanted to talk to *me*.'

Megan could be on to something. Bridget nods at Sasha: another strand for the young detective to run with, see where it leads.

Bridget thanks Megan, and at the same time reminds herself of the importance of staying neutral. Down-to-earth, get-on-with-the-job, calm and helpful: it would be easy to be fooled by Megan's apparent good qualities.

'I like that shade of grey,' Bridget says to Roslyn, pausing when she gets outside. 'What's the name of the colour?'

The older woman presses her lips together. She is the epitome of barely restrained anger.

Megan answers on her behalf. 'Ashville grey. It's nice, isn't it?'

Today has thrown Jess's boyfriend, Alex, into focus, and there is also the need to double-back on Joshua Newson. But standing in front of Bridget is the personification of another cold hard fact. A mother's love is a force of nature: primal, fierce and boundless.

YOU HAD IT COMING.

Is it possible that Roslyn etched those letters into the gum tree, to remind herself of the reason why she was about to cross the most abominable of lines?

29
MEGAN

'What did they want?' Roslyn demands, watching the detectives getting into their car.

Megan is overdue a discussion with her mum, but this is hardly the ideal time, with Seb halfway up the ladder and heaps to get through before his flight tonight. She keeps her answer simple, brief.

'Thomas Malouf died on Thursday night, and William Newson was shot a few weeks ago. The police believe their deaths are related. Maybe something to do with the trial.'

Colour infuses Roslyn's face. 'What? The trial was twelve years ago, for God's sake. Why can't they leave us alone? Haven't we been through enough?'

'They're just doing their job, Mum. Sometimes they have to ask uncomfortable questions. Two men are dead. Their families are owed some answers.'

'Families?' she splutters. 'Since when did they start caring about families? They never cared about us. *They ruined us.* They made *you* look like the criminal, and your father, your *poor father* …' She flings the sandpaper block away. 'I'm going inside.'

'Don't be upset, Mum. This is just routine.'

Roslyn opens and closes her mouth, as though words fail her. Then she's gone, and Megan and Seb are left looking at each other.

'She's right,' he says darkly, glaring down from the ladder. 'They did ruin us.'

It's not fair to blame the police. They did everything they could, including prosecuting when there was probably not enough evidence to get a conviction. If anything, it's the legal system that let them down: the impossibly high level of proof, the rigidity of the court process, yet the creativity afforded to lawyers to craft their own narrative. But in Roslyn's eyes – and Seb's too, apparently – the legal system and the NSW police are all the one entity.

Megan and Seb continue to work, assuming that their mum will return when she's ready. Megan is overdue a discussion with her brother, too, but there's a risk of their voices carrying inside and Roslyn overhearing. Once again, the brushstrokes are satisfying, therapeutic. Clean paint obliterating the grubbiness of what went before. Thomas Malouf is dead. How does she feel? Not sad. Not even that curious.

When Roslyn finally reappears, she's sullen and begins work down the side of the house. By 6 p.m., they've finished the entire front façade and both sides. The difference is both dramatic and validating; Megan is starting to feel more optimistic about the achievability of the sale price.

'We should get going soon, Seb.' Megan is mindful of the fact that traffic to the airport can be unpredictable.

'Yeah, I'll just have a quick shower. Are you coming, Mum?'

'I'll tidy up here.' This means Roslyn is still out of sorts.

Half an hour later they're on the road. It's the first time brother and sister have been properly alone all weekend. Megan doesn't intend to waste it.

'I'm worried about Mum,' she says bluntly.

'Me too.' He sighs. 'I don't remember her being so easily riled.'

'It's the trial. Anything to do with it makes her go crazy. Even after all these years.'

Seb wasn't there for the trial; he was travelling in South America. Megan is glad he wasn't there, glad he didn't hear all the gory details, or experience the full, crushing impact of the verdict. He's the only one of the family who's normal.

'Seb, I found some stuff on Mum's phone. She had a map open. The street where William Newson lived. And she's been reading all these articles about the shooting.'

219

She glances at her brother just in time to catch his frown. 'Maybe she's curious?'

'Yeah, I guess she is, but it *looks* bad. The detective asked me where Mum was on the night of the shooting. She was in bed when I got home, so I didn't *actually* see her …'

He gets where she's heading. 'Which means she doesn't have an alibi, plus she's got all this incriminating stuff on her phone.'

'So, you can see why I'm worried?'

'Yeah, yeah, I can. But Mum wouldn't know how to shoot a gun, or ride a motorbike. I don't think she'd stand up as a suspect for very long.'

True! It's good to talk, get perspective.

Traffic is sparse; they get a pleasing run of green lights until the M2.

'Have you spoken to Jess recently?' he asks quietly.

'Yeah, I went to see her a couple of weeks ago. She's working in a gym in Artarmon.'

'Still fighting?'

'Nah, she's a trainer now.'

Seb's interest in Jess has always been solicitous. She used to fancy him in the way seventeen-year-old girls fancy unattainable men in their twenties. In the way seventeen-year-old girls think there's nothing sexier than a boy with brooding eyes and long hair, who plays the guitar. In the way that seventeen-year-old girls think they're being subtle when they are, in fact, being utterly transparent. Jess used to dress in ripped jeans and black T-shirts, the same uniform as Seb. She engineered it so she was in the same room as him whenever possible. In fairness to Seb, he always gave her time. Asked her about school and karate, never made her feel like a pest. He even sent her the occasional postcard from his travels.

Seb is staring ahead, still frowning. 'So, I guess the police have been to see Jess, too?'

'Apparently. But I'm not the first person she'd tell. Things have never been the same between us.'

They've entered the Lane Cove Tunnel. The radio goes scratchy; Seb turns it off. An articulated truck trundles past in the next lane, scarily close. Neither of them speaks, both thinking about the same thing: their father's funeral. The ugly scene between Roslyn and Jess outside the church that turned a painful day into an excruciating one. It signified the end of Megan's friendship with Jess and a fault line in her relationship with her mother.

On exiting the tunnel, Seb changes the subject to something easier. Cassie is talking about returning to work now that Tia is approaching her first birthday. Seb will be the primary carer for his daughter and continuing to pick up whatever night-time gigs he can get. Finances will be better (Cassie earns a lot more than he does), which means he'll be able to come to Sydney more often.

'What I really want is for Mum to get down to see you,' Megan says, flicking on her indicator to overtake.

'Once the house is sold, there's nothing to tie her to Sydney – she could live in Melbourne for a while. A change of scene would do her good. Might help her let go of all the sadness and anger.'

'Cassie and I would love to have her. An extra pair of hands would be brilliant, short term or medium term or whatever she decides.'

'Great! We're on the same page. Now all we have to do is get the damned house sold.'

Fifteen minutes later they're pulling up outside the domestic terminal. Seb leans across to peck her cheek before jumping out. The boot of the car opens and closes as he extracts his bag. Her brother: the only person she has in the world, besides her mum. It feels slightly dissatisfying every time they catch up; it's never quite enough.

When Megan gets home Roslyn is already in bed. It's only eight; she seems to be going to bed earlier and earlier. Selling the family home is a big upheaval. Maybe her outburst today was more to do with emotional stress than anything. Megan sits on the couch with her phone, which she has barely looked at all day. Three new text messages.

Lucas:

Rachel regained consciousness during the night. She was discharged today. Another one saved from the jaws of death. xxx

Seb:

Never even asked you about your love life. Are you seeing anyone? When do I get to play disapproving older brother?

Jess:

Have you heard about Thomas Malouf? We need to talk. When can we meet up?

30
BRIDGET

Bridget is in Shane's bad books. She worked all weekend, leaving meals, household chores and teenager management to him. Now she's flying out the door, and he's left to deal with the Monday-morning scramble. The kids are *technically* old enough to get themselves ready for school. The reality is they show less independence and initiative than ten-year-olds.

'Sorry,' Bridget says, scouring a drawer for her car keys. 'Got a huge day. Feel like I'm on the verge of a massive breakthrough.'

Shane's sigh is resigned. His job comes second, he understands that. Nothing is more urgent than a murder investigation (potentially a double-murder investigation, in this instance).

Homicide is now leading the investigation into

Thomas Malouf's death, and Katrina has allocated more resources accordingly. Two additional detective constables, and Dave Nesbitt, seconded from Chatswood, are now full time on the case. Bridget arrives in the office to find that her old academy friend has hijacked the empty desk next to hers. He's examining CCTV footage from Artarmon station, his nose almost touching the computer screen as he endeavours to catalogue every detail.

'Here's Malouf, arriving at the station. He's jumpy. Keeps looking over his shoulder. Taking his hands in and out of his pockets. Goes to platform two, changes his mind and heads for platform one. Classic sign that something's up. Who decides to go in the opposite direction all of a sudden, unless they're not sure about their whereabouts?'

Dave keeps up a running commentary that Bridget finds both irritating and reassuring. She can trust him not to miss anything, although she might eventually have to tell him to shut the hell up.

'Hey, Bridge, take a look at this.'

She jumps up to peer over Dave's shoulder. 'What am I looking at?'

'This individual here. Walking behind Malouf on his way into the station. They're on platform two, and hey presto, here they are on platform one a minute or so later. Just like Malouf.'

The figure is blurry and dressed in a nondescript manner. Dark puffer jacket with hood. Head downcast. None of Dave's frames have a clear shot of the face. The mystery person is standing close enough to be conversing with Malouf in one of the frames, but it's impossible to tell from the angle of their heads.

'Something was going on. Some kind of game was being played. I think Thomas Malouf jumped because he felt he had no other choice. Or else he was given a helping hand. It wasn't an accident.'

The problem is that there's very poor coverage of the actual event. Far end of the platform, obscured by the toilet block and other commuters. They can see Malouf's body lurching forward, but no amount of enhancing or freezing can determine if the momentum was his own, or provided by someone else.

Bridget's lips press together. 'I never thought it was an accident, Dave … Or a coincidence that both Newson and Malouf are dead within weeks of each other.'

'Coincidences are often not coincidences at all,' he recites without taking his eyes off the screen.

'Exactly. Do what you can to find out who that person is. I can't even tell if it's a man or a woman.'

The figure on the screen is not especially tall or muscular and the puffer jacket disguises the shoulders, which can be a good indicator of gender. The gait does look a bit masculine. Bridget suddenly remembers the manner in which Jessica Foster sauntered across the gym yesterday morning: legs further apart than you'd usually see in a female. Lucky for Jessica, she has plenty of witnesses who can confirm that she was at the gym at the precise time of both deaths.

Bridget spends the next hour briefing Patrick, Sasha and the new members of the team on the various lines of inquiry. Alex Leary. Roslyn Lowe. Fergus Herrmann. Laura Dundas. Joshua Newson and his mother. They must keep the William Newson investigation ticking over, even though Bridget's gut is telling her that the answers will ultimately lie with Thomas Malouf. Newson had a lot of people who were unhappy with him. Malouf, from what they know so far, was a much simpler individual: account manager in the training sector, committed to his social life and the recreational use of cocaine. So easy to pass off his death as a suicide, but Bridget knows there is much more to the story. He worked in North Sydney and lived, alone, in Mosman. He had no business at Artarmon station at 8 p.m. on a Thursday evening. Uncovering what prompted him to be at that station at that time will uncover the facts behind his death and William Newson's death, too. Bridget is convinced of it. Because they're linked. They have to be.

'Hey, Dave, want to take a break from the screen? I think it's time we had a chat with the Malouf family.'

Dave doesn't need to be asked twice. He is thrilled to be working full time on the investigation. 'Let's go, Bridge.'

The Malouf family home is in Gordon: a brash, two-storey house that stands out from its neighbours, which are mostly single-level Federation-era homes. A water feature in the front garden, an imposing second-floor balcony, three luxury cars parked in the driveway.

'Never guess Dad's a property developer,' Dave says sarcastically.

The front door is double-size and the bell can be heard echoing inside the house. The door is opened by a youngish man, presumably Thomas's brother, Leo: mid-twenties, brown hair, soft features.

'Detective Sergeants Bridget Kennedy and David Nesbitt from Homicide. It's Leo, isn't it? Can we come inside for a minute?'

'I'll get my dad,' he says abruptly.

Bridget and Dave are left standing on the threshold. A number of conclusions can be drawn from Leo Malouf's reluctance to invite them in. A lack of manners. Deference to his father, given that it's his house. Or trust issues with the police.

Leo's father comes to the door: early sixties, grey-black hair, swarthy skin. He offers his hand to shake.

'Joe Malouf. Leo said you're from Homicide?'

'Yes, we've taken the case over from local police. We have some questions.'

Joe regards them warily. 'I've got a full house this morning. Family and friends consoling my wife ... We'll have to talk here.'

No settling in for a long chat, then. Bridget whittles down her questions to the most important ones. 'Can you tell us what frame of mind Thomas was in? Was he worried about anything?'

'Thomas enjoyed life, had a good circle of friends. He was an upbeat fellow.'

'Did he have a girlfriend or partner?'

Joe shakes his head. 'His mother wanted him to settle down, but he wasn't ready.'

'Any financial problems you're aware of?'

'Not at all. He had a good job. Besides, he always knew he could come to us if he ran into trouble.'

The cushioning effect of family wealth. Lucky for Thomas. And Leo.

'So, no long-term effects from the rape trial?' Bridget asks, inwardly wincing at her bluntness. This is what comes of not being able to sit down and ease into things.

Joe's jaw clenches. 'Thomas put it behind him. We all did. Nasty business. Nasty girls.'

Bridget recoils. *Nasty girls.* Is that how Joe and the rest of the family saw it?

Dave puts forward the next question. 'We're investigating whether William Newson's recent death is related to Thomas's. Do you have any information to offer on that possibility?'

Joe is resolute. 'No information.'

Bridget and Dave are back in the car within minutes. Bridget hesitates before driving off, staring up at the big glass windows on the second floor. In one of those bedrooms, two seventeen-year-old girls were allegedly raped. *What really happened that night?*

'It all started in this house,' she says, half to herself.

Nasty business. Nasty girls. Megan mentioned yesterday that she and Jess are no longer close. It suddenly feels important to know why the friendship fell apart.

229

31
JESS

Megan's dad's funeral. He was only sixty-one, two years younger than Jess's dad. He'd had cancer and – quite unfathomably – declined chemotherapy treatment. So, there was a strange atmosphere in the church. A 'what if' question undermining the rhythm of the service. What if he'd had chemo and cooperated with the doctors and oncologists? What if he'd fought his illness instead of succumbing to it? What if this funeral never needed to happen? Megan wouldn't have red-rimmed eyes from crying; Seb wouldn't need to chew on his lip to contain his emotions; Roslyn wouldn't look as though she'd keel over at any minute from the weight of her grief.

While the priest went through the motions, Jess closed her eyes and thought about the man who had died. A man who had seemed very ordinary and accessible when she first met him. A man who was proud of Megan in such a simple, uncomplicated way. A man who was so much more vulnerable and brittle than he appeared on first impressions. Peter Lowe was a burly man, a builder who was used to hefting things around. He had big, rough hands that looked like they could handle anything; the fact was, they couldn't.

Jess joined the line of people to pay her respects once the service was over. Roslyn, Seb and Megan stood in the church porch. Rain was lashing sideways at the windows; the weather seemed to suit the occasion.

'Sorry for your loss,' the people in front of her were saying.

Jess didn't know what to say. Maybe squeezing each of their hands would relay her sadness and sympathy, and relieve some of her guilt? Because she was another 'what-if'. What if she had gone home when Megan asked to go home? What if she had respected Megan's wishes and contained the damage to just the two of them? Megan had always been more intuitive than her; she should have listened.

'You!' Roslyn gasped when it was Jess's turn. '*You!*'

'Mum!' Megan whispered urgently. 'Shush!'

'How dare you show your face … This is *all your fault*.' Roslyn's voice was gaining strength. 'What kind of friend are you, anyway? If you'd been a good friend, my husband would still be alive today.'

'Mum! Stop!' Megan pleaded. 'That's not fair.'

It was fair. Jess's bad decisions had played an undeni-able part in the premature death of a beloved husband and father.

Seb took his mother's arm, tried to get her to back down. Roslyn stood her ground.

'Get out of here!' she screamed in anguish. '*Go!*'

Jess went. She ran.

Megan sent a text later that night.

I'm sorry. I don't know what came over Mum.

Jess replied:

I'm sorry, too. I should have realised I wasn't welcome.

And that was that; they didn't see each other or com-municate again until the night William Newson was shot. Some damage is beyond repair. Deep foun-dational cracks at the time of the trial that led to a catastrophic rupture at a suburban funeral many years later. An insurance company would have looked at the wreck of their friendship and declared it an unequivo-cal write-off.

It's Monday morning. Jess is awake early again, thanks to Alex.

'Can't you be quieter?' she grumbles, covering her eyes with her hand.

'Sorry, babe,' he says breathlessly. 'In a bit of a rush. Can't be late for your mother.'

He's pulling out drawer after drawer, obviously searching for something. 'For God's sake, what are you looking for?'

'A work T-shirt that doesn't have holes in it.'

Despite herself, she smiles. He's trying to impress her mother. Her very aloof mother, who is not easy to impress.

'Put on something, *anything*, and stop clattering around!'

The work at her parents' house is in its second week. Alex has spent a lot of money on materials – bricks, paving, cement, topsoil – and is worried about cash flow.

'Did you do your invoicing last night?' she asks.

'No.'

Jess is irritated but unsurprised. She is also fully awake now. 'Fuck's sake, Alex. You said you'd do a partial invoice. You could've given it to Mum this morning and had money in the bank by tomorrow.'

'I'll wait till the job's finished.'

'Why? You've got to treat her like any other client.'

'But she's not like any other client.' He plants a warm kiss on her forehead. 'She's fifty times more intimidating.'

Can't argue with that. Alex's noise follows him to the kitchen, where cabinet doors are being opened and closed in the same frantic manner. What is he looking for now? Finally, the front door slams and he is gone.

The flat is deliciously quiet in his wake. It's just after

6 a.m. A lazy morning stretches ahead; Jess doesn't need to be at the gym until lunchtime. She closes her eyes, even though there's little chance of falling back to sleep. Her thoughts circle before snagging on her mum and dad. She understands them better now than she did at seventeen. Megan's parents felt more real, more relatable, back then. Compare their fathers, for instance: a builder and a surgeon. Men who work with their hands, and that was the extent of what they had in common. Money, confidence, status: all the things that protected Jess's father were absent in Peter Lowe. Then their mothers: a housewife and a concert pianist. Roslyn so passionate and involved, Margaret cold and contained.

The day that Roslyn had to be escorted from the courtroom symbolised the differences. William Newson had called Jess and Megan liars; Roslyn went berserk.

'Stop saying those terrible things about my daughter!' she cried, not caring that she was in contempt of court and causing a massive scene.

Jess's parents remained dispassionate, as though they didn't have an opinion one way or the other about her ability to tell, or sustain, lies. She sat there, wishing that her parents believed in her half as much as Roslyn and Peter believed in Megan.

But Roslyn's passion had a flip side, which Jess realised nine years later as she ran from a church porch into near-torrential rain. Suddenly, Jess was the person who Roslyn was calling out. When you're put on the spot like that, very publicly, it's hard to summon a defence. Yes, Jess was in the wrong, but Megan was in the wrong too. She cost them a week, a whole week of resisting while Jess begged her to go to the police. A week in which they showered morning and night, washing away vital evidence. A week in which swelling and redness had time to recede. A week in which the clothes they'd worn had been washed, as had the sheets of the bed where it happened. Body fluids, fingernail scrapings, traces of potential drugs: all gone. All that was left was their word against the boys' word. Their 'flimsy, unreliable' – according to William Newson – word. Jess was in the wrong, but so was Megan. They could have won the case if she hadn't dragged her feet.

Jess is on the verge of falling back to sleep when her phone beeps with an incoming text. Her eyes fly open. She has been waiting for this: Megan's response.

> Yes, we should talk. I've got a day off today. Let me know when you're free.

That's twice they'll see each other in as many weeks. Is it stupid to hope? It's too late to salvage their friendship, but maybe forgiveness is within reach.

32
BRIDGET

Bridget arrives back at headquarters armed with a tray of takeaway coffees. Nothing like good coffee to help revive the troops.

She knocks on Katrina's door. 'Skinny flat white delivered with an update, if you have the time.'

'Excellent. Come in.'

Bridget helps herself to a seat. 'Lots of progress to report. Dylan O'Shea is coming in later this morning – hopefully he'll give us some insight into the dynamics at the time of the trial. Dave has a person of interest who was at the station at the same time as Thomas Malouf. We're enhancing images to show to colleagues and family to see if we can get an ID. I talked to Megan and Jessica over the weekend. Their alibis are pretty water-tight, so I'm branching into the families. Definitely some resentment from Megan's mum. She works in a car rental company. Guess what's directly across the road from her workplace …'

Katrina shakes her head, evidently not in the mood for guessing games.

'That motorcycle café. You know the one.'

Katrina nods and grimaces. A café slash motorcycle accessories shop. A reputed hub for drug and other illegal dealings. The shop has been closed down and reopened numerous times, its ownership changing with dizzying frequency.

'And Jessica's parents?'

'Her family is well-to-do, which means plenty of money to pay someone to do their dirty work. Her partner, Alex, also deserves a closer look.'

Katrina sips from her coffee and regards the white-board on her wall. The names are still intact since their meeting last week: Suzanne Newson, Joshua Newson, Fergus Herrmann, Laura Dundas, Emily Wickham, Megan Lowe and Jessica Foster.

'Any names we can take off?'

'Not really.'

Sasha has confirmed that Fergus Herrmann was at work but there is doubt about his specific location. His delivery truck doesn't have a tracking device – which is a bit suspicious, because most delivery vehicles do these days – so he really could have been anywhere. Sasha is checking CCTV from the Pacific Highway to see if there's evidence of the truck being in the area.

Of course, the bike could have been stored in the back, which would explain its disappearance after the shooting. They haven't been able to confirm connections between Fergus and a bikie gang, but Bridget maintains her suspicions. The distinctive beard. The faded angel-wing tattoo. A bikie gang would explain where the weapon came from, and the context for how a distraught father could become a violent killer.

Laura Dundas: maybe her name can be removed? Patrick spent a large part of Sunday driving to the Blue Mountains and speaking to Laura and her family in person. According to Patrick, the arts student was vague and lethargic – side effects from a heavy dose of antidepressants – and displayed none of the passion that had propelled her to protest outside the courthouse and break into Newson's chambers. The family were protective of Laura, but cooperated in terms of establishing their whereabouts on the night of the murder. No guns or motorcycles were registered to the property.

But … from near-nude protests to psychiatric treatment, one extreme to the other. Bridget isn't quite ready to put a line through Laura's name.

Katrina runs a hand through her hair, dishevelling her usually immaculate bob. 'How about Joshua and Suzanne Newson?'

'Still possibilities. William Newson was a wealthy man – Joshua and his brothers will inherit all that wealth. Suzanne abhorred her husband – her motivation would be hate rather than money.'

Bridget tells Katrina about the flowers that Joshua sent Megan. 'Apparently, he wanted to know if his father had any dying words. Maybe understanding all the details helps Joshua cope ... or maybe he's afraid his father said something incriminating.'

'Impossible to know without asking him outright,' Katrina muses.

Bridget's instincts are to hold off. 'He doesn't know I know about the flowers. Let's wait and see if he makes another move.'

'Agreed.'

Bridget finishes off with a mention of the Malouf family. 'Pretty frosty reception this morning. You'd think they'd want the police investigating every possibility. Maybe it was because we called at a bad time ... they had visitors.'

Katrina sets down her coffee and frowns at the whiteboard. 'So, we need to add three or four names, and take none away?'

'Er ... yes ...'

The detective inspector raises one thin silver eyebrow. 'And you're calling this progress?'

Dylan O'Shea is waiting in one of the interview rooms downstairs. Bridget asks Dave to join her; the meeting with Katrina has left her feeling less confident of the direction she's taking. Not Katrina's fault. The detective inspector is doing her job, a degree of scepticism being part of it.

Dylan stands up to shake her hand, then Dave's. His skin is pasty white, his curly hair on the wild side: he looks like an overgrown university student.

They all sit down. 'Thanks for coming in, Dylan. This is an informal chat. We're not recording and you're not a person of interest.'

'Sure.' His eyes are bleary, betraying a night with little sleep. 'What would you like … to know?'

'Can you start by telling us the last time you saw Thomas Malouf?'

'The middle of March. It was a school catch-up. Just drinks in one of the … pubs in the city. There's usually one every few m-months. I … don't always go.' His reply is relatively stutter free; it's obviously a question he anticipated being asked.

'How did Thomas seem to you that night?'

'The same as … always. Boasting about chicks, cars and real-real-estate.'

'So, you're no longer close friends?'

Dylan shakes his head emphatically. 'Don't know why we were in the first p-place. He's always been a d-d-jerk.'

Bridget recalls one of the things she read in the court transcript. A message that Thomas had sent the morning after the party: *What a fucking night. Two virgins! Sick.* The message was sent to a group of ten school friends, their responses crude and derogatory. Were these the same men who gathered on a regular basis for drinks in the city? Bridget could only hope that their attitudes to

240

women had become more respectful. Although, given Dylan's comments, bragging about sexual conquests was not something Thomas had grown out of.

Bridget is not here to go over what happened on the night of the party. The court transcripts painted a very vivid picture, some of which – as the mother of teenage children – has kept her awake at night. What she needs to know is what happened afterwards.

'How did you feel when the trial was over? Was it a relief? Did it take long to get back on your feet?'

'Yeah, I was r-relieved, but I wasn't cel-celebrating. The Maloufs threw a party to … celebrate the verdict. Thomas was annoyed when I didn't show up. What was there to celebrate? Yeah, we didn't get thrown in jail, but our lives were … fucked. In many ways, the verdict didn't matter. Our names were out there, in the p-public domain. It felt like the whole c-c-country knew what we'd been accused of. I wanted to hide … never show my face again.'

Bridget experiences a flare of sympathy. In NSW the complainant's identity is protected but not the defendant's. The media coverage would be difficult to recover from. Probably easier to make a life overseas, although with the internet you'd always be a few clicks away from being identified. Dylan is right; the verdict would be irrelevant to prospective girlfriends and employers who wouldn't want to take the risk. Obviously, the Maloufs weren't looking into the future when they threw the party. What did the Lowe and Foster families do on the night the verdict was handed down? Cry themselves to sleep? Plan their revenge?

'Did you receive any threats from Megan or Jessica's families following the verdict?'

'No. M-Megan's mum had some outbursts during the trial, but there was n-n-nothing afterwards.'

'What kind of outbursts?'

'Said some s-s-stuff to the media. Escorted from the-the courtroom, that kind of thing.'

'Were you afraid for your safety at any point?'

'Not really … She was just a mum.'

Just a mum. Is Roslyn Lowe being underestimated?

Dave takes over the questioning. Bridget concentrates on reading Dylan's body language. 'When did you last see William Newson?'

'Not since the trial.'

'Jessica Foster mentioned you've been in contact with her.'

His shoulders hunch. 'Yes.'

'Can you elaborate on why?'

'I want to say … s-sorry to her and M-Megan.' His face has turned pink. Embarrassment? Shame? 'I never ap-apologised in person. Mr Newson had us under s-s-strict instructions not to speak to the … com-com-complainants or make any kind of c-c-contact.'

'Why do you feel you owe an apology?' Bridget interjects. 'The verdict cleared you of any wrongdoing.'

He shifts in his seat. He's agitated, his speech deteriorating accordingly. 'The verdict m-m-meant there wasn't enough evidence … I was … drunk, really drunk, and I can't actually r-r-remember that much. What I *do* … remember is Megan t-turning me down earlier in the night, when we were both f-f-f … sober. So, whatever happened afterwards p-p-probably shouldn't have … happened. I've thought … about this a lot. It's one thing con-convincing a j-j-judge and … jury. It's another … convincing yourself that you did n-n-nothing wrong.'

So, there's remorse. That's something, at least. Was Thomas Malouf remorseful, too? Had he done any self-examination in the years following? And how about Megan and Jessica? How are they going to receive this belated apology? Are they in a forgiving frame of mind?

Dylan takes his phone from his pocket, glancing at the screen before putting it away again. Presumably checking the time, or missed work-related calls or messages. He's a software engineer in one of the technology companies in Macquarie Park. She can imagine him in that role; preferring to interact with computers and code rather than people.

'Thank you for being so candid, Dylan. We'll finish up soon. Before you go, I want to talk through some extra security measures. Simple things like letting friends and family know your whereabouts at all times, keeping windows and doors locked and trying not to be alone. Be vigilant. Just until we get to the bottom of exactly what's happening here.'

Ladies and gentlemen of the jury, let's take a moment to recall the evidence submitted on physicality. You saw some photographs on the screen. Megan and Jessica at the karate class where they met each other and began a friendship. Megan sparring with another class member. Jessica breaking a board with her leg – she was only sixteen at the time, but obviously fearless. According to their Sensei's testimony, Megan was extremely strong but lacking in agility. Jessica, on the other hand, had both – she could have gone far in the sport had she more discipline. The evidence highlights the fact that neither of these young ladies were weaklings. They were trained in self-defence, for goodness' sake. If a boy needed to be pushed away, they were capable of that … and much more. These girls knew how to protect themselves. They were not victims. They were willing participants.

33
MEGAN

These girls were willing participants. This became one of William Newson's catchphrases. Every day, as many times as he could manage, he got it in there, gelling the idea in the jury's heads. So unfair that a barrister can stand up and say whatever he wants while the complainant sits there helplessly, with no immediate right of response. Of course, the prosecutor lodged objections, and on a few occasions the jury was asked to leave the room until the judge made a ruling. *These girls were willing participants.* It stuck, like one of those songs you hate yet can't get out of your head.

Lengthy cross-examinations. Precise questions. Everything done and said that night funnelled down, down, down until it became one singular question: had consent been given? The one thing Megan knows for sure is that she did not consent. Therefore, it should have been black-and-white. William Newson excelled at introducing grey, querying their trustworthiness, their motives, even their ability to defend themselves. Thomas testified that he'd merely been bragging in the text (*What a fucking night. Two virgins! Sick.*) and he'd only had – consensual – sex with Jess. Leo Malouf had purportedly been lying awake in his bedroom next door and testified that he heard no sounds of dissent or requests to stop (in fact, he heard laughter and giggling). The fact that the boys had been intoxicated too blurred the whole consent issue. The fact that the girls had waited a week to report the assaults to the police drew question to their motives, as well as having the effect of vital evidence no longer being detectable. The fact that the jury was composed of largely middle-aged to elderly people, with only four women. Megan and Jess were too naïve to understand the jury selection process and the use of pre-emptive challenges. The system had started to work against them even before a word was uttered in the courtroom.

The boys were acquitted. No sentencing. No victim impact statements. No further discourse on the many ways in which the girls had been affected. Those precise questions had left so much unsaid. Megan ended up writing her own victim impact statement as a form of self-therapy: *I was not a 'willing participant'. I did not want to lose my virginity that night. My trust in people, and in the world, has been shattered.* The only person who read her statement was her mother.

Megan is meeting Jess at her apartment, in Pymble. The street is one of leafy trees and old wealth. She parks her ten-year-old Toyota between two fat BMWs.

The lift is small and slow to arrive. Megan is beginning to consider the stairs when the bell finally pings. An elderly man and woman are inside.

'Come on, Harry. We're keeping everyone waiting.'

Megan sticks out her arm to hold the doors open. 'Take your time.'

'Sorry we're so slow, dear. Come on now, Harry.'

Poor Harry looks confused. Dementia? 'Where are we going, Bev?'

'We're going for a walk, Harry.'

Not very far, by the looks of things.

Jess's door is on the latch and Megan knocks lightly before letting herself in. The interior is a surprise. Large windows, high ceilings, soft natural furnishings.

'I'm in the kitchen,' Jess calls out.

The kitchen is a galley one. A large, expensive-looking coffee machine sits on the counter, along with a fresh latte. A teabag and boiling water are brewing in another cup. Jess is wearing gym wear, her hair scraped back in its customary high ponytail.

They take their drinks outside to the balcony, which is another surprise. A vertical garden on one wall, shelves with plant pots on the other. Two chairs with printed cushions. This is a grown-up apartment. It belongs to someone who knows who they are, how they want to live. Megan can't help feeling inadequate by comparison, still living in her childhood bedroom. It's little consolation that her living arrangements are about to change.

'Is that you, Jessica?' a quivery voice calls from next door.

Jess's smile obliterates the sharp angles from her face. 'Morning, Helen. How are you?'

'I'm fine, I'm fine.' A loud sigh. 'Another blue sky. It's a curse!'

Jess smiles again, then whispers, 'Helen is a darling. Alex and I are the youngest here by at least forty years!'

This is a new Jess. A benign, more domesticated Jess. Megan feels sheepish when she thinks back to their meeting at the café. Her blunt accusations. No wonder Jess was affronted.

Megan sits back in her seat. 'So, now Thomas Malouf … What's going on?'

Jess shrugs, drawing attention to her thin shoulders. 'Stuffed if I know! Good thing I have people who can vouch that I was at work both those nights. That detective looked like she didn't believe a word I said! Suppose it didn't help that I was at the train station not long afterwards.'

It's beyond bizarre. Megan being with William Newson during the last hours of his life, and Jess minutes away from where Thomas Malouf died. Something is going on, some sort of masterplan. Can they work it out if they put their heads together?

Megan chooses her words carefully. 'Bridget Kennedy seems suspicious of Mum, too.' She isn't ready to admit that she's had her own doubts about Roslyn.

Jess's eyebrows, tinted a shade too dark for her hair colour, shoot upwards. 'That's ridiculous!'

Megan sips her tea, once again casting around for the right words. 'Mum can't prove she was home on those nights because I was at work. And she said some pretty bad stuff at the trial.'

Megan hasn't checked her mum's search history for a few days, but she's willing to put money on Thomas Malouf featuring heavily.

Jess snorts. 'You don't need to worry about people who proclaim their feelings out loud. It's the ones who let it fester that you need to watch out for!'

That's a fair point, and applies to both Jess and Roslyn. But what about Alex? Does he let things fester? Is there a way to ask Jess without offending her?

Jess has moved on. 'Dylan O'Shea phoned out of the blue. He wants to meet up.'

'He contacted me, too. Are you *actually* going to see him?'

'Yep. Tomorrow.'

Megan cannot think of anything more excruciating than seeing Dylan O'Shea after all these years. No doubt he'll have matured. Instead of one mental image, she'll be haunted by two: the younger version and the older one.

'Is that wise? Given everything that's going on?'

Jess's bony shoulders rise in another shrug. 'I don't really care what's wise. I want to get some things off my chest.'

Megan is caught between admiration and apprehension. 'At least don't go alone!'

The dark eyebrows rise again; Jess's eyebrows and shoulders seem to be in constant movement. 'Are you offering to come?'

'Sorry, I couldn't bear it – and anyway, I have work. But now I'm worried about you.'

'Don't worry about me. I can more than take care of myself.'

True. Not that long ago she was a professional fighter, one of the best in the world. Quite suddenly, Megan wants her to punch Dylan O'Shea. A fist straight in the face, that he didn't see coming. A follow-up to the ribs, where it would hurt the most. Something unwinds in Megan at the thought. Something that's been coiled up for a very long time.

She drains the last of her tea and sets the cup down. 'I'm confused, Jess … Why is this restarting now? Why does it feel like we're being implicated? Is someone trying to punish us or set us up?'

Jess is suddenly still. 'Neither … I actually think someone is trying to vindicate us. It reminds me of Helen's cat, next door.'

Megan is lost. 'What?'

'How it brings its killings to the back door, drops them on the step for someone to find first thing in the morning. As if to say, "Look what I've done! Aren't you proud of me?"'

That's an appalling analogy. But it has an undeniable ring of truth.

A door slams in the apartment.

Alex's voice booms out. 'Hey, babe, you still here? Forgot my phone.'

Megan and Jess stare at each other. Then Jess stands up to go and greet her boyfriend.

34
JESS

These girls knew how to protect themselves. William Newson was correct in that regard. The question that should have been asked was what *stopped* them from protecting themselves, from fighting back? Jess and Megan had bruising and chafing, but nothing that indicated a true struggle. Even if the boys had overpowered them, what happened to their voices? Why didn't they scream the house down?

The possibility of date-rape drugs didn't come up during the trial because there was no trace in their blood or urine samples (which were tested a week later, due to Megan dragging her feet). Jess held the possibility at the back of her mind, though, because it was the only plausible explanation for their docility and patchy memories. Many years later it came to the fore of her mind. She was suffering from a broken nose and several cracked ribs as a result of a fight; the pain was intense. The doctor prescribed painkillers that had a sedative effect, to help her sleep. She woke the next morning with very little memory. She couldn't remember eating dinner, or what time she'd gone to bed. She'd slept in track pants and a sweater, hadn't even loosened her hair from its ponytail. Alex said that she'd been 'out of it', walking and talking but acting really weird. Something clicked in Jess's brain. This had happened to her before.

Yesterday morning, she discussed her theory with Megan, who agreed it was possible that GHB had been put in their drinks.

'It can only be detected in the blood for up to four hours and in the urine for twelve hours, which is why it's the perfect date-rape drug.'

Maybe that week's delay hadn't cost them so much after all. Any trace of drugs would have been gone by the next day.

Megan knew quite a lot about GHB, thanks to her job. 'It has a steep dosage response, as in a tiny increase in dose can have a dramatic increase in effects. Of course, there's no quality control, so you can't be sure what even qualifies as a dose to start with. If there's alcohol in the mix, or over-the-counter medications, it's even *more* dangerous. It's one of the main culprits for accidental overdoses at clubs and parties.'

It felt good to be with Megan, sharing the problem,

throwing around theories. The only interruption was Alex, but he seemed to understand that they were in the middle of something heavy; he found his phone and didn't hang around.

Jess is not dumb. Dylan wants to either plead his innocence or say sorry. Maybe he's in therapy because the guilt has been eating away at him. Maybe he's become religious and wants to atone for his sins. Well, if he's sorry, he should do the decent thing and tell the truth. Jess and Megan have a right to know if they were drugged.

Jess is meeting him at the Pymble Memorial Park. A café or a pub didn't seem right; she is not sure she could stomach coffee or any kind of food. She didn't want him in her apartment and neither did she want to see where he lived. A public park seemed like the only option, although yesterday Megan was concerned that it might be too deserted.

'Will there be people around that time of day? Is there passing traffic?'

Jess is expecting plenty of mums with prams. Yes, there is passing traffic, although the park is shielded due to a slope and some well-placed foliage. Most importantly, she can walk to the train station from there and the fact that she is going to work straight afterwards also removes the question about what to wear: black gym pants and T-shirt, and a dark grey sweater. Not the most flattering colours, given her pale complexion, but uncompromising: bleak, even.

Jess doesn't want to admit to herself that she's nervous. What if she's wrong, and an apology isn't forthcoming? What if he's angry or abusive? Is she ready to fight back, defend herself? She checks her phone: ten minutes until she needs to leave. She spends it tidying Alex's clothes off the floor – he is such a slob sometimes – and giving the bathroom a quick once-over. She never thought she'd be the house-proud type. Things change when you have your own place. When it's your hard work and money going into the mortgage and furnishings. If Alex doesn't start cleaning up after himself, she'll threaten to charge him rent. Speaking of Alex, she feels guilty that she didn't tell him where she is going today. She was scared he'd stop her or – worse – insist on coming along. Alex would lash out at Dylan, he wouldn't be able to help himself, and then she wouldn't get what she wants: answers. Now it seems like a big omission, not telling him. Too late now, though.

Two minutes to go. Jess checks her backpack to make sure she has her wallet and phone. A loud buzzing sound causes her heart to leap: the intercom. There's someone at the door downstairs. Does Dylan know where she lives?

'Who is it?' Her voice comes out high-pitched and nervous.

'Me, Natasha. I'm so pleased you're home. Can I come up?'

Fuck! Her sister, who she barely sees from one month

to the next, chooses *now* for a visit. Baby Lucy starts to wail, letting Jess know that she is out there too.

'Sorry, I should have called ahead.' Natasha is being drowned out by Lucy's wails. 'This is a bad time, isn't it?'

Yep, it's a bad time. But this might never happen again. Her sister turning up unannounced at her door. Her super-organised, super-competent sister, who sounds like she is at the end of her tether.

Jess presses the button to unlock the front door. 'What a nice surprise! Come up … I'll put on the kettle.'

Is this a flying visit or something longer? Should she text Dylan to let him know she's running late? Fuck him. She owes him nothing.

35
BRIDGET

Another funeral. Another sunny morning and crayon-blue sky. The church is at full capacity: Bridget and Sasha only managed to get seats because of two chivalrous middle-aged gentlemen who insisted on giving up theirs. It's obvious that the Maloufs are an extensive family, a mini-community in their own right. Everyone here knows each other and they're not afraid to show their grief: sobbing, nose-blowing and throat-clearing provide a backing track to the Catholic service. Bridget can easily imagine these people at the party that was thrown after the verdict. Bellowing congratulations to Thomas, backslapping him and each other, filling themselves with food and becoming intoxicated on pure relief. Telling themselves whatever they needed to tell themselves to make the situation more palatable.

The eulogy is delivered by Leo Malouf. His words come across as stiff and utilitarian. 'My brother lived life in the fast lane. He wanted to experience everything, wasn't afraid of anything ...'

'Fast lane' is code for recreational drug use, which may have deteriorated Thomas's decision-making abilities on that night, or seen him hanging around with the wrong sort of people.

'I was always in his shadow, the annoying younger brother, but I didn't mind ...'

Leo's words and tone are saying two different things. Maybe being stiff is the only way he can keep his emotions in check. Or maybe he wasn't close to his brother and is struggling with what to say. People display grief in very different ways, but even taking that into account, Bridget is not getting the sense that the brothers were close. She tries to visualise fifteen-year-old Leo testifying back in 2007. Did he use the same flat voice, lacking in vigour and conviction? Did he tell *the truth* when he testified? He was in the bedroom next door. Did he really hear nothing at all?

After the service, the casket is shouldered by Leo, Joe and other male relatives. It's hard not to imagine the mangled state of the remains within. Are the other mourners thinking the same thing? The family trails after the coffin, linking arms.

'Such a terrible accident,' an elderly woman sobs, and is comforted by a middle-aged woman, perhaps her daughter. 'So young to be taken.'

The family is not seeing this death for what it is: a suicide or a murder. After the burial, they'll consume food and drinks, sharing anecdotes and rewriting the narrative, like they did in 2007. They are old hands at fooling themselves.

The coffin has been placed in the hearse. The crowd is dispersing to drive to the cemetery, a few kilometres away. Bridget takes Sasha's elbow and turns to leave but someone is blocking their way. Someone dressed in a black suit.

'You're not welcome here,' Leo Malouf hisses in her ear.

He slides away before she can inform him that they were just about to leave.

Back at headquarters, Patrick has managed to retrieve the old case files, including the video-recorded police interviews.

'There's a lot of stuff here. Where do you want to start?'

'I want to see Thomas Malouf's interview,' Bridget says. 'He can't talk for himself now – let's see what he had to say then.'

Dave and Sasha pull up seats; everyone's curious. Thomas and his lawyer appear on Patrick's screen. Thomas is wearing a white shirt, turned up at the sleeves. Floppy fair hair, slight smirk, extraordinarily composed for an eighteen-year-old kid. The lawyer is more tense, fidgeting with paperwork while Thomas is read his rights and cautioned that what he says may be used as evidence against him. The lawyer would have instructed William Newson at a later point, when it became evident that the case would go to trial.

After supplying his name, date of birth and address, Thomas is asked for his version of events. He leans back in his seat. 'Yeah, I had a party. Fifty or sixty people. Everyone had a good time.'

Thomas is questioned about Megan and Jessica's presence at the party. 'Yeah, the two of them were drinking, dancing, didn't want to go home. Ended up in my parents' bedroom, saying they were tired, but they weren't there to sleep … Look, it was one hundred per cent consensual. Why do girls tell lies about this shit?'

Bridget watches the rest of the interview with a strong sense of distaste. Thomas Malouf is unapologetic and strangely unapprehensive. Is it because he knew he could rely on his younger brother to back his story? Pity there's no video of Leo. All they have are his written statement and the court transcript. Leo's evidence was pivotal. If he had heard a muffled cry or any hint of a struggle in the bedroom next door, the whole case would have been turned on its head.

Cold hard fact: Leo Malouf was almost as important to this case as the defendants and complainants. Did testifying for his brother drive them closer, or push them apart? Bridget has had two less-than-friendly encounters with Leo. Is it due to grief, or something else?

Patrick loads Dylan O'Shea's interview next, which is in stark contrast to his friend's. Dylan's a mess. Blushing, quivering, apologising. 'I'm so sorry. I can barely remember anything. I'm so sorry.'

Jesus. One extreme to the other. Bridget returns to her desk and tries to gather her thoughts. Where to next?

Patrick materialises just a few minutes later, as though in answer to her question. 'Take a look at this. Found it in one of the old files. Sent in a few weeks after the verdict, by Roslyn Lowe. A victim impact statement – Megan wrote it as a form of therapy. Roslyn wanted the detective working on the case to see it, to keep it in mind for future sexual assault investigations by the police.'

VICTIM IMPACT STATEMENT OF MEGAN LOWE: GIRL A

I thought that losing my virginity would be romantic. I imagined a boyfriend who was handsome, tender and committed. I imagined a luxurious hotel room with scented candles and background music. An occasion I'd always remember and cherish. Jess and I lost our virginity to boys we didn't like, let alone love. We lost our virginity side by side, too out-of-it to realise what was actually happening. Instead of feeling cherished, we were bruised, ashamed, and spent weeks worrying about pregnancy and STDs. Thomas's text suggests that I was raped by him as well as Dylan. Everyone needs to know that I was not a 'willing participant' for either of those boys. I did not want to lose my virginity that night; I was tired, I just wanted to sleep. I woke up to a nightmare. My trust in people, and in the world, has been shattered. I feel damaged and

worthless and dirty. I find it hard to maintain focus, to see
any meaning to life. The only way forward for me is to go
somewhere else: another city, country, continent. A place
where I can pretend that I'm not, and never was, Girl A.

36
MEGAN

Megan has been rostered with Kaz for the next few months. They've worked together before. Kaz is older, mid-forties, with short wavy hair and scrutinising eyes. She used to work in a high-flying corporate role but gave it up to retrain as a paramedic. Kaz lacks Lucas's extraordinary empathy, but patients respond just as well to her honesty and authority.

Around lunchtime Megan and Kaz get called to an office building in St Ives, where a pregnant woman (thirty-four weeks' gone) has started bleeding. The route takes them past Memorial Park, where Jess had arranged to meet Dylan. Megan has the opportunity to assess how visible the park is to passing traffic. The answer is: not very. She is relieved that Jess didn't end up going.

'Natasha never turns to anyone for help, least of all

me,' Jess said when Megan phoned to find out what Dylan had wanted. 'I just couldn't send her away. And, oh my God, Lucy might be the cutest baby in the world but her screams can shatter glass.'

Natasha was a remote figure when they were teenagers, so focused on her medical degree that she barely reared her head to join in at mealtimes. Megan was half frightened and half in awe of her (and never quite sure if Natasha even knew her name). Megan is glad that Natasha and Jess are becoming closer, and especially glad that Natasha's surprise visit prevented Jess from going to the park. The more she thinks about it, the more it makes her suspicious. Meeting in a 'public place' that's actually quite secluded. And why now, after all this time? What does Dylan want? It's easy to underestimate him. The stumbling words. The petrified look on his face. His white trembling hands. He conveyed both remorse and distress as he sat in the witness box. He played the part perfectly; it was far too easy for the jury to feel sorry for him.

A woman is waiting outside the office block, to show them where to go. 'We're on the third floor. Jennifer seemed perfectly fine. It started out of nowhere.'

'First baby?' Kaz enquires.

'Yes,' she says breathlessly. 'How did you know?'

'Just an educated guess.'

Jennifer is splayed in an armchair that someone has dragged into the boardroom from somewhere else, a bloody towel scrunched between her legs.

'Jennifer, how are you doing? My name's Kaz and this is Megan. Can you feel the baby at the moment?'

'Yeah. He's wriggling like crazy.'

That's good news. Babies of this gestation should be moving pretty continuously. The bad news is that late-pregnancy bleeding can be an indication of placental abruption or uterine rupture.

'How about contractions?'

'I've been cramping up since I started bleeding.'

The cramping could be either contractions or abdominal pain associated with a haemorrhage. Jennifer needs to be taken to Maternity urgently.

'How did you feel this morning when you woke up?'

'I had a backache. Thought nothing of it.'

First-time mothers often miss the signs of impending labour: backache and lower abdominal pressure. Some of them have been faithfully reading pregnancy books, chapter by chapter, to correspond with the current stage of their pregnancy. But some pregnancies don't follow the book, or skip ahead a few chapters, and next thing there's a baby on the way.

Kaz continues to fire off questions while Megan concentrates on Jennifer's vital signs. Her blood pressure is low and her skin is clammy, indications that she has lost a fair amount of blood.

'How old are you, Jennifer?'

'Thirty-two … Is my baby going to be okay?'

Kaz is her usual matter-of-fact self. 'I'm not going to

lie to you, darl. Bleeding at this stage is a bit of a worry … Has anyone called your partner?'

'Yes,' the colleague answers, from where she's standing at the doorway. 'He's on his way.'

'Tell him to go directly to Royal North Shore Maternity. Bring Jennifer's overnight bag and things for the baby.'

The delivery will be an emergency C-section because of the blood loss and the baby's distress. In the back of the ambulance, they manoeuvre Jennifer so that her right hip is elevated and check again to make sure there's no evidence of cord prolapse. She has begun to have proper contractions. Time is of the essence: they do not want a vaginal delivery, given the risks to mother and baby.

Megan jumps behind the wheel while Kaz attends to Jennifer and her baby.

'You'd be doing me a big favour if you can hold off having this bub until we reach the hospital, darl. Is that a deal?'

'I'll try my best,' Jennifer pants in response.

The lunchtime traffic is gridlocked. Cars try to make space when they hear the wail of the siren, but they can only do so much. At one intersection, Megan has no choice but to go down the opposite side of the road, always a heart-in-mouth scenario – all it takes is one driver to barge through without noticing them.

'Focus on your breathing,' Kaz says from behind. 'Inhale slowly through your nose, exhale through the mouth in a long sigh … I'm not seeing any bits of baby presenting, so that's good! Let's keep that bub inside.'

Kaz has made all the medical interventions she can; psychological interventions are all that's left. 'You're doing great, darl. Squeeze the hell out of my hand. We're nearly there now.'

The baby, a boy, is born by C-section forty minutes later. Megan and Kaz receive word just as they're arriving back at base. The baby is healthy except for his lungs, which are underdeveloped. Jennifer is in recovery after the surgery and a blood transfusion.

'Thank God for that.' Kaz breathes a sigh of relief. 'That was a close one.'

They go straight to the kitchen for tea and chocolate biscuits. Adrenalin rapidly gives way to exhaustion in the aftermath of an emergency.

'To Jennifer and her baby boy,' Kaz says, and they clink their mismatched mugs.

'So, this is where you two are hiding.' It's Sakar, one of the senior paramedics.

'Just celebrating a close call with a mum and bub.' Kaz wipes some biscuit crumbs from her navy pants. 'How many babies have you delivered in your day, Sakar?'

Sakar has thirty-odd years on the job; he's a good person to share war stories with. 'Twenty-four. I count them. Each one is a miracle.'

'Any with placental abruption and severe bleeding?'

'No, you got me there. Hey, I have something for you both.'

Sakar hands them identical cream envelopes. Megan's first thought is that it's another card from Joshua Newson, which is irrational, because why would Kaz get one too? She freezes, unable to open the envelope. Kaz shows no such reticence. She takes out the folded paper and reads aloud: 'Lucas and Daniella are delighted to announce their engagement ...'

37
BRIDGET

Thursday morning brings some promising developments. Sasha turns up at Bridget's desk looking extremely pleased with herself.

'Sasha, what have you got for me?'

'Two things, actually. A payment of five thousand dollars to Emily Wickham that wasn't salary related. Plus, you know those flowers that Megan received from Joshua? Well, turns out it was our Ms Wickham who organised them. Makes you wonder, doesn't it? Is it Joshua who wants to know about his father's final words or is it Emily? Is Emily pulling Joshua's strings?'

It does make you wonder. Five thousand dollars: is it enough money to mean something?

'When was the transfer made?'

'About a month before Newson's death. From his

personal bank account, not the business one. We didn't highlight it on first review because it didn't seem big enough. But maybe it's the tip of something?'

'Maybe. See if you can find any other payments. Backdate to when she started working for him.'

The next development comes later in the morning, from Dave. He flops down on her visitor's seat, a self-satisfied grin on his broad face.

'Got something mega interesting for you, Bridge!'

'The identity of our mystery man at the train station?' Bridget asks hopefully, scanning an email before pressing send.

'No, sorry, facial images too indistinct. No, it's to do with the Newson side of things.'

'What is it?'

'Only that Suzanne Newson is in a relationship with her old next-door neighbour, Diana Simon.'

Bridget's hands stiffen on her keyboard. The nosy neighbour and Suzanne Newson a couple? That *is* something interesting. 'And how do you know this?'

'Suzanne's phone records. The same number kept reappearing. Did some digging on social media and found a photo that says "more than just friends".'

Dave is triumphant. It's a fresh angle. It's a plausible motive – Suzanne or Diana wanting to remove the pesky ex-husband from the picture. It suggests that the deaths are unrelated; the answer to William Newson's shooting may not lie with Thomas Malouf after all. And it's yet another name to add to the whiteboard in the detective inspector's office. Bridget can hear Katrina's sardonic tone: *And you're calling this progress?*

She makes an impulsive decision. 'Might be time for another visit to Suzanne Newson. Want to come along?'

'Can't. Meeting one of the tech guys in half an hour. He's in demand, don't want to have to reschedule.'

'I'll take Sasha, then.'

Sasha, who has spent the morning wading through bank transactions, is more than happy to take a trip in the car.

Half an hour later they're standing outside Suzanne Newson's bottle-green front door. Bridget knocks and on cue the dog starts barking from inside.

'Mabel, shush!' Suzanne opens the door, and the dog rushes out to greet them, jumping and yelping with excitement. 'Oh, hello again.'

Bridget smiles brightly. 'Hello, Suzanne. Sorry to drop by unannounced. This is my colleague, Detective Constable Sasha McEvoy. Do you have a minute?'

'Is there news?' Suzanne's plump face is creased with what appears to be genuine concern.

'No news. Still following up various leads. Just want to clarify your relationship with Diana Simon.'

'Oh ...' Suzanne seems to deflate. She steps back from the doorway, to make space for them to pass. 'You better come in, then.'

Bridget and Sasha follow Suzanne into the kitchen-living area. Bridget makes directly for the photographs displayed above the TV unit. There's one of Suzanne and another woman holding flutes of champagne: it's exactly as Bridget remembers it.

'So, this is Diana?' she checks. The other woman has strong cheekbones and blonde hair. She looks younger than Suzanne. Bridget overlays the image with her brief sighting of Diana peering from her upstairs window, the day when Bridget discovered the etching on the tree: *YOU HAD IT COMING*. Is that what Diana thought? And Suzanne?

'Yes.' Suzanne's cheeks have turned pink, a similar shade to her cotton shirt. 'Look, neither of us have been attracted to women in the past. Diana just happens to be someone I love very dearly. She feels the same about me ... We have so much in common – gardening, the theatre, our dogs ... Does any of this make sense?'

Bridget recently read a newspaper article about late-blooming lesbians. Women who'd had long-term, successful relationships with men, and later in life had equally successful relationships with women. Rather than having suppressed their true sexuality, the article suggested that women's sexuality is fluid and can shift over time.

But Bridget is not here to 'make sense' of Suzanne's sexual identity. She's here to figure out if it provided motivation for the murder of her ex-husband three weeks ago.

'How did your sons take the news that you and Diana were in a relationship?'

'Badly,' Suzanne admits with a heavy sigh. 'Especially

Joshua. He lives in Sydney – it's in his face more than the other two. Diana's kids aren't thrilled either, to be honest.'

Is this the real reason why Quentin and Riley chose to stay with Joshua instead of their mother when they returned home for the funeral? Proximity to good restaurants wasn't a likely factor after all, which means they're not as shallow as Bridget thought, but also means they're less open-minded.

'And how did Mr Newson respond?'

'William thought I'd lost my mind. He wanted me to see a psychologist.'

The two women look happy in the photograph. Comfortable in themselves and with each other. But Bridget knows enough not to be duped by a photograph. Smiles and glasses of bubbly in the picture frame, and all the ugly stuff – ex-husbands, seething children, contentious divorce settlements – conveniently cropped out.

Bridget turns so she's looking Suzanne full in the face. 'So, this was the real reason behind the disintegration of your marriage?'

Suzanne's denial is vehement. 'No! My relationship with Diana began at least six months after the separation. I think I mentioned before that William started to represent repeat offenders? That was the tipping point for me. I couldn't reconcile myself to his job, or – eventually – to him.'

Sasha clears her throat, seeking permission to speak. Bridget nods.

'Can you tell us who the repeat offenders were?' the young woman asks tentatively.

Suzanne wouldn't know names. Any discussion would have been in general terms due to client confidentiality.

Suzanne looks from Sasha to Bridget and back to Sasha again, her eyes pinpricks in her cushiony face. 'Thomas Malouf, for one.'

Well, so much for client confidentiality!

Suzanne is perceptive enough to know exactly what Bridget's thinking. 'William wasn't indiscreet ... I know it was wrong of me, but I used to read some of the files he brought home.'

Bridget takes a moment to marshal her thoughts. Forget confidentiality and Suzanne's means of obtaining the information. This is a significant revelation. Just as Bridget was at the point of separating the deaths of William Newson and Thomas Malouf, here is something linking them together again.

'Thomas Malouf?' she double checks, to buy some time. 'From the Malouf–O'Shea trial in 2007?'

Suzanne's nod is definitive. 'I couldn't believe it when his name popped up again. I was so cross with William. The second case didn't even go to trial. My husband got Thomas off on a technicality and, of course, his previous sexual history bore no relevance. My husband was enabling a monster.'

A monster indeed. Thomas Malouf clearly didn't feel remorse about what happened with Megan and Jess all those years ago. He didn't see the 'not guilty' verdict as a warning to keep on the straight and narrow. He saw it as a green light to do whatever he wanted.

'Thomas Malouf was buried yesterday,' Bridget says, sitting down on the floral sofa. 'Tell us everything you know about this other case.'

38
JESS

'Tyler, don't tell me you forgot your mouthguard again. Come on, mate. We've had this discussion. Just tell us if you don't want to spar, and tell us if you don't want to be here at all, for heaven's sake … I can talk to your mum for you.'

Tyler mutters something indecipherable in response. What is it with this kid? Is he scared of his mother? Or maybe it's the father who is exerting pressure. Parents send their kids to youth boxing for different reasons: to toughen them up, to calm them down, to provide an outlet for aggression, frustration or genuine athletic ability. Boxing helps with all of the above, but more than anything it instils discipline. There are clear rules and protocol. The coach is the boss. No back-answering, no messing around, no half measures. Most kids, even the unruly ones, conform. What is the problem with Tyler?

On the other end of the spectrum there's Andy: overweight and lacking in natural ability, but here of his own volition and giving it everything he has. Andy arrived fifteen minutes early, and is already warming up with the skipping rope. Andy has ambition, a goal to gain cred with the kids at school; Tyler can't seem to summon enough ambition to tie his shoelaces.

'I'm going to bring a spare mouthguard to the next class.' Jess tries to look the kid in the eye but it's easier said than done. His gaze bounces away before she manages to hold it down. 'So, there'll be no more excuses, mate. You'll either have to spar or tell me what's going on.'

It's obvious that he'll never become a boxer, not even at a social level, but it might be possible to teach him a different skill: to be honest with himself.

'Some days I'm more like a life coach than a bloody boxing coach,' Jess joked to Natasha when she turned up unexpectedly.

'What would you say to someone like me?' her sister countered, clasping her hands around her coffee mug. 'I could do with some life coaching at the moment.'

Jess glanced at Lucy, so angelic in her pram … now that she had succumbed to a badly needed nap. Apparently, Jess had been a difficult baby too, doggedly fighting sleep. Apparently, she became happier once she was able to crawl around, the movement reducing her frustration and wearing her out for longer sleeps. This is what her mum told Natasha in an attempt at consoling her: *Lucy might be just like Jessica; things will get easier once she starts moving.*

'Someone like you ... Mmm ...' She assessed her sister in the same way she'd assess a prospective gym member. Translucent skin, gritty eyes, leftover baby weight. If Natasha came into the gym, she'd be torn between devising a gentle routine to ease her in or sending her straight home for a long sleep. 'Well, it all depends on what's driving you through the door. It wouldn't be a need to prove yourself, because you're the most accomplished person I know. And it wouldn't be fitness or strength, because running is more your thing ... No, you'd be there because you feel frustrated and want to hit something.'

Natasha sucked in her breath, displaying her surprise.

'Don't be surprised.' Jess smiled. 'Even an idiot can see what's going on. You're a super-organised person and have excelled at everything ... until the unpredictability of being a mum. When did you last get out for a run, Nat?'

Her sister scrunched her face. 'Not since before Lucy.'

'You need to get back to it.' Jess smiled again, to show that she understood it wouldn't be easy. 'Try to run a couple of times a week, but don't go too hard. Your body is still recovering. You need to be kind to it.'

Natasha's sigh was full of weariness. 'Oliver gets home so late and I'm bone tired by then.'

Bloody Oliver. Carrying on like nothing has changed. 'Oliver can come home on time once or twice a week. He must make some sacrifices, too. I think the stock market will survive.'

Exhibit A: the hard-learned maturity and diplomacy of Jessica Foster. The old Jess would have said something scathing about Natasha's husband, which – no matter how true – would have put her sister instantly offside.

'You're a good agony aunt,' Natasha said as she was leaving. 'Thanks for listening, and the coffee. I'll dust off my running shoes.'

Speaking of footwear, Tyler is still wearing his school brogues.

'Are you planning to change those?' Jess asks sarcastically. 'Come on, mate. Enough delaying tactics. Get your runners on and over to the mat quick smart.'

Billy turns up towards the end of youth class. Jess hasn't seen him since Sunday. He's wearing a dark-grey suit, a white shirt and a weary smile. His gym bag is slung over his shoulder.

'How was the business trip?' she asks. It's getting harder and harder to keep him at arm's length. The forced intimacy from all the extra training sessions, not forgetting that strange stand-off with the detective, when he got all lawyer-like and protective.

Billy sighs. 'Not as successful as I hoped. Couldn't get the parties to come to an agreement.'

For some reason, she finds his lack of success pleasing. 'Well, you better get changed. You've got a lot of work to do if you don't want to get smashed next week.'

The fight will be at the local community hall. Vince has lined up fights for Lachlan and Jordy, too, and he's encouraging all members to attend, including the youth class and their parents. A boxer's first official fight is like a religious celebration: a coming-of-age or a welcome-to-the-fold. Sometimes their first fight is also their last – if they decide they aren't cut out for it – or it's the start of an ache that doesn't go away until they next hear the clang of the bell. Jess's first fight at nineteen was against a twenty-two-year-old from Queensland. Jess went into the fight as the underdog and came out, predictably, without her arm being raised in victory. She fought well, though, and the result was close. Vince was thrilled with her performance. All she could think about was her next fight.

Billy emerges from the change cubicle wearing his black sweatsuit and groin guard. 'Heard anything more from that detective?'

'Nope.' She chucks him a skipping rope, which lands at his feet. 'Come on, mate. You need to make up for the last few days. Sitting on your arse in the office when you should have been training.'

Billy starts skipping, and soon is too out of breath to ask any more questions. Jess has been on tenterhooks all week, half expecting Bridget Kennedy to stage another ambush, in addition to waiting for Dylan O'Shea to get back to her. He sent a text about ten minutes after their arranged meeting time at the park:

Are u coming?

Jess didn't answer until after Natasha and Lucy left for home:

Sorry, something came up last minute. Can we reschedule?

No reply since. Dylan's obviously pissed off and Jess hasn't pressed him; she has come to the realisation that she should run any further arrangements past Alex.

'That's enough skipping, Billy. Get on your gloves. Time to start hitting.'

Alex is going to take a lot of convincing. He won't want her to meet Dylan. At a minimum, he'll insist on coming with her. There are two reasons why this won't work: Alex's glowering presence will get in the way of an honest discussion; and Jess is frightened of what he'll do if he loses his cool.

Alex can be deceptively laidback to those who don't know him well. Beneath the casual exterior exists a rarely ignited temper, a dangerous strength.

39
BRIDGET

'Hello. I'm here to see Emily Wickham. It's Detective Sergeant Bridget Kennedy.'

'Is Emily expecting you?' the receptionist enquires pleasantly, a different young woman to last time.

'No, she's not,' Bridget replies in an equally pleasant tone. She deliberately didn't make an appointment or call ahead. Today she wants William Newson's assistant to be a little more on the back foot. Less rehearsed. Less word perfect. More real.

Bridget takes a seat on one of the plush armchairs, and once again appreciates the large artwork on the far wall. It's a different piece to last time: Aboriginal style with thousands of tiny white, black and ochre dots. Painstaking detail paired with a simple colour palette. How long has this particular piece been on display?

Is everything in this reception, including the young women behind the desk, on constant rotation?

Emily appears within a couple of minutes: blonde, slender, her dainty feet encased in teetering shoes. Her cheeks are slightly flushed.

'Detective Kennedy. I'm so sorry, I'm just about to go into a meeting … Is it something quick?'

Bridget stands up and smooths down her trousers. 'Just a file I'd like to see. And a chat, whenever you're free.'

'Which file?' Emily seems frazzled, as though retrieving a file is beyond her capacity right now. Why so busy all of a sudden? Last time they spoke, she was uncertain about her future with the practice.

'Thomas Malouf. The complainant was a woman called Hayley Webster.'

'I remember it.' Emily tucks a strand of straight blonde hair behind her ear. 'About two years ago. The charges were dropped. I'll see if I can quickly locate the file.'

Bridget sits back down. Her eyes veer back to the painting and her thoughts veer to her daughter, who has submitted her university preferences and is putting the finishing touches to her portfolio. Each piece has been laboured over … and cried over. Bridget can't help worrying what will happen if Cara doesn't get her first – or even second! – preference.

'Let it play out, Bridge,' Shane said this morning. 'It is what it is.'

He's right, and it's not like Bridget to be a helicopter parent.

Emily has returned, victoriously clutching a thin manila file. 'Here it is.' The flush on her cheeks has deepened. 'Lucky it wasn't archived. Shall I find you an empty room?'

She's being genuinely helpful, despite being under pressure for time. Bridget warms to her; she knows that rushed feeling all too well.

'No, thanks. I'm absolutely fine here. Much quieter – and more comfortable – than what I'm used to at headquarters. I'll see—'

'Emily?' A deep voice interrupts Bridget mid-flow. Joshua Newson. Neither she nor Emily noticed his approach. Bridget catches the flash of irritation on his face. 'Detective, I didn't know you were coming in today. Emily, you should have said—'

'It was a surprise visit,' Bridget interjects. 'Just needed to see one of your father's files.'

'What file?' he asks sharply, looking from Bridget to Emily.

'The Malouf one, from 2017.' Emily's voice is wobbly. Suddenly she seems less self-assured and more vulnerable. Less the ultra-professional assistant and more a girl.

Joshua pushes his glasses further up his nose. Then glances, pointedly, at his expensive watch. The time seems to deter him from making further objections.

'We have to go,' he says to Emily, while staring at Bridget, hinting that she should also depart.

Does Emily work for him now? Is that why they're attending meetings together? It would also explain why Emily organised those flowers for Megan.

'I'm happy to wait here,' Bridget says cheerfully, and sits down to prove the point.

She watches Emily and Joshua walk towards the security door leading to the offices beyond. Emily looks even tinier next to Joshua's oversize frame; she's half running in her high shoes to keep up. Did Joshua claim his father's executive assistant in the same manner he'll claim his inheritance? How does Emily feel about it? From father to son. From sexual assault cases to drug offences. From someone who made her feel valued to someone who makes her feel under pressure. Perhaps Bridget is reading too much into Emily's body language. Perhaps she is thrilled about the job security and seems flustered purely because she's trying too hard to impress her new boss.

Bridget opens the manila file and begins to read. Hayley Webster was a twenty-three-year-old nurse on a night out with colleagues when she met Thomas Malouf at a city-centre nightclub. Hayley admitted that she found him attractive, but she had a boyfriend and was interested in nothing more than dancing. Hayley's friends went home about 2 a.m. but Hayley didn't go with them; she caught a taxi to her apartment in Redfern about an hour later, with Thomas. She remembers him kissing her in the taxi, and having sex when they got back to the apartment, although she'd told him – repeatedly – that she had a boyfriend. Late the next morning – when Thomas was long gone – Hayley realised how oddly compliant she'd been about the sex. The whole night, after she'd met him, felt like a dream. Hayley called her friends, who confirmed she'd been acting strangely. Hayley, a nurse, knew the protocol: she went straight to hospital, to have her blood and urine tested, and then to her local police station.

The police laid charges, which were later dropped due to insufficient evidence to allow for a reasonable chance of conviction. The nightclub's CCTV showed Hayley on the dance floor and at the bar. Dancing suggestively with Thomas, in between glugging back gin and tonics. A statement from the taxi driver said they'd been behaving 'amorously' in the back of his vehicle. The blood and urine tests showed no illicit substances, and the medical examination showed no evidence of bruising or physical harm. Essentially, it could not be proved that the victim was not consenting, and neither could it be proved that the defendant was *aware* that the victim was not consenting.

Nowhere in the file did it mention that this was Thomas Malouf's second time being accused of sexual assault. Bridget knows that the sexual history of the complainant is not always admissible, but what about the sexual history of the defendant? Was this an oversight by the police, or was it – unbelievably! – deemed irrelevant when determining if there was enough evidence? William Newson knew, though. He knew that this was

Thomas's second time round. He knew that before Hayley Webster there was Jessica Foster, and potentially Megan Lowe, although Thomas never admitted to having sex with Megan. How on earth did the defence barrister sleep at night? Did he ever stop to think of future victims he was putting at risk by continuing to get Thomas Malouf out of trouble? The right to legal representation is a civil right, as is the acknowledgement that the defendant is innocent until proven guilty. William Newson might have persuaded himself about Thomas's innocence the first time, but not the second.

Emily reappears about forty-five minutes later. She sits carefully on the armchair next to Bridget's; her fitted skirt doesn't allow for sudden movements.

'Did you get what you needed?' she asks with a weary air that's well beyond her years.

The answer is yes, and no. Hayley Webster has reason to be very angry with both Newson and Malouf. Bridget has yet another name to add to the whiteboard; and she needs another suspect like a hole in the head.

Bridget holds up the file. 'This was Thomas Malouf's second time, did you know?'

'No.' The young woman seems genuinely shocked. 'I can't remember reading that anywhere in the file ...'

'That's because it *isn't* in the file. The first charge was long before your time.' Bridget changes tack suddenly, hoping to catch Emily off guard. 'We've been investigating Mr Newson's banking transactions and found one concerning you.'

Emily's reaction is immediate. Her face turns bright red before she covers it with her hands. 'Oh God! I didn't want that money! I *told him* I didn't need it!'

So, the money transfer was unwelcome? What was going on between these two? 'If you didn't want or need it, why did he give it to you?'

'Because I was getting married.' She comes out from behind her hands. 'Because he saw himself as a father figure. Because he had trouble believing I could stand on my own two feet.'

'A father figure?'

Emily sighs rather loudly. 'He's known me since I was fourteen. We were part of a programme where successful business people become mentors for disadvantaged youths. I was in foster care at the time and he took me under his wing, coaxed me to study during my final years of high school. When I didn't get enough points for University of Sydney, he advised me to consider going to Newcastle. He helped with my fees and accommodation costs, and he gave me a job when I finished my degree. I owe everything to him.'

Emily's background is nothing like the privileged one Bridget had imagined. It took grit and the helping hand of William Newson to get where she is today. Quite a few hats he was wearing: father figure, mentor, boss, saviour.

'So, the money was a wedding gift?'

'Yes. But I really didn't want it. He'd done enough for me. Besides, people see things like that and draw all the wrong conclusions. They assume there must be a sexual relationship or some sort of manipulation going on. I promise you, I'm not that kind of girl.'

Bridget believes her. At least, she thinks she does. 'How did Suzanne and the kids react? Did they mind Mr Newson supporting you financially at university?'

Another audible sigh. 'Suzanne was always lovely, Joshua and his brothers less so. William would invite me around to the house the odd time. Joshua was super possessive about his dad, and the other two were really awkward with me. William wasn't always attuned to the undercurrents.'

So, Joshua wanted his dad to himself. Middle-child syndrome? Insecurity? Possessiveness is a very plausible motive for murder.

'If it wasn't for William, I'd have left school by Year 10. I'd be in some dead-end job with barely enough money to pay my rent.'

Bridget gazes at the young woman, whose hands are clasped together on her lap. So well-spoken, well-dressed and professional. All thanks to William Newson, apparently.

Who was he? The good guy or the bad guy? A heartless, morally questionable lawyer – or a fair-minded, charitable family man? If Bridget can figure out who he really was, she might also have a better chance of figuring out why he was murdered in cold blood while putting out his rubbish bins.

40
MEGAN

It's not an official engagement party, just drinks, no gifts. If Lucas had given more notice Megan could have arranged to be working. As it was, she had Friday night free and everyone knew it.

What to wear? Something arresting, that will catch his eye and make him wonder what the hell he's doing marrying Daniella? Or something sedate, an outfit that will make her blend into the background: where she obviously belongs.

Black skinny jeans, black flowy top, black suede boots. More make-up than usual: a mask she can hide behind.

'All in black?' Roslyn comments on seeing the outfit. 'You look like you're going to a funeral.'

It does feel like someone has died. Megan woke this

morning with a sense of catastrophe. *Lucas is engaged. Lucas is getting married. Lucas and Daniella are a permanent fixture. There's no hope. There never was, you idiot!*

The drinks are upstairs in a popular pub in North Sydney. There's a night-view of the Harbour Bridge, and access to a balcony with outdoor heaters. Kaz thrusts an oversized glass of wine into her hand as soon as she arrives. She takes an uncharacteristically large glug: Dutch courage. How long does she need to stay in order to be polite? Kaz and the others look like they're up for a big night.

Megan's eyes scan the room for Lucas. There he is, his arm around Daniella's tiny waist. She looks stunning in a forest-green jumpsuit and high strappy shoes. Daniella is slim compared to Megan's sturdiness. She's blonde-haired compared to Megan's dark-brown. She's the one Lucas loves; Megan is just the work friend.

Lucas spots her and smiles widely. He is coming over. Another large glug of wine to brace herself. The alcohol goes straight to her head; she's not much of a drinker.

He leans in, kisses her cheek. 'I didn't see you come in.'

'Just got here,' she says, feeling heat rush to her face. 'Congratulations.'

He met Daniella just a month before meeting Megan. Four weeks: that's all that was in it. With different timing, it could have been Megan celebrating tonight. Perhaps she is fooling herself.

'Long or short engagement,' Sakar asks, joining their conversation.

'Short.' Lucas grins. 'We're both ready to take the leap.'

Sakar laughs, so does Megan, even though her laugh is more like a cough. There's a permanent lump in her throat these last few days.

Sakar and Lucas start to talk shop: a bad house fire that required several ambulances. Multiple casualties suffering from smoke inhalation and burns. A woman in peri-arrest, who needed to be intubated. Trying to avoid members of the same family being split up and dispatched to different hospitals.

'I kept reassuring the kids,' Lucas says to Sakar, his voice heavy with empathy. 'Told them everything was going to be okay, that they'd see Mum in hospital.'

Where can I find another you? Megan asks silently. *Someone a fraction as caring? Someone a fraction as gorgeous, inside and out? Where can I find another you? Where?*

Because she has looked and looked and looked. The fact is, she has slept with a lot of men. Mostly one-night stands, only a few proper relationships. It's obvious, even to her, that she tried to obliterate the significance of the rape by throwing herself into other sexual experiences. The men came in all shapes, sizes, ages and nationalities. She had her heart broken a few times and took it on the chin: the pain was welcome. She broke some hearts herself, and that felt quite cathartic, as though she'd reclaimed a part of herself.

What a fucking night. Two virgins! Sick. It's a hard thing to obliterate.

Lucas and Sakar are still talking about the house fire.

'The family dog raised the alarm, barking his head off until Mum woke up. Poor thing was taken to the vet, suffering smoke inhalation too.'

Lucas has no inkling of her feelings, which is good because the last thing she needs is his pity.

She wakes on Saturday morning with a headache and a heartache. She tries to swallow; the lump is still there. *Lucas is getting married.*

For the last three years she has been conducting a relationship in her head. For the last three years she has put other men on hold – avoiding getting serious with anyone – wanting to be available should Lucas and Daniella ever break up. For the last three years she has been deluding herself.

She hauls herself out of bed, navigating her way around packing boxes. Everything feels like it's coming to an end. This house. The future that she imagined with Lucas. Even her past is disintegrating; Thomas Malouf and William Newson are dead.

The bathroom mirror tells the truth. The dregs of last night's mascara. Undertones of pallor to her skin. Flaky lips and bleak eyes. How many drinks last night? Three? Four? A lot for her. She doesn't drink much for a reason.

Ten minutes later she is sitting outside on the deck

with a strong cup of tea and a slice of wholegrain toast. Roslyn left a note on the counter: *Gone to buy more packing tape*. Megan is glad of the empty house, glad to be able to lick her wounds and contemplate where to go to from here.

The house is going on the market next week. Removalists are booked and practically everything is going into storage. This is what she wanted, so why does she feel so directionless and off kilter? *Pathetic.*

As for Lucas, she has wasted the last three years loving him, hoping against hope that fate would intervene and make them a couple. *Beyond pathetic.*

The caffeine and air are starting to take effect. Now that her head is clearing, anger is taking hold. She is furious with herself.

It's time to get your shit together. Stop falling for the wrong men. Stop making excuses for your bad judgement.

It's a busy day ahead. There's packing to finish and some final touches with the painting. Not forgetting that she should dedicate some time to finding somewhere new to live. Better get going. Rinse her cup at the kitchen sink. Back to her bedroom to get dressed. Why is she rummaging through boxes of clothes for gym wear? Why is she lacing up runners, and rushing out the door as though being chased by someone?

Twenty minutes later she arrives at the industrial estate where Jess works. She sits in the car for a minute, gazing sightlessly at the half-mast roller door.

Lucas is getting married. It's time to get your shit together.

Megan slams the car door, the sound reverberating around the half-empty car park. Her breath is coming in short angry gasps. She ducks under the roller door; the gym started its life as a warehouse. The air thrums with the beat of Billie Eilish's 'Bad Guy'. Boxers, wet patches under their arms, are sparring in the ring. Skipping ropes whistle through the air. Some kind of class is going on over at the mat.

Jess is striding towards her, ponytail bouncing, a question on her pale face. 'Megan? What are you doing here?'

Megan exhales the breath she has been holding since finding out about the engagement. 'I want to hit something. I want to hit something really, really hard.'

41
JESS

Jess can guess why Megan is here. She turned up like this before, years ago. A married man had let her down. The relationship had come to a predictable end. She was disappointed, hurt, wanting to lash out.

Today, Jess doesn't ask her who it is, or what he has done.

'You can join the intermediate class.' She points her to the mat. 'We're only five minutes in.'

As with most of the classes, there's a rotation system in operation. Megan starts on the agility ladders, stumbling her way at first, but quickly getting the hang of it. Then it's two minutes of skipping, followed by squatting against the wall, then an exercise that involves jumping from side to side, to build up calf muscles. Megan's wearing a vest and leggings, like most of the other women, and is keeping up with the pace. Her core fitness is good, but anger can get you a long way, too. Jess should know.

Finally, it's Megan's turn on the punching bags. Jess hands her some elasticated wraps and a pair of gloves. She wipes sweat from her face with her arm before letting loose.

'Two slow ones, then through,' Jess directs. 'That's it. Keep it tight. Now, jab with the left and straight right. Good, keep it up … One, two, rip … One, two, uppercut … One, two, rip, uppercut …'

Megan is hitting the bag strongly. Is it another married man or some other doomed relationship? Everyone has different ways of retaliating when they get hurt. Jess used her fists, while Megan used sex. In the ring, Jess could unleash her aggression and frustration, and the harder she fought, the calmer her mind became. Stretching the limits of her endurance and pain tolerance restored her self-respect. Now she suspects that she healed better than Megan did.

The session ends about forty minutes later. A babble of chatter breaks out; the members know each other well from years of attending these Saturday-morning classes.

Megan surrenders her gloves and the wrap. 'That was exactly what I needed. Sorry for turning up out of the blue.'

Vince is close by, working on Billy's technique using the floor-to-ceiling ball.

'Turn up anytime you want,' he says, pausing his critique of Billy's defensive reflexes. 'It's nice to see you again.'

Vince never forgets a face.

'Thank you.' Megan smiles, a trickle of sweat running down her temple.

'We have a fight night at the community hall next week,' Vince says, his gaze refocused on Billy. 'This man is having his debut. It's going to be a big night. You should come.'

Megan is visibly taken aback by the invitation. 'I – I'm not sure I—'

'Meet Billy,' Jess chimes in. 'When he's not in a sweatsuit, he's in a suit and tie. You should come to the fight, Megan. It's not every day you see a lawyer getting beaten up.'

'Hey!' Billy objects, without losing rhythm on the ball. 'What did I do to deserve that?'

'Just being a lawyer is enough,' Jess says, only half joking. 'Megan's opinion of your profession is just as bad as mine.'

Jess's shift finishes at lunchtime and she heads over to her parents' house. Alex's ute is parked in the driveway, Natasha's Audi directly behind it. There's a huge mound of soil on the front lawn, along with a tangle of half-assembled irrigation pipes and driplines. What started as a relatively small job has been getting bigger and bigger. Extra garden beds. More paving. A new irrigation system, which seems pointless given the current water restrictions.

Jess is surveying the chaos when Alex appears from around the side of the house with a wheelbarrow. 'Hey, babe.'

He's filthy, streaks of dirt on his face and a worrying twinkle in his eye.

'Don't you dare come anywhere near me,' she warns him, edging away.

He lunges. She shrieks and runs for it. Reaching the safety of the front door, she turns to blow him a kiss.

Her dad, Natasha and Lucy are in the kitchen. They seem startled by her breathless arrival.

'Alex chased me,' she explains, because the three of them share the same uncomprehending frown. 'Sometimes he's just an oversized kid.'

Lucy is nestled in her granddad's arms, and seems happy despite the tiny frown. Natasha is nursing a cup of tea and looks white-faced with exhaustion. In the background, Jess can hear a two-handed scale being played on the piano; Margaret must have a student.

'Nice to see you, sweetheart,' Richard says. 'Have you come from work?'

'Yep.' She switches on the kettle. 'What are you three up to?'

'Shooting the breeze,' Richard replies, sounding more like a surfer than a heart surgeon. 'I was just about to take Lucy for a walk. Hopefully get her off to sleep.'

The family is starting to understand that Lucy and

sleep are a tricky combination. Walks in the pram, drives in the car, Granddad lending a hand, whatever it takes.

Richard deposits Lucy in her pram, and familiarises himself with the brakes before setting off at what promises to be a jaunty pace.

'I'm starving,' Jess says, opening the fridge. 'Want something to eat?'

Natasha shakes her head, and watches while Jess assembles a ham and cheese sandwich.

'It's real work, isn't it?' Natasha says, gazing out the window. Jess looks out. Alex is depositing a barrowload into one of the new garden beds by the pool.

'Sure is. Real and *very* dirty.'

'He'll make a good dad. He knows how to get stuck in.'

Jess rolls her eyes. 'Listen to you! Suddenly, every male is being judged on their potential as a father.'

Her sister grins ruefully. 'It's like I have this whole new lens on life. It's okay to tell me to shut up. I know I'm being annoying.'

Jess knows what she's getting at, though. Oliver deals with numbers, share prices and stock markets every day. Maybe if he got his hands dirty once in a while, or had to work up a sweat, he would be better equipped for pitching in with Lucy. That said, Jess is sure there are plenty of stockbrokers who make great hands-on dads.

Alex passes by the window again. He still hasn't

asked Margaret for an instalment payment. They argued about it again last night, and Jess came here today with the intention of dropping a hint. Maybe when her mum's lesson is finished. The student is still labouring through chromatic scales. Margaret is a stickler, maintaining that scales, albeit tedious, are essential for strength and agility. She and Vince have that in common: the belief that technique enables excellence.

Jess and Natasha chat about Lucy as Alex goes back and forth, back and forth. His T-shirt hitches up, exposing his lower back as he tips the wheelbarrow forward, and yet another load of dark soil is dumped into one of the brand-new garden beds. Plenty of loads to come, going by the enormous mound of earth out the front. Margaret has been haphazardly adding to the scope of the job. If Alex had known at the outset it was going to be this big, he would've hired some help.

Natasha cocks her head to one side. 'Christ, what is Mum up to with this massive garden project? Is she trying to bury a body out there?'

42
BRIDGET

Hayley Webster lives in a high-rise block of apartments in Redfern, the same place she lived when she met Thomas Malouf at a nightclub two years ago. The apartment block is modern, well-maintained, and located within a few hundred metres of a notorious public-housing block. The last time Bridget was in this area, she was investigating the death of a thirty-seven-year-old woman who was pushed from a balcony by her partner, who'd hallucinated that she was attacking him. The scene was a shocking one: the woman's broken body on the pavement, her partner – an ice-addict – too far gone to understand the finality of what he'd done. He got fourteen years.

Sasha rings the bell and they wait. It's 6 p.m. on Saturday night. There's a strong possibility that Hayley is at work. Nurses work their fair share of weekends, like detectives.

'Hello?' A youngish female voice crackles from the intercom.

'Is that Hayley?'

'Yes.'

'This is Detective Sergeant Bridget Kennedy and Detective Constable Sasha McEvoy. We want to have a chat about Thomas Malouf. It shouldn't take long. Can we come up?'

'Do you have identification?' the voice asks warily.

'Of course.' Bridget flashes her ID in the direction of the security camera positioned above the doorway. 'Can you see that?'

'Yeah. Come in.'

Hayley's apartment is on the fifth floor. She is waiting by the door when they emerge from the lift: petite, shoulder-length dark hair, guarded expression. She's wearing leggings and an oversized sweater; she doesn't look like she's on her way out tonight.

The apartment is small and feminine. Faux-fur cushions, glittery picture frames, a discarded lip-gloss on the coffee table. Two aubergine-coloured sofas. Bridget and Sasha occupy one, and Hayley Webster sits on the other.

'Thanks for seeing us,' Bridget begins. 'We're investigating the murder of William Newson and the death of Thomas Malouf. Both men were known to you. Were you aware that they've died?'

She nods. 'William Newson was on my newsfeed. It's not every day that you read about someone you know being murdered. There was less about Thomas Malouf – I almost missed it.'

'When did you last see the two men?' Bridget asks, watching her carefully.

'I never actually met William Newson,' she admits with a shrug. 'I knew his name, that he was Thomas Malouf's lawyer, and that he had an impressive track record. As for Thomas, I didn't set eyes on him after that night. Everything was handled through police and lawyers. I guess I would have seen him if we'd actually made it to court.'

'It said in your file that there was no trace of drugs found in your urine or bloodstream,' Bridget challenges, although she's aware that date-rape drugs can be gone from the system within a few hours.

Another nod, followed by another shrug. 'Your body *knows*, even if no trace has been left, even when you can't rely on your mind to properly remember. I knew something was wrong the minute I woke up the next morning.'

'Can you tell us where you were three weeks ago on Tuesday August twentieth?'

'I was at work.'

'Which hospital do you work in, Hayley?'

Redfern is well-situated for Royal Prince Alfred and St Vincent's. Doctors, nurses and medical staff would find the suburb a convenient place to live, if not the safest after nightfall.

'I'm not in a hospital,' she says, her eyes downcast. 'I don't work as a nurse any more. I decided I wasn't cut out for it. I retrained – I'm in a call centre with the health department now. It's easier at the end of a phone. I was diagnosed with post-traumatic stress syndrome.'

Sasha asks if there's someone who can verify that Hayley was at work, and records the details in her notebook. She and Hayley are close in age. Sasha goes clubbing some weekends, and it's obvious from her expression that she can easily imagine herself in Hayley's position: choosing the wrong guy to dance with.

Bridget and Sasha say goodbye shortly afterwards and walk briskly to their car. Two doors down they pass a heroin addict shooting up. Redfern is becoming more gentrified, but pockets of poverty, violence and drug addiction constantly undermine the efforts of town planners and police.

'What did you think of that?' Bridget asks, when they're safely in the car and on their way.

'I felt sorry for her,' the young detective replies. 'Hard to move on from something like that. Charges being dropped when you *know* the person is guilty. Seeing them get off scot-free. It's just not right.'

Thomas Malouf got off scot-free ... but William Newson didn't. He paid the ultimate price: his thirty-five-year marriage. His wife divorced him because of Hayley Webster.

'You know that Malouf's sexual history wasn't deemed relevant?' Bridget says, stopping at a

306

T-intersection. 'The fact that this was his second time being accused wasn't weighed up in the decision to drop charges.'

Sasha's mouth is an angry line. 'The unfairness is enough to make you go crazy.'

Bridget spends Sunday at home, even though her mind is in the office, mulling over the names on Katrina's whiteboard, in particular the newest addition: Hayley Webster. *Did* the unfairness make Hayley go crazy? The charges being dropped is one thing. PTSD and being unable to work as a nurse are another thing altogether: the course of a life changed for ever. Hayley was adamant that she was drugged, but it's human nature to find excuses for our bad decisions. Is it possible that Thomas Malouf was unfortunate enough to be falsely accused on two separate occasions, ten years apart? And how much digging – if any – did Hayley Webster do into his background? Did she find out about two other girls – nameless, thanks to identity protection – whose case *did* make it to court, but still didn't result in a conviction? Would such knowledge have made her even crazier? The fact that she lives in Redfern could be relevant. Crime, violence and poverty conveniently on her doorstep. Not that hard to procure a gun ... or find someone willing to kill for a price.

In the afternoon, Bridget drives her daughter to Chatswood, to shop for a dress for her Year 12 formal. Forget Hayley for the next few hours. Focus on Cara.

Her daughter is on the cusp of finishing school, striking out in the world. Classes will finish next week, then it's a couple of weeks' study leave, followed by the dreaded exams. Cara seems more focused on the formal than the exams, which could be a blessing.

'What do you think?' she asks, emerging in a full-length sky-blue dress, the plunging neckline exposing the undersides of her breasts. *Good thing her father isn't here*, Bridget thinks. Shane would have to be resuscitated.

'Turn around,' Bridget says, mustering a casual tone. 'I'm not sure about how the back is falling ...'

Her next choice is emerald green – a beautiful shade that complements her auburn hair – with an equally revealing drape neck.

'Gorgeous colour. Maybe a bit too much fabric with the fall ...' Good thing Bridget doesn't have to pass a lie-detector.

They go to a different store and select another armful of dresses to try on. Then on to a different shopping centre, which has lots of small boutiques. Short dresses, maxi dresses, lace, satin, all with one thing in common: low-cut necklines and exposed backs. How is one meant to wear a bra?

'You don't wear a bra, Mum,' Cara informs her in a condescending tone. 'You use those stick-on cups.'

Another image of Shane being resuscitated.

It has been more than two hours. Cara is getting frustrated and Bridget is getting impatient. Hunger is making them snippy with each other. Then they find it: a maxi dress with navy sequins. A slit starting high on the leg, not too much cleavage on show. There's a teary moment of mother-daughter bonding, followed by a different type of eye-watering on viewing the price tag.

'Let's get something to eat before we look at shoes,' Bridget says, burying the receipt in her handbag.

They're eating sushi at one of the food courts when Bridget's phone begins to ring. It's Dave. She mentioned to him that she had an important date with her daughter. Dave has a family, too; he understands the delicate dance between home and work. Shane is extremely competent, but Cara needs her mother for this one.

'What is it?' Bridget's mind is full of sequins, silicone bra cups, and shoes that achieve the dual purpose of elegance and comfort (which everyone knows is impossible!).

'Sorry to interrupt, Bridge. I've got something huge.' Bridget can only just make out what he is saying against the background noise of the food court. 'We've found the Yamaha and the gun.'

Did she hear him correctly? She presses the phone to her ear. 'Together? In the same place?'

Dave confirms it: the motorbike and gun have been found in a storage facility in Brookvale. Thomas Malouf's name is on the paperwork.

'Secure the scene,' Bridget commands. 'Don't let anyone touch anything until forensics get there. I'm on my way.'

She hangs up. Cara is staring at her. Oh dear.

'It's okay, I was getting tired anyway.' Cara stands up, her unfinished sushi box in hand. 'Can you drop me home on your way?'

'Sure. Sorry. We'll get the shoes next weekend.'

The investigation looks like it will be wrapped up by then. Bridget didn't see this coming.

Thomas Malouf killed his barrister. Then he killed himself.

43
MEGAN

The home stylist arrives on Monday morning. Clipboard in hand, she moves from room to room, her frown becoming more pronounced as she goes. She ends with a declaration that none of the furniture is up to standard except the beds, which can be disguised with good linen and cushions.

'The right furniture will accentuate the space. First impressions are vital!'

Then she tells Megan how much it's going to cost for furniture rental and a six-week campaign.

Megan phones Seb later in the morning. 'Good thing Mum was at work. She'd have said a flat no. I signed up for it. Plus I booked the removalists for Friday.'

'What if it takes longer than six weeks to sell?'

'Don't even go there.'

'I'll come on Friday to help,' he says impulsively. 'I'll get an early flight.'

'Great! I'll be coming off a twelve-hour shift, so I won't be much good.'

Her shift hours are 6 p.m. to 6 a.m. this week, her least favourite timeslot. Starting work as everyone else is finishing. Driving home as dawn is breaking, knowing you need to go straight to bed when all your instincts are telling you otherwise. Forcing yourself to sleep, forcing yourself to wake up, forcing yourself to stay awake. But it's only for four days, then four days off to compensate.

Megan is excited to see her brother so soon. She checks the time: hours to go before her shift starts and plenty of work to do. Seb's old bedroom is next to be tackled. She has been avoiding it; it's been used as a dumping ground for years. Dust mites in the air and a faintly musty smell: not quite the first impressions the stylist was talking about. Megan opens the window before setting to work. The wardrobe is so full its doors don't properly close. She clears everything from the rails on to the bed. Mostly spill-over from her wardrobe and Roslyn's. A few old things of Seb's: a leather jacket he used to live in and a pair of old Levi's. Some of her dad's clothes, too. Did Roslyn forget they were here, or couldn't she bear to part with them?

Megan has been trying not to think about her dad during this process. He mortgaged himself to the hilt to save this house. In his mind, it was all they had left. Selling feels like a huge betrayal.

Sorry, Dad. I hope you can't see any of this.

The top shelf of the wardrobe is out of her reach; she goes to fetch the step ladder from the garage. Lifting and manoeuvring the ladder reminds her muscles how sore they are from the boxing on Saturday. But it has to be said: hitting something hard really did help. She is still sad about Lucas. She is still asking herself 'what if', but accepts there is no way to change the timing of when they met. Her face was taut and dry when she woke this morning, a reminder that she'd cried herself to sleep again, but she opened her eyes with fresh resolve.

He was never mine. It was all in my head. I'll get over this.

The contents of the top shelf are eclectic. Most of it has been there a long, long time. Mouldy skiwear. A few bulky sweaters. Some dusty photo albums. Megan sweeps what she can to the floor, and goes up and down the ladder half a dozen times with the rest. Once it's empty, she wipes it down with a damp cloth, then folds the ladder away.

The room looks worse than when she started: a cyclone of clothes on the bed, balls of fluff on the carpet, the air thick with dust. It's funny that out of all the stuff in this room, Seb owns the least. She puts his things in a pile – he can go through it when he gets here Friday. On impulse, she sits down on a corner of the bed and flicks through the photo albums. School photos, all the way from a cheeky five-year-old with a gap in his front teeth to the long-haired handsome boy who graduated.

Seb with his beloved guitar, eyes staring at sheet music while his fingers automatically picked the correct chords. Seb and his beleaguered football team, who – as she remembers it – very rarely won their games.

A few pieces of paper are wedged in the back of one of the albums.

Certificate of Achievement for Music and Performance: Sebastian Lowe

Travel Itinerary Nepal: Sebastian Lowe

Apprehended Personal Violence Order: Sebastian Lowe

Her breath catches in shock. An AVO? A familiar name jumps out from the closely spaced text: Thomas Malouf. Oh God, oh God, oh God!

The document is dated more than a year after the trial. What did Seb do to Thomas Malouf? Does this mean her brother has a criminal record?

How did she not know about this? Does she really want to know now?

APPREHENDED PERSONAL VIOLENCE ORDER – SEBASTIAN LOWE CRIMES (DOMESTIC AND PERSONAL VIOLENCE) ACT 2007

Sebastian Lowe you must follow the orders below. It is a criminal offence not to follow these orders.

*The Orders have been made to protect **Thomas Malouf**.*

Orders about Behaviour

1. *You must not do any of the following to Thomas Malouf:*
   A) *assault or threaten him*
   B) *stalk, harass or intimidate him*
   C) *deliberately or recklessly destroy or damage anything that belongs to him*

2. *You must not approach Thomas Malouf or contact him in any way, unless the contact is:*

A) *through a lawyer, or*

B) *to attend accredited or court-approved counselling, mediation or conciliation, or*

C) *as ordered by this or another court*

D) *as agreed in writing between you and Thomas Malouf*

Orders about where you cannot go
You must not go within 100 metres of:

A) *any place where Thomas Malouf lives, or*

B) *any place where Thomas Malouf works*

44
JESS

It's youth class, and hooray: Tyler finally remembered his mouthguard.

'I'm proud of you,' Jess tells him. 'Don't ask me why, but I am! Come on, I'll pair you with Andy.'

Alarm registers on his face. Andy is older and bigger. Tyler wouldn't know that Andy is more puppy fat than muscle, or that his coordination and reflexes aren't exactly razor-sharp. What Andy does have is a kind heart; Jess can rely on him to go easy on Tyler.

'Okay, mate, this is how it works. One of you hits and the other catches the hit. That means you're practising hitting and, just as important, you're practising defence, but we don't do both at the same time. Now, I want you to hit first. Come at Andy. That's right. Push off the right foot. Jab from out there. Long arm. Great work.'

Andy isn't moving around that much, making it easier for Tyler to connect. The younger boy is warming to the task, bouncing, trying to push off his feet, throwing with intent. The best things about boxing are right here on display. A kid who lacks motivation suddenly finding it in the ring. Another kid, with a poor self-image and more to prove than anyone else, taking a back seat so the other can succeed. Respect. Mateship. Physical satisfaction.

'Go on, Tyler. Shove it at Andy, he's not going to hit you back. Power comes from your hips. If you rotate, you get more power … Twenty seconds left … Jab, jab … Hands up, Andy, protect your head … Time.'

Jess gives them a couple of minutes to catch their breath, then the roles are reversed.

'Just practising your catching now, Tyler. See him coming, catch. Don't try to push it away, catch the hit like a ball … Catch, turn … Catch, turn … Don't forget to move … You can't stand in front of him like that, mate. He's too big!'

Defence is harder to teach. Tyler keeps dropping his left hand and needs reminding it's just as good as his right when it comes to protecting himself. He gets left and right mixed up, too, something that happens across all age groups.

When the round is finished, Jess calls Jayden into the ring to be Andy's next opponent.

'Tyler, come over here with me and watch Andy's next round.'

Andy stands tall while he waits for Jayden to get his gloves on. He isn't often held up as an exemplar to others; Jess can practically see his self-confidence inflating.

'I want you to keep an eye on two things, Tyler. Andy's feet. See how he keeps them below his shoulders all the time? Now watch how he catches the punch. Jayden has a really long reach, so Andy can't afford to let one hand slip. See?'

Andy does another round with Jayden, and Jess sends Tyler to practise on the tear-drop bag. She finishes the class with the usual core work on the mat.

'Well done, everyone. Really great session this afternoon. Now don't forget to get around to the community hall on Saturday night. The boys need your support, you'll learn heaps from watching and it's a really fun night.'

Andy and Tyler are beaming and nodding. This is one of those days when Jess loves her job more than anything in the world.

Her shift finishes after youth class. She walks briskly to the train station, sits on one of the benches. The next train is in four minutes. Her attention is caught by some teenagers on the far platform – the city-bound side. They're in formal wear, the girls in sleek dresses and high heels and the boys in slimline suits. It's that time of year: school formals and socials. Young people fretting about who to ask and what to wear. This lot are probably on their way to a harbour cruise or some other city-centre venue. The train is a practical solution: no point hiring a limo only to get stuck in rush-hour traffic. Jess didn't attend her Year 12 formal, neither did Megan. The dresses they'd bought (too far in advance) hung unworn in their wardrobes. The boys they'd planned to ask never got invited. Jess could barely motivate herself to shower and brush her hair; attending the formal, or any kind of social event, seemed impossible.

Thomas Malouf and Dylan O'Shea went to theirs. Jess accidentally came across photos on social media, and there they were: wearing trendy suits and standing alongside girls who she immediately wanted to warn off them. Thomas and Dylan had been charged at that point, but it was still up in the air if the case would proceed to prosecution. But there they were, all suited up for a rite-of-passage in which she and Megan felt unable to participate. It stung. Resentment festered over the following years; Jess realised she could never reclaim that point in time, that precipice between being a schoolgirl and a young woman, or the giddy whoosh of freedom on finishing school and celebrating it accordingly. She wasn't a girly-girl, but the dress and make-up were part of that rite-of-passage, and she'd missed out on them.

'I'll take you to a dinner dance,' Alex promised, a few months after they met. The conversation came up at the farm. Jess loved it there: the animals, the fresh air, Alex's down-to-earth parents, seeing him outside the constraints of the city, herding cows astride a dirt bike, his huge hands helping with the birth of a calf. At night they drank beer on the veranda, and talked honestly under the protective cloak of the black sky and abundant stars.

'You? At a dinner dance? In a *suit*?' Jess laughed off his offer.

But he followed through and arranged tickets for a city-centre charity ball. Jess got her hair and make-up done and spent a staggering amount on a dress. Alex bought a suit (the only one he owns to this day) and even hired a limo. They drank champagne in the back, and Jess told him she loved him. Here was someone special, someone who wanted to right a wrong, even if it meant being totally out of his comfort zone.

Alex didn't reciprocate with, 'I love you, too.'

He pulled her closer, his breath heavy in her ear. 'I've got your back, babe … I've got your back.'

Stronger than a thousand proclamations of love.

45
BRIDGET

'Well, case closed?' Katrina enquires in her usual direct manner. The detective inspector is sitting behind her desk, pen tapping, waiting for Bridget's briefing.

'Certainly looks that way,' Bridget says, taking one of the two visitors' seats. 'I'm waiting for the official report from forensics but it looks like we have the right motorbike and gun. Thomas Malouf had been using the storage facility for years, so no suspicious new lease or anything like that. It's not a very high-tech facility, no PIN codes just plain old locks, so it's hard to determine exactly when the Yamaha was left there. We're going through CCTV, but so far there's no activity we can see on the day of the shooting or the day after, which means we have to comb through potentially two weeks of footage.'

Katrina jerks her head towards the list of names still on her whiteboard. 'So, they're all irrelevant?'

Bridget runs her eye down through the names. Suzanne and Joshua Newson. Diana Simon. Megan Lowe, Jessica Foster and various family members. Fergus Herrmann, Laura Dundas, Hayley Webster and others who suffered because William Newson was so adept at proving there wasn't enough evidence.

'The biggest question I have now is *why*,' she says. 'Maybe, between them, they hold the answer.'

Why did Malouf kill William Newson, the man who saved his bacon not once but twice? Did he resent Newson, blame him in some way for the direction his life had taken? Did his guilty conscience finally catch up with him, haunted by what he'd done to Hayley, Jessica and who knows how many others? Was he part of some religious sect, one that advocated atonement, an eye for an eye or some nonsense like that? And why did he hang on more than two weeks before committing suicide? It's not as if the police had been closing in and he was at risk of being caught. He had a gun, for God's sake, so why jump in front of a train? None of it makes much sense.

Bridget crosses her legs, then uncrosses them again. She's feeling fidgety and directionless. It's the come-down that happens when an investigation is all but solved. Normal pace feels weird after all the long hours and intensity.

'What else did you find in the storage unit?' Katrina asks.

'Mainly furniture. I understand Thomas inherited the pieces from his grandparents and wanted to keep them until he owned a home that was big enough.'

'Doesn't sound like the actions of someone who was planning to kill himself,' Katrina points out.

True, but suicide is often a spur-of-the-moment decision, and maybe that's exactly why nothing is making sense. Thomas's financial affairs were not in order, also implying his death hadn't been planned. His credit card statement – the one where they found the monthly charge that alerted them to the storage unit's existence – was overdue, as were other bills. Crockery was found in his kitchen sink, his bed was left unmade, it didn't look like his flat had been prepared in any way for his imminent death. And there was no note, at least none they could find.

'Okay, let's wait for forensics,' Katrina says, leaning back in her chair. 'Your team can take their foot off the pedal. No more overtime or weekends. Just tie up what loose ends you have while we wait.'

'It's an apparition. It cannot be my wife. It's only five thirty. Can I touch you, see if you're real?'

'Shut up, Shane.'

Bridget deposits her handbag on the floor and takes a moment to look around. In the open-plan kitchen, her long-suffering husband has paused in the middle of prepping vegetables for dinner. Parked in front of the television is her neglected fifteen-year-old son, his attention divided between a futuristic-looking show and his iPhone. In the front room, visible through the glass of the French doors, is Cara, studying for her upcoming exams (her Year Advisor recommended that her studying space be somewhere other than her bedroom). It's daylight. Bridget can't remember the last time she arrived home from work in daylight.

'Well, it must be case solved if we're seeing you this early,' Shane says, chopping some carrots with a deftness she didn't know him capable of.

'That's the thing,' she says with a half-yawn, half-sigh. 'I really don't know if it is. Still lots of unanswered questions.' She shoots him a tired smile and asks half-heartedly, 'Anything I can help with?'

'All under control. Just check in with the offspring, if you like.'

Bridget sits down next to Ethan, who pauses the show he's watching to give perfunctory answers to her enquiries about school and his general well-being. Cara is more receptive when Bridget pokes her head inside the front room.

'How's it going in here?'

'Hey, Mum.' Cara looks up from her work, flicking her hair out of her eyes. 'Getting lots done. Just about to take a break.'

'Can I get you anything to eat or drink?'

'Nah. Dad made me something earlier. I can wait till dinner.'

Bridget feels a wave of appreciation for Shane. 'How

about we lock in some time on the weekend to get those shoes?'

'I promised Gina I'd go shopping with her. She's going to help me with shoes and I'm going to help her choose a dress. Then we're popping into that student travel place, to see if we can get a deal on flights for schoolies … Actually, I meant to tell you there's a party Saturday night. Could either you or Dad give me and Gina a lift?'

Bridget is struck by what an intensely busy time this is for her daughter. Studying to an extent she never has before, managing her blossoming social life, and making travel plans for when the exams are over. This is exactly the stage that Megan Lowe and Jessica Foster were at when they met Thomas Malouf and Dylan O'Shea. That intense period of life suddenly juxtaposed with sexual assault, and everything – their exam results, their friendships and social networks, their futures – jeopardised as a result.

'Sure, I should be able to do that,' she says, planting a kiss on the top of her daughter's head.

It comes to Bridget later that evening, while she is doing the washing-up. An argument breaks out between Cara and Ethan over some 'borrowed' earphones.

'I can't believe you just helped yourself. I've spent the last half-hour trying to find them. For God's sake, Ethan.'

'Mine are missing. I needed to listen to something for school. I was just about to put them back.'

'What happened to asking before taking? Stop going

326

into my room and helping yourself to whatever you want. You have *no right*.'

'Stop overreacting, okay? It's just earphones, that's all.'

Cara proceeds to detail the violation of human rights from her brother's trespassing and 'theft', and something occurs to Bridget. Since time began, siblings have entered each other's bedrooms, taken each other's things. The storage facility might have been in Thomas Malouf's name, but what was stopping Leo from 'helping himself' to the space? But instead of 'taking', he could have left something behind: tools of a crime.

One other thing about siblings: they nurse their grievances passionately. Cara can recall every slight from Ethan from the moment he was born, and vice versa. Bridget is the same with her own brother and sister. Nothing gets forgotten, or fully forgiven; it's all dredged up whenever there's an argument.

Did Leo Malouf bear a longstanding grudge? Was he resentful about testifying at the trial? What was the *true cost* of his testimony? A lifetime of guilt and unhappiness? Continued 'bullying' from his older brother? Did William Newson put pressure on Leo in any way? Was the fifteen-year-old a willing witness or a reluctant one?

Katrina specifically said to ease off on overtime but old habits die hard. Bridget hurriedly dries her hands and grabs her phone. Shane steps in to referee as she composes a text to Dave and the rest of the team:

Let's take a closer look at Leo Malouf.

46
MEGAN

Her shift finishes at 6 a.m., just as the sun is rising. It started off busy: the pollen count was high and asthma sufferers everywhere needed extra help. Usually a nebuliser is enough to open up the airways. Witnessing someone gasping for breath can be worse than blood or tissue exposure: breathing is the essence of humanity. It's always a huge relief when the nebuliser starts to take effect.

After the busy start, things settled down: a woman with chest pains, a teen with mental health issues, then nothing at all. Megan and Kaz spent the last few hours watching reruns of old comedies, and filling themselves with caffeine and sugar to stay awake; sometimes being quiet is more taxing than being busy.

Now Megan is in the car, on the way home, and the city is waking up. Early-morning joggers bouncing along footpaths, traffic thickening on the city-bound side of the road. Down in Melbourne, Seb's flight has already taken off. He'll be at the house in a couple of hours, to help the removalists … and to answer her questions. An AVO: *what the hell?*

Megan hasn't broached it with her mum; she barely sees her when she's on the graveyard shift. There's a strong possibility Roslyn doesn't know and Megan certainly doesn't want to be the one to tell her.

She is suddenly tired. Really, really tired. The rape, the trial, the continuing reverberations. Twelve years later and it's still going on, sucking her dry.

One of yesterday's asthma cases was particularly bad: a young mother who was at her usual gym class when she started to have trouble breathing. They tried a nebuliser, then a steroid, then an injection of adrenalin. She was still coughing, wheezing and worrying about her family.

'I need to go home,' she rasped. 'My kids …'

'Don't talk, just breathe,' Kaz said. 'Breathe …'

Megan's head is spinning. Surely, she had the right to know about the AVO? What happened was obviously because of her, for God's sake! What did Seb do to Thomas Malouf? Why Thomas and not Dylan?

Don't think, just breathe. Don't think, just breathe. Breathe …

Seb gives her a big hug when he arrives. She hugs him back, while silently asking the question: *Do I even know*

329

you? He's dressed for Melbourne weather: jeans, boots and a heavy jacket. He discards the jacket on the back of a chair.

'Freezing and pouring in Melbourne this morning. Sydney is like being in a different country.'

'Sounds like you should move back,' Roslyn says chirpily. She has taken the day off work and exudes energy. Megan expected her mum to be emotional and resistant to stripping the house bare; instead, she seems keen to get things underway. Ironically, Megan is sad and deflated, exhaustion exacerbating everything.

'Nice try, Mum. But I get better gigs in Melbourne, and Cassie would never leave her job. Righto! How long do we have till they get here?'

'Three hours,' Megan says with a weary sigh. 'They're booked for midday.'

By the time the removalist truck backs into the driveway, the house is virtually empty except for the larger pieces of furniture. Boxes are waiting outside to be loaded into the truck. Items that are not going into storage have been stockpiled in the garage. It's been weeks of planning, culling and packing, culminating in this forlorn, hollow house. The stylist's furnishings will arrive on Monday and they'll go from one extreme to another: the house will look better than it ever did. There's sadness in that, too.

The three of them watch as the truck rumbles away.

'I'm going for a shower,' Megan decides. 'It'll either

wake me up or put me to sleep. We'll see which way it goes!'

Her bedroom has bare essentials only. The bed, an armchair that wasn't vetoed by the stylist, and a small selection of clothes hanging in the built-in wardrobe. She selects a clean pair of jeans and a fleece sweater.

The shower revives her. The emptiness of the house is a fresh assault on coming out of the bathroom. A profound silence compounds the bareness. Have Seb and Roslyn gone out?

Megan raps on the door of her brother's room. 'Are you in there?'

'Come in,' he calls in return.

He's lying on the bed, pillows propped behind him, looking at his phone.

'There's nowhere to even sit out there!' she says, plonking herself down on the side of his bed. 'Where's Mum?'

'Gone to the charity shop with a car-full.' Seb puts his phone on his lap, screen facing down. 'She seems fine, doesn't she? I thought she'd struggle today.'

'She's a trooper,' Megan agrees, before admitting, '*I'm* finding it hard … I keep thinking about Dad … How disappointed he'd be.'

Seb's gaze shifts away. 'I know, he's been on my mind, too.'

They sit in silence, remembering. How their dad fought to keep the house. The toll on his health and eventually his ability to work. The unavoidable truth: he might still be alive today if he'd cut his losses.

331

The photo albums and leather jacket are on the bed, where Megan left them.

'You taking these back to Melbourne?'

'Yeah, Cassie loves looking at old photos. Might wear the jacket at one of my gigs.'

Her brother has some explaining to do. Stop skirting around. Just come out with it. 'I found something, Seb ...' She picks up the relevant album and extracts the offending document, laying it down on the bed between them. 'Why didn't I know about this AVO?'

Guilt floods his face. He searches for words, comes up with, 'Because I didn't want to upset you ... or have you think I was making things even worse ...'

'What did you do, exactly?'

'Beat him up a bit.'

Megan didn't know that her brother was capable of beating someone up! He is the broody type rather than the fiery type, as far as she knows.

'Why Thomas and not Dylan?'

He grimaces. 'Oh, I thumped O'Shea too but he didn't report me to the police. I guess he thought he had it coming.' Then a flash of defiance. 'I went doubly hard on Malouf, I belted him for you *and* Dad ...'

Now she is starting to understand. Seb's double-fold frustration. Her brother wasn't as unaffected by the trial as she believed him to be.

'Did Mum and Dad know about this?'

Seb looks horrified. 'God, no, they had more than enough on their plate.'

'Do you have a criminal record because of it?'

He shakes his head. 'Once I kept to the terms, it didn't go on my record.'

Violence is wrong, she knows this better than anyone. But escaping justice is wrong, too.

She reaches across to hug him. 'Thank you. I wish I'd known about this. It makes me feel better to know they got hurt too.'

47
BRIDGET

Dave has a satisfied glint in his eye. 'Leo Malouf: some traffic offences that resulted in a couple of court appearances. Got off with minimal fines, despite one of the incidents causing serious injury to the other party. I'm seeing a pattern ...'

Bridget has been preparing for a court appearance on Monday relating to a different investigation. She mentally changes gears. 'Go on.'

'Apparently, Leo had top-notch legal representation, as did Thomas for his misdemeanours ... which got me thinking. I checked the database for Joe, the father, and quite a few entries for him, too. He's a property developer, disputes and litigation go with the territory, but as I said, a pattern ... This is a family who're used to being in court, who've all the right numbers in their phones should they get into trouble.'

Bridget knows that type of family all too well. 'What if one of them was at *real* threat of going to prison this time? What if Newson declined a job? That could be motivation for killing him. Maybe even explains why Thomas jumped in front of a train.'

'Yeah, but I can't find any current charges on the database. But as you know, disputes can happen through different channels, or be completely off record.'

Dave is right. Only matters involving police make it on to the database.

'Keep at it. Make inquiries through employee, industrial and any other channels you can think of.'

A short while later a copy of the forensics report lands in Bridget's inbox, distracting her from the court matter once again. The contents are at the same time disappointing and suspicious. No latent fingerprints detected on either the gun or the motorcycle. If Thomas planned to kill himself, why bother with gloves, or scrupulously cleaning away fingerprints? Leo, on the other hand, would have more incentive to ensure that no trace had been left.

Katrina's instruction was to close off loose ends. The Maloufs are not a loose end: they're a new line of inquiry. A long history with police, lawyers and courts.

Did something not quite go to plan this time?

'Bridget, a minute please,' Katrina calls from her office door.

It's early afternoon. Bridget has resumed preparing

for Monday's court appearance. She needs to refresh her memory … this particular case has taken a long time to get to this stage. Katrina's urgent tone suggests that her attention will be diverted for more than a few minutes. She pushes her seat back from her desk.

'What's up?' she asks, closing the door behind her.

'I've just received a call from a case officer who's taken a missing person's report.' Katrina's colour is higher than usual. 'I think you'll be extremely interested, but not surprised, to find out who it is.'

Bridget is caught between dread and anticipation. 'Who?'

'Dylan O'Shea … The report was made by his parents.'

Bridget's mouth opens and closes without any words coming out. Dylan O'Shea. *Of course.* She knew he was at risk, and yet somehow lost sight of the fact over the last few days. Oh, Jesus! She should have insisted on Dylan being more careful. Case not closed. Case not remotely closed.

Katrina is still speaking. 'As you probably know, Dylan still lives at home with his parents. He ate breakfast and chatted with his father before leaving for work yesterday – he catches a bus to the closest train station. But he never made it to work, and neither did he return home in the evening. His phone appears to be switched off and he's not been returning concerned calls and texts. His parents and colleagues have said this is very unlike him. Foul play is suspected.'

Foul play is not just suspected, it's almost a given.

Newson, Malouf and now O'Shea: a trifecta. Have they another dead body on their hands? Will it turn up in the vicinity of Megan or Jessica, like the other two? Is there time to intervene, to save Dylan?

Bridget finds her voice. 'I feel responsible. I should have done more. I allowed myself to get sidetracked.'

'If you're responsible, then I am too,' Katrina says, looking rattled. 'This swings the pendulum back to the Lowe and Foster families.'

The list is still on the whiteboard, with that small gap before Megan and Jessica's names. *A twelve-year-old case.* What happened to make it relevant enough to cause two, possibly three, deaths?

The fact is that Megan and Jessica have alibis, which means the answer must lie with those closest to them. Bridget mentally compiles her to-do list.

Roslyn Lowe, the angry mum: get access to her house before all those boxes and potential evidence disappear.

Alex Leary, the boyfriend: contact Hunter police to drop into the family farm and verify that the motorcycles and guns on the property match what's registered to the address.

The Maloufs: what does Dylan mean to them, if anything? Maybe it's time to ask Leo to come in for a 'voluntary' chat? Although, Leo didn't give the impression of being very chatty at the funeral: *You're not welcome here.*

'I need warrants,' Bridget says to her boss. 'For the homes of Megan Lowe and Jessica Foster, for a start.'

'We already have the weapon and the vehicle,' Katrina protests. 'We need reasonable grounds to believe that further evidence will be found before we can apply for a warrant. You know that.'

'Everything points back to these two women and their families,' Bridget argues. 'Plus, I know for a fact that Jessica had plans to meet up with Dylan.'

Katrina folds her arms. 'I'll support the one for Jessica but you need to get more on Megan.'

More on Megan. Bridget gives the task to Sasha – clever, dogged Sasha – who works off the assumption that if Dylan phoned Jess to arrange a meeting, it's likely he phoned Megan, too. Sasha immediately logs an urgent request with the telecommunications provider and a response comes through within a couple of hours. *More on Megan.* Her number is listed in Dylan's phone records; in fact, he contacted Megan first.

'A phone call is hardly a valid basis for a search warrant,' Katrina says cuttingly, when Bridget returns to her office.

'True. But as far as I know, Megan and Dylan haven't had contact for years, so it *is* suspicious. It's crucial we get into that house for a look around, Katrina. They're putting it up for sale soon.'

The detective inspector – begrudgingly – signs her name and then the rush is on to find an approving magistrate late on a Friday afternoon.

48
JESS

Still no word from Dylan. Jess texts him, suggesting Sunday, same place and time. Now all she has to do is convince Alex; she is not prepared to go behind his back a second time. As expected, he doesn't take it very well.

'You've been in contact with him? You want to fucking see him? Are you mental?'

'I just want some blanks filled in, that's all … Is that such a bad thing?'

They're in the kitchen, not the best location. Too confined; Alex seems even larger when he's angry.

'He raped your friend and got away with it,' he yells, his face a dangerous shade of purple. 'That's what fucking happened, the small details don't matter.'

'They *do* matter!' she shouts back. 'Everything about

that night is blurry. I don't know if it was because of the alcohol or whether I was drugged. I don't know if I had a valid excuse for letting Megan down, or whether I was just a bad friend. It torments me. I. Need. To. Know.'

'So you're going to ask *him*? He lied in court. You really expect *him* to tell you what happened?'

'I think he's sorry. Maybe sorry enough to admit the truth.'

'You're fucking deluded!' he roars in her face. 'I can't believe I'm hearing this.'

'I'm not asking you, Alex. I'm *telling* you. As a courtesy.'

'I'm your partner, not a *courtesy*. You should value my opinion. *You should listen to me.*'

'You don't understand. You have no fucking idea what it's like for me.'

Jess swings around on her heel and stalks to the bedroom, where she slams the door so hard the entire apartment reverberates. She sits on the bed, breathing heavily, listening to Alex banging around the kitchen. A pot crashing down on the stove. Some cutlery clattering into the sink. She is shaking all over.

It's her decision, not his.

She wants him to know, but she doesn't need his approval.

He doesn't understand, he can't begin to.

She closes her eyes, summons her seventeen-year-old self. There she is, wearing tight jeans and a skimpy top that she'd 'borrowed' from Natasha's wardrobe without asking. There she is, wriggling her way free from Thomas Malouf's proprietary arm, deciding that she'd had enough of his wandering eye. There she is again, flirting with another group of boys, dancing with uncharacteristic abandon, arms in the air. She's floating above the room. She can see Thomas and he's kissing someone else, and she really doesn't care. Now someone is kissing her – one of the boys she's dancing with – and she kisses him back with the same abandon. Fast-forward and she's staggering up the stairs, woozy, lips swollen. She suspects that she kissed more than one boy in the end but she's on her own now. *She could swear that she's on her own.* She has finally remembered her responsibilities to Megan. *God, she hopes so.* What happens once she finds Megan in the bedroom? Either she can't rouse her or she doesn't even try, deciding to have a nap herself. Thomas and Dylan aren't with her. *She's alone.* She is *almost* positive of that fact.

Jess couldn't live with herself if she'd led them to Megan. But she has doubts, grave doubts, and a thousand questions. Where had all her inhibitions gone, for a start? What was going on with all the dancing (she is *not* an arms-in-the-air kind of girl) and pashing more than one boy? How about that weird out-of-body sensation she remembers? As for the sex, there are disjointed memories of a body pressing heavily on hers, of grunting and breath pungent with alcohol, and feeling leaden and unable to stop it from happening. Jess knows Dylan O'Shea has some of the answers, and she hopes they'll help her understand what led to what, and forgive herself with regards to Megan.

Someone is knocking rather loudly. Probably Helen next door, checking that Jess and Alex haven't killed each other. Jess will have to apologise, reassure her. She rises from the bed with a sigh, opens the bedroom door. Alex has beaten her to it. He glances over his shoulder before lifting the security chain, and they exchange a look of mutual embarrassment. Upsetting elderly neighbours isn't their thing. Neither is screaming and slamming doors.

'Hello. Alex, isn't it? Detective Sergeant Bridget Kennedy and Detective Constable Sasha McEvoy. Is Jessica home?'

Oh God. What now? Could the timing possibly be any worse? It's 5 p.m. on Friday night; shouldn't the detective be finished for the week? Shouldn't they all?

'I'm here.' Jess comes forward to position herself next to Alex. His arm snakes around her waist: his way of saying sorry for losing his rag.

The detective is holding out a piece of paper. 'Jessica Foster, this is an occupier's notice to search and enter 31/165 Stanton Street. The warrant was applied for on the basis of having reasonable grounds to believe that we'll find evidence relating to the disappearance of Dylan O'Shea.'

Shock roots her to the spot. A warrant! Evidence! Dylan O'Shea! What do they think they're going to find here? Dylan can't have disappeared; Jess has questions she needs fucking answered.

'Move, Jess.' Alex manoeuvres her out of the way. 'You've got to let them in.'

49
BRIDGET

Jessica and her boyfriend, Alex, stand mutely in the living room. His hand rests on her shoulder; they both seem shell-shocked. The apartment is well-proportioned and thoughtfully furnished. Bridget already knows that the deeds are in Jessica's name.

Sasha starts on the bedroom, while Bridget stays with the couple.

'We need to seize your phone,' she informs the young woman, not unsympathetically; she understands that it's a major inconvenience. 'The texts between you and Dylan could be important evidence.'

'We never even met in the end.' Jessica's eyes flick upwards to her boyfriend, who is considerably taller than her. There's a strange dynamic between them. An unfinished argument? 'I didn't turn up the first time

– my sister called around unexpectedly – and he didn't respond when I tried to reschedule.'

'We shouldn't need to keep your phone for very long, then,' Bridget states matter-of-factly.

Jessica could be lying. If they *did* meet up, she could have been the last person to see Dylan O'Shea. Alternatively, her boyfriend might have taken a dim view of the proposed meeting.

Sasha finds a small amount of cannabis in a bedroom drawer, which Alex admits to owning. Bridget advises him that he'll be issued with a caution; he doesn't seem overly perturbed. On closer scrutiny, it's hard to tell if his blank expression is shock, as she first thought, or extreme nonchalance. He's hard to read.

'What do you do for work, Alex?'

'I'm a landscaper.'

'And there's a family farm in the Hunter Valley, is that right?'

'Yeah.' He looks surprised that she knows this fact.

'Been back there recently?'

'Not for a few months. Work's been busy.'

'Got some motorbikes on the farm?'

'Yeah, a few.'

'Yamahas?'

'Suzukis. And a Honda.'

The search of Megan Lowe's property is being conducted concurrently by Dave and Patrick. Everyone's Friday-night plans have gone by the wayside. Hopefully, they'll have something to show for it.

Sasha emerges from the bedroom again, holding a black puffer jacket aloft. 'Which of you owns this?'

Jess glares at her boyfriend. 'For God's sake, Alex, you told me you'd given that back to Ramsey.'

He blushes; it's obvious he's been caught out in a lie. 'Ramsey said it isn't his. Thought I better hang on to it till someone claims it.'

'These stains look quite like blood.' Sasha's soft voice contains a thread of steel.

Alex's blush deepens. His nonchalance – if it was that! – has worn off. 'Could be. I work with contractors all the time. They leave stuff behind – tools, clothes, whatever. Cutting yourself is common. Stupid but common.'

Sasha places the jacket in an evidence bag and moves into the kitchen.

'What's kept in here?' Bridget taps the top of a metal filing cabinet, tucked away in a corner of the living room.

'Just paperwork for the business. Invoices and receipts and stuff.'

Bridget opens the first drawer, takes out a handful of grimy invoices. The first few documents contain a delivery address in Pymble.

'Is this where you're working at the moment, Alex?'

'Yeah,' he says after a noticeable pause.

She turns around so she can see his face. 'Is this a long-term client or a new job?'

Another pause. 'It's Jess's parents' place. I've been working there the last few weeks.'

His face says it all. He knows this complicates things. He knows that she's likely to attach significance to it.

'Do you know where Dylan O'Shea is, Alex?'

Jessica takes a sharp breath.

Alex's bushy eyebrows knit together. 'No fuckin' idea.'

Bridget holds his stare, her neck straining uncomfortably. He's intimidatingly tall: a strapping country boy. Bridget had a six-month relationship with a country boy while she was at the academy. One of her abiding memories was that he loved animals but detested human beings, including her in the end. Country boys nurture their grudges as much as their crops. Some have a tendency to take justice into their own roughened hands.

'You sure about that?'

'Don't even know what he looks like.'

Country boys can lie, too. Their open faces can trick you.

'Is there a garage or storage unit downstairs?'

'No, street parking only.'

Bridget is already aware that there is only one vehicle – a Toyota Hilux ute – registered to the address. 'I'd like a quick look at your work vehicle, please.'

A flicker of something on his face – annoyance? defiance? – before his hand plunges into his jeans pocket to retrieve his keys.

The ute is parked a few doors down, sandwiched between two Mercedes. Dusk is creeping in but there is still enough light for Bridget to do an inventory of the contents in the tray of the vehicle. Everyday gardening equipment such as shovels, rakes and pruning shears. An electric hedge trimmer, pressure hose and chainsaw. A few bags of cement and – of most concern – a large container of bleach.

Bridget concludes two things: it's time for Alex Leary to be formally questioned, and his vehicle needs to be taken in for forensic examination.

50
BRIDGET

The interview begins at 8 p.m., with Bridget announcing the time for the benefit of the recording. Alex declines his right to legal representation and dismisses her warning about anything he says being potentially used as evidence against him.

'I just want to get home. Let's get this fuckin' over with.'

Bridget can sympathise; she wants to get home too. Sasha, by contrast, is fresh faced and eager. Bridget tries to channel her young colleague's energy.

'Alex, can you tell us if you've had any recent contact with Dylan O'Shea?'

'No. None.'

'Can you describe your movements yesterday and today?'

'Went to work at Jess's parents' place. Started at seven thirty, got home four thirtyish, had dinner, a few beers, went to bed.'

'Did you speak to either of Jess's parents? Can they confirm that you were at the property?'

'Yeah. Margaret, Jess's mum, made me a few cups of coffee during the day. We spoke about the job and she added on some extras, which is becoming a habit. Her money, I guess.'

'Did you leave the property at any stage during the day?'

'Popped out to the hardware store and to get some lunch. That's about it.'

'Can you tell me the purpose of the container of bleach you keep in your ute?'

Alex jerks back in his seat. 'It's used to clean moss and mould from bricks and pavers ... Fuckin' hell, do you think I used it to clean up evidence or something?'

That's precisely Bridget's line of thought. She deflects his question with another of her own. 'Jessica said that you picked her up from Artarmon train station on Thursday September fifth. Can you confirm that this is correct?'

'Look, I've no idea of specific dates but, yeah, I picked her up from the station a couple of weeks ago. The trains weren't running.'

'Did you go inside the station at any point?'

'No.'

'Can you recall what you were wearing that night?'

'Are you serious?' He glares at her. 'I don't keep a fuckin' record of what I wear.'

'Is it possible you were wearing a black puffer jacket similar to the one found in your home tonight?'

His response is emphatic. 'Not possible. I don't have a jacket like that.'

The interview concludes just after 9 p.m. Bridget thanks him for his cooperation and informs him that he's free to go; there's not enough evidence to detain him any longer. He scowls as he stands up, his height all the more pronounced in the small interview room. Sasha escorts him out.

Back at her desk, Bridget is getting her thoughts in order when she receives a phone call from Anna, one of the forensics team.

'Hi, Bridget. Sorry, know it's late, but I thought you'd want to know straight away. The stains on that jacket are blood spatters.'

'Thanks. How long before we can tell if the blood is Newson's, Malouf's or O'Shea's?'

'Couple of days.'

According to Alex, the blood could be from any random contractor who cut himself on the job, and the bleach is used in the course of his work. But in Bridget's world, the concurrent presence of blood and bleach never fail to set off alarm bells.

Cold hard fact: a landscaper would have more opportunity than anyone else to bury a body.

*

Early on Saturday morning, Bridget receives a preliminary report from the tech department regarding a laptop seized from Megan Lowe's house.

> Search history contains news articles about William Newson's death and a map of his neighbourhood in Killara. In addition, there's Facebook activity relating to Thomas Malouf and Dylan O'Shea. The activity is not just recent: it dates back years.

The laptop belongs to Roslyn Lowe.

Now Bridget and Dave are parked outside the property in Hornsby. It's 8 a.m. A jogger is running along the grass verge, and the neighbour across the road is making arcs with his garden hose. Bridget experiences a fleeting rush of guilt regarding her neglected fitness levels and her arid, thirsty garden at home.

'Let's go,' says Dave, springing out of the car with an enthusiasm that belies the fact that they were both in the office until almost eleven last night. Bridget's exit is hesitant: she's questioning what she's doing here. Every time she thinks she is getting a handle on the case, it takes another turn, pirouetting out of reach. Alex's ute is currently undergoing forensic examination, with traces of blood already detected on one of the spades. It's evident that Bridget is going to need another warrant, for the place he presumably last used the spade: Jessica's family home. Yet, with all that going on, Bridget is here, outside this other more ordinary house that will soon – conveniently? – have brand-new owners. Last night she felt quite convinced that Jessica's boyfriend was implicated; this morning it's Megan's mother who is setting off alarm bells. *A mother's love is a force of nature. A mother's wrath has no boundaries.* Bridget has no clue how either Alex or Roslyn align with the motorbike and gun being found in Thomas Malouf's storage facility. It's making her head spin. What is she missing? A small crucial piece of information that ties everything together, or something bigger and more fundamental?

Megan answers the door. She's dressed in pyjamas, her dark-brown hair mussed from sleep. She looks vulnerable, embarrassed, startled, annoyed: the range of emotions Bridget herself would experience if she opened her front door to two detectives while still in her nightwear.

'Good morning. Sorry for the early call. Is your mum at home?'

'She's working today,' Megan says, then adds, 'to make up for having yesterday off.'

A choice: leave now and phone Roslyn later to arrange a formal interview; or see if anything can be gleaned from her daughter. Dave used the word 'hostile' when describing Roslyn's reaction to last night's search. A chat with Megan might be more productive.

'Do you mind if we come in?'

A blink of chocolate-coloured eyes. 'Sure. But it's not going to be comfortable. There's literally nowhere to sit!'

She's not lying. The living room, which is the first room off the hallway, is entirely empty except for a TV screen on the wall. A door opens further down the hallway. Tattooed arms, unkempt hair and flashing eyes. It's the brother: Sebastian. What's he doing here again? Doesn't he live in Melbourne?

'What's going on?' he demands, looking at everyone in turn, his eyes stopping on his sister.

'They just want to talk,' Megan answers, a quiver detectable in her voice.

'You don't *have* to talk, Megan. You don't have to do *anything*. Mum's right. This is harassment.'

Hostility can be born from fear, or a loss of control, or entrenched anger. Providing detail can dispel some of the first two at least.

Bridget takes a breath. 'Look, it's just a quick chat about your mum's laptop and some of the stuff she's been looking at. But you're right. You're under no obligation to speak to us.'

Megan sighs. Her brother scowls. Bridget is suspicious that they're both well aware of their mother's online activity.

'Let's get out of the hall,' Megan says in a calm voice.

They follow her into the kitchen, converging around the L-shaped countertop.

Bridget is forthright. 'Can either of you explain why there are hundreds of searches relating to two deceased men and another missing man on your mum's laptop?'

Silence. Megan and Seb exchange a long meaningful

look. She wants to explain; he is loath. Bridget waits it out.

'It's not how it looks,' Megan says eventually, breaking eye contact with her brother.

'Isn't it?' Bridget locks her into a stare.

'Mum is a bit obsessed. She lost a lot because of the trial. But she would never hurt anyone ...'

Bridget recalls the victim impact statement that Megan wrote as part of her therapy. She said that she'd woken up to a nightmare, that her trust in people, and in the world, had been shattered. Roslyn forwarded the impact statement to the investigating detectives, insisting it be placed on file, because Roslyn had found herself living a nightmare, too: no mother in the world wants to hear their daughter referred to as Girl A.

'Your mum's workplace is directly across the road from the Motorcycle Accessories Café. Does she have associations with any of its clientele?'

Another – alarmed – look between brother and sister.

'Of course not!' Megan's denial is underscored with uncertainty.

'I hear they do good coffee,' Bridget continues, transferring her stare to Megan's brother. 'Some interesting personalities hanging around that café. You can buy more than coffee and motorcycle parts, if you know what I mean.'

Seb's face darkens; her meaning is not lost on him. Megan's brother never made it on to Katrina's whiteboard because he lives in Melbourne. Yet here he is.

And he was here last time, too. *Melbourne is a mere flight away.*

Megan's dark eyes are pleading. 'I promise this is not as bad as it looks. Listen …'

51
MEGAN

The first sign of trouble came nine months after the trial. Her dad, Peter, had taken on a contract to repair a common property driveway. It was a large, complex job. A few weeks after completion, he received a letter of complaint from the owner, stating that cracks and bubbles were starting to form along the edges of the retaining walls. Megan was in Cambodia at the time, and heard about it from Roslyn over the phone.

'Your father rectified the work, but he doesn't understand what went wrong. It looks like the waterproof membrane failed to bond, but he's used it many times before without any problems.'

Megan remembers the conversation quite clearly, because a driveway dispute seemed like such a first-world problem. Phnom Penh had swarms of children, orphaned and barefoot, who pulled at her clothes and begged for money, food or, their ultimate dream, to be adopted.

Megan and Roslyn spoke again about a week later. 'The owner is still not happy. He's taking your father to the New South Wales Fair Trading Tribunal. He wants compensation.'

'How much?'

'Four hundred thousand.'

'What?' Megan laughed because it sounded so ludicrous, because she had faith in her father's workmanship, and because it still seemed unimportant in comparison to what she'd seen that day at Stung Meanchey, the garbage dump outside Phnom Penh: children scavenging through garbage, looking for plastic, glass and metal to sell to the small local recycling businesses. They not only 'worked' at the dump, they lived there, their makeshift houses perched on mounds of rubbish, a few of them killed each year, rolled over by garbage trucks.

Roslyn sent an email following the tribunal hearing: *Your father has been ordered to pay the compensation. The Tribunal Member said he failed to properly investigate the condition of the concrete slab, the moisture content, and traffic usage. The insurance company are resisting because they weren't informed of the dispute soon enough. This is a disaster.*

Megan started to pay attention: $400,000 was a life-changing sum of money. Had her dad been careless or distracted when undertaking the work? Why didn't he inform the insurance company straight away? Was this 'disaster', indirectly, all her fault?

That doesn't sound like Dad. What happens now?

Now it goes to the NSW Civil and Administrative Tribunal.

Does Dad need a lawyer?

Not at this stage. You're meant to represent yourself. But it's really taking its toll. He's been very stressed and not himself at all. I'm worried about him.

Her dad lost the second hearing and went to see a lawyer about appealing. He was told it would be extremely costly, and there was no guarantee he would win. The dispute was not a clear-cut one and the owner had obtained expert opinions that would hold weight unless Peter could produce some experts of his own.

We've got no money to take this further, Roslyn emailed. *We're already out of pocket from the rectification work. Losing would mean we're up for the other side's legal costs, too. The insurance company isn't budging.*

Peter remortgaged the house to pay the $400,000. His reputation and financial stability were shattered. He sank into depression. The world was a bad place. People couldn't be trusted. What was the point in working hard all your life? His mental health deteriorated until he was unable to summon the confidence to work. In Roslyn's opinion, his depression led to the cancer. Probably not true, but it definitely affected his capacity to fight the disease, and made him resist getting proper treatment. Nothing was worthwhile. Everything was a conspiracy against him; even the doctors and nurses who were doing their very best.

Megan stayed in Cambodia for four weeks. She went on another 'tour' of the garbage dump and this time was struck by the children's happy smiles. Living like this – the putrid smell, the mud and dirt, managing to exist from what other people threw away – they still smiled. There was a pretty girl in a long clean dress and Megan slipped her some money. The girl symbolised hope and inventiveness, despite dire circumstances.

Roslyn called on the day she was due to leave for Vietnam. The other girls in the dormitory growled on being woken up by the loud ring tone. Megan turned off the volume, and scuttled outside to the corridor.

'It was the Maloufs,' Roslyn cried. 'The owner of the building is a relative of theirs. They set your father up.'

'What?' Megan asked groggily, leaning against the wall to prop herself up. She'd had a late night and felt queasy from an impromptu farewell party, which involved shots of vodka in the hostel's common room.

'The Maloufs were behind the whole thing,' Roslyn screeched in her ear, doing her headache no favours.

'How do you know?' she asked in disbelief.

'I did some investigation of my own because I needed your father to feel better about himself. I found out that the site was well-known for its water problems, which meant any kind of construction on that driveway would've had issues. And I found out that the owner is married to one of Thomas Malouf's aunts.'

Megan's stomach plummeted. This was no coincidence. It couldn't be.

'I confronted him, the owner.' Roslyn sounded deranged. 'I told him that I knew who he really was, and the terrible effect the dispute had on Peter. Do you know what he said to me, Megan? Do you know what he *actually* said?'

'What?' she whispered, closing her eyes with dread.

'He said "Reputations are easy to fuck with, aren't they?"'

Bile rose in her throat. 'What did he mean?'

'I asked him! Apparently, Thomas missed out on a cadetship with one of the banks. He was all set to start but the bank suddenly changed its mind. Another job offer was retracted after a background check. Thomas's reputation was damaged, so they thought your father was fair game.'

The Maloufs wanted revenge. Winning the trial evidently wasn't enough.

Megan's thoughts leapt to the girl in the dump who had been wearing that impossibly clean dress. How did she do it? How did she stay clean when she had all that filth around her?

'I'm sorry, Mum. This is all my fault.'

Then, before she could help it, her stomach heaved and she threw up all over the corridor.

52
JESS

The Maloufs tried to sabotage Jess's father, too. They searched their extensive network until they unearthed someone whom Richard Foster had operated on; as one of the top surgeons in the city it wasn't that hard. A lawsuit was manufactured, and an online smear campaign launched. But malpractice in heart surgery is harder to pull off than malpractice in the building industry. Richard knew his way around the pitfalls of professional indemnity insurance and immediately informed his broker. He'd been sued before, and had an experienced lawyer he could afford to engage. The patient claimed that she didn't receive appropriate post-op care, a flaky assertion given her good health and the fact that her pacemaker was working faultlessly. After some argy-bargy between the lawyers, the complainant had no choice but to withdraw or risk significant legal costs when she inevitably lost in court.

The possibility of the complainant being related to Thomas Malouf didn't cross their minds. She was just a cantankerous old woman, who had cost Richard in legal fees and annoyance.

Until Megan sent an email from Vietnam: *You know that money my dad had to pay? Just discovered it was a set-up by the Maloufs to get back at us. The owner of the property is married to Thomas's aunt! Feel sick to my stomach. Mum and Dad had to remortgage and it's all my fault!*

Jess showed the email to her father and he asked his lawyer to investigate further. The cantankerous old woman was, in fact, a cousin of Thomas Malouf's grandfather.

Jess was aghast when her dad confirmed the connection. 'Oh my God, how far will these people go?'

'Don't worry about it,' he said, giving her shoulder a squeeze. 'The lawyers had dealt with it anyway.'

Jess *did* worry about it. The differences between Megan's family and hers had never been more stark: her family possessing the money and resources to fight off the attack by the Maloufs; Megan's family left ruined.

This is what led to Roslyn going crazy at her husband's funeral all those years later.

'How dare you show your face … This is *all your fault*,' she shrieked, when Jess tried to pay her respects. 'What kind of friend are you, anyway? You should have gone home with Megan. If you'd been a good friend, my husband would still be alive today.'

Every word of which was true.

It's midday, Saturday. They're closing the gym for the afternoon and meeting at the community hall later in the evening. Everyone is jumpy with anticipation, even Vince, who has been through this more times than he can remember. Billy is here, flouting their advice to conserve energy and stay at home. He is doing hip stretches, one knee on the mat, an arm curved over his head in an oddly graceful pose. Jess vacuums around him.

'One minute I think I'm going to get thrashed, and the next I'm imagining victory …' He turns his upper body towards her. 'Can't decide if I'm scared shitless or beside myself with excitement.'

She knows that feeling all too well. The combination of fear and excitement, fuelling a surge of adrenalin on stepping into the ring. She is nervous for him, and more than a little jealous. He's starting off, while her career is over. He won't reach professional level – he doesn't have the talent, and besides he already has a career in law – but at least he can fight at an amateur level, a massive achievement in itself.

You're still in the game, she tells herself. *Even if you're no longer the centre player. You're giving back to the sport.*

'Get out of here, for God's sake! You're in my way. You can feel scared shitless at home.'

They laugh, with only the tiniest hint of hysteria. How well he does tonight is testament to Jess and Vince, and everything they've taught him. Jess is less worried about Jordy and Lachlan, who are fighting too. They're more experienced, know what to expect.

The phone rings at the desk and Vince picks it up, saying a gruff hello.

'It's for you,' he says, holding out the receiver to Jess.

Probably Alex. He was rattled this morning when they kissed goodbye. Jess was rattled, too. That stupid puffer jacket. Why did he lie about it? What was the point? Her name was on the warrant, but it was obvious that the detectives were only interested in Alex, taking him in for questioning and towing the ute away. It was hard this morning to find the focus to go into work. But they're both dogged like that, won't let themselves be beaten.

She frowns and turns off the vacuum.

'Hello?'

'Jess, it's Natasha.' Her sister's voice has a tell-tale quiver. Something is clearly wrong. 'I've been trying to call you on your mobile. I'm at Mum and Dad's. You need to come over here.'

'What's going on?'

'Detectives are outside in the garden, talking to Alex. I think they have a warrant. They're going to dig the place up.'

53
BRIDGET

The garden has been sectioned off and a cadaver dog, trained to smell human decomposition, is being led around by its handler.

Bridget's eyes track the dog, a German Shepherd called Louis, his ears pricked and nose to the ground. He is trained to sit down if he detects anything. Louis makes short work of the expansive lawn and garden beds, disappearing behind trees and shrubs only to reappear again. He comes to a stop by the pool gate, waiting for his handler to allow him entry.

Dave voices Bridget's thoughts. 'Nothing in those new garden beds, then. Maybe Louis will have more luck around the pool.'

The Foster family are watching proceedings from the kitchen window. The well-off mother and father,

Margaret and Richard. Jess, who arrived a few minutes ago, and her sister, with a young baby propped on her shoulder. Alex, arms folded, face smouldering. Bridget can imagine the complaints that will make their way to Katrina. She sighs. Her mind is torn between what's going on here – the dog, the team of specialist officers, all present at her instigation – and what she learned this morning at Megan's house. *This is not as bad as it looks …*

Megan's intention was to explain her mother's interest in the three men – William, Thomas and Dylan – but what she revealed lent Roslyn more motive than anything. Roslyn's daughter had been violated. Her husband had lost his business and his will to live. Devastating financial consequences are still being paid today. Roslyn has every right to be mad. Is selling the house a means to free up money to pay a debt to a contract killer? Maybe Roslyn decided that her revenge would be every bit as elaborate as the Maloufs'.

Bridget closes her eyes, imagining herself in Roslyn's shoes, the mother of Girl A. Hot rage courses through her. Revenge is a natural extension of rage. The timing is important, though. Why now? Years of resentment and hatred hurtling to a climax that coincided with the sale of her beloved family home? Or some other trigger: William Newson in the newspapers yet again; Laura Dundas, shivering and defiant in her bikini, holding up her placard. Roslyn's internet history had links to the articles. *Not again*, she must have thought.

Bridget's head hurts from the effort of piecing it

together. She's getting nowhere. It's possible that sympathy for Roslyn is getting in the way of her objectivity.

'The Maloufs destroyed Megan's father,' she says, turning to Dave for inspiration, ideas, anything. 'What kind of family would do such a thing?'

'The kind of family that closes ranks to defend their interests,' he says simply. 'The kind of family that you shouldn't cross.'

Bridget remembers Thomas Malouf's funeral, his relatives spinning their own story on the cause of his death. And the party they threw after the 'not guilty' verdict: treating his acquittal as a victory, a celebration. It was wrong, *so wrong*. How did they justify themselves? How could their view of things be so skewed?

'That family has a thirst for revenge. They think they're above the law. They're dangerous, Dave ... Let's bring Leo Malouf in for questioning.'

'I'll ring him as soon as we're done here,' Dave promises, 'set something up for tomorrow.'

The dog and his handler are finished with the pool area: nothing untoward has been detected. Louis is praised and put back on his lead. No dead bodies, but that doesn't mean there isn't something to be found – a murder weapon? clothing? – under all that fresh earth in the garden beds. Bridget orders the specialist officers to commence digging. Animosity reeks through the glass pane of the kitchen window. Just Alex and Jess standing there now.

Maybe Bridget should ask Katrina to take her off

the case. She is struggling to maintain impartiality, not just in relation to Roslyn. It's easy to sympathise with Megan and Jess as well, to take their side. Cara is the exact age they were when they went to that fateful house party. Such a tender age, such a pivotal age. All Bridget can see is what they lost as a result of that night – their virginity, their sense of security, their belief in the justice system and good prevailing over bad. The damage extended into their families, their friendships and relationships today.

Jessica's pale face stares from the window: Girl B, a term that's far too narrow and clinical to apply to her.

Margaret reappears, miming something to Jessica and Alex, her hand gesticulating to make her point. Then Bridget has a left-field, crazy thought. *What if she has been focusing on the wrong mother?*

It's 4 p.m. when Bridget calls it a day, the specialist officers no longer requiring her presence. Nothing has been found other than an old T-shirt, caked in dirt, once a light colour, perhaps pale blue. Alex claimed the T-shirt was his, a rag used to wipe his hands. Forensic examination might tell another story.

Bridget is tired to the point of being delirious. She calls Shane from the car, and leaves a voicemail when he doesn't pick up.

'It's me. Just popping into the office for half an hour then I'm done, promise. I'll pick up dinner on my way home. Pizza? Thai? Ask the kids and let me know. Bye-ee.'

The office is deserted, except for Sasha, who is bea-vering away at her desk. No sign of Katrina, thank God. Bridget couldn't face her boss right now. Another wasted warrant. Another avenue closed. No answers forthcoming.

'What a hellish day,' Bridget says, dumping her handbag on her desk. 'So much for no more overtime or weekends. Ha!'

Sasha stands up and comes over to Bridget's cubicle. 'I was just about to call you, actually.'

'You were?'

The young woman's eyes are flashing. 'I've been tying up loose ends, one of which was confirming Hayley Webster's alibi for the night Newson was shot.'

Hayley Webster. The ex-nurse. Thomas Malouf's second victim. His second time being charged, at least.

Bridget has all but forgotten about Hayley. Now here she is, popping up again. That's precisely the problem with this case: it's been impossible to fully exclude any of the suspects.

'And?' Bridget prompts, curiosity triumphing over her weariness.

'Well, she was at work, as she said she was. At a call centre, just like she said … But not any old call centre.'

Bridget narrows her eyes. 'What do you mean?'

'Hayley Webster is an emergency medical dispatcher. She works in the ambulance control centre. She decides which ambulances go where.'

Bridget realises two things at once: it wasn't a

coincidence after all that Megan Lowe was the attending paramedic at the shooting; and she won't be going home in the near future, or picking up dinner for her family.

54
MEGAN

Megan and her brother have made countless trips to the local charity shops and as a result the garage is virtually empty, like the rest of the house. The stylist will install metal storage units and a workbench when she comes on Monday, to appeal to DIY enthusiasts.

Seb runs a hand through his long hair, leaving a streak of dirt on his forehead. 'Even the bloody garage is getting styled. What's wrong with having it messy and dingy, like a normal garage?'

'It's all about first impressions and potential lifestyle.' Megan wipes dust from the knees of her jeans. 'That's it for today. Good job.'

They high-five each other. It's been a productive afternoon, although it took a while to find their rhythm after the dramatic start to the day. Megan cried a bit as she told the detectives what had happened to her father, and she detected compassion in their eyes. They would not be permitted to openly sympathise. Megan knows – from her own job – how hard it can be to maintain that veneer of professionalism.

'I'm starving,' her brother says, his long arms raised in the air as he yawns. 'What are we doing about food?'

Eating at home is out of the question: no tables or chairs, an almost empty fridge. Roslyn is going to a friend's sixtieth tonight, so they're on their own. The friend is a close one and Roslyn couldn't pull out, despite being distressed to learn that they'd had yet another visit from police.

'They came again? I'm their suspect? *Me?* Oh my God, they're hopeless.'

Roslyn was wearing her work uniform: white blouse, navy trousers, wild eyes.

Megan asked her about the motorcycle café.

'Never set foot in the place,' Roslyn declared. 'Don't tell me they think I paid one of those bikies to knock off William Newson? Hopeless! No idea what they're doing. Then or now!'

Megan has to agree. The idea of her mum consorting with bikies is preposterous. The suggestion that she paid for a contract killing is beyond preposterous; it's impossible.

'There's no money,' she explained this morning. 'Our financial situation is dire.'

'It can be surprisingly cheap to hire these people,' Bridget Kennedy countered.

'There's no money. For anything.'

Bridget and her colleague understood by the time Megan finished explaining. Sympathy was written on their faces; they didn't need to express it with words.

'You choose the restaurant,' Megan replies now to her brother. 'But there's somewhere I want to go after we've eaten.'

Seb raises an eyebrow. 'The pub? Sounds good to me.'

She laughs and shakes her head. 'Not the pub. There's a fight I want to see …'

It's been on her mind since Vince mentioned it last weekend, with Jess chiming in. Something shifted in Megan. Everything had been dredged to the surface: her repressed shame, sadness, anger. The invitation felt like a new door opening up. The invitation felt like it was originating from Jess, not Vince.

'It's at the community hall in Artarmon. Just two amateurs, as far as I know, but it means something to Jess, and I wouldn't mind going along …'

Seb holds her gaze in the murky light of the garage. He knows what this is. A step towards reconciliation. A show of solidarity. He always had time for Jess, and she would be stoked to see him, too.

'I'm up for that,' he says with a crooked smile. 'Just need a shower before we head out.'

*

Megan is waiting for him when he comes out of the shower, the pieces of paper – evidence – laid out on the kitchen countertop. She found them in the recycling bin, the distinctive font catching her eye: the AVO, in roughly torn pieces.

'Seb, in here,' she calls when she hears the bathroom door.

Her brother materialises, bare-chested, droplets of water on his shoulders and chest. She has the sudden sensation of not knowing who he is, what thoughts are in his head, *what he is capable of doing*. She feels stupid, for so readily dismissing the AVO, her actions belatedly approving the violence.

Megan indicates the jagged pieces of paper. 'Why did you tear up the AVO? Were you trying to hide it from the police?'

He's startled, caught off guard. His eyes jump around guiltily.

'No. The cops would have it on their database, if they looked.'

'Why then?'

He thinks for a moment. 'I heard the knock on the door, the warrant being read out, and I knew the cops would find it pretty quickly – there's not much here, is there? I didn't care about them, I cared about Mum; I didn't want her finding out like that. So, I hid it in my clothes, recycled it later on.' He grins, more sure of himself now. 'Great detective work, Megs. Maybe you should change career.'

55
JESS

Natasha gives Jess and Alex a lift home. The atmosphere in the car is horror-stricken. Nobody makes a sound, not even Lucy. Some situations can't be adequately responded to with words. Waking up naked on bloodstained sheets. A sombre-faced doctor stating that you've suffered too many concussions to continue fighting. The sight of a sniffer dog wandering around your parents' back garden, trying to detect the smell of a decaying body.

'See you tonight,' Natasha says, squeezing Jess's arm before she gets out of the car.

Jess is confused, before remembering that her sister is coming to watch the fight. What seemed like an excellent idea yesterday is now bordering on absurd. Right now, Jess can't even see *herself* at the fight. She can barely think straight, see-sawing between incredulity and horror.

Inside the apartment, she checks the time. Less than two hours to go. How can she coach Billy in this frame of mind? How can she remind him to keep his knees over his feet, and not get lazy with his hands? How can she assess the technical weaknesses of his opponent?

Alex is as shaken as her. He begins pacing around the living room. 'Your mum and dad kept looking at me like I was some kind of fuckin' murderer.'

This isn't true. Jess knows because she was watching them carefully. Margaret behaved like she always does when she's under threat: she goes cold. Richard was unnerved, yes, but his reaction was justified and not specifically directed towards Alex.

'They weren't, Alex, they really weren't.' Jess has collapsed on to the sofa; she doesn't have the strength to stand. 'Anyway, they're under just as much suspicion as you are. In theory, any one of you could be out to avenge what happened to me.'

Alex is circling; she has never seen him so agitated. 'I'm not denying I wouldn't smash O'Shea in the face if I ever met him, but murdering and burying him ...' He shudders at the thought. 'Fuck's sake, I can't even handle it when I stumble across a dead animal.'

Alex has upended the grave of many a deceased pet during the course of his work. He's a lot softer than his appearance would suggest.

Jess checks her watch again. Time is ticking on. 'What

am I going to do? Should I ring Vince? He'll under-stand, won't he? Billy will be on the back foot, though. Typical lawyer – he'll baulk at any change in plans.'

Alex stops moving and stares at her as though she's mad. 'This fight means the world to you, Jess. You've been training that dude for months. Are you going to let O'Shea ruin this as well?'

He's right. Not going tonight means that she is the one losing out. But how can she coach Billy like this? She'll be a liability to him, unless she can get her shit together.

'Will you come with me?' she whispers, looking up at him beseechingly. 'Please, Alex?'

'Aw, babe, I just want to stay home and get pissed. It's been a crap day. Last night too, getting grilled by the fuckin' cops.'

Their eyes lock. He sighs and yields.

'All right, all right, but we're going out afterwards and getting drunk.'

He disappears to shower and get changed. Jess stays on the sofa, hands clasped tightly together. She admits it: she wanted to kill William Newson when he said all those derogatory things, when he obscured the truth with his lies and innuendo. She was furious, and she wanted to hurt him, really badly. But once the trial was over, those feelings didn't linger beyond a couple of months. Who killed him? Why? Where is Dylan O'Shea?

Jess shakes her head violently. She can't solve this

now. Billy is her priority for the next few hours. He has worked hard for this fight; he deserves her best.

Alex reappears; it never takes him long to get ready. But seeing him in his fresh shirt and jeans sends her into another spin. The shirt is the same one he was wearing the night he picked her up from the train station, the night Thomas Malouf died. She noticed then because she'd never seen it before.

'Is that a new shirt?' she asks tremulously.

He glances down at it, as though he has only just noticed it himself. 'Got it a few weeks ago.'

He lied about the puffer jacket. Is he lying about this, too? Where did it come from? Alex doesn't shop for clothes very frequently.

It strikes Jess that her boyfriend could have known all along about her plans to meet Dylan, because he knows the passcode for her phone. His anger last night: was it because he was genuinely concerned about her meeting Dylan, or a front for something far more disturbing? He'd been out with Ramsey – supposedly – on the night William Newson was shot, that bloodstained jacket turning up soon afterwards. And why had he been wearing a brand-new shirt on the night Thomas Malouf died? Had he needed to change clothes urgently?

Fuck! Enough! She is not going there. This is Alex. *He has her back.* To the extent of going to Billy's fight tonight after having the twenty-four hours from hell.

She stands up, and hugs him hard. He smells of shower gel and safety.

56
BRIDGET

The clock on the dash turns over to 5 p.m. just as Bridget cuts the engine on the car. It's still bright: the days are starting to lengthen. Bridget and Sasha attract furtive glances from a dodgy-looking group gathered across the street. Bridget blanks out what they might be up to – drug taking or dealing, most likely – and the two women walk quickly towards the entrance of the Redfern high-rise where Hayley Webster lives.

'What are the chances she's home?' Sasha asks, as the lift whizzes them upwards. Another resident – clearly not very security conscious – held the front door open on his way out. Hayley has no idea they're on their way.

'Who knows?' Bridget shrugs. 'We'll wait, if need be.'

Bridget's weariness is forgotten. She's buzzing with adrenalin; this is the breakthrough she's been waiting for. The question that niggled since day one: how Megan Lowe found herself at the deathbed of William Newson. Bridget never believed it to be coincidence, or fate.

Bridget thumps the door with the ball of her hand. 'Hayley, are you in there? Open up, please. It's Detective Sergeant Kennedy.'

Movement can be heard on the other side. A rustle of clothes. Light footsteps. A pause, perhaps to look through the peephole. Then the security chain being unhooked.

Hayley Webster is in uniform. Blue short-sleeved shirt with a crest on the arm: Ambulance NSW, Control Centre.

'I'm on my way out to work,' she says feebly, unable to meet their eyes. 'My shift starts at five thirty.'

'Well, you'd better call and let them know you're running late,' Bridget retorts and steps inside.

The flat is compact and feminine, as she remembers it. Hayley's handbag is perched on the arm of one of the matching sofas. The young woman picks it up, extracts her phone, and makes a call.

'Robert, it's Hayley. I'm going to be late.' Bridget detects a tremor in her hand as she holds the phone to her ear. 'Hopefully no longer than an hour. Sorry … I'm helping police with an investigation … I'll explain when I get in.'

They sit down in the same positions as before, Bridget and Sasha on one of the sofas and Hayley on the other.

The young woman's composure is rapidly deteriorating. The game is up and she knows it.

'Here we are again.' Bridget adopts her sternest tone; she can afford no more time wasting. 'You left some things out the last time we spoke, Hayley. No more skirting around the facts or I'll have you charged with aiding and abetting a crime, at the very least … Did you receive a triple-zero call on the night of August twentieth relating to the shooting of William Newson?'

Hayley shakes her head. 'I'm in dispatch, I don't receive the calls.'

'Did you *dispatch* the ambulance to the scene, then?'

'The system dispatches the ambulance … But I used the override function.'

Bridget takes a moment to acknowledge the admission. 'Why did you use the override function, Hayley? Did Megan request it?'

'Not Megan, Dylan …' Tears pool in her eyes, before dripping on to her flushed cheeks. 'Oh God, I'm going to lose my job, aren't I? I can't believe I let him talk me into it …'

Bridget is blindsided. Dylan? How did Dylan talk Hayley into anything? How did he even know about Hayley's existence? He maintained that he and Thomas were no longer in regular contact. Was that a lie?

'I swear he didn't tell me any details, other than the location and time … I had no idea someone was going to be *shot* … I used the override function and that was all … *I swear* that was all …'

'Backtrack a second. When did you meet Dylan? Was it the same night you met Thomas? At the nightclub?'

'No, no.' Hayley uses her fingertips to wipe under each eye. 'It was earlier this year. Around March. He found me.'

Bridget briefly looks at Sasha and sees her own confusion mirrored on the young detective's face. 'More details, Hayley. *How* did he "find" you? *Why* did he "find" you?'

'They'd had a school catch-up,' she whispers, fresh tears clouding her eyes. 'Apparently, Thomas was high on cocaine and trying to hit on every woman in sight – fortunately, the women were smart enough to keep away. He got more bitter as the night went on. He started to rant about me, calling me a "stupid fucking bitch" for going to the police. Dylan was appalled, but pretended to be sympathetic and kept him talking until he got my name. Then he messaged me and asked to meet up. He said he was one of Thomas's victims too!'

Bridget bulges with incredulity. '*What?* Why would he say *that*? He was an accomplice, not a victim!'

Hayley's red-rimmed eyes bounce between Bridget and Sasha. 'Thomas gave Dylan GHB too. To loosen him up, apparently.'

Bridget holds her breath. 'And Dylan told you this for a fact?'

Hayley nods vehemently. 'He explained about the court case, about those other two girls, how Thomas had been spiking drinks as far back as then. Even more bizarre and awful, was that Dylan had been drugged too, with a smaller dose. And he had no clue, only that all his inhibitions were suddenly gone … He was a victim, too.'

Members of the jury, I spoke earlier about the character of these young ladies and how it helps us understand their behaviour in a wider context. Now let's discuss the character of the young men who are accused. You have heard testimony from Thomas Malouf's football coach regarding his leadership on the field and commendable encouragement of other players. Dylan O'Shea also displayed admirable qualities, both at school and at his part-time job. Remember the words of his employer: 'Dylan is the most gentle, honest and respectful of boys. He wouldn't hurt a fly.' And that, ladies and gentlemen, concludes the defence's closing address.

57
BRIDGET

The drive across the city will take thirty-four minutes, according to the navigation system. Sasha puts her foot to the pedal while Bridget makes some calls. She tries Katrina twice and catches her the second time.

'Sasha and I are on our way to Dylan O'Shea's house. We need to do a more comprehensive search.'

Bridget visited the house when the missing person report came in. She spoke with the parents and took a cursory look around Dylan's bedroom. This time she needs to employ a different lens. Dylan had prior knowledge of the attack on William Newson. Dylan saw himself as a *victim* of Thomas Malouf. These facts, if true, turn everything on its head. These facts, if true, mean that Dylan is implicated up to his eyeballs.

'Do not even think of asking me to approve another

warrant,' Katrina warns, and Bridget is glad that the detective inspector is not on speaker: bureaucracy can have a disillusioning effect on young detectives like Sasha.

'I'll see how far I get with the parents,' she says, looking out the window as the car emerges on to Sydney Harbour Bridge. 'If they're really concerned about their son, they won't be worried about paperwork.'

Traffic on the bridge is thick but moving quickly. Sasha zips in and out of lanes with confidence. Her face is intent and animated: she is enjoying this. Bridget, on the other hand, is waning slightly. She has covered practically the entire city today, from Hornsby to Pymble to Parramatta to Redfern, and now back to Pymble again. It's been one of those strange disorienting days, where too much has happened to process it all.

She takes a moment to rally herself before calling Dave. 'Where are you?'

'At a family barbecue,' he replies warily.

'I need you back in the office. Sorry.'

His sigh is resigned. 'I thought you might say that.'

She spends the next five minutes instructing Dave on what needs doing. Verification of contact between Dylan and Hayley Webster. Information on how call-centre personnel can override the ambulance dispatch system. A timeline of Dylan O'Shea's movements on 20 August, the evening of the shooting. A review of his bank statements for suspicious transactions that could relate to the purchase of a gun or motorcycle.

They've exited the freeway. Six kilometres to go.

Bridget's imagination is bursting at what they might find when they get there. How much do the parents know? What could be lurking in the garage and sheds, places she didn't think necessary to check last time as Dylan had said goodbye in the morning and supposedly left the house?

'Dylan knowing about the shooting is one thing,' she murmurs. 'Pulling the trigger is quite another … We must remember that.'

Sasha flicks on the indicator to turn right and thrums her fingers on the steering wheel while she waits for a break in the oncoming traffic. 'If it *was* Dylan, what were the motorbike and gun doing in Thomas's storage facility?'

'Good question … Maybe Dylan and Thomas were in cahoots and Thomas couldn't live with himself afterwards and decided to end it all.'

'Maybe …' Sasha says doubtfully, pressing heavily on the accelerator to make the turn, the tight margin causing Bridget to wince. 'But Thomas doesn't come across as the remorseful type, does he?'

'No, he doesn't.'

The O'Shea family dwelling is on the high side of the street, a dozen or so sandstone steps leading to the front door.

Sasha rings the bell and they wait. Mr O'Shea opens the door. He is pale-skinned, with the same unruly hair as his son.

'Oh, it's you.' His face registers recognition when he sees Bridget. Then dread seeps into it. 'It's not bad news, is it?'

'No,' she assures him, with a restrained smile. 'No news yet. But we have some further questions to ask and would like to take another look around, if you don't mind.'

'Of course I don't mind. Come in. My wife is out.'

So far so good. Cooperation makes everything so much easier. Warrants are a bureaucratic pain in the ass.

The house is furnished with heavy antique furniture and chintz fabrics. There are original watercolours on the walls of the front room and Bridget is reminded that Dylan, Thomas and Jess all come from privileged backgrounds. Megan was the odd one out. Still is.

Mr O'Shea, despite being cooperative, divulges little information of use.

'Have you ever met or heard Dylan speak about a young woman called Hayley Webster?' Bridget searches for – and fails to find – recognition at the mention of Hayley's name.

'No. Dylan isn't much good with women. Never so much as had a proper girlfriend.'

'Do you know if Dylan and Thomas got back in contact?'

Mr O'Shea frowns and purses his lips. 'I doubt it. Dylan doesn't like Thomas very much at all.'

'Does Dylan own or know how to ride a motorbike?'

The older man is visibly puzzled. 'He had one in his

early twenties. Few nasty falls and sold it after a couple of years. Why is this relevant?'

'Do you know Dylan's whereabouts on the evening of Tuesday, August twentieth? Approximately four and a half weeks ago,' she adds, to help him navigate back through the weeks.

He shakes his head before answering. 'Dylan is a grown man. He might live at home, but he keeps to his own schedule. Besides, it's difficult to recollect what happened last week, let alone August!'

With Mr O'Shea's permission, Bridget and Sasha have another, more thorough, look in Dylan's bedroom. The room is sparse and rather sad, encapsulating how a neat unimaginative single male adult might live. In one of the bedside drawers, Bridget finds various membership and loyalty cards, one of which is for a shooting range. The shiny bright-blue card is obviously quite new. Hairs stand up at the back of her neck.

She flashes it in front of his father. 'Did you know that Dylan was a member of this club?'

'No ... but the club is legal, isn't it?'

'Yes. Of course.'

'As I said, he's a grown man. He doesn't need to tell me everything.' Mr O'Shea's words are at odds with his tone. Doubt is creeping in.

Bridget and Sasha, with Mr O'Shea in tow, proceed to the garage. It contains a car, a few bicycles, some cast-off furniture and an unpleasant odour. Bridget notices a shabby brown door inset into the sandstone wall.

'What's in there?' she asks, stopping in her tracks.

'Just a storeroom. We don't use it much. Too damp and dingy.'

'Can we have a look?'

'Of course. Of course.'

The door handle is rusty and grimy. Bridget turns it and the door opens a mere crack before the stench forces her back.

Jesus … Oh no …

She knows that pungent, distinctive smell. It's the scent of her job, the scent of rotting flesh. Bridget swallows the urge to gag and holds out her arm, to prevent Sasha and Mr O'Shea from going any further.

'Wait … don't …'

The older man barges through, clicking a light switch inside the doorway.

His howl is one of pure agony. 'Dylan, what have you done, boy? What have you done!'

58
BRIDGET

'He was here all the time … he never left at all …' Mr O'Shea is sobbing into his hands. A uniformed officer is sitting next to him, on camping chairs located from elsewhere in the garage, patting him on the back. 'Why would he do this to us, in his own home, with his mother and father upstairs? Why couldn't he talk to us?'

Dylan had obviously reached the stage where words wouldn't suffice, the stage where he thought the world didn't need him or care for him, where he believed himself beyond help or redemption. A piece of rope looped around an overhead beam, a chair that was kicked away when no longer needed. He would have felt lightheaded after a few seconds, his hearing and vision fading before eventually losing consciousness. A few minutes until death and irreversible oblivion.

The house is swarming with paramedics, forensics and uniformed officers. There are four emergency vehicles parked outside: two police cars, an ambulance and fire truck. Family services are on their way. Mrs O'Shea still isn't home but her arrival is imminent. According to her husband, she went for a walk to clear her head. Unfortunately, she didn't take her phone with her, so all they can do is await her return. Poor, poor woman.

Kate, one of the forensic specialists, emerges from the storeroom holding a box in one hand and a set of plastic gloves in the other.

'You might want to look at this,' she says to Bridget. 'We found it next to the body.'

Bridget snaps on the gloves before opening the old shoebox. There are three things inside: Dylan's phone, with his passcode written on a Post-it; a solitary key, with a tag saying 'storage unit'; and a plain white envelope, which she assumes contains either a suicide note or a confession.

Bridget steps outside with the envelope, away from the distraction of Mr O'Shea's keening. Night has fallen. The temperature has plummeted. She turns on the torch function on her phone, carefully unfolds two typed sheets of paper and begins to read.

My name is Dylan O'Shea. This is my statement …

Tiny drops pepper the paper. The same tiny drops are on the sleeves of her jacket. They're coming from the dark starless sky: drizzle.

'Excuse me. Can you tell me what's happening?'

A woman in her sixties has materialised and is standing in the driveway, surveying the haphazardly parked emergency vehicles. She's illuminated with borrowed light from the garage: coiffed grey-blonde hair, face white with terror, the mist lending her an ethereal air. Her eyes instinctively fix on the sheets of paper clutched in Bridget's hand, somehow understanding that they contain the answer to her question.

Dylan's mother is home.

My name is Dylan O'Shea. This is my statement. On August 20th, I shot William Newson twice outside his house. I also intended to shoot Thomas Malouf but found the experience unsatisfying. I wanted more from Thomas. I wanted a confession, an acknowledgement of the wrongs he'd done. I wanted to see him terrified and helpless, like I'd felt during the trial. I planted the motorbike and gun in his storage unit, took photos of 'the evidence' and told him he was going to get locked up for murder. He laughed in my face, said that his lawyer would get him off. Then I told him about a recording I had on my phone, where he'd admitted to giving women GHB. I played the recording for him, but he laughed again, said there was no way a court would allow it as admissible evidence. It became obvious that I couldn't scare him, or get him to confess, or get any reaction at all other than mockery, and so I pushed him in front of that train.

I've murdered two men, and the truth is I'm not sorry; I'm actually proud that I saw it through. You've no idea what it took. All the planning, knowing there was a good chance I wouldn't have the guts when it came to it. Thinking constantly about my mum and dad, who deserve so much better. Not sleeping properly for months. It started that school night-out in March. I hadn't seen Thomas or any of that gang for years, but I went along because I was at a real low point. Late in the night I was sitting next to Thomas. He was snorting cocaine, talking incessantly. He told me about Hayley, and the more he blabbered the more I realised that it wasn't just Jess, Megan and Hayley: he'd raped other women, too. Then he said something like this: 'Don't look so shocked, Dumbo. GHB is magic stuff – you should know. You were so fucking uptight at that party, remember? So I did you a favour, put some in your drink. And it worked, you bonked that bitch stupid. You should try having some again. Might get some action, eh?'

He started thrusting his hips, laughing raucously. Suddenly it all made sense. How everything about the party night was blurry and surreal. How my awkwardness mysteriously disappeared. How I ended up having sex with Megan, even though she'd rejected me earlier. She hadn't changed her mind; she'd been semi-conscious, and I'd been too drugged to notice or care. Thomas had engineered it all. He'd ruined my life as much as hers.

I shot William Newson because he enabled Thomas, twice. Our barrister never delved into what really happened on the night of the party, he glossed over the details and focused more on what the girls did wrong than what we did wrong. At the time I found this disconcerting but I was too scared to resist the process. I didn't want to go to prison, that's all I could think about. I was sorry and ashamed, but incredibly relieved when we were acquitted. I thought I could walk out of court, leave it all behind me, and finally start my life. But something like that doesn't go away. It affected every relationship I had, every job I interviewed for. To be upfront or not. To tell the truth, or hope they'd never find out. I'd thought of myself as a decent bloke, but I didn't trust myself any more. I felt dirty, ashamed, and scared of doing the wrong thing again. Thomas felt none of those things; in his mind he was invincible. Meeting Hayley Webster was an eye-opener: here was another real-life victim, proof that Newson was enabling Thomas. Who next? Other guilty blokes were walking free, too. Google Laura Dundas and you'll see what I mean. Newson needed to be stopped as much as Thomas did.

I decided early on that Megan and Jess should be involved. If William was going to need an ambulance, who better than Megan? There was even a chance he might recognise her and apologise, but he was too far gone for that. Then I arranged to meet Thomas at Artarmon station with the idea of having him confess in front of Jess – but he laughed at me, changed platforms to get the train home, and you know the rest. I wanted Megan and Jess to know that justice was finally being served. And I also want them to know that I hate myself even more than they hate me. The guilt and shame have only got stronger over the years. I don't want to go to prison now any more than I did back then, and so there's only one way to end this.

Mum and Dad, I'm sorry about everything. The

embarrassment I caused you. The fact that you never really trusted me again. All the money you had to fork out in legal fees. One of you is going to find my body and I'm sorry about that, too. I intended to use Thomas's storage unit but the police have it cordoned off. At least now you know about the drugs and that it wasn't all my fault. I've killed two men and you're going to be devastated. Please forgive me but believe this: these men being dead is a good thing. The world is a better safer place.

I finally did something right.

59
MEGAN

Jess is delighted to see them. 'You came! I can't believe you came! You too, Seb. This is great.'

They're standing in the foyer of the community hall, where an area has been sectioned off for the fighters and their coaches. Alex is here too, and Jess's sister, Natasha. Megan introduces Seb and they form their own little group.

'The canteen is open, if you want drinks,' Jess says, fidgeting with the lanyard around her neck. 'If I were you, I'd go through to the hall pretty soon. The seats are filling up. I'd better get back to Billy. See you later!'

Billy, wearing blue, is sitting on a plastic chair, on the receiving end of a pep talk from Vince. He is listening and nodding, but his inky eyes stare in their direction.

Megan assumes his opponent's in red. Which one is it? Each looks as terrifying as the next.

'Who's for a drink?' Alex asks, and takes orders before zigzagging through the crowd towards the canteen. He returns holding four cans in his huge hands.

'To old friends,' he says, raising his can of Coke with a hang-dog expression that suggests he doesn't often find himself at no-alcohol events.

'And sisters and brothers,' adds Natasha, clinking enthusiastically.

Megan and Seb share a smile, and echo the toast. 'To old friends, and sisters and brothers.'

Pink's 'Try' is booming through the sound system, the lyrics apt for the occasion. It's 7.45 p.m.: fifteen minutes until the first fight. Billy is fourth in the order. They join the line for the hall, paying the ticket price at the door in exchange for a fluoro-green wristband. Officials in white shirts and black trousers sit at tables on each side of the boxing ring. The atmosphere is electric. Voices, camaraderie and anticipation rise above the music. This is a grassroots event. The crowd is a mish-mash of ages, mainly comprised of friends, family and fellow gym members. There is the strong sense that everyone, from kids to pensioners, shares a love of the sport.

'Ladies and gentlemen, welcome, welcome, welcome. We've got sixteen bouts for your entertainment tonight, including some belts up for grabs. We'll be kicking off in a few minutes with some action in the heavyweight division.'

They find seats, towards the back. Alex and Seb are talking and laughing; they've hit it off. Megan feels another shift within herself. She has been unfair to Jess's boyfriend, suspecting him of all sorts of awful things. And here he is, being so friendly and genuine. *Sorry, Alex.*

The lights in the hall dim, the ring illuminated with floodlights on each of the corners. The heavyweights are waiting to be called. They're enormous: ninety kilos, according to the announcer. Megan is half enthralled and half appalled at the spectacle that's about to unfold.

'Megs? Have you got a sec?' Jess has materialised, her expression anxious. 'Billy's complaining about a niggle in his shoulder … would you mind having a look?'

'You know I'm not a physiotherapist, right?'

'Yeah, of course. I think it's all in his head. He's nervous but won't admit it. Fucking lawyers. Never tell the truth.'

They laugh without a trace of bitterness. Megan hands her Coke to Seb for safekeeping, and follows Jess out of the hall and back to the sectioned-off area in the foyer.

'Which shoulder?' she asks, looking into Billy's almost-black eyes. 'What's the problem?'

'Left one. Jarred it while I was warming up.'

Gently, she manoeuvres the arm in a few directions, checking the impact on his shoulder. 'Doesn't look like anything serious … Which one is your opponent?'

Billy nods towards a competitor wearing a red vest

and shorts, shadow boxing a few metres away. His hair is shaved and he has a mean-looking face.

'Shit.'

'Thanks for the vote of confidence.' He grins.

'How about a massage to loosen up the shoulder?' Megan offers, more as a sympathy gesture than anything.

'Great. Thanks.'

Jess produces some gel from the medical kit. Billy's skin is taut, tanned and warm. His shoulders rise and fall in line with his breathing. Megan's breathing unconsciously syncs with his. The music pulses in her ears, fills her heart. Sometimes life presents a randomly exquisite moment. She goes with it.

60
JESS

Boxing is about trying to hurt someone, while abiding to a strict set of rules. Boxing is about intimidation and aggression, to give yourself an edge. You've got to have someone to hate in that ring. If it's not your opponent, then you need to imagine someone else in their place.

'Have you got someone?' she asks Billy. 'Someone you hate and want to hurt?'

'Yeah. Yeah.'

Jess hopes Billy can summon some real aggression because Kyle, his opponent, looks dangerous. His shoulders are broad and powerful and he's a few inches taller. This is his third amateur fight; experience is on his side, too.

Three rounds of three minutes each. Billy and Kyle receive some pre-fight instructions from the referee.

They're poised to begin, eyeing each other from behind raised gloves. Billy has swagger, but Jess can tell he's scared shitless. She's scared, too. He's the first person she's coached to this level. It's her debut, too. The presence of Alex, Natasha, Megan and Seb is gratifying, but adding to her nerves.

The clang of the bell and they're off. Billy and Kyle dance around each other, the referee watching closely. A half-hearted jab by Kyle, which Billy defends easily. He's doing well. Being patient. Using the space.

'Come on, Kyle,' someone shouts from the crowd. The music has been turned down, the babble of voices acting as a soundtrack.

Two more jabs, which Billy defends, before landing a cracking right hook.

'That's it, mate,' Jess responds. 'Keep working. Don't let him get away. Stay there and work!'

The bell rings. The first round is over. Billy returns to the corner and she hands him his drink bottle and a towel.

'Great defence, mate. Don't let him pressure you. But don't give him too much time either.'

He nods, mopping the sweat from his face.

'Ladies and gentlemen, get ready for the second round of action between these two light middleweights.'

Billy and Kyle are more wary in the second, ducking, bouncing and sizing each other up. Billy is in a defensive stance; he'll need to get some shots in if he wants to win this. Just as Jess is thinking this, he goes for Kyle's head, completely misses and leaves himself open. Kyle pushes him back on the ropes, which rattle loudly. He lands some jabs straight on the ribs, and one to the face.

The referee orders them to stop, and begins to count. 'One, two, three …'

'First count of the night,' the announcer declares. 'Doesn't mean much in amateur boxing. Only one point.'

'Keep him away,' Jess shouts, as the fight resumes. 'Use your feet, Billy. Move.'

And Billy moves. He manages to redeem himself with the judges by landing a couple of jabs before the second round is called.

Billy returns to the corner for a drink and a lecture. 'Don't get lazy with your hands, mate. You don't have to go for the big shots every time.'

He has a bust lip; he got off lightly. He gulps some water, dries his face.

'Third and deciding round,' the announcer calls. 'This is a close bout, ladies and gentlemen.'

'Smash him, Billy!' a woman screeches; she sounds suspiciously like Natasha.

Jess tunes out the woman and the crowd. 'Straight punches, mate. You're free-range right. Faster hands. That's too late.

'Keep him away. You're standing too tall. Get lower, mate, *lower*.'

Billy's right in there, jab for jab, uppercut for upper-cut. Billy has style and ingenuity; Kyle has experience and strength. Billy is better at defence, Kyle is better at hitting. It's close, very close.

'Ladies and gentlemen, that's the end of the final round and definitely a rematch in the making. We'll have an official decision shortly.'

Jess undoes Billy's headgear and helps remove his gloves. The referee checks his hands, and those of his opponent. Then he positions them on either side of him, to await the announcement of the decision.

'Ladies and gentlemen, the winner by way of split decision goes to the man in the red corner, all the way from Orange, New South Wales, Kyle Landon!'

'Welcome to the world of split decisions,' Jess sighs, clapping Billy on the back. 'Not a bad result for your first fight. Well done, mate.'

'Thanks.' He grins, his face glowing with blood, sweat and relief.

Jess's eyes locate Megan in the crowd. Her face is animated, she looks like she's enjoying herself. Megan is part of the reason Jess arrived at Vince's doorstep twelve years ago, seeking a fight she at least had a fair chance of winning. Now this, a new phase in her coaching career. It feels fitting that Megan is here. They've come full circle.

All the handshakes are done, and the next pair of fighters are waiting their turn in the ring.

'Come on,' Jess says. 'Let's get some ice on that nice shiner you've got coming through.'

61
BRIDGET

Whether it's suicide or homicide, there's the same shock, confusion, guilt, anger and devastation. The endless 'what if' questions. Something that could have been done or said or noticed that would have diverted to a different outcome. Families left shattered. Friends and colleagues dangerously unanchored. Ripple effects felt for a lifetime.

Bridget has called Katrina and given her the latest news. Three investigations solved at once: the detective inspector is as pleased as one can be in the circumstances. The rational part of Bridget's mind tells her to leave Megan and Jess until tomorrow, but the emotional part can't wait until then. She's invested in these women; she can't leave them waiting any more than she could leave Cara waiting. Jess's phone rings out, and Bridget belatedly remembers that it was seized last night. Megan answers hers after a few rings.

'Megan, it's Detective Sergeant Bridget Kennedy … Are you at home?'

'No.' There is a lot of background noise: cheering and whistling. 'Is something wrong?'

'Where are you? I have an important update.'

'I'm at the community hall in Artarmon. Jess is here, too.'

'Give me twenty minutes,' Bridget says, already moving.

She calls Shane from the car, giving him a brief explanation for her continued failure to arrive home.

'Katrina has promised me a few days off next week,' she says, a yawn escaping at the same time. The wipers slick mesmerisingly from one side to the other. She shakes her head until she's appropriately alert.

Shane's tone is sombre over the speakers. 'I guess we'll see you at some stage tonight. Be careful. Love you.'

He is wonderful, her husband. The wheels would come off without him. Next week she has some serious making up to do, with him and the kids.

The car park adjacent to the community hall is close to full. The rain is coming down more heavily. Bridget pauses for a moment on getting out of the car, raising her face, giving the rain the welcome it deserves. It stings her skin, cold, reviving. The air smells of mingled dust and water. She takes a deep breath before following the sound of voices and loud music. The foyer of the hall has a canteen and a sectioned-off makeshift dressing room, competitors wearing either red or blue, coaches and support staff in dark-coloured polo-shirts.

Bridget smooths down her hair; it tends to go frizzy in the rain. The smell of hot food reminds her how hungry she is. It would appear that the main action is happening next door, in the hall. An announcer's voice booms over the sound system.

'Ladies and gentlemen, the winner by way of referee stops contest is the fighter in the blue corner ...'

She spots Jess's pale blonde head in the provisional dressing room. Next to her, sitting down, is a familiar-looking man in his twenties, his face smeared with sweat and blood: the lawyer. Megan is bent over him; she seems to be examining one of his eyes.

Bridget manoeuvres her way through the crowd and Jess turns her head sharply, as though sensing her approach. She frowns, touches Megan's arm, murmurs something in her ear. Megan straightens, swiping a strand of dark hair away from her eyes.

'Hello. Sorry to gatecrash like this.' In normal circumstances, Bridget would ask the lawyer to leave so she could have a private word, but he looks rather worse for wear. It seems equally impossible to ask Jess and Megan to leave him to his own devices. There are people everywhere, but the noise level offers a certain degree of privacy. 'I'm here to let you know that Dylan O'Shea has died ...'

'Oh.' Megan's eyes are wide, her mouth agape. 'Oh my God.'

Jess is tight-lipped. Her shock is contained, but just as forceful.

'His body was found at his home this evening, along with a written statement in which he admits to shooting William Newson and framing Thomas Malouf for the crime.'

Megan grabs on to the back of the lawyer's chair to steady herself. Jess is untethered, dazed, white as a sheet. Music booms from the hall next door.

Bridget forges on. 'The statement confirms that you were both given GHB on the night of the party. The twist is that Dylan was drugged too, although he didn't discover this until recently—'

'What the fuck?' Jess's eyes narrow with disbelief. 'What does Dylan being drugged have to do with anything?'

'Thomas gave him a lesser dose, just enough to loosen his inhibitions – his actions that night were certainly compromised by the drug. Dylan never got over what happened. According to his father, he never had a proper relationship with a girl, didn't pursue close friendships, and kept a low profile at work – he was constantly fearful that someone would find out. The shame and guilt had a significant toll on his mental health. A few months ago, he discovered that Thomas had drugged him, that Thomas was still using GHB to prey on other women, and that William Newson had got him off another charge. It would seem that these developments sent Dylan over the edge.'

'Oh my God.' Megan's brown eyes are blurry with tears. 'I never thought I'd feel sorry for Dylan O'Shea!'

Jess is fighting the urge to cry, her mouth trembling with the effort. 'Don't feel sorry for him. Don't! What type of person does this kind of shit?'

'Someone deranged.' The male voice takes Bridget by surprise. Billy: she'd forgotten about him. 'Someone who believes their actions to be justified when any sane person knows differently ... Where did he get the gun?'

The question is calm and deliberate. Bridget realises that Billy doesn't care about where the gun came from: his intention is to diffuse some of the emotion with cold hard facts, a technique she often employs herself.

'Both the gun and the motorcycle were stolen. At this point we're assuming that Dylan acquired them through the black market. We've already found evidence of membership to a shooting club.'

Billy nods. The ensuing silence contains the beginnings of acceptance. This is the point where Bridget might step forward to hug the women if she weren't acting in a professional capacity. The hug would portray the depth of her sympathy, as well as her emotional connection to the case and her admiration for them both. Words feel like a poor substitute. She chooses them carefully.

'I know this has been a difficult few weeks. I've had to ask intrusive and upsetting questions, dredging

411

up bad memories. I just want to say how brave you are. When I'm not at work, I'm mum to a seventeen-year-old girl and a fifteen-year-old boy. If my kids turn out like either of you, I'll be the proudest mum in the world.'

62
ONE MONTH LATER
MEGAN

The girl, Hannah, is only sixteen. She regains consciousness on the way to the hospital. Confusion registers in her bloodshot eyes, followed quickly by horror.

'You're all right.' Megan squeezes her hand. 'You're safe. Everything is fine.'

Tears well. Her mouth trembles.

'Sorry. I'm so stupid. My parents …'

'Your mum and dad are meeting us at the hospital. They've had a shock but they'll be okay once they know *you're* okay.'

Hannah's skin is cold and clammy, despite the foil blanket tucked around her. Her heart rate is slow, her pulse irregular. An IV is attached to the pale smooth skin in the crook of her elbow.

Megan gently wipes some vomit from the girl's chin, a task that's part and parcel of most Saturday-night shifts. She doesn't mind, even though the smell sticks to her skin and clothes. She's going to Billy's place straight after work; she'll have a shower there.

It's slightly startling when she thinks about Billy, and how quickly he's become embedded in her life. It started with drinks on the night of his fight – with Seb, Jess and Alex – before catapulting into a full-blown relationship. Billy is smart, uncomplicated and certain about what he thinks and feels. Megan doesn't have to second-guess him, or be on standby for him to let her down: he makes his feelings very obvious.

'I really like you,' he said on that first night, a little bit drunk but clearly genuine. 'I mean really, really, *really* like you.'

In response, Megan has opened up about her own feelings, including her remorse over Dylan, how she vacillates between anger and guilt and sorrow. If she'd spoken to him, granted him the opportunity to tell his side of the story, would that have changed how things turned out?

'Why don't you talk to his family?' Billy advised. 'It might help you and them.'

Poor heartbroken Mr and Mrs O'Shea. Megan's chat with them was both revealing and cathartic. She discovered, among other things, that the Malouf family had bullied Dylan in the months leading up to the trial. *You'd better stick to the story, or else … We'll ruin your life if you ruin Thomas's life ...Just shut up and do what the lawyer tells you to do.* The bullying had intensified Dylan's feelings of helplessness and fear. Who knew what his testimony would have been without their influence? A guilty verdict, albeit disastrous for the boys at the time, could have saved three lives twelve years down the line.

'How's everything back there?' Kaz calls from the front of the vehicle.

'All good,' Megan replies, giving Hannah a reassuring smile.

'Mum and Dad are going to kill me,' she croaks miserably.

Megan spots some more vomit on her top, scrubs at it. 'Just tell them the truth. You drank too much. You misjudged the effect it would have. We all make mistakes. I know I have.'

63
JESS

Jess helps Alex with the baby carrier while Lucy watches wide-eyed from her car seat.

'There, I think that's how it goes.' Jess double checks each strap before lifting Lucy in, facing her towards Alex's chest. The baby grins and kicks her legs. She can hold her head up now, and is very interested in the world around her. 'You like it in there, do you? Ready for a nice walk in the bush?'

Natasha and Oliver are at a wedding today, and Jess and Alex are babysitting. Jess grabs the baby backpack (containing nappies, baby wipes, a pre-prepared bottle, spare clothes and a hundred other necessities) from the back seat and locks the ute.

'Okay, missy, let's go. You can look around for a little bit but then you're going to have a nap. Agreed?'

Lucy gurgles and kicks her legs even more enthusiastically.

Alex glances down at her with a wry smile. 'No chance. She looks ready to party.'

Jess gives her niece a look of mock sternness before leading the way to one of the flat, less challenging tracks in the national park. It's Sunday lunchtime. There are a few other walkers around, who smile when they see the baby bouncing against Alex. The track is mostly in shade and the air is pure and sharp. Jess breathes it in. It's good to be out in the fresh air, in nature. And it's good to be able to help Natasha out. She and her sister have become close these last few weeks, and Natasha has become Alex's advocate, singing his praises at every opportunity. Having Natasha onside has changed the family dynamic. Margaret seems less critical, Jess is less defensive, visits less strained.

The ground is hard and dry underfoot; there still hasn't been near enough rain. Jess smiles as she walks. She is happy, content. More than anything, she is grateful. To Dylan for leaving that letter and supplying the answers she needed to forgive herself. To Billy, for winning his second fight, and for being exactly what Megan deserves in a partner. To Alex, who takes everything in life in his stride, and who is so thoughtful and caring when it matters.

'Hey, Jess,' he whispers from behind. 'Think I heard a snore.'

Jess stops to check. Lucy's head is pressed against his

T-shirt. Eyelashes fan her soft cheeks. Her tiny mouth emits another sound, something between a sigh and a snore.

'Fast asleep,' Jess pronounces.

She and Alex share a proud grin. They can do this. They'll make good parents one day. On Jess's ring finger is a small solitaire, modest and discreet. Alex asked her to marry him last night. She said yes. Nobody knows yet. Except Lucy.

64
BRIDGET

Who knew that watering could be so therapeutic? Standing with a hose in one's hand. Seeing the soil darken and puddle. Breathing in the scent of flowers and fresh air. The satisfaction of a green, well-tended garden. The unexpected joy it brings. The simplicity: water equals growth. Not many things in life are so simple or so responsive.

Bridget's week off work extended into four. The case took an enormous toll, emotionally and physically: she was completely burnt out. She has spent the time nurturing her garden and her family, as well as processing the case and its many nuances. *YOU HAD IT COMING:* that ominous almost-undetected message etched into the smooth bark of the tree trunk. William Newson didn't have it coming, at least not in Bridget's view. He was doing his job, upholding his unwavering belief in the assumption of innocence, and the civil right to legal representation. The problem was that Thomas Malouf didn't deserve his services, because Thomas wasn't innocent. Did *he* have it coming? Possibly, but he was never convicted of his crimes and Bridget would much rather justice through the proper channels: another trial on the strength of that incriminating voice recording, a hefty prison sentence, his family finally capitulating to the law. And what about Dylan O'Shea? How did he get to the point where his sense of right and wrong was so warped that he thought the only answer – for all of them – was death? It's a tragedy of epic proportions. Three families blown asunder. Why is it so hard for men to talk? Dylan's parents were there and willing to listen, and yet he never said a word to alert them to the fact that he was in a dark, dangerous place. Men need to learn to talk, to share their problems. Bridget has used her time off to prise her way into Ethan's internal life, coaxing him to chat after school and before bedtime. The phrase 'getting blood from a stone' applies. Cara has been the opposite, revelling in her mother's presence at home, freely unloading her worries about the HSC exams and who to invite to the formal. This time with her children has been precious, and well overdue.

Despite being on leave, Bridget felt compelled to check in with everyone impacted by the case. Suzanne Newson said she was grateful to have resolution for the sake of her sons. Joshua was emotional on the phone, but still managed to ask a lot of questions, some of which Bridget is still seeking answers to. Emily Wickham has since resigned to take a position in a large city-centre law firm. Hayley Webster didn't survive the internal review at the Ambulance Control Centre and lost her job. Bridget believes that Hayley didn't know the specifics of what Dylan was planning, but she had facilitated and failed to report a serious crime, and Bridget had no choice but to charge her accordingly. Nevertheless, Bridget is hoping for a suspended sentence or something equally light. *Hayley is a victim, too; surely, the poor girl has been through enough?* The case has tested her professionalism in so many respects.

Bridget arcs the hose clockwise, showering the front garden bed with water. Last week she removed the dead wood from the underbelly of the lavender bushes; it cracked gratifyingly in her hands. A few of the gardenia bushes were beyond redeeming. She replaced them with cordylines, which have added colour and structure and fill her with pleasure every time she sees them.

She'll never know for sure about that etching on the tree trunk. Did Dylan do it as a last-minute validation of the terrible crime he was about to commit? Perhaps he did it to stop his hands from shaking, or to make those long minutes of waiting go a little faster? Maybe it was his way of saying 'I was here', or even a bid to stop himself from chickening out. Bridget suspects the latter, but she will never know for certain. She can only surmise.

It's a balmy spring afternoon. Bridget's wearing cut-off denim shorts and a tank top, newly defined muscles on her arms and legs. She has been attending a beginners' class at Jess's gym. The circuit involves skipping, squats, boxing, and the agility ladder, which she never fails to get tangled in.

Bridget immediately detected Jess's new engagement ring on Monday and offered her congratulations. Then she asked after Megan.

'Oh, Megan is great. Madly in love. You've met him – Billy.'

Jess says boxing is about having someone to hate, someone you want to punch and hurt.

Bridget is not motivated by hate. The most important thing is having someone to love. Someone who can make you forget about the terrible things you see every day, who reaffirms your belief in greater goodness.

Bridget loves Shane, Cara and Ethan. Weirdly and very belatedly, she also loves her garden.

ACKNOWLEDGEMENTS

I'll start by admitting that this was a challenging one! I never intended to have a detective as a main character, or to delve so deeply into police procedure, but the story took hold and demanded it. Maybe the fact that this is my tenth novel had something to do with it. Maybe the 'universe' decided it was time to shake things up a bit? Well, that certainly happened! (Says she, smoothing herself down after a wild rollercoaster ride.)

I owe a huge debt to the following people for their technical assistance and for fielding my obscure questions so good-naturedly: Kate Jenkins, Seth Gibbard, Chris Drew, Craig Campbell, Paul Anderson, Donna Heagney, Jess Wootton, Peter Yeomans and Zali Steggall. Any errors are entirely my own (however, there are several occasions when I had to stretch the truth in order to give the story momentum).

Thank you to my writer friends: Petronella McGovern, for reading the manuscript *twice* and giving truly excellent suggestions; Dianne Blacklock and Liane Moriarty, for being unfailingly supportive through all the ups and downs of the writing life. Thank you to the other authors who have reached out and supported me over the years. It's so lovely to be part of this generous supportive global community.

Enormous thanks to my alpha and beta readers, who braved the early drafts and provided unflinching feedback: Erin Downey, Conor Carroll, Rob Carroll, John Newson, Christina Chipman and Merran Harte.

Thank you, Brian Cook from The Author's Agent. Hooray: we've made it to the ten-novel milestone. I still remember our first phone conversation as though it were yesterday.

Thank you to my publisher, Miranda Jewess, for always getting straight to the point and not wasting time (a lady after my own heart). Thank you to all the dedicated team at Profile, Viper and Allen & Unwin.

Thank you to my family in Ireland and Australia. I don't think there are any family-sourced anecdotes in this book … you guys need to come up with some fresh material! Thank you, Amanda Longmore, for feeding the hordes. Thank you, Ashling Carroll, for your video-editing skills. Thank you, PJ (the family dog), whose daily walks facilitate much of my thinking and plotting.

To my readers. Thank you for your encouraging messages, reviews and word-of-mouth recommendations.

This novel put me well outside my comfort zone and was a learning experience in many respects. I hope you enjoy it. xx Ber

ABOUT THE AUTHOR

B.M. Carroll was born in Blarney, a small village in Ireland. The third child of six, reading was her favourite pastime (and still is!). Ber moved to Sydney in 1995 and spent her early career working in finance. Her work colleagues were speechless when she revealed that she had written a novel that was soon to be published. Ber now writes full time and is the author of ten novels, including *Who We Were*, published by Viper in 2020. Find her on Twitter @bmcarrollauthor or at www.bercarroll.com.

NEVILLE SHONE was at the height of his career as a university teacher and researcher, bringing up a young family, a keen sportsman and amateur entertainer, when an operation to remove a spinal tumour rendered him almost immobile and in constant pain. His career and social life ended abruptly, bringing him close to despair. This is reflected in his book *Coping Successfully with Pain*, first published by Sheldon Press in 1992, but the real story is about his fight back and the techniques of pain management which enabled him to regain his mobility, his zest for life, and to escape from his prison of pain. After several revisions, *Coping Successfully with Pain* is now in its third edition, in which Neville Shone included a chapter on the relationship between diet and chronic pain. *The Chronic Pain Diet Book* continues this theme and is based on the 15 years' research he has made into the subject. Neville continues to help people caught up in the pain trap through his involvement with pain charities. He has appeared on many radio and television programmes on the subject of pain and has acted as adviser to a number of TV documentary makers. Neville is also the author of *Cancer – a Family Affair*, published by Sheldon Press in 1995.

Visit his website on <www.painlesspain.co.uk>.

Overcoming Common Problems Series

Selected titles

A full list of titles is available from Sheldon Press,
36 Causton Street, London SW1P 4ST and on our website at
www.sheldonpress.co.uk

101 Questions to Ask Your Doctor
Dr Tom Smith

Asperger Syndrome in Adults
Dr Ruth Searle

Assertiveness: Step by step
Dr Windy Dryden and Daniel Constantinou

Birth Over 35
Sheila Kitzinger

Body Language: What you need to know
David Cohen

Breast Cancer: Your treatment choices
Dr Terry Priestman

Bulimia, Binge-eating and their Treatment
Professor J. Hubert Lacey, Dr Bryony Bamford
and Amy Brown

The Cancer Survivor's Handbook
Dr Terry Priestman

The Chronic Pain Diet Book
Neville Shone

Cider Vinegar
Margaret Hills

Coeliac Disease: What you need to know
Alex Gazzola

**Coping Successfully with Chronic Illness:
Your healing plan**
Neville Shone

Coping Successfully with Pain
Neville Shone

Coping Successfully with Prostate Cancer
Dr Tom Smith

Coping Successfully with Shyness
Margaret Oakes, Professor Robert Bor
and Dr Carina Eriksen

Coping Successfully with Ulcerative Colitis
Peter Cartwright

Coping Successfully with Varicose Veins
Christine Craggs-Hinton

Coping Successfully with Your Hiatus Hernia
Dr Tom Smith

Coping When Your Child Has Cerebral Palsy
Jill Eckersley

Coping with Anaemia
Dr Tom Smith

Coping with Asthma in Adults
Mark Greener

**Coping with Birth Trauma and Postnatal
Depression**
Lucy Jolin

Coping with Bronchitis and Emphysema
Dr Tom Smith

Coping with Candida
Shirley Trickett

Coping with Chemotherapy
Dr Terry Priestman

Coping with Chronic Fatigue
Trudie Chalder

Coping with Difficult Families
Dr Jane McGregor and Tim McGregor

Coping with Diverticulitis
Peter Cartwright

Coping with Drug Problems in the Family
Lucy Jolin

Coping with Dyspraxia
Jill Eckersley

Coping with Early-onset Dementia
Jill Eckersley

Coping with Eating Disorders and Body Image
Christine Craggs-Hinton

Coping with Epilepsy
Dr Pamela Crawford and Fiona Marshall

Coping with Gout
Christine Craggs-Hinton

Coping with Guilt
Dr Windy Dryden

Coping with Headaches and Migraine
Alison Frith

Coping with Heartburn and Reflux
Dr Tom Smith

Coping with Life after Stroke
Dr Mareeni Raymond

**Coping with Life's Challenges: Moving on
from adversity**
Dr Windy Dryden

Coping with Liver Disease
Mark Greener